Exquisite Aberrations

Stories Selected & Edited by

Laurie Moran

&

Amber Newberry

DEDICATION

To the characters pushed to the margins: we hope you find yourself in these stories.
Be the hero. Be the villain. Be yourself.

CONTENTS

ACKNOWLEDGMENTS

Proofread by Bret Valdez

BEATRICE
Ellery D. Margay

Non potest esse nisi unus.

Beatrice was coming. Beatrice the liar. Beatrice the thief. Beatrice who had long held the title of best friend, yet had done little to earn or to keep it. Beatrice was coming to my island, the secluded sanitarium of sea and stone, to which, at my weakest, I had retreated—coming, now, to disrupt my peace. Even as I waited in my favorite easy-chair, still as the dead and twice as tense, she was drawing nearer, ever nearer.

In my mind's eye, I pictured her—a modern-day pilgrim perched at the bow of the 5 o'clock ferry, the last from the Port of Seattle. As though viewing a new world, she'd look out on Puget Sound—its mirror-glass surface; its emerald depths; the constellation of craggy islets, turned, as the sun set, to mist-cloaked silhouettes on a horizon awash in violet and gold. Would she see beauty, as I had?

Perhaps it would be a welcome change, having her here. I would show her the secret trail that wound through the madrones and the beach where the clam-diggers worked, and we'd explore the hidden burial plot, and the ramshackle barn atop the hill. Perhaps, if my health permitted, we might even learn to sail. Then I remembered her fright of whales, and knew she'd never ride at the prow, but indoors away from the water—and she'd no doubt arrive as she always had: stinking of liquor and the street, and the ill-remembered past.

Beatrice the charmer; the trickster; the snake. I loved her like a sister, and hated her like the bitterest of enemies.

When, by telephone, she'd first mentioned coming, I had dismissed it as idle talk. She would never leave New York; she was a fixture there—as welded to the city as Lady Liberty herself. She wouldn't travel 3,000 miles to this windswept horseshoe in the west—not to reside nearly a full day's journey from the distractions of civilization. Not Beatrice with her thirst for mischief and the meaner of life's pleasures.

But she had been adamant.

"Daria," she'd said, "I need a fresh start. Tell me again about the island. Didn't you say it's a place where someone could...disappear?"

I had confirmed that it was indeed such a place—that it was where folks went who didn't want to be found, and it was rife with smugglers and thieves and moonshiners on account.

"And your house there—it's spacious?"

It was, I had admitted, but only the upper floor was habitable, and not a foot of it was mine. It belonged to my sister, Thera, and her husband, Alonso, and I'd already imposed heavily on their kindness. Why, they'd given up their own master bedroom—the dimmest and quietest—so that I might rest and recover undisturbed. She'd pressed me no further that day, and I'd assumed my meaning had been clear. But only two weeks later she'd called again, this time from the lobby of a dockside inn. She'd ridden the rails to Seattle, and planned to rent her own little shack upon reaching the island. Lord only knew how she had come by the funds.

"And just where will you stay in the meantime?" I'd demanded.

"Well, I was hoping, Daria...and you know me, I can sleep any old place, but I was *hoping* that I might stay with you. Only until I find other arrangements of course."

Of course. And, helpless, I'd agreed—and asked Alonso if he would fetch her from the ferry in the Model T. Thera, elated at the prospect of company, had tidied the house and made herbed dumplings, and had carefully primped her auburn curls in preparation for the outing. She didn't belong on the island, my sister. She was not a star-gazing loner like the man she'd married, nor was she an invalid like me, and I knew she pined in secret for the flapper's life she'd left behind.

"Won't you come with us?" she'd urged. "Aren't you just *a bit* excited?"

But I'd remained, as always, in my chair by the parlor windows, staring at a copy of *Kidnapped,* unable to make sense of the words. Beatrice was coming—no, Beatrice was *here!*—and nobody, *nobody* understood.

I heard rather than saw her arrive, for Beatrice's voice is distinctive—a high, babyish chirp, the sort one would expect a mouse to use if indeed a mouse could speak—and it carried crisply from the yard in the still autumn night. She'd changed little since I'd left New York more than a year before: the same stained coat of drab green; the tattered gray cloche pulled low; the long, lank, straw-colored hair, unwashed, no doubt, since Brooklyn.

Beatrice had never been called a great beauty. Her nose was high and vaguely hooked, her chin a touch too soft—and she was miniature, scarcely taller than a little girl, with queer, gawky knees that seemed, whenever she stood at ease, to have bent in the wrong direction. But her clear green eyes were large and lively, and her smile, with its impish charisma, held a power to charm partly owed to its quirks.

"Daria!" she cried, frisking forward to embrace me, and I forgot, as always, the slights of the past, and was glad that she had come.

Something stirred in the satchel at her shoulder, and she lifted the flap to reveal a tiny dun-colored dog, its human-like brows knitted in fear.

"This is Joe-Joe," she said, plucking the quivering creature from its cocoon and kissing its runty snout. "He's my baaayby."

"I didn't say you could bring a dog here, Bea. Their fur makes Thera sneeze."

"Oh, it'll be alright for a few days," said Thera. "Only keep him out of my studio; he's not to make a mess of my paints."

Beatrice fell asleep in the parlor that night, curled on the rug before the fire. For a moment, I studied her—watched the rolling glow of the dying embers reflected in the stark planes of her face. She looked older, now, than her twenty-five years, her skin roughened by long excess and the indignities of the street. From his nest in the crook of her arm, Joe-Joe glared at me, his black seal's eyes and button nose twitching with mistrust.

The following day, we walked the grounds. I showed Beatrice the house, the immense dark-wood mansion in which I passed my days. I introduced her to its hidden nooks and spoke at length on its peculiarities, of which there were many. It was called Linger Longer, I told her, and it was one of the very first homes on the island.

Then, in the pale light of northern fall, we strolled through the woods, down the narrow lane below the house, to the lonely old dock at its end. Bea lit a cigarette and we stood for a time, leaning against the creaking rails, and staring out across the glassy bay at the clean, white village of Eastsound huddled along its rim. In his canvas satchel, Joe-Joe trembled and whined. Bea seemed to go nowhere without him these days, a fact which nettled me more than I cared admit.

We turned, from there, toward Crescent Beach, a desolate strip of rocky sand, just to the east of the house; and I wondered, upon reaching it, why I'd brought her there, for as beaches went, this one had always been a touch unwholesome. At low tide, as it was that day, the waterline was cluttered with kelp and the bodies of deceased crustaceans, ever stinking, ever swarming with midges and blowflies. Above, where the coarse grasses grew, lay a boneyard of bleached and limbless logs—the remnants of mighty evergreens that had long ago succumbed to the roiling waves. It was a melancholy scene, smacking of endings and decay, and I wished we hadn't come, for I was already very tired.

"That there is the edge of Madrona Point," I told Beatrice, gesturing back toward the rocky bluffs. "See how it juts into the Sound, like a tonsil...? We live in the center of the horseshoe; that's why the water's so still..."

But she wasn't listening. She was staring along the shore toward the clam-diggers, and the oystermen beyond, and I wondered if she'd been touched by the island fever, the unease that sets in as it dawns that one is trapped—corralled on all sides like a rat on a ledge.

In returning, we followed the little-used track road that cut through the dense mixed woods, connecting the beach with our estate. How fatigued I'd grown; how my heart pounded and my breath burned; how my feet dragged like stone as I toiled up the muddy slope. But when we reached Linger Longer, my friend was not ready to rest. She insisted on seeing the barn, and the archery range where I practiced on rare good days, and though I could think of nothing but my bed, I grudgingly obliged.

At the barn, I tugged open the great sliding door and let Beatrice have a peek.

"It's Alonso's studio," I said, "where he develops his photographs and tinkers with his contraptions."

"Ah, but what is that?" she asked, peering into the gloom toward an object in the far-right corner. This was a large round target of black and red felt, its center stuck with six silver daggers.

"They're mine. I was learning to throw like they do in the circus."

"I want to try it!"

"We will," I promised, "soon, but not today."

Just beyond the barn, lay the pine-shrouded burial plot of the family Wynne, and it was there that I rested, slumped against the mossy headstone of an infant named Mabel. Beatrice hopped briskly from grave to grave, reading aloud the names of their occupants.

"Wendell K. Wynne...Elma Odlin...Maude Mary Wynne...Lorelei Wynne...Stanhope Wynne..."

"Stanhope Wynne once owned this place," I said. "He was a surgeon and a dentist, and for decades kept a private practice on the lower floor. Much of his equipment—ghastly stuff—was still there when Alonso and Thera arrived."

"Is that why the lower floor isn't used?"

"No, that's because of the rot. The house stood vacant for some years, and parts of it were overrun by mold and rats, and...well, Thera said they discovered an entire *family* of raccoons downstairs—"

"But it's such a handsome old place; why should it stand vacant?"

She had quit her meandering, and now stood peering through the foliage toward the object of our discussion. Handsome it was—handsome, not beautiful, for it was neither graceful Victorian nor lilting gingerbread. There was something almost maritime in its design—something in the solid wood siding, the innumerable casement windows, and the oil lanterns hung therein that gave the impression of an earthbound ship—a stately galleon, crawled ashore to nest among the trees.

"Humans are superstitious creatures," I said. "No one wants to sleep or dine where others have died. It's happened in all old homes, of course, but it's impossible to ignore when living in what was once an operating room. That, and there was a tragedy. One of the Wynne girls had an accident, and was never found—"

"Which girl? Does she have a stone?"

"That one, there—Lorelei, the sister of Russel Wynne, who sold the property. Apparently, he was so keen to run off to sunny California, that he gave the place up for a crackerjack price. And of course, that only encouraged the rumors—because the truth is, no one is *sure* what happened to Lorelei. Some will tell you she drowned, others that she fell from the cliffs along Madrona Point Trail. The most outrageous theory is that, after a quarrel, Russel locked her in the Nothing Room, and just *left* her there."

"The Nothing Room?"

"Ah, yes. It's visible from here if you look closely. See the narrow door set into the upper wall—how there ought to be steps or a veranda below it? Well, as far as we know, there never has been. It's only a door with no purpose, and we can't guess what's inside. *Nothing*, or so the neighbors say, but the door has swollen tightly shut, and we've never been able to look for ourselves."

This piqued Bea's curiosity, and she insisted that we open it, by any means necessary.

"Another time," I told her, "when I'm not so tired."

In the morning I was ill, not with cold or flu, but with the nervous exhaustion that had long mystified my doctors. Two years past, it had struck without warning, turning my steely nerves to jelly and my dancing feet to lead, and I'd abandoned Broadway for the seclusion of the island— for what good was an actress who slept through rehearsals?—who quaked at the sound of applause?

The fatigue proved unshakable that day. For hours I remained beneath my quilts, weak and feverish, listening to Beatrice, who stood outside my bedroom door, chattering away on Thera's new telephone, no doubt to Todd or Shawna, her bootlegging chums from the Bronx. One could always guess to whom Bea was speaking, for in tone, accent, and favored words, she would unconsciously *become* them—and, oh, but she was a grand mimic! Indeed, it had been with shock and some measure of disgust that I'd first observed this habit, and at times I still wondered if, behind the ever-morphing mask, she possessed a true face of her own.

Later, when the sun had set, she crept into my room.

"Thera and I walked to town today," she said. "I asked after rooms to rent, but…I don't know what I'll do. They're all so *expensive*, Daria. Perhaps, if there were *two* renters…"

"I'm not renting with you," I said. "I'm not well enough yet to care for myself. Thera cooks and does the shopping; she's my guardian angel, and I wouldn't get along without her."

"What is your plan then—to stay here, where you're only a guest?"

"Well, I had thought of moving to Deer Harbor when my health improves. There's a lovely marina where I could rent my own boat. I so want to learn to sail, and it would be peaceful on the water."

But rather than improving, my health seemed only to worsen. The fatigue was stubborn, the fevers frequent; I couldn't practice archery with Bea or bob about in the dinghy with her and Thera, and we never did pry open the door of the Nothing Room or learn to throw knives like they do in the circus. Days slipped by, silently turning to weeks, then months. I passed Halloween in bed reading *The Count of Monte Cristo*, and on Thanksgiving, when all of Eastsound feasted at the Oddfellow's hall, I remained in my easy-chair with a basket of felt and leather trim, for I had taken, in my idleness, to fashioning hats.

Beatrice, in these lonesome times, provided precious little company. She spent her days in town, bantering with weekenders and befriending the locals, returning to Linger Longer only to sleep and to partake of Thera's cooking. After dinner, we'd take our cigarettes in the parlor, the casement windows open to the crisp night air, and we'd watch the silver wisps of smoke curl lazily into the dark. Bea would ramble—about the thrills of the day and the splendid new people she'd met. She had always been well-liked, no less so by the notoriously clannish islanders, and it took her a remarkably short time not only to finagle a serving job in a respectable home, but to announce that she was moving. A young friend of hers, Alfie, had offered her the use of his boat—"a real orchid of a yacht moored out at Deer Harbor"—and I wondered what had become of the girl who used to tremble at the sight of salt water.

I won't say that I was envious; while a home on the marina had been a fond wish of mine, neither I nor my housemates would be sorry to see her go. Alonso complained of the telephone charges and the disappearance of his silver razor, though the latter, he insisted, could not have been the work of Beatrice Chip, career pickpocket, for she had reformed her ways and would never steal from friends. Thera took issue with Bea's treatment of me—"she doesn't visit with you; you'd think she only came to evade the law!"—and lamented the increasing emptiness of our pantry. The household breathed a sigh of relief the day Bea and Joe-Joe took their leave—but our respite was to be short-lived, for it was that very night that the sleepwalking began.

At first it was harmless enough. At eleven, I rose and wandered into Thera's studio where she sat before a portrait of Alonso, adding a life-like gleam to each of his black curls. I'd often watched her paint, for in the airy room, with its ornamental screens, its high glass walls, and pastel silks, I had always felt at peace—and she'd therefore noticed nothing out of the ordinary, not till she'd turned and seen my eyes, which appeared to be staring at nothing at all.

"Our ma was a somnambulist, too," she'd said, leading me gently back to my bed. "Nothing bad ever came of it—nothing dangerous at least."

But I never had taken after our ma.

A week later, I was found standing over the stove, a spatula in hand and a single egg sizzling merrily away on the griddle. The night that followed, my sister was wakened by a draft of wintry air, and she and Alonso, upon entering my room, had found the French doors thrown wide. Without a light, I had strayed onto the veranda, climbed atop the rotting wooden rail—and stood poised as if to leap.

After this, I confess I was frightened to sleep alone in my cavernous bedroom with its countless adjoining hazards. Along the far wall lay my worktable and hat-making tools, sharpened for cutting and gauging. To the right was the kitchen—fire and knives!—and to the left the frost-slick balcony, and the infinite perils of the outdoors. I wouldn't so much as shut my eyes, not until Thera, who was an exceptionally light sleeper, offered to stay in my bed. There were no further incidents till the night of Christmas Eve, when Beatrice came for dinner, and the mulled wine flowed.

It ought to have been perfect—a white Christmas of fairy tale charm. After our feast and figgy pudding, we had gathered around the fire, exchanging gifts and listening to Bea's humorous tales of the nautical life. Often she mentioned Alfie, her young landlord, and I wondered if there was something between them, and was glad to see her looking happier, and far healthier—even rather stylish in the fine black cloche I'd given her. I mustn't begrudge her the boat, I thought—must be grateful instead that she was away from New York, and the vices that had nearly destroyed her.

Then, turning to me, she said: "by the way, Daria, I've been learning to sail," and for the first time, I caught sight of *the look*. It was only a flash, really—a momentary glimmer about the features, gone well before I'd discerned what it was. But I didn't forget it, rummy as I was with eggnog and wine, and later, when I'd retired to bed, alone—for Thera wanted only Alonso's company—I pondered long into the night on its significance.

It had been *glee*, tinged perhaps with something more. Smugness?—no, *triumph*!—a look that might suit a conquering general or the victor of a duel to the death. And I was sure I wasn't mistaken, though I sorely wished I were, for it was hardly an expression one wants to see on the face of one's closest friend. It was born of jealousy, no doubt. Beatrice had always envied me: my talent, ambition, family bonds—and the insipid flattery and attentions heaped upon me by my audience. Though I had always sensed her resentments, Bea had absorbed it all in silence. Now she was reveling in my downfall—the rising star brought low!—and I didn't like it one bit. I would *not* be the Edmond Dantes to her Fernand Mondego.

When next I opened my eyes, I was no longer in my bed. I was upright and shivering in frigid blue gloom, wondering, even as awareness returned, if I were in fact still dreaming. But no; I could distinctly feel my frozen feet, toes numbed by the new-fallen snow through which I must have tread, and the rough wood beneath my heels—and it came to me that I was in the old barn. I could see with waking clarity the gaps between the weathered boards, for through them streamed shafts of wan moonlight, and the stronger glow of the back porch lamp.

I wasn't dreaming, but I *had* been not a moment before—a nightmare, vague in detail, yet poignant in emotion. There had been a frightened girl and an angry boy, the glint of a blade and a calm black sea, churned to milky froth by the thrashing of desperate limbs; slick white hands and wordless gasps, pale silk unfurling, slowly, slowly, in the tide, beneath the indifferent watch of a million stars.

Still reeling, I fumbled blindly for a light—and when at last the ceiling lamp flicked on, I was met with an eerie sight: across the dusty floor led an unwavering path of neat wet foot prints, ending at the target in the far corner. One of the knives had been plucked from the felt, and carelessly dropped beneath.

And though I told no one of the dream or the incident, I was to spend Christmas Day in a frenzy of nerves.

"Cabin fever," said Thera. "Why don't you and Beatrice go to Friday Harbor tomorrow, have a haircut and see how your hats are selling in the shops?"

Well, Bea thought this an inspired idea, and I *was* in need of a haircut, and on the following morning, we made the short voyage to San Juan Island, and the bustling village of Friday Harbor.

"How would you like it?" asked the hairdresser, at the only salon in town.

"Short."

"Like a flapper?"

"Shorter," I said, "like Charlie Chaplin or Nils Asther."

The request gave her some pause—like a gentleman's?—was I *certain?*—but she eventually obliged, exclaiming, when she'd finished, how fetching I looked—how elegant and modern. Beatrice, unsure of what she wanted, agreed to a neat bob, which she subsequently requested shortened, not once, but thrice. The result was a style very like mine, albeit in a far less dramatic color than my raven black—and she didn't like it at all.

"I look like a dowdy schoolmarm," she'd fretted, hiding the sandy wisps beneath her filthy gray cloche.

"Why don't you wear your *new* hat?" I asked.

"I can't. This one was a gift from a dear friend back home, and I won't take it off—not till it *falls* off."

She was cuckoo as a clock, I thought—but I said no more of it, and on the evening ferry, we rode home apart, neither desirous of company. Bea paced the inner deck; I stood at the prow in the icy wind, staring into the roiling wake, where, lit by the cabin lights, the waves glowed palest jade. I wondered how it would feel to fall—to sink into the bubbles as one sinks into a bed—for I was tired in a way no sleep could cure.

That night, when Beatrice had gone home, the nightmare came again. I'd like to say it was clearer, the events less muddled and the faces visible— but it wasn't and they weren't, and I was vexed to reflect, upon waking, that only one new detail had emerged. I'd recognized the setting—the bone-white logs, the dark fringe of seaweed that rimmed the shore, like fur on a lady's coat. It had been none other than Crescent Beach where, in the ashen moonlight, a girl had run and a boy had followed—murder in his heart and in his hands. Just who were they, these slender silhouettes, dressed in white?

I sensed, in a purely visceral way, that it was more than a simple dream, for the very witnessing of it had left me sick, haunted for hours by a lingering sillage of evil. At breakfast, I asked Thera if there had been crimes on the island, killings and the like, but she was of little help.

"Here?" she scoffed. "I haven't heard of any."

But Thera had arrived less than a year before me; what did she know? It was time to seek the counsel of locals, and this I soon did on the days I was able. I called on the neighbors across the lane; I chatted with the grocers and the shopkeepers; I questioned the archivists and the white-haired librarians. Each said the same—that the criminals of Eastsound were smugglers and moonshiners, very seldom killers. Of accidents, however, there had been many. The disappearance of Lorelei Wynne was frequently mentioned, often in hushed tones, though accounts of her death were conflicting at best.

"You know that grave of hers is empty," said Scotty Hughes from over the hill. "They never did find her body, poor child."

What had she been like? I'd inquired. Had she been large or small? Had her hair been dark like that of the dream girl?

"Aye, it *was* dark, and she was pretty and slim, just like you. Have you talked with Ike Whitelee? He knew little Lori, and her brother Russ, better than anyone. He's a policeman now...lives out in Olga."

Well, I fully intended to meet this Mr. Whitelee—to drive to Olga myself if need be—but my traitorous body had other ideas.

The morning that followed, it was clear I'd been walking. I awoke exhausted, my ankles scratched, my feet black with mud, and I stayed in my bed the length of the day. Consequently, it was Thera who, whilst bringing my lunch, first noticed the rash.

"What's that on your face?" she asked. "Do we have bedbugs?"

A glance in my hand mirror revealed that she was right. Spattered across my nose and cheekbones, like a crop of demon freckles, were countless raised rosy spots, and no sooner had I seen them than they began to itch. My first thought was the pox; I was dying, no doubt, or had at the very least contracted the measles. But, as my sister pointed out, there were no other symptoms. Likely it had resulted from a brush with some unfriendly plant during my nocturnal ramblings, or had indeed been the work of bedbugs. My quilts were laundered, and my face well cleansed, and Thera, optimistic as ever, told me the rash would be gone in the morning.

But it was not gone. In the night the spots multiplied, spreading across my brow, my chin, my neck, with the speed of a biblical plague—and it itched, God help me. It itched like a thousand worms writhing just beneath the skin, and I tore and picked and scratched with abandon, rending holes that would surely scar. Thera mixed poultices of mud and clay, and I spent long hours in the bath, soaking the innumerable welts that dotted my chest and back. Each morning, I consulted the mirror, and was repeatedly disappointed. The rash persisted, and with each passing day, my hope and dignity further dwindled.

I wanted only solitude during this time, ashamed of my monstrous appearance—yet at my sister's invitation, Bea came often. She'd use the bath and the telephone, and she'd peer at me where I lay curled and vulnerable in the old leather easy-chair, clothed in nothing but a robe and the cracked gray poultice. She'd brag about her friends and their adventures, and the new furnishings she'd bought, for she was working in the home of General Anderson now, and he paid handsomely. She'd tell me of her new longbow and her sabre lessons with the instructor *I* had mentioned, and say what a pity it was that I couldn't learn swordplay, because she was having an absolute ball. She spoke of her sailing trips, decadent dinners with her best girl Priscilla, and sunny picnics on the slopes of Mt. Constitution, from where, on a clear day, one could see Canada—and most days *were* clear, for upon us was a gentle but glorious spring, in which I could take no part.

Through glass, I watched as Bea assumed my goals, my interests, the hobbies and skills I'd long cultivated—with one purpose, it seemed: to become me, or rather a better version than ever I had managed. She dyed her hair dark, and bought black Chanel and silk scarves and button-top boots, and an ivory cigarette holder just like mine—and she'd don this new finery and stand bobbing over my bed like a dainty carrion bird, dressed head to toe as Daria Slane.

I ought to have sent her away, for what true friend would revel in the suffering of the other? But in prolonged seclusion, the mind plays tricks, and I doubted my own impressions. I was, after all, the only one who'd seen *the look*—the smug half smile, the gleaming eye—for it would vanish, mirage-like, when Thera approached, and I could imagine no sane way to describe it. And so I let her come, dreading, in secret, the spiritual disquietude inflicted by each visit. It continued, this parody of friendship, until one evening in June, just after Bea's birthday, when she'd knocked unannounced at the door of Linger Longer, wearing an expensive black cloche.

"That hat," I said, "was it a present?"

"No, I bought it. Isn't it just ducky?"

"Sure is. Just as ducky as the one I made you, with my own hands, from Italian felt—the one you never wore."

"Don't cast a kitten, Daria. It's only a hat. Can I come in? I simply have to tell you about—"

"No! I'm too tired for visitors. You'd better find your way home." And I shut and locked the door, and drew the curtains.

"It's probably envy," said my sister later. "She resents your creativity. It's harder to counterfeit than a haircut or a scarf."

I didn't care, I said; Beatrice was not to be invited home again, and Thera, ever my loyal champion, reluctantly honored my wishes. When she and Bea's paths would cross—as was wont to happen in tiny Eastsound— she'd explain that I'd taken a turn for the worse, that I was far too tired and my nerves too raw, for the entertainment of guests.

At first these excuses were true enough, but with each passing week their veracity declined. A restless energy was brewing, gradually supplanting the ball-and-chain fatigue that had long held me captive. My feet grew lighter, steadier, and while I was plagued still by nightmares and spells of sleepwalking, a fog began to clear that I hadn't known was there. I longed to leave the house. In the still summer nights, I would stand on the veranda, from where one could hear the calls of orcas beneath the waters offshore, or catch a whiff of salt air; and I'd wish that the ancient madrones and pines were but a few feet shorter, so that I might look out on the Sound.

By late October, I could bear it no more. I would attend the annual Halloween walk, I decided, dressed as a bandit in a cloak and a mask, so as to keep my affliction concealed. But when I tried on the gown I'd meant to wear, brocade mourning garb from the days of Queen Victoria, I was overcome by a curious feeling that had little to do with the rash: *revulsion* at the shape of the thing. An acute discomfort at the fullness of skirt, the snugness at the waist and bosom, and an unaccountable loathing for the sight of my own figure in the mirror.

Flinging the garment to the floor, I tried several more in varying styles, all with the same uncanny certainty that they were somehow wrong, and that I looked wrong in them. I wasn't used to clothes anymore, I reasoned. I had, after all, spent months in only a robe. Then, in a dim corner of the hall closet, my eyes fell on Alonso's double-breasted suit. I didn't try it on—its owner, while boasting a fine fashion sense, stood several inches shorter than I, and it would never have hung right. But at the back of my brain, where instinct sleeps, a queer little flame was ignited, and I asked Thera to nip down to the secondhand store and buy me an outfit just like it, in the slimmest size they had.

It was a scruffy thing, my first suit—pin-striped black with an unfashionable excess of pockets—and Thera looked at me askance as I dressed.

"Why not be a *lady* bandit?" she said. "I still don't understand."

"Neither do I," I replied, for I could not yet find the words to explain. I only knew that I didn't want to be a lady bandit, because I didn't want to be a lady *at all*—and for the first time in my life, I didn't have to. There were no longer fans to impress, no patrons to woo or expectations to honor. There was only little old me, and a blank slate.

I went to town that evening in a capital mood, aglow beneath my mask with a previously unknown serenity, and in the morning awoke refreshed, despite some festive excesses. My dreams had been pleasant, and I'd remained in my bed, not having risen a' once. And when Thera brought my eggs on toast, it was discovered that a miracle had occurred in the night.

"Your skin—it's better!" she exclaimed, and as ever she was right. All that remained of the abominable rash were scattered scabs and wounds—the pink and scarlet leavings of my own fingernails—and I nearly sobbed with relief. At last, at last, I was free!

The scars healed quickly and I wasted no time. Almost daily, I ventured over the hill to the shops, to peddle my hats and my ladies' clothes, and to compile a more fitting wardrobe. By late November, I'd turned quite the profit, and had become the sharpest dressed young fellow west of the Cascades. I bought pleated trousers and suspenders, neckties of paisley and silk; waistcoats and silver cuff links and a long black coat of merino wool. I starched my collars and slicked my hair and bound my chest to boyish flatness—all while my housemates looked on in confusion, no doubt viewing my metamorphosis as a bout of passing madness.

"I don't understand you, Daria," wailed Thera. "Why would you want to change yourself when you're so beautiful—so *feminine*?"

And we'd quarrel, and I'd ask that she call me Avery, for I'd never cared for the name of Daria. Avery Slane, the great thespian reborn—and it was armed with this new moniker and my best black Homburg hat that I strolled straight down Main Street to the tiny Puget Theatre, heedless as ever to the curious stares of the small-minded island folk. Actors, after all, were entitled to their caprices.

According to a poster on the door, there was soon to be a play—a production of Peter Pan—and I was engrossed in reading the fine print when who should emerge but Beatrice.

"Daria! I've missed you. Are you better now? You must be, because here you are, out and about..." As she spoke she studied me, bug-eyed, with frenetic interest.

Much better indeed, I told her. I'd been sleeping like a baby—no nightmares at all. And just what had brought her to the theatre?

"I popped in to say hello to General Anderson's wife, Lydia, who's on the committee. They're doing Peter Pan! Will you audition?"

"Certainly will," I said.

"Which role—Wendy? Tinkerbell?"

"I'd like the title role if I'm to do it at all."

"Of course. With this striking new look of yours, why shouldn't you play Peter? Fellas won't be dogging your heels this time, but you never did want a man, did you? Not, at least, in *that* way."

I smiled, suddenly very fond of my old friend. She knew me—better, at times, than I knew myself—and, in the spirit of the moment, I invited her to supper on Saturday.

But when that night came, and Bea arrived, she was no longer the same Bea I had met downtown—no longer the girl in beaded Chanel. Unashamed, she stood before me in a tailored suit of stark black wool, a paisley necktie at her throat. Her hair had been freshly darkened, and slicked back from her brow, and her head adorned in a brand new hat—a black Homburg precisely like mine.

I nearly shut the door again—nearly turned her away without a word. But I didn't. I stared, agape, frozen by rage and something like fear. She had traded one skin for another, the old me for the new.

"Where did you find those clothes?" I heard myself say. "Rob a little boy, did you?"

She giggled, and slipped past me into the kitchen, Joe-Joe emitting a peevish snarl from the satchel on her shoulder.

We supped in the formal dining room—Thera, Alonso, Beatrice, and I—my companions chatting amiably over my sister's fragrant borscht, oblivious to my gathering ire.

"This is an interesting new look, Beatrice," said my sister. "What does that beau of yours think?"

"Alfie isn't my beau," said Bea. "You know, I've never wanted a man— not, at least, in *that* way...and it's a difficult way to be, on the street, where everyone wants something from you."

Alonso and Thera nodded their sympathy, and I said nothing—only stared into my bowl, stirring the blood red broth and thinking of the Sound—the vast fathomless trench into which any sin might sink.

I dreamed of Crescent Beach that night—saw once again the kelp-choked shore, two figures locked in struggle and a shining blade dropped; the pale hands on a pale throat, ivory silk unfurling in the lapping of black waves. *Lorelei.* Somewhere there existed proof of her brother's crime—and it would be here at Linger Longer.

When I awoke, it was with a jolt, and I knew I had strayed from my bed. All was stifling black, yet I was sure I wasn't in the house or the barn—at least no corner I had explored. The air was different; stale and frozen, imbued throughout with a scent like death—the sickly must of air untouched for years by living lungs. Extending a hand, I felt raw wood, dust, nails—and close behind another wall, and another. Then, thoroughly disoriented, I discovered a door. Hope surged as I grasped the knob, only to plummet soon after when it would not budge!

Panic took me and I screamed, pounding at the unyielding boards and shouting the names of Thera and Alonso—each sound seemingly muffled by the walls of my prison. What if I'd wandered downstairs—locked myself in some closet, far from anyone who might hear me? I'd smother here in the blinding dark, while above they searched in vain.

Then, from below, came raised voices! There was a thud—a metallic object striking the door—and I stepped backward, wincing as my bare feet stirred ancient filth. I heard a scrape, a grunt of exertion, the crack of splintering wood, and the door sprung outward, revealing the worried face of my rescuer, Alonso, who stood perched on a ladder, pry bar in hand. Dawn was creeping over the tops of the trees, and I saw where I had been: locked, alone, in the Nothing Room, for how long, I couldn't say.

Weak and babbling, I was half led, half carried into the parlor, and set before the fire. Thera, fussing, brought blankets and a tincture for my nerves, and Bea sat beside me, patting my back in an awkward pantomime of concern.

"You sure can scream," she said, "like a dying rabbit. Bet they heard you from town!"

Presently, a knock sounded at the kitchen door, and a policeman was shown in, scruffy and fair-haired, his nose red from the cold.

"I called him," said Thera. "I wasn't sure Alonso could free you by himself."

The officer, one Sergeant Whitelee, insisted that he have a word with me, curious as to what exactly had transpired. How had I scaled the wall?—prized open the door? And why on earth should I want to do either?

I couldn't answer—only muttered halfheartedly that I'd been looking for Lorelei Wynne, dreaming of the night that Russel killed her—and that some people, while dreaming, do very odd things.

"What do *you* know of Russ Wynne?" he said.

"Nothing...only I—I saw them, fighting...There was a knife, but he lost it, or perhaps couldn't use it...and then...he was so angry. He couldn't be stopped..." I trailed off, embarrassed, for I'd recognized the name: this was Ike Whitelee, childhood friend of the unfortunate siblings Wynne, and he was glowering at me with patent disdain.

"Russ never hurt Lori. Russ never hurt *anyone*. These lies—they're vile, and you shouldn't repeat them."

"They say her body was never found—"

"She went into the Sound—what would you expect? They were picnicking on the water—Russ and little Lori—and their skiff was tossed by a pod of transient orcas. Russ surfaced and Lori didn't. He thought she'd been pulled below, dragged down by one of the whales—and he was never the same after. Could hardly *speak* of the tragedy."

I apologized, of course, for my thoughtlessness, but couldn't resist asking the thing that I'd meant to all along: what did Russ Wynne look like?

"He's big, bearded...We all called him the friendly giant."

I thought of the boy on the beach, a delicate figure in white—and I confess that my heart sank. He had never been Russel Wynne, nor had his victim been Lorelei.

"You must let this go," said my sister, at afternoon tea. "You'll make yourself sick over a *dream*. And Daria, dear...I don't think you should have Beatrice here anymore."

"Why?"

"I saw something while she was comforting you...a look that crossed her face. And you may not believe it, but...it appeared that she was *gloating!*"

Truth be told, I thought little of Beatrice or the nightmare in the following weeks. The auditions were at hand, and I spent them preparing, rehearsing songs and monologues, even purchasing a fay green coat to better evoke Pan.

When the day arrived, all went swimmingly. The part was mine, I had no doubt; my performance had been impeccable, and I strode proudly through town, my spirits soaring high over the ice-crusted streets.

When I arrived home, Thera met me at the door. "Daria...don't go in there yet—"

"You should call me Avery," I said, brushing past her in annoyance. "Soon everyone else will know that name."

She was acting queer, anxious almost, and the reason was soon plain; for whom should I find in the parlor, smoking leisurely by the open window, but Beatrice—and she was wearing a fay green coat. For one hideous moment, we regarded each other, her features all atwitch with hateful triumph. Then she smiled and embraced me, and asked if I'd heard the news.

"What news?" But I already knew the answer, and my heart quickened in dread.

"I'm going to play Peter Pan!"

"H—how?"

"Oh, I auditioned this morning and they *loved* me—Lydia Anderson told me so! They'll go through with the rest for formality's sake, but she said they couldn't imagine a more perfect Peter, and the part is mine if I want it!"

Thera laid a comforting hand on my shoulder; Joe-Joe snarled from his perch on my leather easy-chair—and I paid no mind to either. All that existed in that moment was the face of Beatrice Chip—traitor, impostor, shameless saboteuse—her twinkle-eyed smirk framed by a dizzying surge of red.

"I'll call myself Adrian," she chattered. "It's a better stage name than Beatrice, don't you think? Less *girly*? Oh, and Avery...Tabby is throwing a party tonight to celebrate. You know Tabby's house—the yellow gingerbread just off Crescent Beach? Alfie and Priscilla are coming and they have nowhere to park their new breezer, so I was wondering, Avery, since your front drive is mostly empty—"

"Get out," I said.

"But...Avery—"

"Get out! Take your mutt, and get out of my house—and don't ever come back."

But she did come back, not days or weeks, but *hours* later, and it was not to beg my pardon. I heard them in the drive: the roar and silencing of a motor, the echo of laughter, gay and boisterous as though all was right with the world. I considered dashing outside, banishing her once more from the property; but I had already dressed for bed, and so I did the thing I would live to regret; I turned out the light, and went to sleep.

The nightmare came with a vengeance—the morbid play unfolding as it always had before—except, that is, for its ending. As the stranglehold was loosened, I looked down upon the victim, her young life drifting out to sea, and at last I saw her face. It was Beatrice, her body limp in the gentle waves, surrounded by the sodden silk of a long nightgown—for she *had* been a girl after all—and the murderer above her, from whose eyes I bore witness, could be none other than myself!

My feet were muddy when I woke, and the white satin of my new pajama suit was uncomfortably damp and stiff. Yet when I told Thera of my worries, she dismissed them in a huff. The nightmare, she said, had been a manifestation of yesterday's turmoil. Likely I'd wandered the grounds, as I was wont to do while dreaming, and been drenched in the early morning downpour. I was inclined to accept her logic; after all no knives were missing from the kitchen, and the fancy car had left the drive, presumably with Beatrice inside.

But a nagging doubt persisted, and at noon I fetched my warmest coat, and made for Crescent Beach. In the bitter winds and rough high tide, it was empty as a desert isle. No footprints marred the rain-washed sand; no body rolled on the breakers or lay tangled in the kelp. Relieved, I was about to turn back when, at once, two anomalies caught my eye. Thera and Alonso's hand-painted dinghy, which had for months remained tethered to the roots of a driftwood log, was now absent; and at the far end of the beach there was movement—a dun-colored speck, racing to and fro along the rising spume. It was Joe-Joe.

That evening, as I had feared, the good Sergeant Whitelee came calling—and he had both news and questions. A quaintly painted dinghy had been found, knocking against the western dock, and it had been identified by a neighbor, Tabby Moran, as ours. She'd been searching for a mutual friend, Beatrice Chip, who had vanished sometime in the night, leaving all her clothes and her beloved dog behind in Tabby's guest room.

"I'm sure she hasn't gone far," said Alonso. "She has strange habits, our Bea, but she always comes back."

"Everyone adores Beatrice," said Thera. "There's not a soul on the island who'd hurt her."

"There's no evidence yet of violence," said Whitelee. "We think she's gone into hiding, set the scene to look like she's met with an accident or that she's split for Victoria—"

"But *why*?" I demanded.

"Come now! As her friends you must know? The charming Miss Chip was smuggling hooch, and we were closing in. Now we've got our work cut out for us, because it's just as you folks say: *everyone* loves Beatrice. She's got the island in the palm of her hand."

Well, my housemates seized this theory and held it close, for it was infinitely preferable to any other. I tried my best to follow suit, but my suspicions robbed me of sleep. I lay awake watching the sky grow light, listening to the carols of the robins—and it was then, with a jolt, that I remembered: *Kitchen knives were not the only blades on the grounds of Linger Longer.*

The barn was dark when I wrenched open the doors, but the flood of electric light soon showed me what I'd dreaded. In the far corner, where in the target had stood six daggers, five now remained.

I packed my bags that afternoon amid Thera's spirited protests.

"It's not proof!" she cried. "You may have wanted to, may have believed at the time that you *were*, but you didn't do it!—you *wouldn't*! Somewhere here you acted it out—like a play in the theatre of dreams—and it will be here on the property that we'll find that knife; you'll see!"

I only shrugged, for it made no matter where it lay—whether in the woods or the waves, as harmless prop or would-be weapon. Only the Sound knew what had happened that night—the great silent Sound and a little dun dog, and I feared the testament of neither.

The time had simply come—and it was by the light of a waxing moon that I boarded the evening ferry, my destination uncertain and my feet as light as wind. The island belonged to Beatrice, and, dead or alive, she could keep it.

FLAYMIRE'S LIGHT
Die Booth

Flaymire Hall was built on the headland, cannibalized from the very stone it stood upon and the timbers of wrecked ships. A ghastly edifice: staring, with a hundred blank-eyed windows, out to sea. Every winter the waves took another bite from the cliffs of Dislendowr, pulling Flaymire ever closer to their wet maw. But the house brooded unmoved, inching— from the moment it was raised—towards its doom.

The house had always been in the Bessemer family. It was built in 1615, more than a century hence, ostensibly by Thomas Bessemer, but more truly by his wife, Constance, who designed the three wings whilst her husband hunted and gambled. The family fortune had its foundations in gambling. "Now, I fear, Edwards," said Ann, the last of the Bessemer line, "that our luck has truly turned." She dropped a chit upon the licking fire, watched the paper char and curl, its ashes twisting up the chimney on the cold, sucking moan of the wind.

Edwards cleared his throat, a habitual practice that more often than not caught into a cough, now muffled by his nap-worn velvet coat-sleeve.

"Yes, Edwards," Ann agreed. "Your father always said 'we make our own luck.'" She glanced at her companion, whose handsome, white-whiskered countenance now so strongly resembled his late patriarch, the elder Edwards of her distant girlhood. "I think that your father lived in happier, more prosperous times, my friend." Sighing, Ann pulled the fringed silk of her shawl closer about her and glanced around the room. The firelight capered, casting weird shadows about the turret chamber, so crowded with antique furniture and treasured artefacts that it seemed they must be barricading themselves in. "We are, I fear, finally insolvent. Every farthing I own is mixed into this mortar, buried in this earth. There are no expenses left to cut—we already live like hermits in these two rooms." She let forth another despairing sigh, but schooled it to a smile at Edwards's frown. "Of course, I cannot dismiss you like the other staff." The old man shook his head, vehemently, reaching for her hand. "I venture I could sell some furniture..." She looked around the room again, at the lacquer and oak and brass-inlaid ebony—all her favorite pieces, not dormant under dust-sheets in the cold, locked wings of the house. Edwards wagged his head vigorously once more, and his tremulous grip on her hands grew tighter. She turned to regard him, gravely. "I could take a husband." Slowly, the old man tilted his chin. "Only if the suitor is right, of course—Oh!"

Both of them turned towards the windows. The pummeling storm outside rattled the casements: all that could be seen beyond was darkness, the inky blue of sky uninterrupted by tree or horizon. Then came the sound again; the distinct cry of voices carried on the mourning wind. Ann covered her mouth with one hand. "Oh, I do so hope that another ship is not lost." Again, the urgent shout carried to them, above the clamor of the gale. "They say the spirit walks abroad these days. When Young Arthur fetched the mail, he told me of it. Maggie Hammett saw it, with its lantern burning, in the lane beyond the drive. He said that some of the farm laborers sighted it in the churchyard. No longer content to just lure ships from our roof, it seems. Edwards, I don't like it. What can it all mean? It feels like ill-tidings. Already we are receiving fewer visitors: the villagers are afraid." Edwards patted her arm, consolingly, but his expression was troubled. He glanced towards the chamber door, back at Ann once again. She nodded. "Of course. Go and check. Let me know if there is an accident—but Edwards? Do be careful." The ornate iron latch clicked, heavily, as Edwards let himself out, the draft through the door setting the candles all guttering. Ann shivered. She picked her way to the windows—she could see nothing save for an ominous, glittering string of torchlight, far down on the beach—and closed the faded brocade drapes. Similar curtains of heavy red velvet surrounded her bed, fighting a forlorn battle against the drafts that insinuated through every crack and keyhole of the house. Ann closed the drapes halfway, tucked her feet beneath her on the bed and reached for her book. After a few minutes with only the lament of the wind and the distant shouts from the beach for company, she heard the too-familiar sound of weeping.

It took a week for the villagers to clear the wreckage from the beach. Edwards had returned later that night to appraise her—soaked through from the storm, his pale blue eyes reddened, no doubt from the merciless whip of wind—that another clipper had run aground on the rocks off the cove and was in two already. On brighter days, at low tide, Ann would walk the blustery yellow sands below the house, but not in the weeks after a wreck. To see the splinters of ship-timber, the scraps of cargo washed aground, filled her with too keen a melancholy to bear. On occasion, more than spoilt cargo washed up. Sometimes the sea took weeks to give up its dead, and the bloated and battered remains that rolled slowly from the ocean's embrace were not something that Ann wished to happen upon.

There were also the smugglers.

They would not be called 'wreckers' for they maintained with venom that the Flaymire ghost with its phantom lamp did all the wrecking for them. They were *salvagers*: a sly, furtive knot of folk who appeared as soon as a ship broke on the rocks, wading into the shallows with nets and rope to snag the unlucky cargo and any other treasure they could lay hands on, like so many ghoulish fishermen, spiriting their scavenged catch away onto the dark pathways up the headland.

That is why, upon hearing a knock resound upon Flaymire's great studded front door, that Ann startled and almost stalled Edwards from answering it. It was not yet late of hour, but the sun had already extinguished itself in the stormy waters of the horizon, staining the sea blood-red. Visitors from the village grew ever more infrequent now that they feared the estate's roaming ghost and certainly did not call so late in the evening. Unless, of course, there had been another accident. Ann descended the staircase halfway, leaning on the bannister to listen. The door gave a dolorous groan as Edwards heaved it open. It was not the wreckers who stood there in the rain.

As Ann reached the foot of the stairs, Edwards stood aside and gestured, to introduce a young man whom Ann had not seen before. The youth in question bowed smartly and offered his hand. "Mister Maurice Callow, ma'am," said he, and his voice was melodious and sweet. A mist of droplets turned his flaxen curls to gold in the candlelight. His fingers were cold as the murderous ocean, and white as bone against Ann's own brown skin.

"I am sorry to trouble you, my lady," said he, in a quiet, deliberate voice. He turned to nod courteously to Edwards. "Kind gentleman. My brother has met with an accident, you see, in the lane beyond your boundary. This was the nearest house."

"Dear me! What happened? He's not hurt?"

Maurice Callow shook his head. "Only a twisted ankle, I fancy. He came off his horse." A frown rumpled his fair eyebrows. "Strange: Charles is quite the horseman; I've never seen him take a tumble for so slight a reason before."

A crawling feeling slid across Ann's shoulders. "What reason...?"

"A light, that's all. Someone bearing a lantern along the lane. It seemed for some reason to startle the beast."

Ann shivered, and caught Edwards's eye. "We'll come with you to fetch him directly."

Callow looked alarmed. "I really don't wish to trouble you, Mrs—"

"Miss Bessemer."

"Miss Bessemer." The glance of his pale eyes, the bleached blue of glass washed smooth by the sea, made Ann feel *seen*. "It's filthy weather out there: I wouldn't want your man, let alone your gentle self, getting an undue soaking. Only, if I may bring my brother in to rest, and perhaps tether our mounts in your stables, then I would be most grateful."

"Of course, bring him in." She watched him leave, and then paced the floor until the door (which Edwards had shut to, to keep out the worst of the cold) swung open once more and Callow entered, his arms about his limping companion.

"You are twins?" The words left Ann's lips almost before she thought them, so strong was the resemblance.

"Yes, miss." Maurice's breath came harder, from his run back to the road, and supporting his injured sibling back to the house. "May I present to you, my brother Mister Charles Callow."

"Pleased to make your acquaintance, Miss Bessemer."

"Mr. Callow. No, please—don't get up." Charles Callow appeared, superficially, identical to his brother—although a certain flintiness of gaze made itself instantly apparent to Ann, that was wholly absent in Maurice. They were dressed much alike, in smart riding attire that spoke of quality: Maurice in gray and Charles in bottle green. The handsome riding boots that Maurice knelt to assist his brother out of ("Lest your ankle swell and prevent its removal presently, my dear.") were exquisitely made and appeared new. Charles's handshake was no warmer than Maurice's, but was more firm: Ann had heard this to be a good quality in a young man, yet could not help but reserve judgement. There was an air about Charles of an inquisitive parrot cocking its head: beautiful, and fascinating, but one was unsure whether it might bite. "You'll stay the night, of course."

"We couldn't possibly trouble you," Maurice said. He cast a glance at his brother who fixed him with the same direct stare.

"It's no trouble," Ann said. Then, honestly: "We get so few visitors these days, really you would be indulging us with your company. Please, let Edwards show you to our guest rooms, and then we may all take some supper."

Charles Callow smiled, a dazzling, sweet smile that quickly turned pained as Maurice helped him to stand, favoring his uninjured foot. "We thank you for your generosity, dear lady, and accept with gratitude."

Ann watched the three of them carefully ascend the sweep of the great staircase. Charles's ankle did not look disfigured, but perhaps the swelling had yet to come out.

They dined on water-souchy with slices of bread and butter. Discreetly, Ann watched the brothers' faces, searching for any disdain at the homeliness of the meal, but found none. Indeed, they both appeared enthusiastic in their appetite, as if hungry from a long and arduous journey. This conjecture was borne up when they three settled to brandy in front of the sitting-room fire. "We were on our way to Porth Steren, before the accident. We've been traveling a long while."

With no bags, Ann thought, but said nothing. She folded further into her shawl, struggling not to shiver: the room was cold, the fact that it was not generally in use all too evident from the chill that permeated furniture so lately shrouded in dust sheets. The fire in the hearth was obviously young, not yet blazing enough to throw much heat. Either the twins were too polite to give indication of noticing these sorry things, or they didn't feel the cold. Either way, Ann did not feel in the position to judge them on their luggage or lack thereof. "Do you have family there, Mr. Callow?" she inquired instead.

Maurice looked at the carpet, hastily swept and in need of beating. Charles replied, "No, miss. We are recently alone in this world."

"Oh. I'm sorry."

He shook his head. Ann thought she saw the faintest hint of a smile tug the corners of his mouth. "Things are what they are. That's the reason, partly, for our journey, though. With Mother gone now, we are looking to relocate from the city. Society life is diverting enough, but we wish to build our own estates. Perhaps to marry."

"I am also without family," Ann ventured, after a moment. She paused, then added, "Except, Edwards is very much like family to me." At that, Maurice definitely did smile, his fair face lighting up with it, like a lily turned towards the sun.

In the subsequent hours, Ann learned much more about the Callow twins: how they were named for the old king and his nephew, their love for horses and hounds, what subjects each favored in their books, and which composers they liked best. It occurred to Ann, after such time had passed so quickly and unchecked, that she was quite shocked to glimpse the past-midnight clock, that her young guests were identical in appearance alone. Charles was, he informed her, born a clear hour ahead of his brother, and it was Charles who indeed carried the most of the conversation. Maurice was quieter and seemed more solemn. "My brother is not like other men," Charles said, a twinkle in his icy-blue eyes that was difficult to read. Maurice shook his head, affably, yet he looked a little discomfited. "But, dear Maurice, you are not!" He leaned forward a little in his chair, the warmth of the fire that now jumped in the grate and twinkled above with motes of burning dust—and perhaps the brandy, and maybe something else entirely—pinking his pale cheeks. "Would you believe, Miss Bessemer, that when my brother here was born, they fancied him...?"

"Charles," Maurice said, quietly stern.

"Dead!" Charles breathed. His brother sighed, pinching the bridge of his nose. "Yes, not only did he show up a full hour late, but they thought him quite dead, for a good five minutes, before he revived. Like a magic trick!" He smiled, with all of his straight, pearly teeth. "You've always been a man of hidden talents, haven't you, Maurice?"

"If you say so, dear brother. But I'm certain that Miss Bessemer doesn't wish to hear any more about me."

"Quite. I must change the subject." Charles agreed. Ann glanced from one man to the other, trying to peer into the pauses between their exchanges. "The hour grows late. Listen to that wind! How it howls in the chimneys like a fey hound that's lost its master. I fancy that lantern-bearer who so startled my Marmaduke in the lane today was truly a spirit."

"Well, there is talk..." Ann began. Something felt not-quite-right: as if she were somehow betraying Flaymire to talk of it to new acquaintances. As if speaking of ghosts might make them the more real.

Charles Callow nodded to her, that blush of color like petals still upon his cheeks. "Go on."

He looked so young, so earnest, that it troubled Ann's heart strangely. "Gentlemen, I will not deceive you. I love my home as I loved my family, but this is an ill-omened house. Accident and misfortune plague this place: they have dogged it for decades. On wild, wet nights, a spirit stalks the parapets, holding an eerie light. When the moon is waning, you can hear the fiend weeping. Oh! Dislendowr was always a treacherous coast, but more ships than ever meet their doom here now, due to that unhappy specter."

"On wild, wet nights, such as this one?" Charles Callow asked. He did not appear afraid. He looked hopeful. "When the moon is devoured down to a rind?"

"Charles," Maurice said again, a note of warning creeping now into his soft voice.

Charles merely grinned at him. "Whose echo is it bejewels the crown of your house with corpse-fire?"

Ann's glance flitted nervously betwixt the two. "Perhaps this isn't the nicest conversation before retiring, after all," she said, and she saw that instant that Maurice's expression softened.

"Not at all, dear lady," he assured her. "Please, go on."

"Yes, tell us, do," said Charles, all eager.

"Before I was born," Ann began, twisting the fringe of her shawl between her fingers. "Nearly sixty years ago, I believe, a young priest fell to his death from the parapet and onto the cliffs below. I've been told my whole life that it is his ghost that paces in the gloom. And now the villagers say..."

She trailed off, those creeping shivers of unease running their fingers through her hair once again. Charles finished for her, "That his figure has been seen in the lanes too?"

"Aye, and the graveyard beside the chapel. It's too awful to contemplate." A sudden rush of emotion threatened to overwhelm her: long months of worry straining the dam of her resolve.

It was as if Charles could read her mind. He fell to one knee on the dusty carpet, and taking one of her hands in his, said fervently, "There, there, dear lady. You are no longer alone and no longer must bear this terrible burden by yourself."

I wasn't alone before, Ann wanted to say. *I have Edwards*. Instead, she shook her head, resigned. "This is a cursed house. You should stay away, for the sake of your sanity."

"We would not think of leaving you unprotected, sweet mistress, until this curse has been lifted." He turned brightly to his brother, who was still seated on the plush green velvet of a Rococo couch. "You see, Maurice: that *was* a spirit surprised us in the lane."

Maurice returned a tight smile. "The hour grows ever later: I fear we keep Miss Bessemer up past her usual time of retirement. Here, brother—I will help you to bed."

"Dear Maurice, I'm in no need of assistance—I'm not a child." His voice and smile were sweet, but his eyes still held that chip of flint that looked capable to cut.

"I meant only, because of your ankle."

Charles Callow paused, half risen. "My ankle. Of course." He stood, smoothly, and nodded. "In truth, it is much better now, but you are quite right, Maurice. It's best that I have aid in climbing the staircase."

"Then we bid you, kind hostess, a good night," Maurice said. As they exited the sitting room, Charles leaning stoic-faced against his brother's shoulder, Ann heard Maurice murmur to him, "That was no ghost in the lane. It was a man."

A tonic though their youthful company had been, Ann found herself relieved when her guests took to bed. Perhaps she was too used now to the quiet of Flaymire, of hearing no living voice but her own, of seeing no living soul but Edwards in his devoted silence. Alone once more, Ann's thoughts untangled themselves. The soft night sounds wove a lullaby: the cadenced tick of the clock, the wind's moan, the hungry snap of the fire. The room was warm for once, and the chair Ann was curled up on, her feet drawn up beneath her skirts and her shawl wrapped snugly, was soft and comfortable. Suddenly, her own cold chamber, and the long, candle-lit walk up the stairs to it, seemed less appealing than simply staying where she was, lulled by the fanning heat of the fire.

Her eyelids were just fluttering shut when she heard a knock at the door—not timid, exactly, but careful. "Edwards? Is that you?"

"Miss Bessemer?" The voice from beyond the door was careful too: clearly Maurice Callow—for already she could not mistake one brother for the other, despite their similarities—wished not to wake the slumbering household, small though it was.

"Mr. Callow." Ann shifted in the chair, rearranging her shawl and sitting properly. She patted the dark cloud of her hair quickly back into some semblance of neatness. "How may I help you?"

In the firelight, his face was painted in shadows. It made him look older. Sadder. "My apologies, miss. I expected you sleeping by now. I only thought I heard..."

"Weeping?" Ann asked, softly. Maurice nodded his fair head.

"Yes, ma'am."

"So you hear it too." All Ann could hear then was the mourning of the wind, the twinned crackle of the fire and rattle of rain against the window-panes. She gestured to the couch opposite her chair and Maurice sat, rubbing his palms against the woolen knees of his breeches.

"I fancy any hearing creature would. Miss Bessemer?" He swallowed: Ann noted the bob of his pale throat in a way that launched a flutter in her belly, as she thought, all of a sudden, upon young men proposing to their sweethearts in chivalrous tales. "May I be frank with you, before my brother is, upon my behalf?"

Her heart thrummed, like a flag in a gale. "Of course."

"I *am* not like other men. On the event of my birth, they thought me not only dead, but also a daughter."

"I am not sure I quite follow, sir, but do go on?"

Maurice nodded. "I came into this world with a particular condition, whereby whilst I have the heart and soul of a man, bodily I bear certain resemblance to the feminine sex."

"My dear Mr. Callow." Ann inclined her head, regarding him gravely: his fair curls and smooth cheeks, his slender figure in his smart gray suit, every inch the Donatello David. "I cannot say other than, it becomes you."

Perhaps he blushed, or maybe it was the firelight. "I thank you, miss. It is not such an inconvenience, except that I shall never father children. Although, I confess, that this fact causes consternation to others more than to myself."

"Well. I myself, so I'm told, am too old to become a mother now—and that is also of more concern to gossips than to me," Ann confided. It felt strange, to be sharing these intimate details with someone other than Edwards; strange, but liberating. "And that is your dark secret? It does not seem so unusual or shameful to me."

"No, miss," said Maurice Callow. "That is not my secret."

He bid goodnight to Ann after that exchange, and once again she was left with only her whirling thoughts for company. Although the sitting room was still snug and hospitable, it now seemed less private than before and Ann, the unexpected conversation having roused her from lethargy, felt more inclined towards her own personal chamber.

The hour crept towards dawn. Ascending the narrow back staircase to the top floor, such a draft snatched at her candle-flame that it was almost snuffed out. Raising the candlestick, Ann paused and took stock. The little flame guttered, leaning far to the left. Carried on the breeze came the familiar sound of sobbing, much louder even than was usual. There was a door ajar.

There was no ghost in the lane. Maurice Callow's words echoed inside her head. Quietly, she followed the chill rush of air to the door that afforded access onto the roof: in the tight circle of candlelight, she saw it held open with a slipper. It was certainly her night of revelations which made her so bold. Cautiously, she set down her candlestick on the floor, and slipped through the low door.

The cold hit her at once, like an ocean wave. A chill wind bit, spitting with it a fine mist of icy rain that clung to Ann's hair, to her eyelashes, blurring her sight. It was a starless night. Fat clouds rolled across a horned moon sharp as the edge of a scythe. Yet Ann could still make out the bare stone steps in front of her—slick with precipitation and dappled with bird droppings—by virtue of an unseen source of light. A terrible, plummeting feeling dropped upon her. She knew she should turn back, but her hand gripped the pitted iron rail against her instinct, her foot set upon the next step, and the next. The sound of wailing grew louder, duetting a lament with the suffering wind. Inexorably, she reached the top of the flight, peeked her head over the edge of the stairwell, to be greeted with a vision she could not fathom.

It was Edwards there on the parapet, wringing his hands in wretched grief, his white hair whipped about his head by the wind, his tears mingling with the salt spray buffeted up from the sea. *Merely Edwards*, Ann thought wildly, illuminated, in spite of the cloud-tumbled sliver of moon, by the sickly glow of that phantom lamp held aloft by the grinning wraith that now turned its ghastly, skeletal face towards her.

There was a knocking sound. Ann frowned into the darkness. She shifted, her limbs aching despite the softness of her bedsheets. Bedsheets! Realization tumbled in all at once. Rubbing sleep-heavy eyes she struggled upright, pushing a pillow behind her to save her back from the unforgiving carvings of the oak headboard. Morning. It must be. It was only so ill-lit still because her bed curtains were drawn. "Come in," she called. Moments later, a light tread on the boards, and she was blinking at wan daylight as Edwards's face appeared between her drawn bed drapes. "Edwards." Her head felt strangely foggy—but then she recalled the brandy she'd drank the night before; not a lot, but certainly more than she was used to. "Have I overslept?"

A slight nod, accompanied by a placating smile. Ann let out a long breath; the presence of her most trusted friend was always a calming influence. "I had the strangest dream." Edwards tilted his head. Ann shook hers. "No, I shan't tell you—you would think me silly if I did. Too much talk of ghosts before bedtime; that is all. Oh—but I feel strange." She stretched her arms, and her frown deepened: pulling back the ruffled reticella cuff of her nightgown, she inspected a darkened bruise on her arm. "Edwards...did something...*happen*, last night?"

A look of sympathy passed over the old man's face. He placed both hands together in an attitude of prayer, leaning his cheek against them, then mimed as if picking up and carrying a child. Ann bit her lower lip. "I fell asleep? And you carried me here, to bed?" An affirmative nod. "So very strange," she murmured, once again, more to herself than her companion.

When Ann made her way downstairs, the twins were already taking tea in the dining room; another chamber unwrapped from its dust-cloths like a corpse from a winding-sheet, hastily cleaned and a fire stoked in the hearth for their guests. The sun shone brighter there through the large windows, but it carried with it no heat, and Ann shivered at the head of the table, troubled by her dreams of phantoms and fainting.

"My dear Miss Bessemer," said Charles Callow. "I hope that you slept well?"

"Please, sir," Ann replied, distractedly. "Do call me Ann."

"I will, miss," said he, his blue eyes alight with all the warmth of the cloudless sky outside. "And gladly."

Charles Callow called her 'Ann' frequently, from that moment.

It became soon apparent to her, over those strange weeks that followed, that Charles Callow's intentions towards her extended to the amorous. The brothers did not so much stay at Flaymire, as they failed to leave. The subject was simply never brought up, Ann realizing abruptly with the advent of her young guests how heavily boredom and solitude had weighed upon her for too many long years. Despite the anchor of Edwards's constant companionship, it was conversation and the company of those closer to her age she craved—although, she estimated, she must be almost twenty years senior to and she'd wager, cleverer by far, than young Charles. Still, he persisted. His attentions were no doubt flattering, but uncomfortable. He never stated outright his intentions, instead deferring to a particular flirtatious coyness that quite set Ann's teeth on edge. His airy compliments and baseless flattery began to feel almost obsequious in nature. Yet, Ann did not broach the subject of the twins taking their leave: for, to dismiss one would be to lose both.

Maurice Callow was a different conundrum entirely.

"Oh!" Ann exclaimed, that day, pressing her palm to her breast as though she might gentle her racing heart that way, like it were a startled beast. Maurice stepped further out of the doorway where he'd appeared, light of tread as a cat, an apologetic look upon his face. "You startled me!"

"Did you think I was the ghost?"

"I thought you were your brother," Ann said, and the tone of her voice left no ambiguity as to her opinion on which was the worse option.

Maurice stifled a smile behind a polite hand, but could not hide the laughing dimples of his cheeks. Composing himself, he nodded towards the flowers that Ann was busy arranging in a large Delft vase with a fluted rim. "They're very pretty."

Nodding, she pressed her nose into a sumptuous scarlet rose. The petals were soft as silk, red as sunset, but the bloom was utterly scentless. Ann tucked it into the vase with its siblings, nestled between red snapdragons and puffs of sweet stock. "Charles fetched them." She twirled a pearly sprig of orange blossom between her fingers. "I think he may be trying to tell me something."

"He wishes to make you his wife."

That concise directness was one of the qualities that most drew Ann to him. She nodded, worrying at her lip with her teeth. "I don't want to marry Charles."

A pensive sigh issued forth from Maurice's chest, and a frown furrowed his brow. "Charles is eligible; charming, young, strong, intelligent, ambitious—why would any woman not wish to wed him?"

"Because I love his brother," Ann said.

She studied Maurice's face for his—surely scandalized—reaction, but received none, save that slow, quiet smile. "I have no money."

"I don't care."

"I will die childless."

"So will I."

The sweet curve of his lips broadened with mirth. "Charles will be cross."

"Let him be."

"My dearest Ann." As quickly as it flourished, his smile faded, his eyes grew solemn. "Do not be so quick to make promises. I have spoken to you of a secret..."

It was as if a cloud passed across the struggling sun. Ann placed the remaining flowers down upon the damask tablecloth and paced the few steps towards him until they were standing face to face. "Knowledge isn't only power. It's currency. There are too many secrets: we hoard them jealously like coins, and count them in the lonely dark."

Maurice Callow nodded once, and took her hand in his. "I will tell you then, dear Ann. And you may judge for yourself.

"You have heard already how, upon the late hour of my birth, I was feared dead. Five minutes I lingered in that space betwixt worlds, and when, at last, took my first breath in this one, I was left with the uncanny sight." He paused, studying Ann's face intently. "Now I remain cursed with it: I see that which ordinary men do not. I, miserable creature, see beyond those dark curtains that separate our world from that of the fey, the eldritch, and the dead as clearly as if they were windows."

Ann was mesmerized. "The night you came, you and your brother, I fancied I saw upon the parapet such a fearful sight...I woke in my own bed, certain it had just been a dream. But now I am not so sure."

"Some echoes are loud enough for all to hear." He gazed at her, his eyes unblinking and full of strange emotion. "Dear Ann, what did you see that night?"

In spite of herself, Ann shuddered. But the press of Maurice's hands over her own was a great comfort, and made her feel much braver. "I saw the ghost, Maurice. The spirit of Flaymire, holding its lantern aloft to lure the ships. Oh! It was a terrible thing: a grisly fiend, fugitive from the tomb. I shudder to think on it, but every moment it haunts my thoughts along with my home. I cannot forget that macabre countenance. It was dressed in priest's habit, but the mold of the grave was upon it, and though the creature was but a shadow, so insubstantial that the storm blew it through and through, it was at once rotting; the gray flesh withered and peeling from its skull, bare teeth chattering, festering pits where eyes should be." She paused to take a shaky breath. "But strangest of all, Edwards was there too. I had taken the sound of weeping to come from the spirit, but it was Edwards whose cheeks ran with tears."

"My dearest, I shall tell you all now: and I do not think that I break your oldest friend's confidence, as I know he would tell you himself, if only he were able."

"My oldest friend?" Ann frowned. "Edwards?"

"Aye, the very man," Maurice said. He led her back across the room, towards a couch where she followed his example and sat, her heart leaping a little higher at what revelation might be next that required she be seated. "The loathsome apparition that you saw was no dream; it was in truth that young priest who fell to his unlucky death all those years ago. As sure as his phantasm fades, his memory is lost to the tide of time. Only Edwards knows him now." Maurice's calm voice seemed to shake with some repressed emotion. "His name was Christopher. Father Christopher was Edwards's true love. But heaven knows that people are not kind. The lovers had to hide their affections, so they would meet in secret upon the roof. Christopher would signal with a lantern when it was prudent for Edwards to come up, but one rain-swept night he slipped upon the wet stone and fell to his death. A tragic accident. Edwards never spoke again, keeping their secret, but he visits the battlements to walk silently alongside his lost love, who is doomed to re-tread those fateful steps there when the moon wanes and the wind howls. Silent, but for Edwards's weeping as he surely expires slowly of a broken heart, for walk together is all they can do—no conversation can pass between a spirit and a man without the uncanny sight."

"It is too sad," Ann said, quietly. "All these years, and I never knew what torment afflicted my dearest friend. But...the ghost seemed so horrible to me. So hideous to look upon, and shining that cruel, false light all across the bay."

Maurice shook his golden head. "You see, the wrecked ships are accident also: piling sorrow upon sorrow; Christopher mourns for those lost lives he had a helpless hand in extinguishing. It is this anguish, and his forgetting by mortal minds, that leads his wraith to fade and rot, becoming ever more ghastly in imitation of the grave." His voice grew contemplative. "The young priest, who has long been moldering in his coffin, and his sweetheart, living yet, but pining to dust!"

For a moment, Ann solemnly regarded their clasped hands, her mind awash with a tumult of thoughts. Presently she spoke. "And Edwards told you all of this. But how?"

"Not Edwards," said Maurice. "Christopher was the one who told me; he speaks to me at night in my chamber."

For an instant Ann reeled with the shock: the notion of that foul specter visiting her gentle Maurice in the dark, of it *entering the house*, was awful beyond belief. But then her thoughts fell again to the tale of grief-stricken love, and her heart ached. "Mr. Callow," she said, gravely, "I have heard your sad story of lost love, and your dark secret, and there is only one way now that I can see fit to proceed." He bowed his head as she rose and stood before him, nodding in an attitude of resigned understanding. Ann placed a hand upon his shoulder. "Maurice, marry me."

"What?" His placid blue eyes grew wild. "I..."

"Will you marry me?" she said again.

A brilliant smile lit the man's face, as he fell to one knee and clasped the hand that had rested upon his shoulder, and kissed it. "Yes. A thousand times yes, dear one."

Laughing in delight, she accepted his loving embrace, before each held the other at arm's length to admire. Finally, Ann was sure, a thin ray of happiness had pierced the ill-fated clouds that hung over Flaymire. "Then, husband, we must make plans to announce our engagement. I shall tell Edwards! And I shall write directly to the parson this afternoon. Perhaps you might tell your brother...?"

"I think perhaps we should wait a day or two and tell him together."

Ann nodded. They both needed to prepare for that revelation. "Then it's settled." Taking up her flowers again, she added a rose to the display. Falling petals scattered across the ivory damask of the tablecloth. It was only when Maurice turned to leave the room that she felt the pang of a prickle, saw a bright bead of blood welling at her fingertip.

The days that passed since then felt filled with more light than before: the windows of the great, gray house on the cliffs seemed larger somehow; the clouds carded across the wide, tumbling ocean looked less opaque and brooding. Ann spent less time in her chamber than she could remember doing in a long while. She rode to the village to deliver letters. She tended to the gardens. She walked laughing along the sands of Dislendowr, arm in arm with Maurice.

She saw strangely little of Charles Callow.

"Miss Ann."

"Mr. Callow. You startled me."

"My apologies." Sauntering into the sitting room, Charles took a seat in the chair alongside Ann's. Both of the twins were, she thought, like cats—in both their subtle footsteps and inscrutable stares. He fixed her now with his, and it took effort for Ann's hands not to shake under his scrutiny, knowing what new secret she now guarded.

"Your brother will be here shortly," she said, and Charles smiled sweetly, but the warmth of it did not reach his eyes. "Will you take tea with me?"

"Thank you, I will." The cup rattled in its saucer as she passed it over, as if the gilded chinoiserie dragons that decorated the fragile porcelain were heaving and coiling around it. "Is there sugar?"

"Of course. One moment." She had to retrieve the sugar basin from the cabinet, so accustomed was she to only preparing tea for one and leaving the unnecessary accoutrements off the tray. Ann did not take sugar with her tea, and up until that point neither brother had requested it. When she returned, Charles was still smiling pleasantly at her, as she dropped a lump of sugar into his offered cup. It was strange, but then, so much about Charles was strange, and she could not dismiss her own pricking feelings of guilt over her still-private engagement to Maurice, that seemed more than ever to weigh as a physical burden upon her shoulders. For a while, they sipped in silence. Then Charles took a slice of bread-and-butter and said, quite conversationally, "I heard you conspiring with my brother."

That feeling of a weight pressing down upon her intensified, dread flooding into her deadening limbs. "I beg your pardon, sir?" Ann said, and her voice sounded slow and far-away.

"This Tuesday gone, in this very room. I know that you are betrothed." Charles set his cup down upon the tray, and stood, seeming suddenly much taller than usual as he leaned over her. Ann tried to stand too, but her strength failed her; she tried to say *what have you done to me?* but her voice wouldn't come. "I am sorry, truly, for the uncouth lengths to which I am forced to go, but you see, you have left me no choice." Slipping an arm around her waist, another beneath her knees, he gathered her up in a dreadful parody of a bridal carry, her head lolling, helpless as a bird's in a gundog's mouth. "The least I owe you is an explanation for my regrettably necessary behavior. You see, my dear, our acquaintance was no accident at all. I needed to meet you. I wanted nothing more than to become your husband: the Master of Flaymire." He crossed the room, and there he stopped, setting her down gently on another chair, before busying himself with something out of her range of sight. Again, Ann tried to scream, to struggle, but to no avail. Whatever potion he must have slipped into her tea while her back was turned had left her conscious but unable to move at all, not even her tongue. Beside her, something sounded a resonant click. "It would have been perfect, had you only not betrayed me." Charles came into view again, crouching down to look her earnestly in the eye. "I searched for so long for the perfect estate, the perfect bride. And you, my dear—an aging, penniless heiress with no prospects and no family and this wealth of land. Well. I even studied the plans to this house, grew to know it like it was my own before I ever set foot here. So you see that it is very difficult for me to give it up to my brother's whim." Producing a length of cloth, he pressed it between her lips, tying the ends firmly behind her head. In her powerless state, she was unable to resist. He leaned her forward and bound her wrists in similar fashion; likewise her ankles. "But when you disappear without a trace, surely fallen from those treacherous cliffs you are so fond of wandering, then this estate will pass to your husband-to-be. And if something were to happen to *him*, well..." He lifted her again, his hands beneath her arms, and Ann saw as she was turned a gap in the oak paneling that had surely never been there before. "Let us hope that nothing has to happen to my brother: that is all."

Her boot heels trailed across the boards; a dreary scraping sound, as he dragged her into the hole in the wall. Inside was a small alcove, like a priest hole, choked with dust and cobwebs. Settling her on her side on the filthy floor, Charles Callow stroked her hair back from her brow and planted a first and final kiss upon it, before he pulled the panel back into place and her world was consumed by darkness.

Ann wasn't certain how long she lay there, surrounded by whispering gloom. There were noises. Unsettling noises. Little scuffles and trickles, like ancient plaster falling where it was dislodged by the draft of air that wound between the boards. At least, she thought, she would not suffocate: but the soft brushes against her bound hands and face felt often more than just the passage of air, and she desperately turned her thoughts from what insects and vermin might be lurking there with her in the dark. Would she die here, still as stone, her bones gnawed by mice and beetles, whilst Charles Callow took her family home? Again, she tried to struggle against her bonds, but she was incapable as a statue: all she could do was stare like one. The view from her prone position was not inspiring. It was too dark to see anything at all inside the partition, but a slight chink between floorboards and paneling afforded her some weak light and a limited view across the polished floor of the sitting room.

She waited.

It felt like an age.

Then, there were voices.

"She's not here?" Maurice asked. Ann tried to cry out; could only whimper around the gag in her mouth, the drug still in her veins.

"I haven't seen her. Not since she asked me to bid you meet her on the cliff walk," said Charles. Shadows passed across the narrow gap beneath the paneling, as one of them paced.

"She wasn't there either," said Maurice. The worry was already audible in his voice.

Charles made a consoling noise. "I'm sure she only tired of waiting and took herself for a promenade alone. Tea is set out; will you join me, brother?"

"Of course."

The floor creaked beneath their footfalls. *No,* Ann tried to cry out, *do not drink the tea!* From deep within the walls, another breeze passed across her numb face, stronger this time and smelling of damp. From without the alcove, she heard Charles say, "Why, brother, what on earth is the matter now?"

The answering tone of Maurice's voice was one that Ann had never heard before. "Where is Ann?"

A puzzled pause. "I have told you: I've not seen her; she must be out walking."

"What have you done with her?" There was the sound of a chair scraping back across the floor, the tinkle of china rattling on the table.

"Done with her?" Charles's voice was incredulous. "What do you mean, 'done with her'?"

"Do not lie to me, brother, I can read your face plain as a broadside. I know that you have taken Ann. Tell me where she is, or—blood or not—I will not be held responsible for my actions."

"Taken her? Rot! How can you think that? How can you know? Oh..." Charles's voice hardened. "Is this what the *spirits* tell you? To turn against your own flesh and blood?"

"The dead do not lie, Charles."

"Then ask your dead man to take you to her, for I will not."

Through the paneling, mere feet away, Ann heard the sudden sounds of a scuffle, hammering footsteps and the ring of breaking crockery. Maurice's voice calling, further away now, "I *will* catch you, sirrah, and I will best you. Take up your sword, for I challenge you to a duel." The whole house seemed to creak in alarm at these events, or perhaps there was just another storm picking up: she thought she heard the drum of rain against the window panes, but perhaps the tears rolling unchecked down her cheeks merely caused her to imagine it.

Again she waited, and may have dozed, or perhaps swooned: whatever the case, Ann jolted to her senses at a sudden noise and realized instantly that she could move again. Her limbs were still weak, uncoordinated from the poison Charles had administered, and it left her no hope of struggling free of her bonds. Still, she could gradually inch to a sitting position, sideways behind the paneling, flinching at the cloying drape of cobwebs across her face. There were voices again, distantly: she strained to hear Maurice, but could make neither him nor Charles out; there seemed to be more than two men talking. Her heart jolted, in alarm and hope. Perhaps folk from the village, alerted by the quarrel? She banged her shoulder against the panel, tried to force it, but it was stuck tight, with precious little room for maneuver. As the voices grew closer, some instinct told her to be still. As they entered the room, she could not only hear them but now also spy them through cracks in the old oak paneling.

It was the wreckers.

"Quiet," an unfamiliar voice hissed, and instinctively Ann held her breath, as if the woman were addressing her. "Your feet are so heavy they'd wake the dead."

Another of them looked around nervously at that. "Don't jest about those things." He said, and crossed himself, his free hand fumbling with the large hessian sack he carried.

The woman rolled her eyes at him, face full of scorn. "It's not the dead we need worry about. Be quiet I say."

"No need." When this man spoke up, the others fell silent. His voice was resonant: it carried clear and rich without him raising it. His beard was so dark that it was almost black and he wore on his head a beautifully knitted cap of cornflower blue, with two long tassels that hung down his back. "The place is empty, I tell you: we're quite safe from discovery. I saw the old fellow leave for market, as usual, then those other two—the youngsters—came out, the one of them shouting about Ann Bessemer going walking along the cliffs. They looked to be having quite the quarrel; I doubt we'll see them back here soon." He raised an eyebrow. "If both of them even come back at all."

"Take heed of Jim Jolly, and let's make haste," another woman said. There appeared, by Ann's reckoning, to be five of them in total, all carrying sacks. "The household might be out, but once the village sees smoke, it'll take more than our Francis dressed up as a specter to keep them frightened away from our route." She picked up a silver spoon from the tea set, examined it briefly, then shined it on the sleeve of her calico print dress and dropped it into the bag she carried. "Here, take what you can carry, and we'll light the place up." A sudden and violent sickness overcame Ann at the words. But she remained motionless, even more afraid of alerting the brutes to her whereabouts than she was of remaining trapped. The woman looked around her. "Shame, really, but needs must, and it has to be now. If the lady marries, then it means people. More staff, more visits, more *noticing*. It'll be the end of our business, friends."

"Aye," the man, Jim, agreed tersely. He walked with purpose, out of Ann's line of sight. She tried to follow his path, but the pattern of cracks in the paneling wouldn't allow it. It was then that she saw, almost hidden from her view and certainly concealed from the intruders, Edwards standing beyond the open door to the hall. He was gone again so quickly that Ann wondered if she may have, in her desperation, imagined him—but she knew in her heart she had not, and her soul rallied with hope.

It felt an eternity as Ann watched them pick over the bones of her life, knowing their intent on burning the leftovers. More than once the thought crossed her mind of knocking on the paneling: perhaps they were not such monsters as to set fire to a house with somebody still inside, or maybe they would even take her for the ghost and flee. But some grim certainty inside her said that they would surely condemn one who had witnessed so much, and so she stayed quiet and still. Hope was deserting her once more when she heard them make ready to leave, and smelled the first acrid whiff of charring cloth. Then, there came a sudden commotion, and she pressed her face eagerly to her spy hole in the paneling.

The first thing she saw was one of the men fall sprawling upon the floor, the force of it sliding him clear across the polished boards. The others sprang forward, and then just as quickly fell back, one of the women holding up her sack of stolen treasure like a shield, against the encroaching tip of a sword.

The commander of the sword advanced: Ann watched the blade slide into view, until she could see Maurice Callow wielding it, his coat torn and hair disheveled, drenched from the downpour outside. At his side stood Charles, in alike sorry state, with a cut upon his cheek, holding en garde his own rapier. Edwards brought up their rear, looking breathless but standing dignified in the face of the invaders.

"Put out that damn fire and come quietly, or you force us to take more extreme measures," Maurice said. Ann felt a flutter of pride as his voice did not waver.

"Oh yes?" The woman in the print dress replied. She lifted her chin and took a step forward. "I count five of us to three of you. Well..." She gave a short, unpleasant laugh, glancing at Edwards. "Two and a half, say." But her eyes widened and her mouth shut as the tip of Maurice's blade moved to her throat.

"And two of us armed," he said. The woman backed away, until her legs bumped into one of the marble side-tables flanking a window. From behind her, a coil of smoke rolled heavily across the room. Ann bit down around the gag in her mouth, her eyes beginning to water.

"Make that three," said the calm, sonorous voice of Jim Jolly, and to Ann's horror, he raised a pistol that pointed directly at Maurice's chest.

"Lower your weapon, sir," said Maurice. His voice was icy.

The pistol's hammer clicked as it was cocked, and Charles Callow moved swiftly in front of his brother. Jim Jolly's lip curled in a sneer, then there was a flash of powder, and a high pitched sound of panic and disbelief rose in Ann's throat.

It was instinct then that spurred Ann to movement. She threw herself bodily at the solid wall in front of her. Lifting her feet, she kicked side-wise at the panel, drumming as loud as she was able. From outside, she heard one of the thieves shout, "What's that? It's the ghost!"

The woman in the print dress replied, "You fool, John Randle, ghosts aren't real." But the man was already running, two of his cronies on his tail. The woman glanced back at Jim. He tipped her a curt nod, and then she too was haring in their wake. They were leaving. Ann had to get out. She shivered at the feeling again of the strange breeze that carried with it the scent of damp earth. The current of air: it surely must indicate an escape route? If she could crawl through the walls, perhaps—but her bound limbs hobbled her, and she found herself transfixed by the scene in the sitting room.

Smoke was filling the air now. On the floor, Maurice cradled Charles's head in his lap. His voice was soft. "Stay awake, dear brother. We need to go outside."

"Maurice."

"Yes, I'm here." Maurice stroked his hair.

"Forgive me." His voice was frail as the ashes that floated around them.

"Charles." The name cracked in half. "I forgive you."

Ann laid her cheek against the still-cool wood of the panel. She knew before she heard Maurice's sob.

"Don't cry, lad," Jim Jolly said, his voice level. "You won't be apart from him long." He glanced over to Ann's hiding place only briefly as she started to hammer once again against the paneling; then he looked back to where he was aiming his pistol, direct at Maurice's head.

The room grew hotter as the flames licked, the air seeming all sucked away. Hell had come to earth. Ann's head spun. As if in a dream, she felt her bonds loosened, that same, incongruous breath of damp coolness brushing her cheek as the gag came undone and she spat it from her mouth and instantly took to coughing as the fumes of the fire hit her. Before she could hammer both fists upon the wall, the panel barricading her popped open with a tiny, dull click. Ann blinked, blinded by smoke and surprise.

Crawling out of her confinement, she glanced about the room. Jim Jolly still had his back to her. His pistol hand did not waver as he began to squeeze the trigger. With no pause for thought, Ann seized the closest weapon to hand, and there was a deafening crack as the pistol shot misfired into the ceiling and Jim Jolly slumped to the ground, the shattered remains of vase and floral display scattered about his bleeding head.

"Ann!"

"My darling." She clasped Maurice's hands and glanced frantically at the fire, now taking swift hold of the furnishings. "We must make haste." She pulled Maurice to his feet, urging him towards the doorway, but he held back.

"My brother..."

"He is gone," she said, sadly. The yellow light of the flames fluttered bronze reflections across Charles's serene face.

"Edwards..."

Edwards. She scanned the infernal room. "Escaped?"

"The pirate." He looked at Jim's slumped form. "We can't just leave him."

"He's likely dead too," said Ann. *And if he is not*, Ann thought, *then he deserves to be: let him burn before we risk ourselves to save that murderer!* Outside the room, the corridor was choked with smoke too, but clearer. As they neared the outside doors there came the vital shout of many voices and Ann's heart leapt.

When they stumbled onto the storm-whipped headland, the village was already out in force. They sat in the back of the blacksmith's cart, wrapped in heavy woolen blankets whilst volunteers braved the burning house and re-emerged with Charles Callow's remains, and with Jim Jolly—dazed and chained—who took his place with the others of his crew already laid under arrest. For once the ever-present wind and rain were in their favor, for the storm was blowing inland, and the rain hammering down damped the flames and soon, whilst the east wing of the house stood smoldering, the central and west remained blessedly untouched.

Clouds of black smoke lingered in the air, blotting out the sunset. Ann called out to delay a hurrying boy and asked, "Arthur, has anybody seen Edwards?"

"Yes, ma'am." He looked at her, then nervously looked away. "You've not heard?"

"Heard what, pray?"

"I'm sorry ma'am, but he's passed away."

Maurice held her tight as she hid her face against his chest. "Not the fire?" he asked.

Arthur said, "No, sir."

"Those ruffians?"

"No, sir," he said again. "He got out soon as the fire started and came to raise the alarm. That's how we knew to come and save the house—he ran into the village and shouted for us all to come quick, and we did. But with all the excitement, he couldn't take the strain. His heart just stopped, sir."

"Wait." Ann raised her head and blinked at the boy. "He *shouted* for you to come?"

"Yes, ma'am. Proper agitated he was, and yelling fit to raise the dead. But he looked peaceful when he went, like he knew his job was done."

When, finally, the jagged silhouette of Flaymire was melting into the deep blue distance of the darkening sky, Maurice asked her, "How did you escape the priest hole?" They'd accepted the insistent offer to stay in the village that night, as 'work's best left on the hall until sun-up' and now the little wooden cart jogged and jolted along the dirt track there.

"Christopher," she said, quietly. "He was never haunting the house. He's been guarding it all along."

They were married when the hawthorn bloomed, and not even the predictable, misting rain could dampen the joy of that day. The west wing of Flaymire was unpacked from its dust cloths and aired out again. The east wing, stones scoured clean by sea winds, relaxed into decay: the dead and the living, in accord side by side.

When the sun extinguished itself in the waves, on fair nights or even foul, you might see the mistress and master of the house taking the air, arm in arm on the battlements of the west wing, gazing together out to sea. And, across the courtyard in the dark mirror of the ruined east wing, their path was paralleled by two flickering shades: reunited in death, and no longer in need of a phantom light by which to find each other.

THE GRAVEKEEPER'S DAUGHTER
C. W. Blackwell

Ginnie Sutton

"Just sit, Clara. You're gonna want to hear it told."

Ginnie twisted the cork from the bottle of brandy and filled Clara's snifter to the rim of the glass, as if she had spent her life filling snifters in a hurry. A Schubert sonata played on the gramophone, strange and beautiful as a summer storm.

"Everything alright?" said Clara. She waited for Ginnie to adjust her bustle over the stool beside her before taking a drink.

"Well, no. It's serious," said Ginnie. "And I wouldn't have believed a word of it if I hadn't seen it myself." She took a sip and squinted at the window as if building the words in her mind. The light had changed suddenly in the room as an afternoon cloud slipped over the sun.

"It's William, ain't it?" said Clara.

"No, the boy's fine. Still mendin' from the accident."

"Thank the Lord."

"He is merciful. This is about the gravekeeper's daughter."

Clara took another sip and nodded. "I know the one. The strange girl with the dark curls. What is her name?"

"Tallulah," said Ginnie. "That's what her mother calls her. I ain't never heard the girl speak, even when she's called upon. She just looks at the ground and rubs her fingers together like it's the only part of her that's alive."

"Reverend Calderwood said her father was some kinda Russian or Polish. Said he worked tending to them graves at the cemetery five years or more."

"Yes, he did. He died in the spring and now his widow Marina does the work, the poor woman. We took pity and hired her for the summer as our maid." Ginnie was still looking out the window and took a bigger sip of brandy than she otherwise would have in polite company. She wiped her mouth and swirled what was left around the bottom of the glass.

"You all right?" said Clara.

"Yeah. Just gotta get it out my craw is all." She poured another drink and just looked at it without bringing it to her mouth. She took a breath and stared hard into her hands. "Well, that woman always comes on Sundays when we're at church, on account of the Polish havin' some other day to worship, Friday or Saturday, I think. Anyway, she brings the girl with her to help. Don't bother us none, since they come and go 'fore we return. Now if you remember, Reverend Calderwood held a short service last Sunday on account of that summer cold he done caught."

"Yes," said Clara. "Go on."

"Well, we come home early and Marina and that strange girl were still tidyin' up the house. Thing is, the girl was just sittin' at the end of this very table with a swarm of flies circlin' around her like she was some kind of dead animal just layin' in the durn road. She was singin' some song ain't none of us ever heard before."

"That's what's been botherin' you so, Ginnie?"

"No," said Ginnie. "What's botherin' me is that Mr. Sutton spent all mornin' swattin' them flies dead as tiny black pebbles and not a single critter was buzzin' when we left for church. I told him he'd need to clean 'em all up if the maid wouldn't do it, but wouldn't you believe it all them things was back up in the air flyin' round that curly-haired girl with not a single dead one layin' in the sill or on the ground or anywheres. Like she just undid it all."

"Like she brought the life back into 'em?" Clara shook her head. "It sounds too peculiar, Ginnie. Maybe they left the window open and more flies got in. It's summertime after all."

"We closed every crack on Mr. Sutton's orders. They was still shut tight when we came home. I'm tellin' you Clara, that girl done brought some curse into my home. You ain't even seen the worst of it."

"You got somethin' to show me, Ginnie?"

Ginnie looked down the hall with her eyes wide and nervous like it wasn't even her own house anymore. She poured another glass of brandy down her throat and coughed into her hand.

"Well, I'll show you on account we're practically family. But you gotta know Mr. Sutton is petitioning Reverend Calderwood for some kind of resolution. Ain't nothin' been agreed to yet, but we expect a visit tomorrow or the next day. Till then, it's a private matter."

Clara tensed up and peered down the hall, trying to see what had frightened Ginnie. "Fine, Ginnie. I'll keep a secret."

Ginnie nodded and went slowly to one of the back rooms. She appeared again shortly with a cigar box held at arm's length. The box was wrapped in a coil of red crochet yarn. Ginnie opened the front door and motioned with her chin for Clara to follow. She laid the box at the base of a walnut tree in the front yard and unwound the yarn, quickly at first and then slower as the material began to loosen from the box.

"Sunday night we heard somethin' scrapin' along the baseboards behind the gramophone," said Ginnie. Her voice was a whisper, just barely audible over the rustle of the walnut leaves. "When William and I looked back there, this is what we found."

She pulled the rest of the yarn from the cigar box and flipped open the lid, then backed away as if letting loose some kind of malady upon the earth. Clara leaned in to look, her feet as far away as she could plant them while still able to peer inside.

There was a mousetrap in the box, fully deployed with a dead rat caught in the steel jaws of the device.

"Looks dead as mutton, Ginnie," said Clara.

"Just wait." Ginnie kicked the box with the toe of her shoe.

There was a scratching sound from inside, and the animal began to writhe against the device. The thing's fur had curled from its skull and it was now lurching from beneath a leathery pelt as if the bones hadn't given up on life and were trying to shake off the dead parts. Its wide, empty sockets and bald skull lifted upward, like it could somehow smell the fresh air with that rotten cavity of a snout. Its legs were just tiny matchstick femurs scrabbling against the sides of the cedarwood.

Clara swayed where she stood and the color washed from her face.

"Good Lord Almighty," said Clara.

Ginnie steadied Clara and looked into her eyes. "You ain't wrong about it, Clara. It's just a different kind of dead, I reckon."

Clara put her hands to her face and shook her head slowly. "You really think this was the girl's doin'?"

Ginnie nodded. "Reckon she found it while she was cleanin' and put the curse on it, just like all them flies. When Calderwood heard about it, he just bobbed his head like he heard it all before. That girl's in league with the devil, I tell you."

Marina Lazarov

When the stew came to a boil, Marina ladled two portions into wooden bowls that were the color of chestnuts. The smell of stock and carrots now filled the mud-brick shanty, and at once it reminded her of her grandmother; quiet and pale and forever shifting from the stove to the table to the cot in the dark corner of the room where she slept, as if each unconscious hour would bring her closer to her eternal reward.

She laid the bowls on the table and went to the window to call the girl. When the girl didn't come, she sat alone with the steam furiously rising from the stew. After a moment, she lifted one of the bowls and walked it outside as the sun scattered through the oak leaves and the insects chittered and whined in the shadowed boughs.

She found the girl sitting on a wool blanket beside her father's grave with her knees pulled to her chest and her arms laced around her shins, humming a song that Marina would sing to her long ago.

"Talushka?" she called, but the girl didn't respond. She hummed like it was some kind of process that had to finish without interruption. "Talushka, supper is ready."

The girl looked up and pressed a finger to her lips and tapped her ear as though listening to the granite headstone. Marina kneeled in the splayed grass and placed the bowl on the ground beside her. She reached for the girl and swept a lock of her black curls behind her ear and thought of her own mother in her youth, before her curls turned gray.

"Talushka, please listen to me," she said. She had served the girl supper in the graveyard every day for six months, but this day there was something that was clambering to be heard, something raw and pure and unanticipated. "I know you are sad for Papa," she said, and when she said it her hands shook as if the words wanted to come out from there. "I know you are sad for wanting the school. I will speak to...to...учителка."

Tallulah's earth-brown eyes pooled with tears and her breath quickened. She lifted a book from atop the wool blanket, slapped the pages to the back cover, and scribbled over it with a knife-honed pencil. *Teacher?* she wrote.

"Yes," said Marina, her own eyes welling. "Tee-cher. I want school again for you."

The girl gazed across the cemetery to the daisy-colored schoolhouse in the distance. She cupped the bottom of the wooden bowl and reached for her mother's hand. Marina led her through the oaks and elms toward the broke-down shack blooming with the smell of stock and carrots and the fading trace of her dead husband's cherry pipe tobacco.

Ambrose Calderwood

Reverend Calderwood sat in a cloister made of pinewood, running the edge of a dagger over his wrist and watching the skin turn white with each scrape. He flicked the tip of the steel at each of the bald scars on his arm, thoughtful and calm as if counting the heads of animals in a herd. He stopped suddenly, as though remembering something he had forgotten, and shuffled through a stack of papers on his desk until he found a page with a handwritten poem. He read it to himself twice, then a third time aloud. As if inspired by the words, he rose, lifted a cane with an ivory knob from beside the door, and went out into the failing light of evening.

Slowly he walked along the road, past the gaslit storefronts and the schoolhouse with its eerie yellow paint that glowed with its own brightness. He walked through a field of tall grass where he could hear the river burbling like the sound of an unending hush. He emerged among a row of houses and went to the third house on the row, where the window was lit with a flickering lantern, and the porch smelled of fresh lacquer and boiled potatoes. He stood at the door and listened for a moment, then knocked with his cane. A man soon appeared, glanced through the door window and pushed it open.

"Reverend Calderwood, please come in," said the man. It was Daniel Fleming, the thresher salesman from St. Louis. He was short, with a wispy beard that grew haphazardly about his cheeks like a boy who had come to the very edge of manhood but had never crossed the line.

"Hello, Daniel," said Calderwood. He laid the cane beside the door and stepped inside.

"Eliza has dinner on the stove. You are welcome to join us."

"No," said Calderwood. He attempted a smile but it only looked dower. "I've already eaten. I've come on official business and have a few questions for Mrs. Fleming."

"Of course," he said. "She's in the kitchen. Please sit down."

Daniel disappeared down the hall and when he returned, Eliza was with him wearing an apron and holding a cooking mitt.

Calderwood was still standing.

"I've interrupted your supper, Eliza," said Calderwood.

"It's no bother," she said. "Sorry we haven't been to church this month. I've been preppin' for school and Daniel has been so busy."

Calderwood lifted his hand and shook his head.

"No need for that," he said. "I intend to make this quick. It's about the gravekeeper's daughter. I know that she was dismissed from your class in the spring."

Eliza and Daniel looked at each other as if waiting for the other to react. Eliza walked to a chair in the room and sat, laying the mitt over her lap.

"Yes. Tallulah," said Eliza. Her face was expressionless, and she was looking only at the space between them.

Daniel walked to her and put his hand on her shoulder. "Forgive us, Reverend. We weren't expecting company," he said.

"I understand. Only certain allegations have been made. I thought you could help."

Eliza looked at Daniel, then back to Calderwood. "I'm afraid the girl was slow," she said. "She couldn't learn the language and was holdin' the other students back." She looked down when she said it, then slipped her cooking mitt over her hand and took it off again just as soon as her finger reached the end of it.

"Slow," repeated Calderwood. His tone was curious. "Remind me of her native language?"

"Bulgarian, if I remember it," said Daniel.

"You know the girl as well, Mr. Fleming?"

"Only 'cause we talked about it, Eliza and I. It was hard on her. My wife has a great affection for the children."

"What else do you know about her?"

"Well," Eliza said. "I know they come up along the river from Louisiana. The girl was born there in Tallulah, near Vicksburg. That's why they done give her the name."

"I see," said Calderwood. He pulled a slip of paper from beneath his coat and unfolded it like a map, then he went to the sill and lifted the lantern so he could see it clearly. "I'd like to read something."

Eliza stood and pointed politely to the kitchen.

"It can wait," said Calderwood. "Please have a seat, Mrs. Fleming." He cleared his throat. "*Rain falls on tilted stones.*" His voice was low and lyrical as if reading from scripture on Sunday morning. "*And ne'er the dead do know. But from their blackened mouths do sing a song once sung by ancient kings, that makes them stir atop their beds and dream they walk'd on earth instead.*"

The Flemings sat and listened as if more words were coming and so didn't give a reaction.

"Do you know who wrote that?" said Calderwood. He was smiling as though he were proud of his own recital. "It was your *slow girl*, Tallulah. Now, in my opinion, it is derivative of Dickinson—and decidedly ungodly—but I would challenge anyone in this town to write something better. It goes on, would you like me to continue?"

"No," said Daniel.

"And why not?"

"'Cause there's somethin' else."

"Oh good, I was hoping as much," said Calderwood. He folded the poem and slipped it back in his pocket.

"I travel a lot, as you know," said Daniel. His voice was flat as if it pained him to talk. "One thing I like to do on the road is collect moths and butterflies. You know, pin 'em to a board like they have at the museums. I bring 'em back to show Eliza, and sometimes I'll show the children."

"I can almost picture it in my mind," said Calderwood. He was grinning and rubbing his hands together, and his eyes seemed to glow in the lamplight as if they somehow burned off the same kind of fuel.

Daniel continued, trance-like as if in confessional. "Last winter I brought some butterflies I caught while prospectin' in Tennessee. Eliza asked me to bring 'em to school, so I did."

"And how did it go?"

Eliza's eyes were closed, and something was now smoking in the kitchen. "The children took an interest," she said.

"And Tallulah?"

"Especially Tallulah," said Eliza. "At lunchtime, she began singin' to them dead things in Bulgarian or what have you. Some melody ain't nobody heard before."

"She was singing to the insects?"

"That's right," she said. "And when Daniel come home and set them things on the table, they was flappin' their wings and curlin' up against the pins like they weren't never dead to begin with."

"I know it sounds peculiar, Reverend," said Daniel. "But that's the truth of it. The Lord's honest truth. I unpinned 'em all and some flew up and over the house and took off in the breeze. For a short time, all them colorful things floatin' over the house seemed, well kinda pretty to me and the missus."

There was now a ghostly gray smoke that hung in the air.

"May I excuse myself?" said Eliza, inching backward to the kitchen.

"Yes, of course. I'll see myself out."

Daniel walked Calderwood to the door anyway and held it open for him. "What are you going to do about the girl?" said Daniel.

Calderwood lifted his cane and bounced it in the air as if guessing its weight. "I think a baptism is in order."

"I see," said Daniel, nodding placidly in the doorway. "You reckon that'll put an end to it?"

"Perhaps," said Calderwood. He planted the cane on the walkway and smiled wide enough to catch the light of the moon in his teeth. "I've found that the longer you hold a sinner under the water, the greater the absolution. If it takes longer than one can naturally hold their breath, well that is no fault of the Lord's."

William Sutton

The boy stood at the edge of the road, watching a carriage pass before him as if the horse and wheels were something to fear, like some kind of nightmare contraption imagined in the stranger passages of Revelations. He followed it with his eyes and as it passed he swatted a clod of dirt with the tip of his crutch, but doing so sent him into a precarious hop, with each stumble more damning than its predecessor, until he was bent and toppling with the crutch slipping sideways in the mud. He teetered for a moment in that awkward pose until an arm looped around him and held him steady.

William turned his head into a faceful of black curls.

"Tallulah?" When the boy said it, there was something in his voice that sounded like he hoped it was her.

Tallulah held the boy by the shoulders until he inched the crutch under his arm and gave him a quiet smile in lieu of a proper greeting.

William looked up and down the street as if counting the people he could see. "I ain't supposed to," he began, but then he paused and looked the girl over.

Tallulah backed away and gazed at the ground.

"Ah heck, it don't sit right by me anyway," he said. "You wanna sit somewhere? My leg is aching and I heard my momma talkin' 'bout you, and it's somethin' you might want to hear if'n you don't already knows it."

Tallulah shrugged and pointed across the cemetery and made her hands undulate from one side to the other as one would describe a river. William understood the meaning. They turned from the road and went slowly through the ankle-high grass among the teetered gravestones to where the willow brush grew and the hiss of the river was loud and urgent. They settled on a stony wash where the river deepened over a jumble of boulders and watched the eddies whirl and shine against the brightening of the sky.

"Momma always says I'm a chatter bug, and well my daddy says it too whenever he comes around, business bein' what it is," said William. "Everybody got so many durn secrets. I say just talk, and let them chips fall where they may, that's what I say." He rested his crutch over his lap and looked at the girl, who was studying his face like he was the only one with a voice in the world. "And you never seem bothered by me. I just like talkin' to you, Tallulah."

The girl touched his hand as if to thank him, and the boy folded his other hand over it, and they sat that way, with their hands overlapped.

"Thing is, I heard Momma talkin' 'bout you and those dead critters we found at the house." His hand had become sweaty and he pulled it away to adjust the crutch on his lap, as if somehow it needed adjusting. "She said Reverend Calderwood wanted to baptize you here in the river. The way she talks about him, well he seems like he'd talk to Mrs. Fleming about you, if'n you stop that singin' and hummin'. Don't know why they're so cross about it. Heck, you got a better singin' voice than any of them old church ladies anyway."

Tallulah crossed her hands in her lap and watched the river spray off the stones on the riverbank.

"I know you ain't a Christian, or at least maybe you're half-Christian—I don't know what you is. But singin' like you do, well if you joined the choir Calderwood would walk you to school himself, I'm sure of it. Mrs. Flemming would be waitin' for you there, big ol' smile on her face."

Tallulah turned to him and looked hard into his eyes, and there was something inside of him that heated up, as if his shoulders were tugging his body that way. Instead, William cleared his throat and fished for something in his coat pocket. When his hand cleared the lining, he was holding a long steel tube with a cap at both ends.

"Ever seen one of these?" asked William.

Tallulah shook her head.

"Got it from my uncle on the Fourth of July. It's a firecracker. A big one."

Tallulah eyed it and turned back to the river.

"Ain't gonna light it off now," said William. "I'm savin' it for the first day of school. That red-haired boy Zacharias is in on it too. If you're there we can light it off together. If not, well I reckon you'll hear it from your momma's house and then you'll know I'm thinkin' 'bout you and wishin' you were there, too."

Tallulah took the firework from the boy and turned it over in her hands. There was a displeasure in her eyes. She opened his coat and put it back into the seam pocket. She pressed the jacket against William's chest, straightened his collar and watched him for a moment. She leaned in and kissed him on the lips. The boy's cheeks turned red as apples and he blinked his eyes. He reached for the girl's hand and just held onto it like he had suddenly found something soft and kind in the world that until then he had only known by rumor and innuendo.

Dell Trafton

It was the hottest day of the year, and the cicadas hissed loud and boastful from the shadows. Dell Trafton stood on a sandy wash along the riverbank, lifting his hat every few minutes to wick the sweat from his bald and freckled scalp. He saw a pair of finches depart a cottonwood tree along the trail, and soon he heard the sound of footsteps over dried leaves. Reverend Calderwood appeared in a white robe with a bible held square to his chest, and the dark-haired girl and her mother followed just a few paces behind. Calderwood led the pair to the edge of the river, and held his hand to it like he could somehow sense its qualities from the nakedness of his palm. He stood until his stillness became strange and electric, then he turned to Trafton with a menacing smile.

"Hello, Marshal Trafton," said Calderwood. His voice had a calm and far-off quality. "This is the day the Lord has made, let us rejoice."

"Hello, Reverend. Amen and hallelujah." Trafton smiled back, but it only failed at his cheekbones.

"Being in the presence of the unholy is never easy," said Calderwood. "But we each have our crosses to bear, isn't that right, marshal?"

Trafton's smile had surrendered completely and was now tightening around his chin. "I got mine," he said. "You and the Lord knows it."

Calderwood placed his hand on Trafton's shoulder and sighed, looking sideways into his eyes. "The Bible celebrates witnesses, marshal. There wouldn't be a book without them, you understand that don't you?"

Trafton nodded and glanced at Marina, who was tucking the girl's hair behind her ears and kissing her forehead. His gaze fell to the silty ground. "Reckon I do, Reverend."

"Good." Calderwood patted the man's cheeks. "The Lord has called you here today. Bear witness, my friend. There is much to say of the pen, but does not our Lord prefer the sword?"

Trafton managed another smile, but when he did so, he was vaguely aware of his thumb brushing the wooden grip of the .38 at his hip.

There was a far-off sound, like cannon fire.

A dozen crows flew overhead.

They watched the birds soar high above the river to some faraway roost.

Calderwood walked to the women on the riverbank. The girl was distracted, smiling and scanning the treeline for the sound she had heard. Calderwood pressed his hand on the girl's back and walked her into the water, the hem of her dress floating like something that had been spilled into the current.

Trafton built a cigarette and lit a match against the rough grain of his belt. As he blew out the first breath of smoke, Calderwood whispered in the girl's ear and tipped her backward against the mirrored surface. Her hair floated and her breath bubbled and broke apart into a smaller froth, but when she was expected to come back up, she remained underwater, her form like some dark root curling from the river bottom.

Marina screamed at Calderwood.

He only stood there, still and passionless as if counting to himself or imagining something far away. When the girl began to thrash, her mother moved into the current, shouting in her native tongue.

"Marshal," Calderwood yelled, and gestured at Marina. The sleeves of his robe were pulled up to his forearms, exposing the bald and striated scars along his wrist. Watching him hold the girl down with that wildness about him, Trafton suddenly understood what the scars meant: they were tally marks, plain as the color of his face. Trophies for each time he reckoned to please the Lord.

Trafton made a show of reaching for the woman, but she passed easily by and stomped deeper as the girl kicked and fought beneath the surface. When Marina neared, Calderwood struck her with the back of his hand and she fell into the current.

Trafton watched the ordeal unfold as if he were somewhere else hearing it told to him, but again he was aware of his hand feeling for the pistol. This time he lifted it from its leather cone and clicked the hammer back, but all he could see at the end of the barrel was the preacher, wet and angry and murderous and he imagined him shot dead in that cold, deep pool where his soul might drown under the weight of its own avarice.

A man's voice shouted from the trail behind them.

Trafton turned and saw three men scrabbling along the riverbank with buckets in their hands, and his first thought was that he had never seen men in this town move so quickly.

"Fire," called the first man. "Fire at the schoolhouse!"

Calderwood released the girl and she launched to the surface, spitting and vomiting with her hair sucked around her face. The men were already at the river dipping their buckets and turning back up the hill. More townsfolk appeared, slipping over the loose trail with pots and jugs and other useless things one might grab in a panic.

Trafton lowered the hammer of his pistol and placed it into his belt, watching the preacher's eyes glower and redden like the whole river was soon to boil over.

Tallulah Lazarov

A tower of smoke curled at the sky beyond the cottonwood trees, gray and crooked as a dead man's finger. Tallulah saw her mother wading toward her, sobbing and bleeding from her mouth.

"I am sorry," Marina cried, wrapping the girl in her arms and heaving. "We leave today. Not this town. Not anymore."

"No," said Tallulah. She just stood there, arms at her sides, watching the sky.

"You speak," said Marina, her eyes dark and wild.

Tallulah looked at her and then at Calderwood, who was now on the riverbank asking a man about the fire. She took her mother's hand and they emerged from the river, through the gathering crowd and up along the trail as people ran beside them in both directions. When they reached the top, an old woman brushed past them and toppled to the ground, spilling a cooking pot filled with river water. The woman scrambled to her feet and looked into the empty pot, and then at the schoolhouse.

"Oh dear God, those poor children," she said, and fled back down the trail.

Tallulah let go of her mother's hand and ran through the cemetery to the edge of the road. A dozen people were running frantic along the front of the schoolhouse, which was now consumed in waves of red-orange flames. Black ribbons of smoke spooled into the air. As the wind shifted, Tallulah could feel the heat wash over her. A single boy lay in the road, coughing and crying and pointing at the conflagration while a woman gave him water and tried to calm him.

Tallulah backed slowly into the cemetery, and as she did so a melody started at her lips. It was nothing more than a hum, like a sonata once played long ago in a place nobody remembered anymore, a place from which everyone had simply moved on and forgotten. She stepped backward with her eyes closed until she stood over her father's grave. She stood with her arms held into the air and her dress still wet and heavy and she sang until the people running by slowed and listened curiously, as if somehow singing was more useful than the pots they carried. She sang louder, the words unfolding like strange flowers that bloomed into the hot air.

Beneath her feet, the earth began to stir.

When it began, it all seemed natural, like some pocket gopher tugging at the roots and making the grass jerk against the soil. But soon all the plots were stirring and the headstones tilted forward and back, and as Tallulah's song rose, the hands of the dead broke through, clawing and growing from the earth as if this world could somehow birth the same body twice.

Word spread of the dead's coming through shrieks and footfalls as the townspeople disappeared into the shadows of the cottonwood, or down along the road with their jugs falling spindrift into the street. And when, at last, they unfolded from their graves, they shook off the gravedirt and descended in a lumbering march to the road where they swayed and waited for the rest to gather.

Tallulah followed the dead like some ancient shepherdess urging them onward over the road, their bones clicking and scraping in the joints as they moved.

Soon there were nearly fifty of them bunched against the schoolhouse, clawing and pushing at the blackening wood until they found purchase through the doorway and disappeared one by one into the flames. For a moment there was only the sound of Tallulah's song and the quake-like rumble of the fire. A lone dog howled somewhere in the distance as if unsettled by what carried in the wind.

Calderwood emerged from the willow brush, his robes wet and dragging through the dirt.

"Witch!" he cried, pointing to the girl. "Look and see what curse this devil has brought us." He turned and shouted at the trees where faces now peered from the haze. "Look and see this leviathan and let us mete out the Lord's justice."

Calderwood reached for the girl and gathered a handful of her hair in his fist, but as he did so, the dead emerged from the schoolhouse with loads of their own. They stepped to the center of the road and laid their charges down, each child crying and gasping and flinging away their smoking clothes. Yet more came, every one of them bringing forth a new figure until the last of them set the schoolteacher down. Her hair was burnt and matted around her scalp. She gasped and sobbed and blessed the dead even as she struggled for a full breath of air.

Marina stood among them with a kitchen knife in her hand, her eyes filled with nearly the same shadow as those swaying beside her.

"Let her go," she said to the preacher.

Calderwood slipped his own blade from beneath his robes and wagged it in the air.

"Let her go?" he snapped. "I'll let her go when she's dead and stumbling alongside this foul herd." He yanked the girl's hair so the veins of her neck showed naked and blue to that choked-out sun. "May Almighty God forever pass his judgment upon the most wicked among us," he shouted.

He had barely finished those words when a pair of decrepit hands slipped around his throat. He made a sound as if to scream, but the pointed fingertips hooked deeper into the softness of his flesh and all that came forth was a wet and angry growl.

Calderwood plunged the blade into his attacker, but it only rattled between the dead man's ribcage. He sliced again at the air as he fell to his knees. More hands raked over him, scratching and pulling him toward the burning structure.

The townsfolk only looked upon the preacher curiously, as if watching a vagrant from some far-off town stumbling drunk in the street.

Calderwood kicked his legs and tried to scream as blood gushed from his throat, but the dead dragged him slowly into the flames until he vanished, the pops and cracks and errant sparks becoming the preacher's final and most dramatic of sermons.

Ivan Lazarov

The dead stood over the children in the road, beckoning the townspeople with boney gestures. And as the people came and knelt beside them, the departed returned to the cemetery, each to their own plot where they settled atop the dirt with their knees tucked and hands balled at their chins.

Tallulah sat with her dress bunched beneath her, hair falling over her face. Marina stood behind her and combed at the curls with her fingernails.

Her mother's hands stopped and pulled away.

An old man approached and crouched beside the girl. He handed Tallulah a wooden ladle filled with water, but she only stared at the ground and waved it away. The man lifted the girl's hand and placed the handle into her palm, some of the water spilling into the dirt.

"Not for you," he said, his voice was just an ancient whisper. He pointed to the other children stirring in the road. "You're not done with it yet. They still need you."

The man touched the top of her head and shuffled slowly to the cemetery gates. Tallulah looked into the ladle and then at the hill where the dead had wandered. The old man stood by the iron arch with his shoulders hanging low beneath his filthy wool suit. His hair was white and full of dirt and his face was gray as ashes.

"Papa," said Tallulah, and she rose to her feet.

The man held up a hand, and pointed down the road. She looked in that direction where the people were giving water to the living and singing some old hymnal that was slow and telluric, as if the melody had been buried someplace deep and was now being tenderly unearthed.

YELLOW CANARY
Allister Nelson

It was a summer afternoon—slow like molasses, with the kind of heat that melts marrow to mush. Death lazed on a riverbank, sharpening his scythe with a whetstone. He attempted to tan, which was difficult when you had the complexion of a corpse.

Something rustled in the brush. Death looked at the forest's edge to find a dirt-smudged girl, watching him from the crook of a tree. She had wild curls, umber skin, and fraying black boots laced to the knee.

Death glided over, plucked a brier rose, and offered it to her. The leaves withered in his grasp.

She studied the inky blackness of his robe, then swung down from her bower.

"A flower for an overcurious girl," he said, voice honey-sweet.

She smelled the woodsmoke and loam that wafted from him, saw the void in his eyes, and recognized Death for what he was. "I don't take things from strangers," she said, stubborn nose pointed skyward.

Death circled the girl, tossing his flower to the side. "It's impolite to refuse gifts, you know."

"It's rude to arrive uninvited."

Kindling flared in his eyes. "No one refuses me; I come and go as I please."

Undaunted, she pinned his face with wood-dark eyes. "You come too often, and you're never wanted. You're a Mormon bicycle boy that knocks at exactly the wrong time."

"And I suppose you're the cookie-peddling Girl Scout?" Death asked, amused.

"Something like that. Maybe if you offered Thin Mints instead of death, you'd be more welcome."

"Don't tell me how to do my job," he began, then paused. "How do you know what I am?"

"I saw you at mom's sickbed. You stood at her wake, collected her soul, and your shade's haunted our house ever since."

Death's lips parted. "I'm sorry for your loss, but such is life's dance."

She shrugged. "I don't blame you. But you shouldn't be here, out in the daylight, sunbathing. This *is* my hideout, after all."

"Not welcome, eh?" Death said, motioning to the woods. "The mayflies are breathing their last, and fruits need ripening for the harvest." He withdrew to the forest's edge. "Things must be reaped."

The girl watched as he touched the branch of an apple tree. The blossoms withered and folded in on themselves, growing fat with the gestating seeds. Soon they bore succulent fruit which he plucked, smiling as he sank shining teeth into an apple's flesh. "Here. Taste the fruit of my work."

She took one hesitantly: it throbbed with potential, tasted like dreamsand. Her eyes widened and the world grew rich, golden with the beauty that suffused it.

"Is this how you see things?"

"Lovely, isn't it?"

"Yeah..."

With that, Death vanished, leaving a withered rose at her feet. She called out his name, breast burning with questions, but only the meadowlark answered.

The summer passed and the girl grew older. She felt the change now, in her bones, like a wild thing. She kept his rose in a vase by her bed. It thrived at her touch, but its petals were black as coal.

Autumn gave way to winter, and a chill crept into her house. Her father, long-mourning, became broken, an automaton going through the motions of life. He wasted like there were worms in his guts, and neither doctor nor machine could diagnose him.

Somber, the girl—not really a girl anymore, though—cared for him. As the nights dragged on, the petals of her rose veined blue. She watched in morbid fascination as it bruised, tinting its water red. Each morning, it was covered in ruddy dew. She licked the droplets, once—they tasted like Communion wine.

The not-yet-woman, no-longer-child did everything she could to delay the inevitable. She watched as her father was sapped of strength. At night, he cried out to his dead wife. "I can feel her now," he told his girl, eyes filmy, like rain on a windshield.

The moon thinned to a sickle and her father's pain waned as he faded.

The girl raged against Death. Her pleas slipped off his ears like rain. Her father sank into dreams, conversing with his love, whom he imagined at the foot of his bed. He was taken to the hospital, and though she was old enough to take care of herself, the girl was too young to be alone.

At the stroke of eleven, through the peals of a summer storm, she watched as the rose wept blood.

The girl rushed to her father's sickbed, bursting into the ICU to find Death. She saw his pale hands, hovering over her father's heart.

"Don't touch him."

She grabbed a scalpel and plunged towards the Reaper, brandishing the blade.

He made no motion to defend himself—Death simply stood there, letting the metal part his flesh. He sighed as she crashed into him, steadying her shaking limbs.

"That hurt." He pried the blade from his empty ribcage.

She pummeled him until her knuckles bled. Death ignored her, watching her father's arrhythmic heart pulse across the screen.

Strength spent, she collapsed to the floor. "Don't take him," she begged.

"Whether I want to or not, it's his time. All the pleas in the world couldn't stop me. Or all the knives." Death smiled softly.

"There must be something you want. Anything, I'll give it to you. I could show you the best spots to tan, God knows you need it—"

"Trying to bribe me, eh? You know that never works. Don't fret—your father'll thrive in the place he's bound."

"Afterwards, where do they go? Where's—well, where's Mom?"

Death toyed with the scalpel. "I don't know, but I can feel the joy of the souls that pass through me when they get there."

She clutched her father's hands. "Happy ending or not, I can't let him go."

"Nor should you. That's what memories are for."

"You don't understand." Tears studded her eyes. "You don't feel emotions like us."

"Look, I've seen millennia of life, since the first cell replicated its DNA in Earth's primordial sea. Creation can be terrible, yes, but even in decay, there's beauty."

She ignored his words, temples throbbing. Her father's pulse grew erratic. She called for the doctors. They rushed in, parting Death like fog.

Death rematerialized, observing as they administered shocks to her father's heart. The tallow of his life sputtered, died: his pulse ran flat.

The girl collapsed to the cold tiles. Nurses laid comforting hands on her shoulders, murmuring assurances. Death let her father's soul flow through the portal of his obsidian heart, into the great beyond.

The man's soul lingered a moment, kissed his daughter's brow, then departed.

The girl stumbled to her car. The hospital had briefed her on the funeral proceedings, asking if she wanted the corpse cremated. She had choked a yes—her father wanted his ashes mingled with her mother's, together, buried as one in a rainy, flowered graveyard.

Rain pelted the pavement. It was warm. Soaking, she sank to the ground, then vomited. Thunder matched her heaving.

A hand brushed the hair from her brow. She lifted heavy lids, vision fluttering as she saw Death. He proffered a bony hand.

"C'mon. You'll catch a cold if you stay here."

"As if I care." She choked on bile. "I've got no one left."

"You've got yourself, and someday, a family. A man to love, children to raise, the world to see. Don't throw away your potential so easily. You're about to bloom. I should know, after all, I'm a gardener."

"Bloom? Like that stupid rose you gave me? It should be dead, but it keeps growing. It's rotting alive."

He winced. "I couldn't give you something living—that's beyond me."

"So you gave me the corpse of a rose? Great."

Death's face twisted. "Get up, please."

She sat there, laughing and sobbing, her eyes slicing him as the scalpel had not. He carried her to her car and opened the door without keys, for no barriers stopped him. He set her down, and then slid into the driver's seat.

Death stared at the alien dashboard, perplexed. He placed a hand upon the wheel. The vehicle transformed into a horse-drawn hearse. More familiar. He took her home.

"Why'd you follow me?" Her arms curled round her legs, nails biting into her forearms.

"Because tonight, you shouldn't be alone."

She stared out at the rain-heavy forest that bordered the road. "Your company won't give me much comfort."

Death bit his lips. He had to remember: she was a wounded animal, licking her cuts. She would lash out with claws and a snarl, even if his intentions were good. He wondered why he'd lingered, after such an unremarkable death. Why he'd given her the rose in the first place. Whimsy, he supposed.

She inhaled sharply.

Death glanced at her drowning eyes. Something stirred in his depths. He remembered her house from the appointment he'd kept months ago, collecting her mother's soul. It was a decrepit sprawling thing, with peeling paint and ramshackle walls. The girl breathed in relief at its sight, rushing from the hearse inside. Death glided across the weed-choked yard.

She heard the air shift behind her in the foyer. "I should've known locks wouldn't stop you," she said wearily, trudging into the cluttered kitchen. She slouched against the refrigerator, eyes drifting to the counter. A meat cleaver shined against it. The blade was almost tempting, nearly whispered to her.

"That'd solve nothing," Death warned, moving to block the knife from her vision.

"Dad gave up," she echoed. "He let misery rule him. Why shouldn't I?"

"Because. You're stronger than him."

"I'm not. I'm scared shitless, miserable, and alone. Mom's death broke Dad, and their loss will break me."

"Trust me, time will heal you. Think of it as growing pains: the old dies, giving way to the new. Your parents just passed on earlier than most."

"You don't get it. I *can't* deal with this." She struggled to her feet. "Get out of my house. You've done enough."

Without a glance back, she stumbled to her room, then collapsed on the bed. Death heard her animal shrieks. He tucked away the gleaming cleaver in a drawer, fixing the knife container so the implements wouldn't budge. He waited until her sobs gave way to fitful sleep.

He entered her room. Death rested a hand on her brow, killing some of her pain. It was bittersweet on his tongue as he crushed it between his teeth. She stirred, a sob escaping her lips, and he pressed his finger against them, letting a peaceful slumber slip down her throat.

The equinox approached, and as the days grew longer, the girl's pain waned. She found her thoughts straying to things beyond sadness. The brighter the sun shone, the more she dreamed of that hot summer day, of apples ripening before her eyes, and the hand that had changed them. Grief became acceptance, and acceptance, understanding.

The girl moved on.

Death watched her, and the rose turned a heavenly blue. She woke each morning to its bittersweet scent, like whispers and fresh rain.

She shed the last vestiges of youth, until one morning she rose in full bloom. Death saw how ripe she had grown and, as always, the temptation to pluck the most beautiful of blossoms arose. To capture her magnificence before it faded. For who else could appreciate it, if not him, who savored it last?

That was why, on occasion, he collected souls before their time. Before their beauty faded, or their talents fell to madness and abuse. Mozart, Hendrix, and Marilyn, to name a few. Botticelli's own Venus, Simonetta Vespucci, he had cut down at the tender age of twenty-two from the blood-blossom of consumption.

Their fame remained immortal, never to fade—perfect ever in death.

It wasn't often he reaped those that burned their tallows at both ends, but it was enough to cause him shame. And the girl would know his intentions; her eyes could cut through his veil.

Even now, she noticed the blots of darkness too large to be her shadow, the scent of woodsmoke that lingered out of place. She smiled at him, though he remained unseen. She smiled at the darkness, as one who knows what it hides. She smiled, without fear, as if greeting an old friend.

He couldn't take her, not now, however much he yearned.

She bloomed so tantalizingly, and the world saw. It noticed the brilliant flower that perfumed the wind: her rosy petals, how she stared at the heavens, swallowing the sun. Some tried to pluck her, others fed her sweet waters and let her scent fill their dreams.

Death watched as hands caressed her with a twinge of envy. He watched them tear her blossoms, uproot her. He watched her wither, starve, and drown. He watched, but never did he touch. And always, he witnessed her bloom again, always more potent than before. She claimed a part of the earth as her own, spread hungry roots, and fed her thirsty dream.

Years came and went. She left her small town nestled in the mountains' crook for the madness of the city, searching. She saw traces of her dream, in the eyes of lovers and the flashing signs of Times Square. It glinted in the rain that kissed asphalt, spiraling down the gutter. Reflected on skyscrapers, it played across windows, dancing just out of reach. Her muse whispered— in the frayed binding of college textbooks, in a busker's melody, and the taste of a hundred coffees.

She tried to master her dream, penning poems delivered in dim cafés, snapping photos of decrepit buildings and people life forgot. Their negatives haunted her mind; the shadows clung to them like skin. The winos and the addicts, the homeless, the insane. The girl watched them reach out to passersby and saw the masses brush them aside. She saw the lights flicker and dampen in their eyes.

It pained her. With every dismissal, the shadows tightened their crushing coils round the forgotten, bringing them one step closer to Death.

The shadows clung to everyone; the closer she looked, the more she noticed. They embraced the burly executive who rode the bus with haggard eyes. The slim girl, the scarred artist, the quiet Chinese grandmother with a tortoiseshell comb in her hair. All were veiled by black. The shadows draped across Wall Street, and a thick smog choked Ground Zero. Sometimes, she could hear the echoes of screams coming from where the Twin Towers once stood.

The girl would blink, and the shadows would disappear. But not for long, never for long, and when she passed by, they emerged like parasites from their owners, turning monstrous heads to watch her. They smirked, eyes threatening, yet she met their gazes, stoic. "You don't scare me," she'd whisper.

Death was impressed. His denizens should have terrified her, but they merely made her catch her breath, then carry on.

He tested her limits. He showed her snatches of the past, letting ghosts flood the streets. She froze in Central Park as the spirits swarmed her, noticed the strange looks of passersby, then gathered herself. She marched up to the nearest spirit and touched its face. Her hand swiped damp mist. Shielding her brow, she strode through the throng of spirits, emerging chilled but otherwise unharmed.

Death stroked his chin, shepherding the spirits back to their graves. He gave a laugh like bones rolling in a grave.

"Nice trick, Grim," she muttered, resuming her jog. It wasn't long until Death overtook her, gliding beside her as she ran.

"It's nothing. I was bored; it's been slow reaping, lately. Everything's so dreadfully peaceful."

"You need a hobby. How about sports?"

"Every team I root for is struck by calamity."

"Then cheer on the team you despise."

"That's no fun."

"Horticulture, then?"

"The more I touch a plant, the quicker it ages, the faster it dies."

"...Taxidermy? That suits you." She paused, breaths heavy, and sipped water.

"No. My passion's dancing." He looked at the billowing clouds. "Unfortunately, everyone I dance with winds up dead."

"I'm sure they've got dance halls in Heaven. Aren't angels natural musicians?"

"I'll be damned if Heaven exists. All I know, yellow canary, is that there's life, and there's the beyond."

"Yellow canary?"

He grinned crookedly. "Like a light in a coal mine."

"What a dumb name." She capped her water. "The shadows that surround everyone: what are they?"

"They're pieces of me, I suppose. Each human carries a seed of darkness inside them, the shadow of death." Death yawned, fanning himself in the heat, and relaxed on a bench, looking at her under lidded eyes.

The girl sat next to him.

A bold pigeon waddled up to her, pink eyes imploring. "So they're parts of you, huh? Talk about devils on shoulders." She reached into her pocket and withdrew some dried crust she kept for such occasions. Holding it out, she let the pigeon nuzzle her fingers and gobble the crumbs down.

"More or less. You know that pigeons are riddled with disease, right?"

She laughed. "Who're you to tell me what's safe? Anyways, talking with you is way more dangerous, but I'm still alive, aren't I?"

"Don't tempt the Reaper."

She looked out across the lush grass and dandelions erupting from cracks in the pavement. "We tempt you just by living."

"That's a depressing outlook."

"Depressing, but true. You must hate watching things, everything, that you can see but never have." She watched the pigeon fly away, leaving a trail of crumbs.

He furrowed his brow. "And it must frustrate you, going through life with something burning within you, driving you to chase something wild, something without a name—a thing you couldn't recognize even if it held you at gunpoint."

Her gaze grew stormy.

Death shifted, uneasy.

"Maybe I don't understand you, or even what I'm after," she finally said. "But life? Life's something I know intimately. But all you can do is watch and wonder what it's like, to live, to breathe, to feel."

"Have you ever danced so madly to life's music your feet bled and you fell down dead? Have you lived, really lived, every moment to its fullest?"

She paused. "No," she admitted. "I haven't."

"Therein lies your failure. Let me tell you a little secret: life's a test that everyone fails. Nothing, great or small, long-lived or fleeting, achieves its greatest potential. It's only the dead that know how to live: with the hindsight of a lifetime, they realize all the things they've done wrong. But it's too late for them. Life's rigged, and everyone loses. Life, unconquerable, yields her secrets to no one. Not even me, its end."

She rubbed her brow. "It's too early in the morning for metaphysics. I can't follow this discussion anymore."

Death laughed, rising. "I don't like philosophy either. We're here, we exist, and any wondering beyond that is a waste of time."

"But I do have a question," she said hastily, before he disappeared yet again. "How is it that you have a personality? You shouldn't be real."

"According to whom?"

"Logic."

"There's a point where things grow so complex, there are no rules. Rhyme takes over, and everything you knew before no longer applies. I don't need reason to justify my existence. I just am."

In a shaft of sun, he ascended, quite dramatically, she thought. She wondered if his ego was the size of the moon. The girl shook her head.

"Good riddance," she muttered, looking around the park at the concerned faces peering back.

She turned white, realizing talking with Death—invisible to others—had made her seem like a bag lady. Blushing, she jogged from the clearing, into the cool shade of the woods. The path was unusually bare, pavement lined with no one but the emerald leaves and the wind rustling beside her. She banished all questions to the recesses of her mind, cutting through the woods with the mindlessness of a bullet. If she went fast enough, she could outrun even him.

Next time, she thought, she would catch Death by surprise. She would be the one to find him.

Fall drew near, and the rose's petals began to wilt. The girl watched as the rose bore fruit, forming a glossy orb. Death's words echoed in her mind, something he had told her in a dream, maybe:

"That Fruit was meant to be eaten by Man. It was Nature's design."

She let the rose hip be, never daring to pluck it. Still, she wondered. What was the fruit of Death? And, once eaten, what would it bring?

The girl yearned for the rugged mountains and freedom of home. The city was smeared with the grime of centuries; the earth beneath it had forgotten how to dream. The shadows were everywhere, chained to stranger's spines. They stared back at her through others' eyes, slithering out of orifices, hissing.

They could smell his fruit on her, the taint of Death. The ripening rose hip's aroma clung to her, drawing things from beyond the veil. She could see demons in the hearts of men, angels in others, and strange snakes twined round stranger's ribs. Evanescent sheens of blood clung to the hands of killers, and stars gleamed in healers' eyes. Souls were laid bare before her, and she saw people's true forms.

Her photographs became ethereal, the gritty made transcendent with her new-found vision: a wizened wino's face, rendered lovingly so the viewer could see the saint's soul within. An icy actress, made vulnerable in the shifting light of the moon. She stitched rainbows out of oil spills and knit crystals from iced sidewalks. Her art touched others, deep in their psyches, and she was hailed as the eye of her generation.

Maybe it was the fruit that affected her so, or maybe her eyes had always been sharp. She'd seen Death, after all. Regardless, her fame spread, and she grew rich off the love of her labor, birthing art and truth.

Death watched as she was swept up into the whirlwind of the world, sent to far-off places to capture life as it unfolded before her camera. Her pictures graced the covers of glossy magazines.

Death leafed through a newspaper bearing her work, sipping his espresso in deep contemplation. There she was again, behind the lens in a war zone, snapping pictures of corrupt politicians. Up close and personal with a drug lord.

She must see them as I do, Death pondered. The maggots of humanity, their insides festering with rot. Her pictures dissected them, exposed the sickness behind their exteriors. He finished his bitter shot of espresso and watched rain kiss the cobblestone canals of Venice, tucked inside a cozy café.

Had he known what he was doing when he'd gifted her with a blossom from the Tree of Life? Perhaps. His actions were rarely conscious ones— they arose from impulse and fate, which were usually one and the same.

He glanced at his reflection in the aged mirror lining the wall. The deaths of infinity stared back at him. Her end wavered before him, a pinch of sand away.

He watched her soul flutter, dancing against the winds of time as the shadow of her exit waltzed closer.

How he longed to extend his hand and lead her shining soul onward. She would resist, slicing away as he danced her to the brink of oblivion.

What an exquisite partner she would be.

Her soul shone in the mirror. Death watched for hours, mesmerized, until day turned dark and the café closed. He clenched the newspaper in his hand, strolling through the streets and whistling to the stars.

Under his mantle of shadow, he seeped into the night. He could smell the Fruit of Life, tracked its scent like a bloodhound across the Atlantic to the chill waters of the Hudson.

She lay asleep in a loft lit by candlelight, naked in the arms of a man. Death hovered at the foot of her bed, glancing at the vase on her nightstand.

The Fruit lay tucked away beneath lilies and baby's breath. He took it in his cold, cold hands, crushed it until its juices flowed. He dabbed the liquid onto her eyelids, pressed it to her lips.

She jolted awake. "You?" she breathed, drawing the blankets around her. "Not now. Not while I'm like this."

"Good evening to you too, canary," Death said, sitting at the foot of her bed. "Nice boy toy you've got. Well-hung too."

"He's my fiancée." She laced her fingers together. "What do you want? Because it can't be my life, or his. I see your shadows now, hanging over everyone. My time hasn't come."

He leaned closer, smile crooked. "Tell me, what do you see these days? Your pictures are captivating. You capture the essence of your subjects. Such discrimination, quite an eye for detail. Where did that talent come from, I wonder?"

"I've always had keen eyes," she said, guarded.

"Have you?"

"I saw you, clinging to the shadows of my house, when everyone else turned a blind eye to your existence. You didn't recognize me, not until I followed you."

Death stiffened. "You followed me? That's not what I remember."

The girl smirked. "Of course I did. I kept tabs on you ever since my mom died, watching your comings and goings, figuring out your haunts. I was hunting you." She laughed. "It was dumb, but I wanted to destroy you."

"Kill death?"

"Yeah, I guess. So no one would have to suffer again. It was idiotic, probably impossible, but I wanted to beat you to a shadow of yourself, so weak you could only claim the old and sick. I know how you operate: you covet beauty. You drain those you desire of life before their time. I wanted to change that."

Death chuckled. "We all have flaws. And unfortunately, I'm unstoppable—incorrigible to boot. But that doesn't prevent the living from raging against death. And it didn't stop you. So tell me, how would you strike out against something you couldn't touch?"

"You're mocking me."

"Maybe a little."

She sighed, tangled curls shining in the candlelight. "There's no way, is there? All we can do is live our damnedest. I remember what you said: life's rigged. In the end, you win. Nothing's immortal." She looked out her window at the velvet sky. "Not even stars. All we can do is burn brightly and try to blind you."

"The brighter the flame, the quicker it burns, and the more moths it draws: dark shadows that want so dearly to possess a little light of their own."

Her face grew stony. "That's impossible. Don't kid yourself, you know it. You may exist, but you can never live, no matter how many souls you tempt. Your dance leads to death. We can't dance you alive."

A shadow passed over his face. "We always want what we can't have," he said. Wistful, remembering: every twist in the danse macabre, the throbbing of hearts in his hand. How mortal faces, once flushed with life, grew wan. He danced them to dust, until their souls slipped through his barren heart like mist, into the great beyond.

"You think life is so grand, don't you?" she said, interrupting his reverie.

"I do. Truly."

"I see—*wait*." She paused, blinking hard. "I can see in the dark. What?" She examined her hands, as distinctive as they were in daylight.

She looked around her room like a startled doe: everything was vivid, clear. She could see shadow against shadow, muted colors where there had once been darkness.

It was too visceral—she closed her eyes, breathing deeply. She could smell her scent, mingled with her fiancée's spice and the earthy, smoky musk of Death, even the incense she'd burned a month ago, lingering in the corners of her room.

The girl remembered a summer long past and an apple ripened before its time. Her eyes snapped open. "Where's the fruit?" she demanded.

Death looked at his fingertips idly. "Oh, I don't know," he said airily, watching the juice shine on her lips.

She followed his gaze, heat rising in her cheeks. Tentatively, she licked her mouth, pupils dilating as the ambrosial taste registered on her tongue. "You didn't."

"Actually, I did. It's time."

"Time for you to leave!"

"No. For you to bear fruit."

Her lips curled into a snarl. "You forced it on me."

"The world needs you."

"What about my needs?"

She slapped him, hard.

He rubbed the red welt on his cheek. "I'd apologize, but I don't want to be insincere."

"All my life, I've cared for others: Mom, Dad, the forgotten—whose faces make me *choke*." She bit her lips. "I work to bring them justice. I see their suffering, every day. It makes me sick." Bile rose in her throat. "All I can do is try to show the world what I see, or else I'll go mad." She choked on her words. "I've never had a choice."

Death smiled. "You sound like me during a drunken rant."

"I," she spat, "am nothing like you."

Her voice echoed through the alleys. A summer wind blew, extinguishing the candles.

Death licked a bit of the rose hip's juice from his fingers. "What does your soul look like?"

She drew the blankets round her, shaking.

"When you see it in the looking glass. What is the shape of your spirit?"

"A mockery, that's what," she whispered. "I'm not yours. I never was."

Death smiled, almost cruel. "I never said you were. But," he said, a hair's length from her, "I'm not alone in this line of work."

Chills danced across her flesh. "You're mad."

"Life's mad. Will you dance to its chaos, with me?"

"I don't want to." The vision of a thousand mirrors screeched through her brain.

Cricket-song filled the silence between them. Death extended his palm.

"Do you have a choice?"

Her feet began to itch, and her heart pumped a staccato rhythm. "Do mirrors lie?" she asked, desperate.

"Not for you."

He took her hand.

Death and the maiden rose, and he led her to the mirror, their silhouettes cut by the moon.

She stared at her soul; then, into his. Their shadows intertwined, counterparts. His great black wings against her soft white ones. Hers a crown of roses, his of thorns. His gaze the vast, all-encompassing pit. And her eyes, just like bark.

Death and the maiden. Two faces of life's coin.

His grip tightened round her. He drew her close. "Do you understand?"

She looked up into his cold eyes. The maiden placed one hand on his shoulder, the other in his outstretched palm. "Does anyone?" she murmured, feeling the pulse of the universe beneath his wrist. The rhythm of his blood. "It just is, from electrons to the stars. The music—the dance."

The empty space in Death's chest—where his heart would have been, where she should be—stirred. "Come with me."

He led her into the sea of the night. A blast of air blew open the window and he whisked her away, out onto the fire escape, above the glittering skyline. The city spilled like jewels below.

She clung to him. "I hate heights."

"Height's relative. You'll forget it soon enough." He spun her from his embrace.

She stumbled, but did not fall. The night caught her, like a silky blanket beneath her feet, and the wind bore her aloft to the heavens above. The beauty of the moon struck her tongueless, and the clouds' vapor shimmered like rainbows in the starlight.

Her body was seized with a primal force, kindling her limbs with fire. She would dance, until her feet wore down to bloody nubs.

A song pulsed through the night, the lamentations of the dead and the cries of those newly born. They mingled with lover's sighs, children's breath, mixing with the symphony of the world, until a chimera filled the sky. At its core was the heartbeat of the universe. It was the music of life.

Death bowed, then waltzed forward and, ever so gently, took her hand. He led her into a sinuous movement with no beginning and no end. The sky was their ballroom, the moon their chandelier.

Her limbs grew cold, and her consciousness ground to dust. Up and down in a waltz gone mad, they spun like two planets with their axes unhinged.

Her feet wept gore, for dancing on stars tears skin. He was talking to her, of the universe and what lay beyond, but she heard only life's song.

She grew exhausted; he was tireless. She had to dance, could do nothing but move. If she stopped, she would die. That, or be born anew.

Dawn came, days and nights passed, yet still she endured, clinging to life with the hunger of a starved lion.

"Are you trying to kill me?" she finally gasped, reaching her limit.

Death laughed so hard the heavens shook. "Feel dead yet, canary?"

She struggled to speak, each breath vital. "I'm numb. I can't remember anything, not my name. I don't even know if I ever had one."

She tripped in exhaustion, and Death caught her with inexorable arms.

She struggled to her feet, resuming the dance.

Death fed off her burning mortality. He licked his lips in hunger. "Just a bit longer. That is, if you can last that long."

He led her in a sequence of spins and interlocking footwork more vicious than all before. It was the dance of predator and prey. Her steps were faulty; the need to escape wracked her brain as he chased her across the sky.

The heavens darkened as thunderheads swelled with rain. Lightning split the sky, blinding her, and Death's laughter joined the chorus of the storm. She was drenched, freezing, her breath crystallized by the wind.

The maiden's blood joined the firmament's tears. She gulped down ozone, clawing at her last reserve of strength.

He watched her eyes dim, breathing in the sweet smell of her almost-death. Water droplets shone like diamonds in her hair and her skin had grown nearly as pale as his own.

He wondered: would she bloom to her full potential, or wither in his embrace? The maiden stared into his hungry eyes. He dipped her low until she was staring up, up, up into the sky. It would be so simple, she thought, soul-weary, to slip into that infinite black.

"Go on," Death murmured, caressing her cheek. "Show it to me. That dream you've been chasing all along,"

The stars in her eyes were nearly extinguished. He felt the slowing pulse beneath her wrist and watched her flesh drain of blood. Just a heartbeat more, and she would be his.

Something within her snapped. "No!" she shouted, slapping his hand from her face. She fled his embrace.

Her eyes shone with new life. She danced counter to the song of the universe, against nature's demand. Her body undulated, hips swaying like Salome. With twisting spider limbs, she wove a web that could trap a falcon in mid-flight.

Death was transfixed, watching as the pulsing thunder began to follow her lead. The embers in her eyes blazed anew. Fearless, she opened her lips, and with the voice of a siren began to sing. The whipping wind was her song.

Her voice was a ripe apple, her melody the rushing ocean. Her song crescendoed, fell, and finally, she sang of him.

He was powerless, obeying each command her words trickled forth. She drove him back to the darkness. The storm dissipated as nature shifted, following her will.

The maiden ordered the sun to burn away every trace of his shadow.

Death stood naked before her, stripped of his power. He shuddered in the light; pain wracked every inch of his being. He fell to his knees, shielding his brow from the maiden's new-found glory, her form silhouetted against the dawn.

Death laughed through gritted teeth: he had melted her to her breaking point, then cast her anew with tongs of glorious life. Her soul, driven wild by the danse macabre, had abandoned its mortality.

She had re-forged herself out of sheer, clawing will: like lead into gold, her human nature was transmuted into that of the divine.

He grinned up at her shining form. "Amazing," he said, tears stinging his eyes. "A worthier partner never graced my arms."

Her voice echoed through the mountains. "Have you damned me?" She looked at the radiance that streamed from her flesh. "This isn't natural," she said, voice shaky. "I'm like you."

"The opposite, actually. Darkness can't drive out darkness. Only light can do that."

He struggled to crawl forwards, the light of glory and life sapping him of strength. His bleeding eyes looked at her form. "You always were her, you know."

"What am I?"

"Everything I'm not. Will you take my hand, canary, and help me stand?"

She took his trembling fingers.

He reeled, her touch like eternity.

Their lips met, soft as falling snow.

Strange thunder stirred in the maiden's heart. Rain mingled with her tears, baptizing her in a storm both harsh and sweet.

Life flowed through Death's lips, and he closed his eyes.

The maiden's memories returned to her. "My name? I remember it. Yours, too. We met in a garden, long ago. We always meet in a garden, I think."

He held her close, as if the winds would rip her away. "I've sung your name to a thousand stars, seen your face in hazy dreams. I've sought you through eternity. Tell me, where have you been hiding, all these lonely years?"

She smiled softly. "I could ask you the same question."

His grin was crooked. "I dreamt of your existence. I thought: how callous was the universe, to create just me, me alone? You're a Terpsichore—the pulsing rhythm of the blood I never had."

"Even if we know our dream, sometimes, we don't recognize them. Life's funny that way."

"Strange, isn't it?"

Death's voice trailed off. He found himself shaking, scared for the first time in his ancient, unlived life. He peered into her pupils, searching for the source of his terror.

She felt lightning race through her veins. The levin bolts struck his thirsting soul, and Death knew, finally, what her strange passion was.

"So this is hope?" he whispered.

He peered into his empty ribs, searching in the bowels of destruction. There, within the depths of the pit, burnt a newborn flame. He unfurled his hand, and the bittersweet fire piped up his arm, licked his palm.

He blew it gently to tendrils of smoke. The embers drifted, crowning her hair.

They were strange to one another, yet born of the same skin.

Alpha and omega.

Death and the maiden.

Entwined.

DEAREST WILLA
Patricia Correll

It was the wrong sort of day for a funeral, any funeral, but especially Lucie's. The sun shone in a cloudless blue sky. It turned the snow into glittering crystal and forced the mourners to squint through their tears.

After the ordeal was finally over, the crowd—for Lucie had many friends—limped slowly through the cemetery gates to the waiting carriages and cabs that lined the street. Willa turned to leave with the rest, but Lucie's husband...her widower, now...laid a hand upon her arm.

"Miss Williams, I hope you will be staying the night? Your parents aren't leaving until morning." John Banville's handsome face was composed, but his fingers were anxiously tight on Willa's wrist. "I'm glad they chose to stay with me. I can't bear the thought of being in that big old house all alone. I know you took the train from Boston this morning. You must be tired. And Lucie loved you so. She always said you were like a sister."

Willa stared at his gloved fingers. She knew that big old house had been purchased with Lucie's inheritance. She knew her parents hadn't approved of the marriage. And she had meant to stay in the town's only hotel tonight. But sweet little Lucie had loved this man. And if she stayed the night, perhaps she could find some token, a favorite book, or a scrap of paper with her handwriting, before she returned home.

And she was tired. So very, very tired.

"Thank you, sir." She touched his hand with her own, pressing harder than necessary. It achieved the desired effect; Banville removed his fingers. "If I might be of some comfort to you, or to my parents, I'll stay."

Some emotion flashed across his face. Surprise, Willa thought, no...dismay. But the man's expression resolved into gratitude so quickly that she wasn't sure she'd seen the other at all.

"I'll send to the hotel for your luggage. My wife would be happy to have you in..." His voice cracked, and he turned away. Willa followed him along the gravel path to the street where her mother and father waited, glancing back only once at the mounded dirt and the great wreaths of hothouse flowers and the gravediggers ambling in like ragged vultures to entomb Lucie's golden hair, her blinded blue eyes.

***

It was striking eleven when Joe Dixon swung his leg over the top rail of the fence. Clouds, gray with unfallen snow, had billowed in as the sun set, so the sky was a solid ceiling of black, interrupted by neither moon nor stars. Dixon carried a cold lantern in one hand, but he wouldn't strike a match until he was deep among the sheltering gravestones. He'd been digging graves here for years. He knew the boneyard in darkness as well as light.

He lit the lantern as soon as he reached the point where he knew the light was invisible from the street. The battered shovel was just where he'd left it, tucked behind the marble mausoleum of some fancy family. Dixon shook his grizzled head as he balanced the shovel over his shoulder. And here that poor pretty girl today, buried in the dirt. He'd seen the Banville house, up on the hill where the rich people lived. There surely was money for a mausoleum. Banville's stinginess made Dixon's job tonight harder.

He weaved through the stones, silent and still as soldiers at attention. Frosted grass crackled softly beneath his feet. The lantern's yellow light showed his breath in white clouds. Cold wormed icy fingers through the rips and frayed holes in his overcoat.

The girl's grave was easy to find—the rich smell of turned earth was even stronger than the nose-numbing cold. No stone yet, but one flower wreath had been left behind, a confection of pink and white. Dixon plucked a white bloom and tucked it into his hatband. After a moment's thought he also took a pink flower, to give to Maggie if he saw her tonight.

He set the lantern at the head of the grave and began to dig. It was slow work, and his hands quickly went numb with cold. He paused to rub them together, callouses scraping. It began to snow, broad flakes that sparkled briefly in the circle of yellow light. Dixon hunched his shoulders and worked faster. It would all be worth it, oh yes, when he had his hands on the woman's rings, with their great sparkling stones. What would a corpse do with such finery anyway?

He dug and dug, stopping to blow on his stiff fingers. The night and the cold and the snow mired the graveyard in silence. Dixon hummed as he worked, snatches of alehouse songs, and then bits of hymns from his childhood when the alehouse ran dry. He wasn't unnerved, no, just the quiet weighed a little heavy this time of night.

Finally, the shovel struck something unyielding. Dixon was shoulder-deep in the hole now, but he recalled the way the coffin had lain when he'd first covered it, and had dug himself a narrow ledge to stand upon so he could shift the lid aside. He reached for the lantern, fingers scrabbling on the frozen grass, and drew it nearer to the edge of the opened grave. He yanked a crowbar from his belt and used it to lever open the coffin lid. The falling snow and his numb fingers made the lid hard to grasp. It slipped and landed painfully on his toe. Dixon cursed. His feet were too cold to feel it now, but after an hour in the alehouse it would be throbbing. At least tonight he wouldn't be hauling the coffin's entire contents away, to be bundled into an associate's cart and driven to the fancy doctor school in Boston.

Dixon heaved up the lid and leaned it against the opposite wall of dirt. He held his breath at first, but when he saw the corpse he gasped and was surprised to smell nothing but earth and wood.

The woman looked as if she was asleep. So often people said that about the dead, trying to pretend the corpse wasn't shriveling or bloating or turning gray before their eyes. Dixon had always snickered at them. But in the pale light, with snowflakes settling on her pink lips and yellow hair, this woman really did seem to be sleeping. She was young too, barely more than a girl. There was no stink, not even a hint of decay. It was warmer here beneath the ground. Dixon rubbed his hands on his coat and crouched over her.

Her slender white hands were folded over her chest, a sparkling rosary threaded between her fingers. One was encircled by both a gold band and another ring with a round blue stone as large as his thumbnail, surrounded by tiny diamonds. Dixon gingerly lifted the woman's stiff fingers. He slipped the rosary from them and dropped it into his only pocket that was without a hole. Then he stretched out her ring finger. Her skin felt faintly warm against his, but that was only because his hands were frozen. He tugged at the rings. Despite the elegant slenderness of her fingers, they stuck fast. He tried to work one broken thumbnail beneath the bands, but it was useless. Well, the bodies often swelled up. He had a solution for that.

The knife's blade had been sharpened so much over the years that it was as thin as a sheet of paper. But it was more than sharp enough. Dixon pressed it into the woman's finger. The blade slid through the flesh. Just before he struck bone he paused. Something wet trickled over his finger, warm enough to breach the numbness. He peered closer, puzzled. Blood, black in the lantern light. Had he cut himself on the knife? No—the cut on the woman's finger leaked blood.

Years of filling graves and opening them again had taught Joe Dixon much about the dead. The dead didn't bleed. At least, not the *naturally* dead. His stomach lurched. He started to rise, to back away. A flicker of movement snagged his gaze. The dead woman's eyelids fluttered. Dixon froze in horror.

The woman's eyes opened. She stared up at the black sky, the swirling snow. Her blue eyes were glassy, but not clouded. Dixon's mouth went dry. Her lips parted. His heart hammered in his chest. Her head turned, her unfocused gaze seeking him, the one who'd torn open her resting place.

Dixon moaned as fear closed its icy fist around him. He jerked to his feet and cracked his head on the coffin lid. Pain sliced through his temple. He lost his balance and fell forward. Darkness clawed at the edges of his vision as he collapsed, his grizzled face landing in the green silk of the corpse's skirt.

***

Lucie reached for the glimmer of light above her head. But it was beginning to fade again, and every movement she made was dreadfully slow, as if she were trying to swim through custard. Lucie focused on the pain, the biting little pain that she thought had woken her, that throbbed somewhere in her body. The light steadied, and she caught it, drew it down around herself.

Her eyelids felt gummy, heavy as rocks. She struggled and finally managed to open them a crack. A yellow strip of light made her head ache. Her arms and legs felt as if they had anchors tied to them. Lucie shifted one, finally, and struck something very close. A few more blinks showed her that the yellow light was faint and fading, and beyond it lay darkness. Small white specks fell toward her face. Something touched her cheek. A cry rose in Lucie's throat, but stuck there. The thing was cold and wet and...a word crawled out of the pudding her mind had become. *Snow.*

Her vision was clearing. She smelled cold and dirt. Why was she lying on the ground outside? Something moved beside her, a brown flurry. There was a cracking sound, and a weight fell across her legs. Lucie caught hold of her panic, concentrating on moving her head. The smell had changed. Now she could smell unwashed skin and the sharp tang of alcohol.

She wiggled her fingers, then shrugged. Feeling began to flow back, and with it her mind grew sharper. To either side rose walls of packed earth, roots twisting out of them like skeletal fingers. The light came from somewhere above, and reflected off a slab of polished wood.

Lucie whimpered as she realized where she was. She struggled to sit, feeling her spine crack as she did. She managed to lift her leaden arms and rub her eyes. One hand ached dully, and blood spiraled down her wrist to stain the skirt of her dress; her green silk, she saw.

The weight across her legs was a man. He filled the entire end of the narrow hole, and the stink of sweat and ale rose from him. All his clothes appeared to be the same muddy brown color. Had he been...digging a grave? Her grave? Why was he so still?

The snow fell faster now. The numbness in her fingers and toes retreated, replaced by a prickling sensation. Lucie braced her hands against the edges of the coffin and drew her legs from beneath the gravedigger. She rose, swaying on knees that threatened to fold every minute. She steadied herself with a loop of tree root. The gravedigger hadn't moved, but she could hear his rasping breath and saw faint clouds of frost issuing from his mouth. The pain radiated from her hand, she saw. Blood trickled from beneath her wedding band. She pressed stiff fingers into the wound to staunch the bleeding, and was shocked by how hot it felt.

The poor man was hurt. Lucie had to get out of here and find help for both of them. She tentatively placed a foot—clad in her favorite silk dancing slippers—on the man's prone shoulder. He made no sound.

"I'm sorry," she tried to say, but her throat felt dry and tight, and only a toad-like croak emerged. Luckily the man's back was broad, and he didn't shift much while Lucie pulled herself out of the grave on arms that wobbled like jelly. Dirt crumbled from the side of the hole, sprinkling her face and hair.

Finally, she lay on the ground, gasping as if she'd nearly drowned, her skirt bunched up around her knees, her feet dangling over the open grave. As she sat up, one of her slippers fell off and tumbled down into the coffin. The snow soaked into her stockings, and covered her bare arms in icy pinpricks. Lucie hugged herself. Questions crowded her mind. Where was John? Why was she being buried? She had a vague memory of fever, sickness, sweating. Had she...died? Was she...?

Sweet Jesus...she parted her lips to pray, but the words stuck in her throat. The church...she staggered to her feet. Her unshod foot sank into the gathering snow nearly to the ankle.

The lantern. Lucie looked back. The gravedigger might need it if he woke, and at the moment it seemed very far away. She could make out the modest figure of the church through the falling snow, like a mother hen gathering in tombstone chicks. Lucie started toward the church, the same one she attended every Sunday, sometimes with her husband. More often without.

The stained-glass windows were dark. She reached the iron-bound door; the metal handle burned her cold fingers. Too weak to pull it open, she threw her entire weight against it. The door stood fast, and Lucie's heart sank as she realized it was locked. The pastor lived in town, many streets away. Lucie huddled in the doorway, shivering convulsively. Tears pricked her eyes, but for some reason they wouldn't fall. She tried to shout for help, but only the ragged croak escaped. Once again, she groped for words to pray, but they eluded her.

Stand up. The voice in her mind wasn't her own. It was one she recognized, one she'd known all her life. Willa's voice, gentle but firm.

No one was coming to save her. Lucie forced herself to stand. She didn't know why she'd been spared, but she couldn't distort God's grace. And the poor gravedigger depended on her.

Lucie staggered away from the church. The snow fell thicker now. Her hair was coming loose from its pins, straggling over her shoulders, over her favorite dancing dress. She weaved between the sentinel gravestones, barking her shins and tearing her skirt. Finally, she reached the path of crushed rock that led to the gate. She stumbled and fell into the iron bars, but her body was so numb with cold that she felt no pain. Frantically she felt for the chain, but it was locked as well. It was too high to climb, though she couldn't have climbed even a stile now. She pulled weakly at the lock, then slumped forward, defeated. Her shoulder slid through the narrow gap between gate and fence. It could just fit. Seized by hope, she squeezed into the space. The bars pressed into her chest. Her skirt caught and tore with a wet ripping sound. Lucie held her breath and pushed. Dizziness struck her, and her stomach twisted, but then she was through. She lost her balance and sprawled into the street, crying out hoarsely. In a panic she scrambled to her feet. She needn't have bothered. No carriages or horses bore down on her. The dark street was deserted.

It was eerily silent. Lucie had rarely been abroad at night, usually bundled into and out of carriages on her way to the theater or a party. Now the snow muffled even her tentative, half-shod footsteps.

Across from the cemetery gate stood a row of shops, dark and shuttered against the cold. Her hazy mind couldn't recall in which direction her home lay. The town wasn't large. Surely, she could find an occupied house nearby and procure help for herself and the gravedigger.

Lucie Banville rubbed her bare arms with her stiff fingers and slowly, clumsily, began to walk.

***

The Banville house was a stately monstrosity built near the end of the previous century. It brandished an air of chill formality. *It was John Banville's house*, Willa thought as she alighted from the carriage. Not Lucie's taste at all. She would have loved one of the ivy-covered stone cottages Willa had seen in France. Not this featureless box with symmetrical windows like empty eyes.

She followed Banville and her parents up the walk. Mother and Father held each other's arms as if they might fall. Well, Lucie might as well have been their daughter too. Willa drew in a sharp breath, her eyes burning. Now Lucie was gone.

As the carriage drove away someone opened one of the tall double doors. Willa squinted her eyes against the heartless sun and made out a woman older than Lucie, in a white cap and apron. She curtsied, smiling broadly. Willa gritted her teeth. How dare she smile when her mistress was dead? Mother and Father didn't seem to notice, sunk as they were in grief.

Banville frowned and gave a little shake of his head. When the servant took Willa's coat and hat her head was demurely bowed, her eyes lowered.

Willa's parents immediately excused themselves to their room. Mother kissed Willa's cheek and squeezed her wrist. "We'll go home in the morning, dear. Will you stay with us a while?"

She nodded and patted Mother's hand, feeling Father's gaze on her. "I've notified the school I'll be gone until next term."

Banville nodded solemnly as they trudged up the stairs. He turned to Willa. "The driver will bring your case from the hotel and Abigail will take it to your room. Have you eaten, Miss Williams? Abigail can bring us some dinner."

Dinner had been nowhere near Willa's thoughts. She'd had no appetite for lunch on the train, though she vaguely recalled drinking coffee and picking at a slab of toast that morning. But now she realized that she was hungry, despite everything. "Yes, thank you."

Again, that look of faint surprise that vanished in an instant. "I'll have Abigail bring us something." He went down the hall, calling for the servant. Willa looked around at the spare corridor, the dark wallpaper and darker wood. She tried to imagine Lucie in this house, receiving visitors through those heavy doors. Lucie with her golden hair and blue eyes, who preferred to wear pink and green, must have looked like an unseasonal butterfly in a dead autumn wood. Willa's throat grew tight at the memory of her laughter, the press of her hand.

Banville returned. "I hope you don't mind eating in my study. It's not really a place for a woman, but the big dining room feels horribly empty now."

Willa followed him into the study. It was lit by glass lamps and warmed by a blazing fire in the hearth—apparently his servant-woman knew him well. It looked like her father's study. Leather chairs, shelves of books. Ranged along one wall were photographs. Among the books were stuffed and dried marine animals, several fish mounted on the walls. He was some kind of scientist, a biologist, Willa recalled.

"Lucie always said you were her favorite cousin. Well, more a sister." Banville repeated as he poured them each a drink. "Oh, sorry. Do you drink?"

"Yes, thanks." Willa took it with the first flush of gratitude she'd felt for the man. "But we truly weren't any relation at all. Our fathers were best friends, so when her parents died in the cholera epidemic and she had no other relatives, my parents took her in." She coughed to hide the sudden break in her voice. She remembered the little girl in her blue coat and frightened expression standing in the front hall, and Father introducing her to Willa and her brothers as their new cousin.

"I'm sorry to meet you this way." Banville held out the glass. Willa took it. The liquid was a warm, inviting amber, the same color as Lucie's hair. "You were in France when we married last year, yes?"

"At art school. I only returned two weeks ago for a holiday. I meant to visit Lucie, but..." Willa sipped the drink. It was sour and warm in her mouth. She hoped Banville would believe she'd been busy, instead of afraid.

Banville nodded. "No one could have predicted Lucie would...she was so young and healthy. But she fell ill suddenly one evening, and by the next sunrise she'd gone home to the Lord."

The phrase, one Willa had often heard variations on, sounded strange in his mouth, almost...mocking? She supposed he might well be angry at the God who had reached so soon for his young wife. She certainly was. "The doctors couldn't even name the illness?"

"No. It was quick, you see. By the time the doctor arrived she was already dead."

Willa glanced up from her drink. Banville was watching her over the rim of his glass with hard eyes. Had he sensed the depth of Willa's shock, her grief? A chasm had opened up inside her, far deeper than she would have felt for any cousin or sister. She looked away. "So, Mr. Banville. What do you do for a profession? Lucie never mentioned it."

Before Banville could answer, a knock sounded at the door, and Abigail entered with a tray of dinner.

***

Martin Becker woke to the urgent press of his bladder. The fire had burned low, but it offered enough light for him to crawl out of bed without stumbling and pull the chamber pot from beneath it. His wife snored on as he relieved himself. In their fourth decade of marriage, with no more children in the house to cry for her at night, Klara slept well and deeply, while Martin woke three or four times in the dark to answer the calls from his body.

When he was finished, he hobbled to the fire to add some wood. It was a frigid night outside, by God. He felt sorry for any beast left out there in the dark.

He dropped a log into the hearth with a shower of sparks. As Martin straightened up, he heard it. He paused, listening. There it was again, a faint scratching at the window. He glanced at his sleeping wife. Surely, he could let a little cat in just for the night, and put it out in the morning before Klara woke? It was really too cruel to leave it out in the snow. He reached for the curtain.

The scratching stopped. Almost immediately it began again, fainter this time. Martin followed the sound to the chilly front room, then to the door that opened onto the street. A proper cat, to come to the door. He smiled.

Again, the scratching stopped. It was replaced by a moan that froze Martin's reaching hand. A high-pitched groaning that hovered on the edge of a wail. It was a sound like nothing the old man had ever heard before in all his long life. It was the cry of a lost soul. Fragments of stories told to him by his grandmother floated to the surface of his mind. Noisy ghosts. Goat-headed demons. Ghosts of murdered Indians. Martin stared at the door in repulsed fascination. The cry rose, desperate, then sank and trailed off. He listened, trembling. But it was not repeated. Quickly he crossed himself and, whispering pleas to Jesus and the saints, limped back to his bed, where he pulled the quilt over his head as he had not done since he was a child.

Beside him, Klara snored on.

***

Lucie sagged against the door. Hope had gripped her when she saw the sign for the silversmith's shop. Kindly old Becker would help her. But her arms were so heavy she couldn't lift them to knock. All she could do was slump against the building and scratch at the window with lacquered nails, then at the door when a gust of wind sent her stumbling forward. No one answered the door. Was Becker away? Lucie opened her mouth to call for help but her tongue was thick and useless in her mouth. All that emerged was a wordless, guttural moaning. She tried to harness her voice, but her lips were too stiff to form words.

She blinked, her eyes burning. Exhaustion tugged at her limbs, urging her to lie down in the snow and sleep. Darkness crept into the corners of her mind, caressing, coaxing...

Don't sleep, Lucie. Keep moving. Come to me.

Not John's voice. Not her husband. Willa. Stupid Willa who had sailed off to Paris and never come back.

How could she go to Willa, an ocean away? Why would she want to?

At least if she could imagine Willa's voice, her brain wasn't completely frozen. Becker's shop was in the commercial section of town. Going up the street and making a right would take her through the Irish quarter, at the bottom of the hill where the Banvilles' house, and others of its ilk, resided. Surely an Irish wife would be awake with a baby and could send someone up the hill to fetch John.

Lucie used one numb elbow to lever herself upright. Shivering furiously, she turned and staggered toward the end of the street, dragging her ruined skirt behind her.

***

The servant took away the remains of their dinner. She swished her skirts as she pushed open the study door with her hip, showing stockinged calves. Willa frowned after her. She shouldn't judge the woman so harshly; she'd only been ill-disposed toward her because of the badly-timed smile. She sighed and pinched the bridge of her nose. Her head ached with weariness.

78

"I know Abigail doesn't have very nice manners." Banville was pouring himself a fourth drink. "Lucie was trying to teach her. I found Abigail in Haiti, widow of an American soldier who'd died there. She was destitute and begged me to bring her home to America and, well, I have a soft heart. She and Lucie became very fond of each other."

"Haiti?" Willa said politely. Another time she might have been interested in his travels. Now she only wanted him to stop talking so she could go to bed. But Banville was flushed with drink, and Willa knew from experience that men in that state would talk about themselves for long minutes at a time.

"The American army spent some years there, after the slave rebellion. I don't suppose you knew that. I study marine animals, and there are some very unique ones living in tropical waters. I took the opportunity of our men being there to go down myself and have a look."

She nodded, feeling her eyelids droop.

But Banville seemed energized by the subject. "They have some strange ideas down there, the Haitians. Yes, very strange."

"Oh?" Willa glanced at the photographs while she waited for Banville to tire of his subject: Banville proudly holding a massive fish in his arms, Banville flanked by two dark-skinned men in front of a jungle of some kind. There was only one of Lucie, in her wedding dress, her jaw clenched, eyes anxious. She had always had trouble standing still long enough for photographs. Willa looked quickly away.

"...even so far as raising the dead."

She turned her back on worried Lucie. "Pardon?"

"The beliefs of the Haitians. They practice a strange kind of religion. They believe their voodoo priests can raise the dead and make them into slaves. Of course it's all pretense, accomplished through the use of a curious poison from a certain fish—"

Willa's face must have shown her confusion and dawning disgust, for he abruptly stopped talking and uttered a nervous little laugh. "I'm sorry, Miss Williams. Here I am talking such nonsense. I apologize. I've been in rather a state since Lucie..."

"I understand."

"It all happened so quickly."

They lapsed into silence. Despite snow falling outside the window, the study was uncomfortably hot. Willa felt Banville watching her, but when she looked up the man was emptying his glass. "I thank you for your hospitality sir, especially in this difficult time. But it's been a long and tiring day—"

"Of course!" He nodded, as if relieved. Perhaps all this time he'd been waiting for her to excuse herself. "Abigail can take you to your room." He went to the door and shouted for her. A moment later Abigail appeared, her face sallow in the light of her lamp. "Take Miss Williams up to her room."

The servant's lips pressed into a thin line. "Yes," she said curtly and turned on her heel. She must be stupid, Willa thought, if she hadn't learned better manners from Lucie in a year.

"Good night, Miss Williams. Thank you for keeping me company in this...unbearable...time." Banville held out his hand.

Willa shook it. Then she followed Abigail out. As they made their way toward the stairs, she asked idly, "What are these other doors?"

"Dining room, kitchen, parlor, day room."

"Miss Lucie's day room?"

Abigail nodded. She led Willa upstairs, to a door at the end of the hall. Inside the fire and lamps were lit.

"Guest room." Abigail turned away without asking if she needed anything else.

Lucie's day room. There would be something there, something she could take, something with Lucie's handwriting or a lace handkerchief. Willa's throat clenched tight, and this time she didn't fight the tears.

***

It was harder now for Lucie to think about where she was going. The snow was coming thicker and faster, blurring her vision. Her silk gown might as well have not been there at all; it was soaked, the silk ruined and in tatters. She was numb all over, her limbs heavy and leaden. The voice in her mind, Willa's voice, had grown fainter. But it persisted.

Come along, little Lucie. Keep walking.

She'd expected some kind of protest from Willa when she'd announced her engagement to John Banville after only three months' acquaintance. She'd not written herself, but knew Aunt and Uncle would have. But there was nothing from faraway Paris. Lucie had been relieved, had told herself she was relieved, but that spark of indignation and hurt had flared and stayed. She didn't care, she insisted to herself. John was fine, with his exciting stories of the exotic Caribbean. And the house had been for their own good. She could live with him as his wife and be content. And never admit to having made a mistake.

Yet now it was Willa urging her on, and not John.

Was Willa here, back in America? Had she been there, at Lucie's...funeral?

Everything was dark. Lucie started awake. Her eyes had been closed. She was so tired, so very tired. If she could curl up somewhere, in a doorway out of the snow, when she woke—

You won't wake, little Lucie. Keep walking.

Panic surged through her. Lucie struggled to move her feet to the nearest house—little more than a shack, really—and threw her body at the door, opening her mouth to cry for help.

***

Mary O'Dare woke with a start. At first, she thought the baby was crying, but when she groped around she felt him, still and breathing deep between her and Kate. Mary held her own breath, listening. The sound came again. A hoarse, guttural cry. The door, only a dozen steps from where she huddled under the blanket with her brother and sister, shuddered on its hinges. Kate's eyes flew open, pale green in the darkness. The sisters stared at each other over the downy head of the baby. Then Kate ducked under the blanket. Mary followed.

The wail rose, trailing off into a moan. Mary knew exactly what it was. Her mama had told her of the old country, and how some of the ghosts had followed them to the new country in big ships. Mary O'Dare knew the warning cry of a *bansidhe* when she heard it.

She began to pray silently as tears welled in her eyes. She prayed for the creature to spare Kate and the baby. She prayed for Mama to come back soon from her job serving at the bar.

The baby woke and began to whimper. Kate slapped her hand over his mouth. Mary squeezed her eyes shut and pleaded for the evil thing outside to pass them by.

***

Willa waited until the clock above the mantel struck midnight. Then she took a candle and slipped out of her borrowed room.

The hallways were carpetless, so she had to walk gingerly to the stairs, on tiptoe in the shoes she hadn't taken off. At the top of the stairs she paused, listening. But the house was dark, breathless and silent as a corpse.

She halted again at the foot of the steps. No light leaked from beneath the study door. The hall, bereft of stars, was blacker than night. Willa followed the fragile light of her candle to Lucie's day room. The door wasn't locked, and it swung open without a creak.

The day room was as dark as the hall. All the curtains were drawn. Willa wandered the room, holding the candle aloft. A fist squeezed her heart every time she saw evidence of Lucie—the twined pink flowers of the carpet, the slender writing desk she must have brought from Willa's parent's house, a painting of Greek dancers above the cold fireplace.

Willa sat at the desk, imagining Lucie perched here, sunlight streaming through the window and setting fire to the usually invisible red strands woven among her yellow hair. Her white hands holding a pen in that odd way she had, between thumb and forefinger only. Her lower lip began to tremble, and Willa lay her head down on her folded arms and cried. This house, John Banville...Lucie had possessed a life Willa knew nothing about. And it was her own fault, for going to Lucie before she left for art school, for confessing her feelings. She'd never forget the way Lucie had pushed her away, her lips trembling in confusion and disgust.

After a time, the tears finally stopped. Willa wiped her eyes with her sleeve like a child. The candle was visibly shorter, and the little room was cold. She should quickly find something of Lucie's to keep and go back to bed, then leave this depressing place as fast as she could, before breakfast. With shaking hands, she pulled open the top drawer of the little desk.

It was a jumble of papers, wax sticks, inkwells, hair pins. Willa's lips curved into a tiny smile. Same Lucie. Her wardrobe had always been a jumble of clothes and shoes, her school desk overflowing with papers. Willa lifted out a few sheets, seeking a list for the grocer, a note to a friend, anything with Lucie's spidery handwriting. She drew out a few blank sheets, one with a hasty sketch of a cat stalking a cartoonishly-proportioned bird that made her smile. Finally, she found a sheet Lucie had written on.

It held only two words. A date, five days previous. Below that-
Dearest Willa,

She stared, stunned. Lucie hadn't written once since Willa left for Paris, and Willa had not dared to write her. Why had she changed her mind? Was it a mistake? Did she know another woman named Willa?

Something was written on the page below that one. She looked. Another date, two months before. *Dear Willa,* ...and another, and another. *Dear Willa, Dearest Willa, Darling Willa.*

The dates stretched back until shortly after Willa had left the country. Lucie had never gotten past the salutations.

She took the stack of paper and folded them carefully. Then she snatched up the candle in trembling fingers and crept to the door.

It swung silently open. Willa slipped into the hall. She'd reached the foot of the stairs when she heard voices.

***

Lucie resisted blinking—it was getting harder and harder to lift her eyelids each time. Her eyes watered furiously, and her cheeks were stiff with frozen tears. Her arms and legs no longer belonged to her; she felt something moving, something attached to her, but there was no feeling and her brain moved too sluggishly to be commanding them.

A lit streetlamp flickered somewhere above her. She swayed before a sign with a name painted on it. She stared blindly for a moment before the letters formed meaning in her mind. *Evergreen.*

That was the street, the road where the great mausoleum of a house stood. The house she hated, where lived the man she didn't love.

But it was home. Lucie sucked in a breath that tore at her lungs. She lurched in the direction the sign indicated, the rags of her skirt dragging through the snow.

***

Willa froze. Sweat broke out on her temples. The voices came from around the corner, leaking from a crack in the door of a room she assumed to be the parlor. The room was dark. Willa hurried up several steps, hoping to escape before anyone noticed her. Then one of the voices said something that made her crouch down behind the banister, listening.

"Do you think it's over yet?"

A woman's voice. The only other women in the house were Mother and Abigail. It had to be the servant.

Banville's voice replied, "By now it surely is. If it so concerns you, perhaps you shouldn't have insisted I do it that way."

"I wouldn't see you damned, you fool! This way it's the gravedigger who killed her, not you."

Willa's mouth went dry. *Kill? Kill her?* They could only mean one person. White fury erupted in her chest, choking her. Willa flung herself down the stairs, heedless of her skirts, and barreled through the parlor door. She held up the candle, exposing two startled faces. They stood indecently close.

Willa's shout was fierce. "What have you done?"

They jerked apart. Banville began, "What—"

"You killed Lucie!"

"Miss Williams—"

Willa surged forward. Abigail squealed and Banville raised his hands, but Willa's outrage lent her speed. She tossed the candle aside, heedless of where it fell. In the sudden darkness Abigail and Banville became darker silhouettes. She closed her fingers around Banville's wrists and dug her long nails into the flesh, forcing him back until his head crashed into the wall. Abigail dithered, her hands fluttering helplessly. Willa ignored her. She thrust her face close to Banville's. The man stank of liquor.

"What did you do to Lucie?" Willa hissed.

Banville twisted, but Willa's fingers were frozen into vises. She sank her nails deeper and deeper, until he growled in pain. "I did nothing, you mad wench!"

"Liar! I heard you!"

"Stop!" Abigail shrieked.

Willa shook Banville. "You killed her!"

"I didn't kill anyone! I put her to sleep, that's all!"

"What do you mean?"

Behind her, Abigail cried, "He didn't kill her! Killing is a sin!"

"Lucie's *alive?*" Willa turned her head to glare at the disheveled servant woman.

Banville laughed shrilly. "Not anymore!" Before Willa could turn her attention back to him, he yanked free and grasped her wrists. Banville shoved her away. Willa staggered backward, taken by surprise. Banville followed, his fists raised.

***

The yard was surrounded by a fence, but no gate, for which Lucie was grateful. She would have thanked God, but her lips seemed frozen half-open, rubbery and lifeless. Even her teeth had ceased chattering.

The great ugly house was not far from the entrance, but she could barely see it through the thick curtain of snow. The cobbles were slick and wrenched her unshod foot painfully sideways. Lucie struggled toward the brooding monolith. Her eyes kept trying to close. They were successful; she didn't realize she'd reached the house until rough brick scraped her face. She pressed her hands into the walls and shuffled sideways, looking for the door.

The remains of her skirt wrapped around her ankles. Lucie tumbled forward and struck something that shivered under her weight. The door! She raised hands she could no longer feel and clubbed the wood. She tried to call for John, or even that wretched Abigail, but her tongue wouldn't move; it sat in her mouth like a dead slug, cold and useless. All she could manage was that hoarse, wordless wail. She screamed and howled and pounded at the door until darkness crowded the edges of her vision and she could no longer hear herself.

***

Willa had just lifted her hands to defend herself when she heard the sound. Despite the scuffle in the parlor, the night and the house were quiet enough that it came to her quite clearly. It was a rising wail, quavering, lost. It brought gooseflesh to Willa's arms and prickled the hair on the back of her neck.

Banville froze, his fingers curved into claws. The rustle of Abigail's skirts stilled; Willa assumed she was similarly paralyzed, but she didn't dare take her gaze from Banville long enough to see.

The cry rose up and up and up. Abigail began to whimper. Willa held her breath. It trailed away, finally, like the last lingering note of some hideous song.

"The wind—" Banville began. But his voice sounded uncertain, and he made no move to complete his attack on Willa.

"It's *her!*" Abigail shrieked. "I told you, John! I told you! You can't hide from God!"

"Shut up, woman!"

Willa backed toward the door. Scream for Father and Mother, that's what she had to—

"Where are you going?" Banville snarled, taking notice of her again. He started after her. Willa turned and dashed into the foyer, lifting her skirts to ease her flight.

"Mother!" she screamed. "Father! Mother!"

Behind her Banville burst through the parlor door. His hand reached out, fingers closing painfully around her arm. Willa was jerked off her feet and fell to the bare floor. Pain shot up her ankle as it twisted beneath her.

A *thud* sounded against the front door. Somewhere in the dark Abigail screamed. Banville's grip weakened. Willa took advantage of his hesitation to stand up and limp away. At the top of the stairs a light appeared.

"Willa? What's wrong?" Her father's voice.

Another thud at the door. More and more, blows raining senselessly, without rhythm. Willa stared at it, her heart racing in her chest.

"Don't open it!" Abigail babbled. "It's *her!*"

Willa glanced around. Another light had appeared beside Father's; Mother, clutching a candle. Her face was white in the flickering flame. Banville stood like a statue, gaping at the door with dread in his face. He hadn't even seemed to notice that he'd lost Willa. Abigail leaned against the wall as if she might faint.

"I fear no ghosts." Her voice was steady and firm. She reached for the brass handle. "Especially not Lucie's."

The hinges creaked and a blast of icy air struck Willa as she opened the door. Abigail screamed again, and she heard her father shouting, but Willa paid them no mind. Something that had been leaning against the door fell over the threshold. Even in the dark, even with the servant's screaming ringing in her ears, with the green dress shredded and her face turning blue, Willa knew her. She flung herself to the ground and wrapped her arms around the bent shoulders.

"Lucie," she sobbed, clutching the other woman tightly to her breast.

***

She woke into sunlight, in the room of her childhood. Where she'd played hide-and-seek with Willa and cried over her schoolwork. Despite the pain in her feet and the bandages around her hands, for the first time in over a year, Lucie Banville was happy.

There was a rap at the door. "Come in," Lucie tried to call. But her throat was still sore, and it came out as a hoarse cough.

It was Willa. Of course it was. She carried a tray with a kettle and a cup, and a hot water bottle. Her hair, usually pinned tightly out of the way, fell over her shoulder in a loose braid. She smiled when she saw Lucie was awake. "I brought some coffee. And this. You're in all the papers, you know. And the broadsheets. And the penny dreadfuls, any day now."

"Thank you," Lucie rasped. Willa set the tray on the bedside table. She hesitated a moment before lifting the quilt and replacing the lukewarm water bottle with the fresh one. Heat flooded Lucie's face, and she looked away.

"The doctor said you were lucky, only losing three toes to frostbite."

She was the same blunt Willa. Lucie laughed, but it sounded like a gasp. Willa looked up in concern. "You'll have to learn to walk without them. That grave robber had frostbite too, but he lost a finger, that's all. They say he's at an asylum now. You gave him quite a fright."

"Will you help me?" Lucie whispered. She held her breath, waiting for Willa's answer. Hoping.

Willa straightened up. She poured Lucie a cup of coffee and perched on the edge of the bed, as if afraid to get too close. She was careful not to brush Lucie's fingers when she handed it to her. Lucie sipped. The sugar and cream only dulled the edge of bitterness, but she gulped it, grateful for the warmth that stilled the nervous flutters in her stomach.

"Of course I will. The new term begins today, but I'm not going back to school until next term. I already told them. I planned to stay anyhow, even when I thought you were..." Willa folded her hands in her lap and stared at them. "We found out what happened to Banville, by the way. Father wasn't fast enough to stop him from bolting, but they caught him on a train to Chicago. He's in jail right now, along with his mistress. It was your money they wanted, but you probably realized that. The poison he used on you came from a puffer fish common in the sea around Haiti, it's used to induce a deathlike state so the voodoo priests—"

Lucie put down the cup of coffee. She burst into tears.

Willa raised her hands in alarm, as if she intended to embrace her but stopped halfway. That only made Lucie cry harder. "Lucie? What's wrong? I thought you'd be happy to hear he was caught."

She sniffled and dragged the sleeve of her nightgown across her eyes. "I'm...I'm sorry. I'm sorry, Willa. I'm sorry for being horrible to you before you left. I'm sorry for going off and marrying John when I barely knew him. I'm sorry for causing all this trouble. I'm sorry I never wrote you. I tried, I did, but..."

"No." Willa caught Lucie's hands and ducked her head to peer into her face. The stiffness she'd held since entering the room was gone, her expression as earnest as Lucie remembered. "It's not your fault, Lucie. You were upset after...after I said what I said, before I left for school. I'm the one who's sorry. I should never—"

Lucie shook her head frantically. Words erupted from her lips and spilled hoarsely into the air between them. "No, I was upset, I was confused...I was *scared*, Willa. But not of you, I could never be scared of you. It was myself that frightened me. I was scared and I ran off and married John Banville because I knew what you were feeling. Only...I thought it was just me. I thought I was...an abnormal woman. I don't mean *you* are, Willa, I just...I don't know. I was shocked when you told me how you felt about me. I thought I was the only one."

Willa's mouth dropped open. She tried to speak, coughed, then managed, "But...now, Lucie?"

"I almost died." She was sharply aware of Willa's fingers on hers, how she absently rubbed her thumb over the bandage on Lucie's now-naked ring finger. Surely, she could feel Lucie's pulse pounding like she'd run a mile? "I've been buried, Willa. John isn't important now. Many things that seemed important before just...don't...anymore. And out there, in the snow, I heard someone. Someone who told me to keep going. A voice in my mind. It was yours, Willa. I don't know *what* that means."

"Listen to me." Willa leaned forward, her grip on Lucie tightening. "Listen, Lucie. In Paris I saw...other ways to live. The women—and the men—who live that way, they're good people. Not monsters. Not sinners. All those things the preachers say, that my parents said...God hasn't *done* anything bad to them. They're *happy*. And if He won't punish them now, here, why should it be any different in Heaven?"

Lucie squeezed her fingers. "I...don't know, Willa. I never loved John, but I don't know if that means..."

"Lucie." Willa laid a hand along the side of her face, gently turning Lucie's head to look at her. Her fingers trembled. "I love you. I told you that before and it hasn't changed. I know you love me, but I don't know if it's as a sister or a friend or...and it doesn't matter one bit. Whatever kind of love it is, I'm happy to have it. I was angry before, but I was angry at myself. For frightening you. If...there are ways, Lucie. Ways to live the way we want, if that's what *you* want. But you don't have to decide now. For now, I want you to recover. And I will do whatever I must to make sure you do. Whenever you need me, I'll be here."

Lucie looked at Willa's wide eyes, her determined mouth. Willa was a terrible liar, she'd always been. Now her gaze was steady and clear. She was telling the truth. Lucie threw her arms around Willa's neck and buried her face in that long brown braid that smelled so familiarly of soap. Willa returned the embrace without hesitation. They stayed that way a long time, each feeling the other breathing, arms tight around each other, warm in the sunlight that streamed through the bedroom windows.

MORTAL CLAY
Nancy Brewka-Clark

Lily stood at the tower window watching for the beams of the Daimler's headlamps. Twilight had set in and pale moths were flitting about in the garden like ghosts. "James," she whispered, "don't you love me anymore?"

"You should ask him."

Lately the voice, always speaking in Russian, had become more taunting. "No."

Lily stroked her forehead as if the calming motion could suppress the insinuating hiss. As usual, she found herself replying in her native tongue even though she hadn't spoken it since she was a little girl. "There is no need."

"Don't be such a coward, Lilya Vladimirovna."

She first began hearing the voice after she and James returned from their European honeymoon four months ago. The great brick mansion on the northern outskirts of Boston with its exquisite views of the Charles River reminded her of the London townhouse in the elegant district of Mayfair where she'd spent the latter part of her childhood. It was the last place on earth she expected to hear the language of her youth.

After trying to block the voice out with the childish remedy of putting her fingers in her ears, she'd come to believe that it was emanating from some part of her own mind. Yet she was unable to silence or control it. These random outbursts created a frightening secret that weighed heavily on her soul. Even so, she didn't dare confide in either Reverend Pilcher or Dr. Burleigh. Both represented institutions which frowned upon fragile young wives who hid behind fictitious ailments to avoid their wifely duties. But that wasn't Lily—no!—she loved her husband.

"Very well. I'll tell you. You sicken him."

"No. Of course not. He loves me." Lily's fingers slipped through her thick black hair to touch the concealed birthmark above her left ear. "I don't know why I have these foolish thoughts."

"You know why."

Red as a Valentine heart, the mark pulsed beneath her fingertips. Twin birthmarks on her left shoulder and left hip began to throb as well.

"Your husband loathes the sight of you, just as your father did."

Lily's father, Vladimir Dishiry, had been a shipping magnate in St. Petersburg, Russia. A handsome, restless man with ancient ties to the once-powerful boyar ruling class, Vladimir often went abroad to further his contacts both East and West.

"And do you blame him?"

On a voyage to London, Vladimir met, wooed, and wed Lily's mother. Angelica Fitzwallace was not only the niece of the ninth earl of Huttlesfield, but an heiress in her own right. Vladimir transported Angelica to his ancient family estate on the banks of the Neva River with the promise that life would be as romantic as a frothy ladies' novel. Instead, the Russian darkness of Dostoyevsky eclipsed whatever joy there might have been.

"You destroyed what he loved best."

In 1885, at the age of twenty-three, Angelica died giving birth to Lily. The tragedy affected Vladimir so deeply that he couldn't bear the presence of his wailing newborn daughter. His shuddering abhorrence at the mere sight of her only worsened with time.

"You stole his happiness."

Lily's care fell to Margaret Redding, Angelica's lady's maid, who saw to it that the little girl's upbringing was as English as possible. When Lily was five years old, Vladimir fell afoul of the local governor in a battle over unpaid tariff fees. He seized on the demands of mounting a lengthy and complicated countersuit as a reason to pack Lily off permanently to her relatives in London.

"You sucked the joy out of his life."

A few months later, Lily's father was killed by a runaway carriage outside the Winter Palace on the way to his hearing. Having no male heir, he left his estate to a distant cousin. In light of the political unrest throughout Russia, Lily's English relatives thought it wise to allow the transaction of property to go unchallenged.

"You caused the death of his line."

Although every year since had seen ominous signs of rebellion against the Romanov dynasty, Tsar Alexander remained on the imperial throne. And now, with the birth of his son Alexei Nikolaevich, there was reason to believe that the dynasty would continue well into the twentieth century and beyond.

"Your husband fears you'll do the same to him."

But none of that meant anything to Lily. She was English through and through, Russian in name only. And now, even that was no longer true. She was Mrs. James Whittier Ackerman III. She had a mansion, jewels, servants, beauty, and youth. Oh, yes, Lily meant to enjoy her new life to the fullest, if only that wretched voice would cease and desist.

"What do you say to that, Lilya Vladimirovna?"

"I must dress for dinner." Rushing to her closet, Lily flung open the double doors. The closet itself was the size of a small room, with a massive iron bar running the length of it upon which dozens of dresses hung.

"No matter what you wear, you'll be hideous in his eyes."

"Never."

She and James both had their own en-suite bedrooms as was customary for their social status, but until recently they'd slept together every night. And on every one of those nights, James had told her how desirable she was and how fortunate he was to have such a beautiful bride. Suddenly, it had all stopped.

"He loves me." Lily blindly thrust aside an armful of satin and taffeta. "Now, go away."

"Hideous, because he knows what lies beneath."

"Go away!"

"Excuse me, madam?" Lavinia, her maid, stood in the doorway.

"Oh, Lavinia." Lily peered over her shoulder, smiling tremulously. "I need you to find me something special to wear tonight. I can't decide."

"Yes, madam." Well trained on Beacon Hill by a family of Boston Brahmins, the maid gave a little bob. Only a few years older than Lily, she radiated an air of confidence coupled with calm efficiency. "One of the Worth gowns, do you think?"

"The emerald green satin with the apple green silk underskirt, please." Remembering the deliriously exciting hours she'd spent in the Paris salon of Worth being fitted in the most exquisite gowns a woman could ever desire, Lily made up her mind. Tonight she would seduce her husband back into her bed. "I'll wear my mother's emerald parure as well."

Once she'd dressed Lily in the breathtaking gown, Lavinia retrieved a dark green velvet box from the center drawer in Lily's vanity. Lily sat down in the dainty French provincial chair with its white and gilt paint so unlike the rest of the oak and maple furnishings in the rest of the mansion. "Here you are, madam."

Lily undid the gold hasp and lifted the lid. A pair of drop earrings, a bracelet, a ring for her right hand, and a necklace, all of shimmering emeralds set in diadems of rose-cut diamonds, gleamed up at her from the white satin. Each piece bore a tiny stamp with the famous House of Fabergé name in Cyrillic as well as the name of Michael Evlampievitch Perchin, the jeweler who created exquisite bejeweled and enameled Easter eggs for the Romanovs.

"Is Mr. Ackerman home yet?" Lily asked casually as she put on her earrings. "I didn't see his auto in the drive."

"He came in just a little while ago, madam." After Lavinia fastened the clasp, her fingers brushed the silken material covering the scar on Lily's shoulder.

For a moment, the maid's hand hovered over the spot.

"You know, madam," Lavinia said, "it's all the fashion now to wear a gown like this off the shoulder. It does produce a lovely décolletage. Shall I—"

"Certainly not." Sorry that she'd snapped at the pretty young woman, Lily added softly, "I have no desire to reveal my birthmark."

Lavinia's hand rose to her mouth. Wide-eyed, she whispered, "Oh, madam, do forgive me. I wasn't thinking."

"This frock is my husband's favorite." Lily stood and walked over to the cheval mirror. Turning from side to side, she smiled. "I wouldn't dare change a thing."

Lavinia clucked her tongue. "The gown's a bit loose, madam."

"I've been very active." Lily choked out a little laugh. "Long walks in the garden do wonders for the figure."

Carefully avoiding her mistress's eye, Lavinia said, "You haven't been out much in the past few weeks. Truth to tell, some were starting to wonder—an heir at last?"

Lily flushed. "When I have such an announcement to make, it will be made through the appropriate channels, not servants' gossip."

Lavinia finished the final hook and eye and gave another bob. "Yes, madam."

***

Halfway through dinner, Lily flung down her napkin. Rage bubbled through her, coupled with an intense desire to weep. James had come to the table with a newspaper and proceeded to read it as if he were dining alone. After reading the editorial page, he'd handed it to a footman and proceeded to attack his roast beef and asparagus with oblivious zeal. "I'm not feeling well. I'm going to bed."

James Ackerman raised his eyebrows, thick and white as his beard and bristling muttonchop sideburns. "What's wrong, dearest?"

Feeling the eyes of the manservants standing at full attention around the massive polished table with its double pairs of gleaming silver candelabra, she forced a smile. "I haven't been sleeping well lately, I'm afraid."

"Oh, my dear girl, you should have told me. I would have called for Dr. Burleigh at once." When James stood, he towered over the table like a colossus. His beautifully tailored evening coat was designed to contrast his broad shoulders with a waist that was still admirably slender. "I'll ring him up now. He'll be here in two shakes of a lamb's tail."

Usually old-fashioned expressions like that struck Lily as amusing. She'd been prepared to accept that there would be some differences between the way a twenty-year-old female and sixty-year-old male looked at things. Tonight, tears welled in her eyes. "I'm not ill, James, just tired."

"Dear, dear," he murmured. "Then a good long sleep's in order." As one of the footmen pulled out her chair for her, he added, "And don't worry, my love. I shan't disturb you."

She froze. "That won't be necessary, James."

"Now, now," he said, "go and get a good night's sleep. We don't want those lovely cheeks of yours to grow pale like faded roses."

***

"Yes, I'm here. But I see he isn't."

Lily lay stiffly in the massive mahogany bed, listening against her will to her invisible tormentor.

"It's beginning."

Her heart fluttered in her breast. "What is?"

"Suspicion."

Lily sat up. Through the south-facing window she could see the fiery glow of the Ackerman kilns still blazing away on Rumney Marsh. As autumn approached, every last man and boy employed at the Ackerman Brickworks labored in overlapping shifts to labor around the clock. It was back-breaking, filthy work that would end as soon as wintry weather set in. Then the clay deposits, some of them one hundred feet deep, would freeze over, untouchable until the spring thaw. The fires would die in the huge beehive kilns made of the same red brick as the Ackerman home that was now also hers. The low-riding schooners that transported millions upon millions of bricks to the docks of South Boston would rock empty at anchor like ghostly cradles.

"That's nonsense. I trust James completely." Lying back down, Lily pulled the Egyptian cotton sheets up to her chin as a cold wave of air wafted over her.

"You have to say that. He's all you have."

"Oh, why won't you leave me alone? Why shouldn't I trust him? If he says he's staying late at the brickworks, or has to return at some ungodly hour, why should I doubt him?"

"So many questions. But I have one for you."

Lily sat up again.

"What do you really know about James Ackerman?"

She put her arms about her knees and rested her head on them. "He's rich."

"Ah. That speaks volumes."

When Lily lifted her face, it was streaked with tears. "My great-uncle approved of our match. They'd known each other for years and years, ever since James studied for a year at Oxford. I couldn't remain a debutante forever. It seemed logical to marry him."

"Logical? That doesn't sound much like love."

"I love him." Lily said it through clenched teeth.

"Then satisfy his greatest need, or you'll join the others."

"What do you mean?"

This time there was nothing but silence.

***

The elderly woman behind the counter of the general store held up a length of cheap cotton. "New to these parts, are you?"

Pretending to finger the ugly material with interest, Lily gave a nervous smile behind the brown veil. It draped down from the brim of the brown velvet hat from which she'd plucked the expensive osprey feathers and eighteen-carat bejeweled pin. "Yes, but we're not staying. My husband's a salesman. He has an appointment at the brickworks."

Praying the woman wouldn't ask what he was selling or why she'd come along on such a trip, Lily added quickly, "Does the Ackerman family still run it?"

"A lot of people are curious about the Ackermans." The woman held the bolt out further, turning it so Lily could see another yard of cloth. "Because of all the terrible goings-on, you know."

Lily's heart missed a beat. "I really don't know anything."

"Poor Mr. Ackerman, he lost both his parents and his twin brother years ago in that horrible fire. It was an explosion, they say. The old mansion was built of brick, too, just like that big castle up there on the hill where he lives now. Happened just after he and his brother came back from the war. Bull Run through Appomattox without a scratch and then, boom."

"An explosion." Lily shivered. "How terrible."

"That's not the half of it." The old woman's eyes gleamed. "He's lost four wives. Such bad luck for such a lovely man. He's got a fifth wife now." The woman flipped the bolt expertly so another yard pooled on the counter. "Young enough to be his granddaughter."

"Are people scandalized?" Lily asked in a tiny voice.

Putting the bolt down, the shopkeeper leaned toward Lily. "James Ackerman would give his right arm for an heir. The brickworks have been in his family for nigh on a hundred and twenty years, ever since old Jacob Ackerman came a-digging right after the War of Independence and found just what he wanted, blue clay and cheap land. Business is booming, but what good is it if he can't pass it on?"

***

Lily lay in bed staring into the darkness. For the fourth night in a row James had failed to join her. The first night, he was out late at a dinner for one of his charities. The second night he spent in Boston at his club. The third, he told her he'd be at the brickworks talking with his foremen about beginning the process of closing up for the winter. And tonight? He simply hadn't come home. Instead of calling, he'd sent a message by courier telling her that once again he had talks with the men that couldn't be put off.

Was this what it had been like for all the other wives? Turning onto her side in her blue silk and lace negligee, she punched the pillows until they formed huge soft mounds around her face. Here she was, literally in their place, and she didn't even know their names. With a gasp, she turned onto her back for fear she'd suffocate herself. What would it be like to die in this bed? Had any of the others died here? Would she, of old age?

Lily yearned to know more, but she certainly couldn't ask the cook or the head housekeeper or the chauffeur or the gardener. They'd all been here a long time but had almost nothing to do with her, preferring to run the house the way their master had always demanded it be run. She didn't dare return to the general store. She did attend the local Episcopal church on Sundays with James, but she couldn't think of a way to ask Reverend Pilcher about her predecessors.

How could she ever find out?

"The graveyard."

"Of course," she said aloud, and finally sank into an uneasy sleep that deepened to dreamless slumber as the lonely night wore on.

***

The day was crisp and clear, the sky an enameled blue. The Anglican church could have been plucked out of the English countryside. A square stone edifice in the Norman style, it appeared to be centuries older than it really was. The impression was enhanced by the mossy gravestones tilted in slanting, irregular rows. Some had been carved with skulls, others with angels. Massive maple trees lined the rutted lane, their leaves glowing like rubies in the sunlight.   But Lily was barely aware of the glorious day as she made her way down a branching path toward a granite tomb the size of a workman's cottage. Panting a little from nerves more than exertion, she stood before the door of the vault to read the inscription on the bronze plaque. So many names, more than a century's worth.

There were James' great-grandparents, his grandparents, his parents, and his brother. She reached out a gloved hand and touched his brother's name: Joseph. The family certainly hadn't been prolific in the reproductive department. One male per generation until the twins, Joseph and James. And then Joseph died so very tragically. He'd only been twenty-two and just back from the war where he'd served as a captain with Company F, the 95th New York Volunteer Infantry.

Her heart beating faster, she studied the female names.
Cynthia Van Ragsdale Ackerman, November 1, 1847-August 12, 1868
Francesca Delano Ackerman, September 4, 1849-January 6, 1878
Marianne Stackpole Ackerman, May 22, 1859-March 11, 1887

Victoria Vanderbilt Ackerman, December 3, 1869-July 14, 1903

"Lily Dishiry Ackerman, 1885-1905," Lily murmured, tracing the invisible characters with her fingertip, and then stopped in horror as she realized what she was doing.

"Hello, there," a voice called. "May I help you?"

The elderly minister was thumping toward her, leaning heavily on his gold-knobbed oaken cane.

As if she were still a student in her London finishing school, Lily dropped a small curtsey. "Good morning, Reverend Pilcher."

"Why, Mrs. Ackerman." For an instant his blue gaze, a bit clouded behind thick lenses, moved toward the bronze plaque with its morbid list. "Out for a walk, are we?"

"Yes." Deciding there was no point in pretending she'd stumbled upon the mausoleum by accident, she said, "I wanted to pay my respects to the others."

"Well, my goodness, that is a charitable thought, indeed." He folded his gloved hands piously before him to lean upon his stick. "Such tragedies. But God works his miracles, bringing you here to fill Mr. Ackerman's golden days with wifely affection."

Lily waved a trembling hand at the plaque. "Did you know all of them?"

"Oh, my, yes. Yes, I did. The boy, too. Your husband's brother, I mean." He sighed heavily. "Joseph was a peach."

"A peach?" she repeated, not certain she'd heard correctly.

He gave her a shy smile. "I don't know if people say such things now, but by that I meant he was a real gentleman. Oh, yes, virile but polite, scholarly and yet athletic. He won scores of honors at Phillips Andover Academy before enlisting in our nation's deadly war between the states. Yet he was modest in all his accomplishments. It was a terrible thing for his parents to lose him, especially his father. The elder son, you know."

"Elder?" Lily frowned. "I thought James and Joseph were twins."

"Born mere minutes apart," Reverend Pilcher said. "But in legal parlance, Joseph was the first born." He looked toward the engraved list of dead wives. "After that dreadful explosion, James actually acquired more than the complete ownership of the brickworks. Cynthia was originally Joseph's fiancée."

Lily gasped.

"Oh, there was nothing sinful about James and Cynthia's union, I assure you," the minister said quickly. "It was perfectly proper for the two young people to marry. They had both overcome great losses. It was natural for them to turn to each other."

"So, they had your blessing," Lily said.

"Of course. She was a lovely young lady." The minister gazed off across the sea of headstones. "Simply beautiful. Within and without, as we say."

Wondering from his wistful tone if he'd thought of courting Cynthia himself, Lily murmured, "Such a loss."

"Indeed." Reverend Pilcher shook his head. "Unfortunately, poor Cynthia began to suffer fits. Terrible thing to witness, choking, snarling, foaming at the mouth. Eventually, a grand mal seizure killed her."

"How terribly sad." Lily stared at the next name on the plaque. "And Francesca?"

"Italian nobility, you know. Poor girl succumbed to an alimentary ailment." He gave a little shrug that might have been censorious. "Dr. Burleigh suspected her foreign diet in her youth led to a build-up of bilious matter."

Lily was finding it difficult to swallow herself. Licking her dry lips, she asked, "And Marianne?"

"Oh, my goodness, she was such an athlete. Do you know, she reminded me of one of those Greek goddesses." Reverend Pilcher chuckled, caught up for a moment in a more pleasant memory. "Put a helmet on her, hand her a sword, and she'd conquer the world."

"She sounds very—" Lily fumbled for an appropriate word. Masculine? Terrifying? "Healthy."

"Indeed." The smile vanished from the minister's face. "She was best known as an accomplished equestrienne. Before the advent of these dreadful motor cars—forgive me, Mrs. Ackerman, I know how your husband enjoys his horseless carriages, but I do fervently pray they're merely a passing fancy, here today, gone tomorrow—the Ackerman stables were famous for their Thoroughbreds."

Although the original stable building still stood, it was now bereft of its stalls. They'd been knocked down to create a garage for not just the Daimler but an Upton Tonneau touring car custom-made right up the coast in Beverly as well as a cute little poppy-red run-about from France. "I had no idea," Lily said.

"No, those days ended when Marianne passed away." Reverend Pilcher sighed heavily. "Accidents happen to the best of us, no matter our pedigree or breeding. A swarm of bees came after her mount during a jump. Just came out of nowhere, a great cloud of them. Whether she could have survived the stings or not, her horse threw her and trampled her."

"To survive one horror only to die by another." Lily bowed her head. "How dreadful."

"As for Victoria, well, she turned out to be of troubled mind." The minister peered at Lily as if seeking pardon for having to cast such an aspersion on her husband's fourth wife. "She came to me on several occasions requesting that I pray with her. Of course, I was happy to do so even though she couldn't or wouldn't tell me what was weighing on her conscience so heavily." The guilt on his face turned to raw grief. "When she didn't appear for our regular session, I thought she'd decided to forego it because she'd rallied. Instead—"

Lily waited, unwilling to do anything that would startle the old man out of his reverie.

"They found her clothing and the note on the bank of the river," he said sadly.

When a pair of squirrels started to chatter in the maple beyond the tomb, Lily finally found her tongue. "Four funerals. How sad."

"Three funerals, my dear Mrs. Ackerman," Reverend Pilcher corrected her gently, "and one memorial service. You see, poor Victoria's body was never found."

***

"Accidents? I don't think so, Lilya."

"What you're implying is despicable." Lily paced around and around the bedroom, obliviously tying and untying knots into her little handkerchief until it began to disintegrate into a ball of threads. Once again James had failed to come home for dinner, and she'd had to sit under the silent gaze of the servants pretending that all was fine. "Keep your wicked opinions to yourself."

"Certainly not. After all, you're a clever one, aren't you, Mrs. Ackerman? Continue to put the facts together and there might not be the need for a sixth Mrs. Ackerman."

"I have no need for you. I should get Reverend Pilcher in here to perform one of those rites that gets rid of ghosts. Oh!"

Lily gaped at the shattered vase lying on the brick fireplace hearth.

"Listen to me, Lilya Vladimirovna."

"Be silent," Lily sobbed. "Leave me alone."

The silence grew heavy as a shroud. Unable to bear the weight of it, Lily fell weeping upon the bed.

"Get up."

It was humiliating, but Lily was actually relieved to hear the voice again. "Why should I?"

"It's time."

Sniffling, Lily swung her legs over the side of the bed. "Time for what?"

A cold draft touched her forehead. *"Follow me."*

Led by the cool air, Lily entered her closet. "Why am I in here?"

"Push your gowns aside."

Lily glared at the brick wall. "There's nothing there."

"Knock."

Her knuckles rapped the bricks. A hollow sound echoed among the folds of velvet, silks, and laces. Lily rapped, put her ear to the wall, and rapped again. "These bricks must be very thin. I believe they're nothing more than a façade." She pounded the wall with both fists before slamming into it with her shoulder. "How do I get in?"

97

"Mind over muscle, Lilya. Are you an ox or a fox?"

"Why can't you just help me?" Lily ran her fingertips lightly over the bricks. When she felt a seam, she followed it until she'd traced a rectangle. "This is actually a door. But how do I open it?"

"You can't. It's been sealed shut."

"Why?" Once again Lily flung herself against the door. "What's behind there?"

"You know in your heart, Lilya. You know."

"No." Lily backed away from the barrier she'd been working so hard to destroy just moments before. "That's mad."

"Say it, Lilya. Say her name."

Spinning around, she stumbled her way out of the closet into the twilight of her silent bedroom.

"If you won't, I will."

Sinking down on the bed, she buried her face in her icy hands.

"Victoria."

"No!"

"Madam?" Lavinia knocked sharply on the bedroom door. "May I come in?"

Wiping at her eyes with the heels of her hands, Lily said, "Yes, of course."

"Forgive me, madam, but I was wondering if you were ready to retire." The maid dropped a curtsey. "It is a bit past your usual time."

"Yes, thank you." Lily stood, turning her back so that the myriad silken buttons of her dinner dress could be undone. "I lost track of time, I'm afraid."

"Oh, my!"

At the maid's exclamation, Lily looked over her shoulder. "What is it?"

"The vase, madam." Lavinia was staring at the shards. "How did it happen?"

"What? Oh, I dropped it."

Lavinia stepped toward the tapestry bell pull attached to a wire running up into the molding. Mounted on the wall next to the pull was a small silver plate concealing a speaking tube. "One of the housemaids must sweep that up."

"No, don't disturb them." Lily waved a hand. "It can wait until morning."

Lavinia rang the bell. "You might forget all about it and cut yourself."

Lily knew that up in the attic servants' quarters a numbered key on a wooden board would be jangling, tugged by the wire running through the walls of the mansion alongside the warren of tubes. She'd rushed up there after hearing the voice for the first time, hoping she was picking up muted conversations that in their piped distortion sounded Russian. But servants never occupied their tiny rooms beneath the eaves during the day—in fact, in many grand homes simply being up there during working hours provided grounds for firing—so she'd found no one.

Flipping open the silver cover, Lavinia waited, tapping her foot. "Hilda, bring a broom and dustpan to Mrs. Ackerman's bedroom. And be quick about it."

There was something different about her maid tonight, Lily thought, observing her sparkling eyes and pink cheeks. Perhaps she'd received good news from a family member, a letter telling of a birth or a proposal. Lily had never thought to question Lavinia about her personal life. One just didn't do those things, not here and certainly not in Mayfair. Hired by James, Lavinia had been installed in the house just before their return from their honeymoon. As James put it, Lily would be pampered from the moment she set foot in her new home.

"You know, madam," Lavinia said as she returned to undressing her mistress, "I thought I heard you talking to someone in here a bit earlier. It's why I didn't come in at the usual time."

Lily froze.

"I didn't wish to interrupt you if you were at prayer." Lavinia let out a little laugh. "Or having an argument."

The chill enveloping Lily evaporated in a flash of anger. "An argument? With whom?"

"Forgive me, Mrs. Ackerman," Lavinia said softly as Lily stepped out of her petticoats. "It's just that often I do hear your voice." She began to unlace Lily's corset. "I always wonder if I should knock."

"I prefer it to eavesdropping," Lily said coldly.

"Oh, you needn't worry about that." Lavinia went to the dresser and pulled open a drawer. "I can't speak Russian."

Maid and mistress stood within inches of each other, one nude and the other holding out a long white flannel nightgown. In the cheval glass Lily's white flesh displayed two heart-shaped marks, one on her shoulder and one on her hip. Only Lavinia and James knew of her blemishes, but Lily suddenly wished only her husband had seen her in such intimacy.

"I wish to have my peach satin negligee," Lily said.

"It's going to be a very cold night," Lavinia replied. "I thought you might want to wear this."

Lily stared at the garment.

"Madam?" Lavinia cocked her head. "Is something wrong?"

Lily raised her eyes in time to catch Lavinia's expression of sly amusement. "Why would I wear that?"

The maid cast a glance at Lily's blemished shoulder, and then her hip. "It will keep you warm when you're sleeping alone."

Shocked by her insolence, Lily slipped into the nightgown, vowing to speak to James in the morning about hiring another maid.

"Oh, and madam, Mr. Ackerman has asked me to inform you that he spoke to Dr. Burleigh about your insomnia." Lavinia produced a stoppered amber bottle from her pocket. "You're to take these pills."

"He said nothing to me." Lily sank down on the bed. "Please leave me now, Lavinia. I'll speak with him in the morning."

The maid tossed her head proudly. "I have my orders."

So, that was what it was, an air of triumph mixed with anticipatory malice she'd brought into the bedroom with her tonight. Lily was about to order her to leave when a timid knock at the door startled them both.

"Enter," Lavinia called.

With a bob, the slight figure in a huge mobcap scurried over to the shards of glass.

"You there, fetch Mrs. Ackerman a glass of water."

"Yes, ma'am."

While the girl was in Lily's bathroom, Lavinia muttered, "He's not having it, you know. The last one was mad as a hatter and she came to an unfortunate end." For an instant, Lavinia's gaze fell upon the closet door. "Imperfection—it's a fatal flaw."

***

Lily marched up to the desk clutching the handle of her purse in both hands to keep them from shaking. "I wish to speak to a detective."

Officer Clarence Higgins didn't lift his head from the big ledger. "Who's asking?"

"I am Mrs. James Ackerman," Lily said, "and I live—"

"No worries, Mrs. Ackerman." The officer jumped up. "We all know where you live. What is it you want to see the chief about?"

"Is he a detective?" she asked.

"He's the chief," the officer said firmly. "He's the one you want to see." He peered over her shoulder. "Is Mr. Ackerman with you?"

She shivered. "No."

"All right, then," Higgins said, backing away while still staring at her. "You wait right here, and I'll fetch the chief."

Looking around the shabby little station, Lily was quite certain she could smell some unsettling odors, the source of which she didn't want to know. The unvarnished floorboards bore stains ranging from deep brown to pale pink, as if someone had tried to scrub up pools of blood. The brick workers' lives were an enigma to her, but she knew enough about life to understand that drunken brawls were a common side effect of hard labor.

"Mrs. Ackerman?" The portly man in the tight blue uniform with bright brass buttons came toward her with a broad smile pasted on his shiny red face. "Chief of Police Lawrence McPhee. What can I do for you?"

"Is there someplace private we can talk?" she whispered.

100

The chief shot a glance at Higgins before giving him a sharp nod. Waving his hand before him, he said, "Please, Mrs. Ackerman, come right down to my office."

Once seated, Lily leaned forward to murmur, "Are you sure no one can hear us?"

The chief blinked hard. "Yes, ma'am."

"Please, you must help me." Lily slid a little closer to his desk on the battered seat of the plain wooden chair. "I wish to gain entrance to a secret room."

McPhee stroked his chin. "Is that so? Where is this room, might I ask?"

"It's at the back of my closet." Opening her purse, she took out a folded piece of paper. "I've drawn you a sketch."

Shaking out the folds, McPhee studied the little map. "What do you expect to find, Mrs. Ackerman?"

Her eyes filled with tears. Clutching her bottom lip with her teeth to keep it from trembling, she paused a long moment. "I can't say."

He folded his pudgy hands. "Why not, Mrs. Ackerman?"

She leaned toward him, tears running down her cheeks. "Just help me. Please."

"Why do you think you need help, Mrs. Ackerman?" The chief poked his head at her like a turtle testing the air outside his shell. "What are you afraid of?"

Lily twisted in her chair as the door behind them banged open.

"Darling!" James Ackerman strode into the room. "What on earth are you doing here?"

"Don't worry, Mrs. Ackerman," Officer Higgins said, almost bursting with self-satisfaction. "You're safe now."

Over Lily's bowed head, James was shaking hands with the chief. "Thank you, Chief McPhee. I'll handle this." Putting a hand on Lily's shoulder, he said, "Come on, now, darling, the auto's just outside. We'll have you home in a jiffy. You'll soon be snug as a bug in a rug. How does that sound, hmm?"

As they left the station, Lily was sure she heard the chief mutter, "That poor fellow sure can pick them, can't he, Higgins."

***

Struggling to lift her head, Lily mumbled through parched lips, "Water."

"Here you go, madam." Lavinia thrust her hand beneath the pillow, lifting it up slightly with one hand while she held the glass with the other. "Careful now. Just a little bit at first. It has your medicine in it. You don't want to spill it." Tilting the glass until it was empty, she said, "There. Soon you'll be fit as a fiddle."

"Thank you." With a sigh, Lily sank back into the softness and shut her eyes. "Tell me again. I know you once told me, but I forgot. What's wrong with me?"

"You had a terrible shock," the maid responded. "You visited the graveyard. Reverend Pilcher was there. He told you about the other poor ladies and you became obsessed with them."

"How is she?"

Lily froze beneath the sheets. James Ackerman had just entered the room. He was her husband. So why did she feel as if her heart might explode with fear? What was it that she knew about him? Why couldn't she remember? Was it something unpleasant? Something frightening? Why couldn't she remember?

"Madam? Madam?" Lavinia bent over her. "Your husband is here to see you. He's very concerned about you."

Lily lay as still as a corpse.

"Excellent." Lavinia straightened. "I just gave her the entire bottle of laudanum. It's more than enough to silence her forever, my love."

Through a growing haze, Lily decided she must have misheard her maid. Why on earth would she use such an intimate endearment to James?

"Dr. Burleigh just telephoned to confirm the extraordinary news, Lavinia. Well done, my beautiful girl."

Lily heard the heavy footsteps approach the bed.

"Oh, James, I'm so very happy," Lavinia murmured.

"Not as happy as I," James Ackerman responded. "Finally, a child."

"Our own precious baby," Lavinia whispered. "One not tainted with filthy foreign blood."

"God, yes. When I saw all that blemished skin on our wedding night, I felt ill. Birthmarks! That was bad enough. But then I wrote to my dear old friend Ruddy Fitzwilliam excoriating him for his filthy trick. 'Tell me, old boy, why did you sell me a pig in a poke?'"

Lavinia burst into laughter, immediately suppressed.

"And what did he do but write me a veritable epistle describing his grand-niece's birth as if it were a tragic misfortune and not a disgusting plot worthy of the Theater du Grand Guignol."

Through stifled snickers, Lavinia managed to gasp, "Lucky James. Your very own monster."

"Siamese twins, and one of them a stillbirth." James barked out a laugh. "It beggars belief. My bride of Frankenstein had been joined at the hip, head, and shoulder to a corpse."

Lavinia snorted. "If I had been that thing's mother, I'd have died at the sight of it, too."

"Despite my own wretched situation, I couldn't help but feel pity for Dishiry. He'd lost his son and heir." James's voice was hoarse with emotion. "The little fellow had the life literally drained out of him by the female succubus who now bears my name."

"Not for long," Lavinia said.

"You are a miracle of perfection," James whispered. "And soon you'll be my wife."

"I long to be in your arms forever," Lavinia moaned.

"Let's leave her now," James murmured, "and let nature take its course. Dr. Burleigh's already made out the death certificate. "

"Heart failure." Lavinia laughed softly. "She's failed you all around, but I won't."

"Come into my arms, my darling," James sighed, "and let me show you how much I adore you."

They were embracing within inches of her sickbed—her deathbed.

"I believe it's time to move our celebration across the hall," James whispered.

Lily heard muted laughter, and then the door clicked shut softly.

Rolling over, she hung off the side of the bed and vomited into the white enamel chamber pot, retching until there was nothing left to heave up.

Finally, wrung out but more alert than she'd been in days, Lily hauled herself out of the bed. Studying the array of beauty tools on her dresser, she picked up her manicure case with its two pairs of sharp scissors and an assortment of files, and stumbled over to the closet. Wrenching open the door, she fell to her knees and began to scrape.

***

"Good God, Burleigh, she's gone!"

"She has to be here, James." Lavinia's voice grew hopeful. "Maybe she jumped out the window. I'll look. Oh, rats. There's nothing there."

"Burleigh, check the closet."

The dresses parted with a screech.

"Come here, Mr. Ackerman."

Crouching on the other side of the jagged hole, Lily held the longest file high in one hand and a pair of manicure scissors in the other.

"Good Lord, how has she managed to ferret her way through the wall?" A fist pounded the section nearest her head. "Lily, listen to me. If you're in there, answer me at once."

The air in the hidden room seethed around her, blowing her hair in spiraling tendrils. The voice calling to her was familiar in its hostile, hateful tone.

Father.

Husband.

Then the voice that had been silent throughout her current ordeal spoke at last.

"Now you know who I am. "

"Yes," Lily whispered, her eyes riveted on the shaking door. "You're my brother."

"In some secret part of you, Lilya Vladimirovna, you always knew I existed. But you couldn't bear the thought of how your body robbed me of nourishment or how your soul enveloped mine. Nor could you bear the guilt of our mother's death or our father's grief. You lived amongst whispers telling of how our bodies were severed from each other, but you refused to understand. You told yourself you were complete."

"Mrs. Ackerman, you are unwell. Let me help you." Dr. Burleigh's voice grew louder. "You must come out of there this instant."

"I'm sorry," Lily whispered.

"Yes, sister, I forgive you. You must defend yourself now. And I must say goodbye."

"Out of my way, Burleigh."

Her husband's head was crowning in the small opening in a horrifying parody of birth. "Damn hole's too small." The head withdrew. A hand came creeping toward her on pale hairy fingers. "Lily, come out here at once."

Her slash was swift and silent.

"Oh, oh, my God, I'm bleeding. Listen, you madwoman, if you're not out here by the count of three, I'll get the hunting rifle and shoot until you're nothing but bloody Swiss cheese."

"Let me see that hand, Mr. Ackerman. Here, wrap this handkerchief around it."

The front doorbell rang far below.

"Good Lord, what a time for a visitor. I'll go down and get rid of them." James' voice grew distant. "You two guard that rat hole. If she tries to creep out, club her with the poker. And, for God's sake, close that closet door and keep it closed until I return."

Lily closed her eyes. There was no point in expending any more energy until she had to fight to the death. She could hear Dr. Burleigh and Lavinia breathing just a few feet away, and then, heavy footsteps pounding down the hallway.

"Is this the lady's bedroom, sir?" Officer Higgins asked.

"Of course it is," James boomed. "And as you can see, it's empty. She's gone."

"God forgive me, I'm too late again," Reverend Pilcher quavered. "You've done her in, too. Shame on you, Jimmy."

"I warn you, sir," James roared, "that I will prosecute you for slander to the full extent of the law. There is no court in the land that would countenance such an outrageous charge, clergyman or not."

"Where is she? Where is Lily? I opened the crypt, Jimmy, and checked the coffins." Reverend Pilcher sighed heavily. "She's not there. But I found Victoria."

"You senile lunatic," James snarled, "you wouldn't know a corpse from a cord of wood."

"Hair, Jimmy." The minister drew out a handkerchief and patted his forehead. "You can always identify a body by the hair. They were all there, Francesca, Marianne, Victoria, and Cynthia." He dabbed at his eyes. "Lovely, lovely Cynthia."

"The thing is," Higgins said, "the bodies had been disturbed. To put it bluntly, parts are missing."

"Desecration," James hissed. "You'll be defrocked, Pilcher. You can spend your last miserable years in jail."

"Hands," the minister murmured. Once again, he patted his forehead. "Jawbones."

"Mr. Ackerman, what have you done with your current wife?" Higgins asked.

James drew himself up to his full height. "I am hardly a character from a fairytale. I am neither Peter the Pumpkin Eater nor Bluebeard. She ran away because she is stark raving mad."

"She was as sane as sane can be when I met her," Reverend Pilcher said.

"As if you'd know," James sneered.

"She said something about surviving. You see, Jimmy, it niggled." The minister plowed on, undeterred by James' murderous glare. "Finally, I remembered what Joseph said just before the explosion. 'I survived being shot at by rebels, but I don't know if I can survive living here with Jimmy. He wants it all, so that he can build himself a dynasty.'"

"Ancient tales," James spat. "Meaningless rot."

"So, where's Mrs. Ackerman?" Higgins persisted. "Just tell us, sir."

Lily crawled to the opening. "Help!"

Lavinia kicked her in the face just as Higgins yanked open the closet door.

"What are you doing in there, Dr. Burleigh?" the officer asked. "And who's she?"

"Keeping an eye on a madwoman. And this is Mrs. Ackerman's devoted and loyal maid. Now go back to your beat, Higgins, and let me do my job."

"That's a lot to swallow," Higgins said. "Would you mind coming out, please?"

Lily watched through swelling slits as two pairs of feet slowly moved away. "I'm in here, Officer Higgins."

Dropping to his knees, Higgins thrust his head through the hole. "Mrs. Ackerman?"

"We're all here. All five of us." Lily pushed a straggling lock of hair from her face, leaving a streak of blood. "Cynthia, Francesca, Marianne, Victoria, and me."

Higgins stared around the circular chamber. "There's no one here but you."

James shouted from the bedroom, "I told you she was mad."

"Come and see," Lily said.

Higgins stood. "Yes, ma'am." Thrusting his right shoulder against the false wall with all his might, he crashed through to stumble toward her. "All right then, show me."

Lily pointed at the brick walls around her.

"Bone fragments." With a little whistle, he ran his hand along the roughly textured bricks closest to him. "Teeth." He peered closer. "Say, here's some fingerprints."

With a cry, James grabbed Lavinia's hand. Shoving Reverend Pilcher aside, he lunged for the bedroom door with the struggling maid in tow.

"I had nothing to do with it," Lavinia shrieked. "Nothing!"

Stumbling through the closet, Officer Higgins leveled his service revolver at the couple. "Step back into the room or I'll shoot. I mean it, Mr. Ackerman. You too, miss."

"I'll have your badge for this," James blustered.

"Where's Burleigh?" Higgins asked just as a motor revved up in the portico below. "Well, we're not going to worry about him. He won't get far." Turning his head, he called, "Mrs. Ackerman? It's safe to come out now."

Lily was truly a sight, swollen eyes, bleeding cut on her cheek, dust in her hair, but she didn't care. She was alive. Father, husband, brother, all had tormented her simply because she existed. And now she was free of them all.

"'Oh, death, where is thy victory? Oh, grave where is thy sting?'" Reverend Pilcher gazed sorrowfully at James. "At the end, even though you despised them for their perceived imperfections, you couldn't bear to part with them, could you, Jimmy?"

"Prove it," James snarled.

"Oh, James," Lily said, aware that she was speaking for those who would never speak again, not even in whispers, "I'm perfectly certain we will."

VAMPIRIK
Russell J. Dorn

Kelsey watched her ex-boyfriend struggle, seemingly at war with his stomach. Judging from the thousand-yard stare, his belly had the upper hand, but still he tried to stuff the last bit of curry chicken and cauliflower into it. *A real trooper*, she thought, not without disgust. Her ex-boyfriend's demeanor had gone sour so quickly, Kelsey figured the rice must've exploded like a grenade in the pit of his belly along with the naan bread. The pitcher of water he'd chugged since they took their seats at the dining room table must've felt more like gasoline on the fire than anything refreshing.

"Indian food is really filling," Kelsey called. She had to speak louder than she wanted given the length of the antique table.

"I'll say." Terry groaned as he swabbed his forehead with his napkin. Though he seemed engrossed in his food, Kelsey thought it would be a good time to ask what she'd been meaning to ask.

"My front door has been having trouble locking."

"You should get that fixed," he said blankly through a mouthful of food.

"I know." Kelsey forced a smile. "Do you think you might take a look at it?"

"I'm not good with that type of thing," he said. "You know that."

"Ah." Kelsey shoved an aloo ki tikki around her plate. "Tell me, Terrance—"

"Terry." He smiled, a white smile, unsoiled by cigarettes. "Has it been so long you forgot how much I hate the name Terrance?"

"Of course not, Terry." Of course she knew that. "What do you do? What's a day in your life like now?"

"What do I do?" he repeated, perhaps simply to show he had heard the question. He held his knife and fork on his plate as if trying to keep his drumstick pinned, though the seasoned chicken leg had no means of running off. His thoughts seemed to scatter in every direction, and Kelsey saw as his eyes followed one thought and finally snared it.

"Read up on the news," he said. "Hope I don't read about one of my buddies cozying up too close to a land mine. Lots of eating. I head down to the Job Connect a few times a week, but the pickings are still pretty slim for veterans."

"Uh huh." Kelsey split her potato cake with her fork.

"I try to hit the gym a few times a week as well. Often, I just use the Iron Gym bar. You know, the one hanging on my bathroom door. Sometimes I don't feel like seeing other people, you know? Or having them see me squeezing out a dozen butterflies with my chest all exposed."

Kelsey saw that his arms were indeed admirable swells—his chest, too. His stomach swelled as well, but with fat, not muscle. His recent breakup with that skank Amber must've served as a catalyst for his exercise routine.

"Do you ever imagine the terrible things you saw over there, in...Iran?"

"Iraq." He nodded. "Too well, yeah. I don't really like to—"

"Dead bodies?"

"Yes, unfortunately. Like I said, though, I don't really—"

"Dead friends?"

"Come on! What is this, Kelsey?" Terry scanned the room, as if in search of hidden cameras or threats. Finally dropping his utensils, he grabbed his coat from the rack as if making to leave. He paused a moment in the foyer before he sat back down. "Dead friends? Why would you ask that? You have no idea what it was like over there."

"I don't, because you always refused to talk about it."

"With good reason."

"A reason I have yet to hear."

"With good reason."

"Jesus."

"Watch it." He lifted a warning finger. "Why do you care so much?"

She saw it coming the moment his face twisted up when he first took in her knee-high mallet boots, black skirt, shirt, and stockings, and the holes in her pale face plugged again with metal rings. She saw the conflict in his eyes, when he traced the sharp, feminine angles of her face, her neatly plucked eyebrows and the little cleavage that she could manage. He still wanted her, he just didn't want to take her home to mom again unless she agreed to put on a sundress or a bejeweled pair of jeans and cowboy boots, with a plaid flannel shirt to top it off, and let the black stripe of her hair grow back out to the same brown as the rest of her A-cut. Unless she put on a show, she wouldn't be accepted. It seemed so odd to her that Terry hadn't felt such a conflict of interest when he enlisted to kill people, as he probably grew up reciting the Ten Commandments.

"Just curious."

"You went too far. You've—just too far. This isn't going to work for me. Seeing you, it's draining. I'm sorry. There are lines you don't cross. I would think a girl your age would know that."

A girl my age, Kelsey repeated in her head.

"It's been fun," Kelsey called after him as he finally turned to leave.

He stopped, fished around in his wallet and tossed a card on the table. A card for the church he volunteered at.

Kelsey grabbed the card after he'd gone far enough away to not see her do so. She used it to pick her teeth. Several minutes later, she grabbed her own coat. She needed to get out of the house. Being the only one there often proved exhausting.

***

By the afternoon, a storm had rolled in. Lightning struck the hills behind Kelsey's withering Victorian home. The flashes of light provoked the shadows in the eaves and gables, sending them into a menacing dance. It wasn't the shadows that worried her, though. It was the wind, beating the old building with unrestrained violence. Kelsey wondered if the house would survive another season of storms. Suddenly, she could hear as a shingle rattled down the roof and watched as it leapt into view and fell heavily to the unkempt landscaping below.

She clamored inside just as the sun set.

Tossing her wet jacket on the coat rack, Kelsey shut the door, twice. After the third time, she gave it a good kick, and this seemed to keep it closed. Frustrated at the door, she marched through the dimly lit dining room, down the dark, narrow hallway, past the vacant study and guest restroom, and into the kitchen where she grabbed a handful of Utz cheese balls from the large plastic barrel on her kitchen table. She had not eaten since her failed date with Terry, unless two coffees at the Barnes & Noble café counted as sustenance. Still hungry, she surveyed the pantry, but found only a variety of dry ramen, some peanut butter, and a yam, which had started to grow purple zigzagging roots. In the fridge, she found a little less: a square of tofu, a quarter of a Pepsi 2-liter bottle, some soymilk, and a few remaining eggs.

She settled for the ramen.

As the noodles cooked, Kelsey listened to the creaking of the house. It had all become like a familiar song to her, but the storm had added an unfamiliar chorus. Rain rapped like an impatient teacher's fingernails at the windows. The copper piping groaned as the house bent in the wind. The hallway floorboards creaked.

The floorboards—?

Finding this unusual, Kelsey peered into the dark hall, but saw no unexpected guests. She returned her attention to her meal and spooned the noodles into a bowl before taking a seat at the table, which shrieked as if the bowl of ramen were too much of a burden for it in its old age.

As soon as she had finished her noodles and put the bowl aside, her cat, Mantis, jumped on her lap and quickly fell into a light sleep, purring. After a few minutes, Kelsey saw the cat's ears prick up and then its head turned towards the hall. As Mantis darted under the kitchen table, Kelsey stood, thinking little of her cat's behavior, and moved to rinse out her bowl.

That's when she heard the creak of a floorboard under step.

She listened, afraid then to check the hall again.

Silence.

Then—

The toilet flushed.

Kelsey spun around knocking the bowl of ramen broth on to the wood floor. She peered into the hall, straining to make out something in the gloom. Peering into the black, she saw it.

Shoulders, she saw shoulders!

Kelsey's eyes slowly adjusted to the dark, too slowly. A silhouette swelled in the dim blue light from the dining room windows, shoulders rising like Kelsey's heart rate, gliding out from her bathroom.

"Who's there?" She felt her pockets for her phone, but she must have left it in her jacket. Fishing around for a weapon she only came up with the fork she'd used for her ramen. She backed up towards the stove. Without looking, she felt around for the knife drawer.

"Please," a voice yawned, low and soft like clean linens. It was almost inhumanly calm. "Please, don't scream. It's too early for screaming."

"Don't scream? You can bet I will."

"I mean no harm." A nervous laugh. "I'm a couch surfer. You know, from the website?" Kelsey pictured brutish arms, arms like Terry's, as much of a weapon as a knife when put up against her slender ones. The man's voice remained calm. "I've been here since this morning. If I wanted to hurt you, don't you think I would have already? Don't you remember the couch surfing service?"

This morning? Kelsey repeated to herself. He'd been there when she'd set out? Surely, he couldn't have gone unnoticed during the day, even in the living room where it stayed dim. Then again, she had started her day late and in a hurry. She could have missed the guy if he slept quietly on the sofa. As a matter of fact, she hadn't needed to go into the living room for several days.

"Turn the light on. I want to see your face. Pacifists don't typically break in to other people's places and hide in the dark."

"Break in? I knocked on the door last evening and it opened, unlocked. I figured something had come up for you." Slowly the man made his way towards the switch on the hallway wall. "I even tried looking for a note, but

I didn't want to make too much noise searching, in case you had just fallen asleep. I had my doubts, but then I saw the sheet on the couch and figured you must have been expecting me after all."

With her heart still thumping hard, Kelsey watched the man inch closer and closer to the light switch.

She knew the cushions of the couch were sleeved with a sheet. Mantis' fur got everywhere, and it was her brother's couch. She just held it for him while he went off to travel the world on a series of couches himself, so she'd slipped the sheet on to protect it, and she always had a few throws laying around, blankets and pillows.

As a clap of thunder pealed out, the light flicked on, and Kelsey squinted to take in the man's features as quickly as possible—his look, his posture, his demeanor—in case he attacked her and tied her up. In case she needed to identify him in a line up. *If* she survived.

The man looked to be in his early thirties but could have been younger. Beards tended to age people in Kelsey's eyes, and he had a thick one—black, like his hair that draped over his broad shoulders, the ends catching here and there on his poncho. Under the beard stretched an innocent smile, and under his widow's peak, soft brown eyes peered out and a hooked nose cut through. Despite the sun-loving impression his gladiator sandals and beach shorts presented, his skin looked very pale for a man of Middle Eastern heritage, with a bar of strange freckles across his nose and dark threads of hair that climbed his shins and calves like lichen.

"I'm just a friend you haven't met, yet," he said. Perhaps noticing the confusion in Kelsey's expression, he clarified, "You know—as most surfers say."

"I don't deal with that site."

"I know. You're Kelsey though, right? Please tell me I got the right house. Oh, man, that would be just my luck. Your brother Daniel set it all up. He said you held down the fort while he continued his adventure. A true inspiration, that one. He's hit all of Europe—"

"—and half of Asia," Kelsey finished.

"Good, this isn't the wrong place. You must have had some idea that I was coming, even if you let Daniel deal with the plans? Hope he didn't think I meant five in the afternoon." The stranger nodded, as he stared off to the side, as if he were thinking of where best to place a bronze memorial of her brother in order to commemorate his great couch surfing deeds.

Kelsey relaxed. The man knew her brother, at least a little through instant messenger. Her stupid, inconsiderate brother. He wouldn't send a lunatic to stay with her, and he'd probably send a heads' up message when he came down from whatever high he was currently indulged in. But her brother knew the guy. She knew that much at least.

"You are?"

"I am? Oh, right! Irik. With an I. Sorry, all the commotion has me forgetting my manners. Forgive me, please. You can call me Irik."

He held out his hand and took a step forward. Cautious still, Kelsey took it and gave it a quick shake.

"Strange name for a Muslim."

"I'm not Muslim. What gave you that idea?"

Kelsey eyed Irik from head to foot.

"Oh, well." The smile slipped from his lips. "I'm not a terrorist either, I'm afraid. Sorry to disappoint."

"I didn't mean it like that."

"Ah." Irik clasped his hands together, looking disappointed in Kelsey.

"Just how long did you and Daniel have it worked out for? You staying here, that is."

Using her brother's name felt strange, but Kelsey didn't want to give the impression that the two of them were close. She also hoped that Irik would take the hint and find another couch.

"Open-ended, actually."

"Wonderful."

Given Irik's pleasant reaction and the smile that tickled the edges of his beard once more, Kelsey guessed he didn't catch the sarcasm in her response. Surprising, as it came off flatter than the Pepsi she offered him. *The guy must be as much of a hippie as his grungy appearance makes him seem*, she thought. *All genuine gaiety and no real-world hardness.*

He sniffed the edge of the glass and held the drink in his lap once he'd taken a seat, not bothering to take a sip.

"I wish I would have known you were coming. We could have avoided all this, and I might have something better to offer you."

"Oh, no—this is great." Irik picked up and jiggled the glass of Pepsi in the air before dropping it back into his pretzeled legs. "So, how's the night life around here?"

"Night life? I took you more for a day, beachy-type of guy. I was going to suggest the lake." It would keep him away for a while at least. "Hour drive by Uber from here."

"I'm more of a night owl." A hint of a frown appeared. "I like sleeping in, you know?"

"We'll that's good, actually. I work into the evenings and sleep in the morning, so we won't have to be waking one another with cooking and what not."

Irik licked his lips as if a hunger suddenly struck him. His eyes flared just as his nostrils did. Kelsey suddenly felt the warm movement of liquid down her nostril and touched her finger to the first drop of blood that came out. "Sorry. It's the dry air." Kelsey stood and rushed to the sink. Ripping a paper towel from the roll, she sunk the end of it into her nostril.

"Yeah." Irik choked on his Pepsi. "Quite dry."

"I was just about to turn in for the night, so feel free to use the television or the computer if you want. I don't have much in the way of food at the moment, but I'll shop tomorrow, or if you want to do your own thing, I understand. I'm still sort of new to the whole couch surfing world."

"I tend to do my own thing. Dine in. Take out."

"That's fine." Kelsey applied more pressure to her nose. She couldn't be sure if he'd said *dine* in or *dive* in. "I'll save you space in the fridge."

"Not necessary."

"No?"

"Thank you for the offer, but I like to try different places around the towns I travel through."

Kelsey nodded and said good night before heading to her bedroom. As she peeled off her jeans and slipped on some sweats, she heard Irik open the front door to leave.

While she had planned to surf the web on her phone for a bit, Kelsey nodded off as soon as her head punched into her pillow. In the middle of the night, something woke her. It wasn't thunder, and the pitter-patter of rain on the roof proved more calming than rousing. It was something else.

She couldn't have actually woken to her name being hissed, could she? A gust of wind might be mistaken for a quiet but harsh splattering of syllables. Or it might be those cheese balls and ramen knotting up her stomach and deceiving her mind. Or the old surrounding oak trees might be reading the Braille of the roof shingles with their knotted fingers, she reasoned.

The intruder hissed her name again—*Kelsey*. The voice came from behind the curtains of her four-poster bed, and when Kelsey shot up and looked, she saw Irik's face, bloody around the mouth and wrapped in the curtains. He grinned ear to ear in a superficial, eerie way.

Kelsey kicked at him, but her foot only met a soft curtain. In an instant, Irik had disappeared. Or, more likely he had never been there, she realized.

Confused but exhausted, Kelsey laid her head back on her pillow.

Sweating, she woke in the afternoon to the retreating clack of thunder and tossed off her covers. Walking to the window she flung it open and took a deep breath of the cool air. The sky remained a deep gray overhead.

Heading downstairs, she found that the kitchen smelled fresh as well, but a different kind of fresh from that of the rain. A bleached, Mr. Clean fresh. Kelsey didn't even have to inspect the counters and floor closely to see that they had been scrubbed clean. The cabinets, too, had been wiped down and now looked a shade or two lighter than normal. Even the microwave had been polished, but not the inside, Kelsey found as she placed a mug of soymilk in it to be heated. Little ramen limbs, specks of various sauces, and grease still clung to the sides. Still, Irik had done good work, even going so far as to carve out the grime in the creases between the counter edges and the stovetop and the pits of the burners themselves.

She didn't want to wake Irik from his dark cocoon of blankets on the couch, but she thought she'd thank him anyway with a nice dinner. After work was done, she decided she'd do her shopping for two after all.

***

"Because everyone likes Italian and I don't feel like mushu eggplant. Simple as that." Kelsey ripped her paycheck from her supervisor's hand. "Jesus, Carl, you already control my hours, do you really feel the need to control what I eat, too? I'm an employee, not an indentured servant. Remember that."

"It's not that," Carl said. "Bite my head off, why don't you! I was offering you the leftovers before we closed the kitchen. You know, for free?"

"Right."

"You try to do something nice for somebody—"

"Something nice? Something nice is what I want to do for my guest. I don't want to give him food poisoning."

"Why do you even work here if that's how you feel about the food?"

"So, I can afford good food. *Vegetarian* food."

Carl sighed. "I always forget."

"This is why you don't have a girlfriend."

Carl spun on his heel and marched towards the kitchen. He hollered out as he turned, "Enjoy your date."

Kelsey raised an eyebrow. She liked seeing Carl squirm when she didn't deny it being a date.

Though cashing her check and shopping took longer than she'd hoped, Kelsey still had dinner ready before Irik returned home from wherever he had gone. Luckily the garlic bread had just finished crisping as he walked in the door. Kelsey had begun to worry he'd be out all night and the food would go cold, the power of her thank-you gesture cooling as well. She nearly dropped the tray of garlic bread when she caught sight of Irik coming in, and suddenly wished she'd been wearing rubber biohazard gloves rather than oven mitts.

Irik's face, arms, and legs—every exposed piece of flesh—had swelled up to almost twice their normal size. Bloated was an understatement, for he looked ready to pop. The rolls of flesh jiggled with a soggy weight, and his eyes were webbed with red veins.

"Good lord! Are you all right?"

"Oh, yeah. I feel great," Irik said. "Must be allergies." A bubble of snot popped in one of his nostrils and both leaked slow streams of mucus over his mustache. Globs dripped to the hair on his chin. Kelsey didn't know what was more disgusting: the fact that he wiped at it with the sleeve of his poncho sweatshirt, or that he followed up this up by licking it clean.

She held back her urge to vomit. "I—uh—I wanted to thank you for cleaning the kitchen, so I made dinner for you."

"Oh," he smiled and the skin that the gesture pulled tight suddenly seemed to turn purple, and there was a creak like shifting leather. "I really shouldn't. I'm full as it is."

Of course he is, she thought. His bloated figure looked sick, though, not full.

"At least try a little. Taste it," Kelsey pleaded. "I don't cook often, so when I do, I find it to be grueling work."

Irik's wide smile settled into a grin. "In that case. I'll nibble on a little of that bread."

"Good idea. Might settle your stomach."

"I'd say it smells great," Irik snatched a piece of garlic breath and took a bite, "but I can't smell a thing."

"Sagebrush, probably. You don't feel sick?"

"Not sick, no. Must be the sagebrush, like you say."

Now that she had convinced Irik to eat, she wished she hadn't. Spider web veins crawled on and off his upper cheeks as he chewed and finally swallowed with what seemed to be a great effort, as if his esophagus had grown weak. Her own stomach felt unsettled. Irik nodded to show he enjoyed the bread, but it was clear he didn't even taste the food and that the act of swallowing pained him. Still, he wandered over to a seat at the kitchen table holding the bread.

Kelsey sat, too.

"This topping, what is it," Irik asked, pointing to the glossy surface of the bread.

"Just a little butter," she said and Irik nodded, "and garlic."

He froze. "Garlic?"

"Well, of course. Can't make garlic bread without garlic." Taking in the alarm on his face, she added, "You aren't allergic, are you? I should have asked."

Irik held up a finger to silence Kelsey. He convulsed, once, twice—he couldn't hold it! He erupted. A fountain of red exploded from his mouth and showered Kelsey. She could feel the thick warmness of it on her scalp, her face, down the lines of her nose, the corners of her mouth, the edge of her chin. She could feel the dense drops fall to her collar bone. Vomit crawled over her breasts before being soaked up by her bra and shirt. Her stomach, too, felt wet and sticky, and the thighs of her jeans hung heavy with the wet weight.

The smell of copper permeated the room.

A moment later, Kelsey fell to her hands and knees and heaved the contents of her own stomach into the puddle of Irik's vomit. She focused on a hazy lump of bread, the lump of bread Irik had swallowed a moment before, and she vomited again and again until she could only gag, dryly, and then she gagged a few more times.

"Red velvet cake," Irik said, though it made no difference. He grabbed Kelsey's shoulder, but she immediately shook him off. "I'm very sorry."

"You're very sorry?" Kelsey repeated, softly. Then a bit more harshly, she said, "You're very sorry?"

"I can't stomach garlic."

"Shower," Kelsey said, standing.

Irik held out his hands, offering to help her, but she shoved him away, gripping her own soggy knee to help herself up.

"I didn't catch that."

"Shower. Move!" Kelsey bellowed, as she tore past Irik and fumbled down the hallway towards the guest bathroom. Once she reached the claw foot tub, she twisted both shower knobs, and without waiting for the water to warm, or even pausing to remove her clothes, she hopped in. The water slowly ate away at the thick coat of red. The fifty or so water streams left craters like artillery fire in the thick paste on her shirt. She wondered if Terrance ever experienced anything so horrific. She squeezed her eyes and mouth tight for a few minutes until the vomit felt diluted enough. After lathering and rinsing three times, then stripping and repeating the process thrice more, Kelsey's thoughts strayed from wanting simply to skin herself to less violent things.

Surely, he'll be too embarrassed to stay, she thought. *Surely. This might even be a blessing in disguise. A slimy, disgusting I-might-have-PTSD-because-of-this disguise.*

However, Irik was not gone when Kelsey finally came out of the bathroom with a towel wrapped around her hair, and another around her torso. In fact, it barely seemed that he'd be able to lift a finger, much less his belongings in order to flee. As if a cartoon character, his once plump face now looked gaunt. All color had faded.

Kelsey fetched the half bottle of whiskey that she kept under the sink and drank straight from it, stepping over the vomit, hoping Irik would clean it up.

"I'm going to bed." Without waiting for a reply, Kelsey dashed upstairs into her room, whiskey still in hand. She drank until the numbness of her belly spread to her limbs, before collapsing back onto her bed, under the spinning ceiling.

When she awoke the following afternoon, Kelsey wandered into the kitchen for a glass of water. The vomit had been cleaned up, but there lingered the scent of it still, under the sharper smell of bleach. Kelsey shook the cat food canister, but her cat didn't come running as it usually did. She filled the food bowl anyway, and then slunk into the living room where she took up a seat on the tall-backed chair. Her head throbbed and it hurt to keep her eyes open, but Kelsey saw Irik asleep on the couch. She'd almost forgotten he had been sleeping there and hoped she wasn't also forgetting a shift at work or something equally as important. As Irik stirred, hearing his host wiggle in an attempt to find comfort on the chair, Kelsey noticed that a tuft of orange fur danced on his lips. She gestured to her own mouth until he got the hint and wiped the fur away saying, "Guess Mantis was smitten with me."

Besides the fur, he looked much better than he had before. Not plump, not skeletal, just normal.

Then a breeze suddenly rushed over Kelsey and she noticed the front door slightly ajar.

Mantis!

Immediately, she began calling out for her cat. Images of road-kill and the neighborhood dogs' jagged rows of teeth danced through her mind. She called louder as if to quiet the disturbing thoughts. For thirty minutes she walked. She searched around the concrete walls and fence perimeter of the nearby apartment complex, and near the gym and community mail lots, as well as the pool, in case Mantis had sought it out for a drink. She peeked over the balconies that she often saw other cats sunbathing at, under parked cars. She searched everywhere she could think of, calling "Mantis, Mantis!" all the while, but to no avail. That cat remained lost.

Kelsey slumped back to her house and leaned on the doorframe. She said, "Why did you leave the door open?"

Irik sat up, covering himself with his blankets until Kelsey shut the door, blocking the dim sunlight. "I didn't. The lock is busted and the wind must have blown it open while I slept."

"You didn't close it?"

"If I had noticed, of course I would have. To be honest, I don't feel safe myself with a busted lock."

"Locks only keep honest people honest. If a burglar wanted in, they'd get in, lock or no lock."

"Well, the wind is without motive. I'm sorry your cat got out."

Kelsey sensed the sincerity in Irik's words. Still fuming, she snubbed the flame of her anger in the cushion of the recliner.

She reclined before looking at Irik. "I shouldn't blame you. I should have fixed that lock by now. It's my fault, and I lashed out at the wrong person."

"It's all right." Irik nodded. "You really loved—I mean, love," a hiccup, "that cat, don't you?

"I do."

"I've never been an animal owner."

"I've never been an animal person until Mantis. She was a stray."

"Why Mantis?"

"She looks like a praying mantis when she curls up her front paws to sleep."

There was something very strange about Irik: charming, even after vomiting several gallons of V8-like paste on her. His eyes smiled wider than his mouth, though that might have been because he never seemed to smile with his teeth showing.

"I wish my ex had been handier—not to mention a decent guy."

"Oh?"

"I don't want to prattle on about my troubles."

"There's nothing I like more than a story. Really."

"In that case." Kelsey smiled. "He's a jealous guy. I don't know if you're Catholic, but he certainly is. What he sees as saving me, I've always seen as controlling."

"Ah."

"Why should he care anyway? I can't imagine him being happy with me for more than a few hours, much less eternity."

"Catholicism is a deal breaker for me, too."

A deal breaker? Kelsey repeated to herself, uneasily. She did not pursue clarification, but rather said, "It's not even that. The religion is just a mask to hide behind, a justification for his manipulative nature."

"Sounds like you got him figured out."

"I guess."

"I can't imagine you regret leaving him."

"What makes you think that I left him?"

"If you didn't, I'd be even more surprised. You see him for what he is, and, well, you're a beautiful girl. I can't imagine anyone walking away from you."

"You are too sweet." Kelsey held back her laughter long enough to say, "Eating too much of that red velvet cake has some positive side effects, I guess."

"I am really sorry about that."

"Water under the bridge." She gritted her teeth. "Let's just forget it ever happened." *Please.* Kelsey searched for the Kahlúa. "I have just the thing to help us with that."

She drank several glasses of the liqueur. Irik abstained.

***

The following afternoon, Kelsey woke with a pounding headache. With a stiff back and weak limbs, she staggered to the bathroom sink where she nearly choked on a cup of water when seeing her reflection. Pale flesh hugged her cheekbones and temple divots. Black bags cradled her red veiny eyes.

"I don't eat meat." She heard Irik laughing uncomfortably when she made her way down the dark hallway. Both Irik and Terry looked towards

Kelsey as she came into view, with helpless and angry faces respectively.

"What are you doing here?" Kelsey's words came out harsher than she had meant them to.

"I got to worrying about you—what, with your door busted, so I came to take a look at it. Then I met Eric, here." Terry had enough tools on him to prove to Kelsey he wasn't lying.

"It's Irik." Crossing her arms, Kelsey felt weak. "I don't like you coming over unannounced."

Terry's jaw stiffened, showing his irritation. "Because of your new boyfriend, here? Is that it?"

"Jesus, Terry." Kelsey ignored the finger Terry raised at her use of his Lord's name. "You're embarrassing yourself. Irik is a couch surfer. That's it."

"I'm going to step out—or rather to the bathroom." Irik stood. "Let you two—"

"Sit your ass down, Aladdin."

"I want you to leave," Kelsey said.

"All right, fine. You can run off. Just don't rig my rig to explode."

"No," Kelsey clarified, "I want *you* to leave, Terry."

"Please do." Irik stood once more.

Angered, Terry took a swing at Irik, who ducked and caught the back of Terry's wrist. With his hand behind his back, Terry yelped in pain until Irik shoved him out the door into the rain, where Terry scrambled to his feet, looking as if he were skating on ice for the first time.

"You'll regret this," Terry shouted as he stormed away.

Kelsey put the back of her hand to her forehead as she gripped the back of the couch for support, feeling faint. She felt drained by Terry's hostility and thought of how much effort it had taken for her to let him feel in control while they dated.

"God, are all men like—like vampires?" Kelsey collapsed into the recliner, as the heavy images crushed down on her. She felt the red velvet cake paste coating her all over again, smelled its metallic tang. Irik's words echoed in her head: *allergic to garlic.* The image of a swollen Irik shrank into that of a gaunt skeleton. The smell of kitchen cleaner accompanied the image of a clean kitchen. The thought of Mantis missing and Irik's rosy cheeks came hand in hand. Even then, Irik seemed to glow, full of life, a sun to the pale moon that Kelsey saw staring back at her in the mirror just a moment before.

A flash of a fang glittered when Irik smiled, ruefully. "Not all men."

"I'm going to lie down for a bit."

Nightmares crept in through Kelsey's ears as she slept. She dreamt of Irik vomiting red paste into her mouth, and then vomiting it back into his, back and forth almost comically. In a half daze, she opened her eyes to see

Irik walking on the ceiling. Suddenly, he dropped down and straddled her. Wrapping his hands around her shoulders, he dug his mouth into her neck, but when Kelsey woke, she found a throw blanket on top of her, not Irik. Still, there was a greater weight on her than the throw. Something was off with her couch surfing guest.

She had texted her brother to ask about Irik before going to bed, but he'd always been slow to respond and had yet to do so.

Kelsey felt an urgent need to act.

***

"You sure look comfortable on your knees," Terry wheezed, walking from a back room to the fountain behind the pews.

"Yeah?" Kelsey sealed her water bottle of holy water. "Maybe I'm busy praying you'll never say something like that again."

"Really? I was hoping you were praying for my forgiveness."

"You're the one who needs to apologize."

"How's your new deadbeat boyfriend?"

"You're the only deadbeat."

Terry's nostrils flared when Kelsey didn't deny Irik being her boyfriend. He was even more fun to watch than her boss.

"You look sick," he said.

"That's why I'm here."

"Life getting you down? Or is Eric stressing you out?"

"It's pronounced Irik, with an I." *For goodness sake*, she thought, *learn it in case I end up missing.*

"All right," he said. "Irik."

Kelsey rubbed the tender spots on her neck. She admired the sunlight glistening through the stained-glass windows for a moment before saying, "I'm just tired of the whole strangers on the couch thing."

"If you want, I can be there when you tell him to leave."

"Don't go all white knight on me, please. I'll be fine. I just need some holy water."

Terry snorted. "Holy water?"

"Yeah, and do you have any crucifixes in the back?"

"We do." He scratched his head, and then sighed after seeing she was serious. "I'll go grab you one." Terry seemed pleasantly confused. He turned back after a few steps. "I'm glad to see you making an effort."

Kelsey nodded. As Terry disappeared into the back room, she rolled her eyes.

***

The banging of the hammer woke Irik. Kelsey straightened the crucifix on her living room wall before stepping back and observing Irik's reaction. His pupils narrowed on the cross. He clenched his teeth together as if in anger.

He is a vampire! Kelsey thought. She suddenly wondered if *Interview with the Vampire* was better placed in the non-fiction section of the library. Her lips curled a little, knowing that the cross was a problem for him. "What's wrong?"

"What's wrong? You're putting up a cross then staring at me to see what I think. If you want me gone—"

"What *do* you think?"

"I think you're being insensitive. You're not even Catholic, are you?"

"Does that make this lose its power over you?"

"Power?" Irik shook his head—a true actor. "What do you mean power?"

Kelsey unscrewed the top of her water bottle. "Then how about this?" She flung the holy water at Irik.

Irik cried out and tore his shirt off, revealing a dark patch of hair over his well-muscled chest that climbed slightly down to his carved abs. Then—

He wrung it out.

"That's my favorite shirt. What's wrong with you?" He scrapped a bit of the water off his stomach and brought it to his nose to smell it. "Water?" He strained to see the cross on the bottle in Kelsey's hands. "I'm an agnostic, not a vampire."

"Hah! So you admit—wait. Agnostic?"

"Yeah, agnostic." Irik used his damp shirt to dry his body. "Guess you and your brother are quite different and he doesn't know you as well as he thinks he does. I thought you were more tolerant than your boyfriend."

"Ex-boyfriend." Kelsey's shoulder's sagged in shame. "I just thought with the blood and with Mantis..."

Irik looked at her with interest.

"Christ! I'm so stupid. I actually thought you were a, well...I mean, garlic made you vomit what looked like blood; my cat goes missing during a night you looked so hungry that you were ready to eat your own arm. You sleep during the day."

"So do you."

"Yeah, but...I've been feeling so weak of late," She gestured to her neck, "and these bite wounds."

"You must have a fever to be talking like this and those are scratch marks. Here, let me feel your forehead."

Kelsey tossed her water bottle to the couch. "But—"

"I'm going to be honest here, Kelsey." Irik began to pace. "If anyone is a vampire, it's you. Now, I don't mean the way you dress in black. I actually dig your style. I mean the way you suck the joy from people. I get the feeling you enjoy making people miserable."

Kelsey remained speechless.

Irik approached Kelsey and took her hand is his. "You obviously assume the worst of people."

"I'm sorry—" Kelsey began, but the front door slamming open stopped her mid-sentence.

"Kelsey!" Terry tore into the room as the busted lock put up no resistance. He held a crowbar in his hands, that much Kelsey could tell, but it was hard to see his face with the sun behind him. "I put it all together. You fear for your life so much you've turned to prayer."

Kelsey couldn't get her tongue to move yet again, dumbfounded, but she managed to pull her hand away from Irik. She hoped Terry hadn't seen, or that if he had, he wouldn't mistake it for intimacy.

She quickly realized he must've.

Without another word, Terry pounced on Irik and began hitting him in the face with the crowbar. Irik took several blows before his knees gave out and the two disappeared behind the couch.

Her legs felt weak.

"Stop!" Kelsey yelled when the shock passed. She lunged and grabbed Terry's arm mid swing as her eyes drank in the swollen, featureless mass of Irik's bloodied face. "Stop! You're killing him."

Terry stopped beating Irik and got to his feet. Together, he and Kelsey watched as Irik's chest went from a violent seizure to utter stillness.

"Jesus Christ," Terry said.

Kelsey thought for a moment of raising her finger like Terry had in order to mock him, but it didn't seem important. She had a hard enough time simply keeping her jaw from going slack.

"What did I do?" Terry clutched his temples, a war waging in his head.

Kelsey let Irik's stillness answer the question as she slowly moved away from the body, towards the front door. She feared what else Terry might do. Looking back from the light of the entrance, she saw Irik's motionless feet and sandals poking out from behind the couch. Seeing this—knowing her unfortunate guest would never journey to another couch again—she found she couldn't manage to move any further than the threshold. She did manage to feel as Mantis came in from outside and rubbed against her leg. Kelsey could also feel the sun coming through the door, warm on her skin.

The sun fell on Irik's exposed feet, too, she noticed just before she saw the smoke.

When the couch first went up in flames, Kelsey thought madly for a moment that it was Irik catching fire from the sunlight, but then she realized that Terry had moved on to setting fire to the curtains. He worked his way around the room, setting doilies and furnished chairs alight.

As Terry turned towards her with a dogged glare, Kelsey wondered if her charred body would be found with a spent cigarette in her four-poster bed or bent over the blackened frame of a couch, a crowbar in hand.

THE PORTRAIT OF THE WITCH
Nicole Vasari

There is nothing left to me of that summer save secrets and dreams—and doubt. If I went back to that house in the Veneto and walked through the echoing, decaying corridors, I would disturb nothing but mice—and myself. There was no door where there should be none and no one—nothing—came through.

Yet my life since then, the better part of a decade, has been spent in the long shadow of that summer. We parted so abruptly and I never saw or spoke to any of them again. I never told anyone what happened. At first, I think I wanted to pretend that nothing had happened, and then it was too late: no one would believe me after so long. Even worse, I began to doubt myself. As I became less certain of what had happened, in some strange way the influence of what had—or had not—happened grew. The less I believe, the more signs I see, the more coincidences occur, the more strange, absurd things recall specific instants to me, the more often I dream...of her.

But I have no proof and no faith. So that now, when I wake to the touch of her hand on my face and see her bending over me—and then start truly awake and disturb Denise asleep in bed beside me, I am not lying when I whisper to her murmured question, "Nothing, it's nothing."

Must I go back, in memory or fact, to the scarred wall and the listing iron gate? To the house beyond dreaming uneasily in the tall grass, to the long, long summer nights it holds within its walls where doors open here and there.

***

The house was basking in the brilliant sunlight when I first saw it, and that, despite all that passed afterward, is my most enduring image of it. How clearly I saw it: a 17th century villa, the faintly crinkled plaster the same mellow burnt orange-gold as the waist-high seeding grass. The porticoed facade was surmounted by a pediment anchored by elegant urns on which balanced nymphs or Hermes. The main, central part of the building was flanked by a pair of long, rambling barchesse. On the left, the arches were crowned by roughly-made, grimacing masks, and on the right by delicately chiseled smiling masks. The long, straight drive was lined by venerable plane trees and weathered sculptures—a mix of genuine classical pieces and 17th and 18th century emulations. Between the impossible whiplash coils of the much later Stile Liberty gate, it at first appeared regal, rising like a monument against the clear blue sky. Yet after a little while, as I sat in the car outside the gate that first afternoon, its monumentality began to seem to me like that of a ruin—something truly desolate, un-romanticized, unreformed by tourism. It had been transformed by isolation from a monument to the wealth and splendor of the family that had built it into a funereal monument from which time had erased even the names of the memorialized. The dazzling, pitiless sunshine showed, even at this distance, the fissures in the plaster and the scabs where it had fallen away entirely, the dirt curtaining the windows, and every hardy, noxious weed that overran the faint track of the drive beyond the tilted gate.

Anita pulled the bell again and again I heard the distant, tuneless clap. Then she got back in the car and pressed hard on the horn.

"Is anyone there?" I asked faintly, but she didn't answer.

I had met Anita almost a year ago, at the beginning of my last year studying abroad at the University of P—. We met at a house party hosted by a mutual acquaintance: I can't imagine we would have met any other way. I was a theater major, specializing in classical Greek staging, the indulged and carefully guarded only daughter of a comfortable, respectable family.

My acceptance at the university had been a point of pride for my father, a tax attorney employed by Ford, a pragmatic man who nevertheless grasped at least the social value of the arts. My mother had taken pains to let us know how poorly she disguised her anxiety at sending me so far away; my aunts in Beirut, at least a decade older than my mother, were enlisted to monitor me as they were the closest to P—. But my aunts, a pair of grand, elegant matriarchs, fashionable women whose black hair grew each year slightly more copper-colored, were decidedly more lenient than my mother hoped. They called every other week but mostly to chide me for having a less active social life than they thought was healthy. They sent young men and women, the children of their friends or far removed relatives, to call on me and take me out to extravagant parties. During the summer vacation, they arrived, always without their husbands, vague figures they rarely mentioned by name, to take me to London and Paris, Madrid and Tangier. They chaperoned me to stores to buy the latest in young women's fashion: dresses and skirts so short I didn't dare wear them to class. They took me to the hairdressers and cosmeticians and sent me out to nightclubs with their friends' sons and daughters. I would return, very early in the morning, to find them awake, playing cards, smoking, and talking softly as the radio played. I would be given a glass of wine and a sweet and some perfectly chosen, expensive gift: a 16th century translation of Euripides rebound in 18th century Moroccan leather, an antique gold ring shaped like a snake clasping its tail with a tiny, square-faceted diamond eye.

Anita was not a student anywhere, although she was well-educated and fluent in all the Cinquencento translations I spent hours at the library unearthing. She was tall and graceful, shaped and posed like a dancer. She had fine golden hair and gray eyes as cool and clear as glass. She was open and frank, entirely careless of the opinion of other people in a way that suggested to me that her family was immensely wealthy. Despite her offhand and candid attitude, there was something oddly hieratic about her behavior, something formal and antique about her gestures. This strange cant to her behavior was at odds, or reflected perfectly by, her very modern tastes. Her apartment was in an imposing Baroque building, the interior of which had been remodeled in the 18th century. Against this backdrop of paneled walls and crystal chandeliers, Anita had modern furniture: sleek white tulip chairs and dizzily printed fabrics. In this apartment, where painted roundels of ribboned shepherds and milkmaids wooing to the encouragement of cherubs looked down on Day-Glo flowers and a celestial Hockney swimming pool, she hosted parties that outstripped the rumors that woke, sluggish with pleasure and guilt, the next day.

That first night I met Anita, we barely spoke at the party after we were introduced, but by chance left at almost the same time. We caught a cab together and by a series of misunderstandings, and the mutual distraction attending our increasingly animated conversation, ended up deposited in a quarter of town opposite where either of us lived. When we eventually found another cab, Anita insisted that I allow her to ask me to stay the night so she could make it up to me with breakfast. That night, exhausted, I slept on her stiff little modern couch, but every other night I spent at Anita's I slept in her room.

Our relationship deepened with the rapidity of youth, and we grew absorbed in each other, or I in her, as only young people can.

Occasionally, Anita disappeared for a few days, on a weekend or a holiday, to visit family in various aggressively antique-sounding corners of Europe. She gave the impression that these visits were smothered in boredom and dusty splendor and because she was involved, I imagined them imbued with romance: picturesquely aged castles and mansions on sleepy estates shaded by mature trees. And so, when my final year at university drew to a close and Anita invited me to spend the latter part of the summer with her at one of her family's homes outside of a small town in Veneto, I accepted.

I had already arranged to travel with my aunts after graduation, and I had agreed to meet my parents in Beirut or Cairo sometime in the fall. I knew my mother hoped to bring me home and my father hoped that I would find either suitable work or that I would have an acceptable suitor to introduce to them. But I could imagine neither returning to Detroit nor marriage. I hoped to have the question settled, without discussion or anguish, by remaining with Anita.

My aunts—Paris, still seething after its failed revolt, bypassed in favor of London—left me in Venice in August. They saw me and my luggage, full of new clothes they had insisted on buying for me, onto the train. I waved to them as the platform slid out of sight, then, in the stifling heat of the carriage, fell asleep and did not stir until the porter woke me at my station.

Anita waited for me outside an immense, battle-scarred Duesenberg. She wore a short shift dress as brightly patterned as the paintings in her apartment. A kind of wide lace shawl was wrapped around her shoulders and over her wide-brimmed hat. Her fine-featured face was half-hidden by a pair of huge white sunglasses.

"Lydia!" She held her arms out to me; she wore little white net gloves and over the gloves glittering rings. "Darling, how I've missed you! Let me take you away."

She pulled me into her arms and kissed me, and then gave rapid instructions to a porter to load my luggage in the Duesenberg. He did not quite meet her eyes but followed her instructions with a discreet efficiency I wouldn't have guessed to find.

"How was your trip?" she asked as we climbed into the car. "Was it slow? I thought I'd be late but I was waiting for ages."

"It was fine," I said, and then, "Where did you *find* this car?"

She laughed: she had a deep, rich laugh, completely at odds with her refined appearance. She turned the key in the ignition and the engine coughed and wheezed and sputtered but refused to turn over. "Oh god, isn't it incredible?"

The outside was bad enough, scratched, dented, stained with rust and bird droppings. The interior was possibly worse: the seats were shredded as if a wildcat had been trapped inside and the rents left by its frenzy had been patched together with rags and duct tape.

"We found it in the garage," Anita explained. "I had no idea it was there. It's probably been there for almost forty years. I think it must have belonged to the people who had the house before. We've been working on it off and on because—oh, it's a stupid story but we don't have another car so we didn't really have a choice. Kirsten said she'd get her father to send us one but then he'd have one of his people poking around."

The engine finally turned over and we both shouted in surprise. "Here we go! Do you think we'll make it?"

"I'll give us even odds."

Anita drove badly but not cautiously. She gunned the immense, shabby car through the narrow streets of the town and hit the country road fast enough to rattle some piece of the car off.

"Was that vital? Lydia, look back and tell me what I've lost."

I peered through the back window. "I can't see anything. Do you have more parts?"

"I don't know. I said we've been fixing it up, but really I meant everyone else."

"Who else is there?" I asked. I wasn't exactly disappointed; despite my absorption with Anita, I had never quite grown jealous. I had hoped to have at least a few serious discussions about my future and whether we could consider anything like our future, and I knew the presence of other people would limit my opportunities for such a conversation.

"Just Kirsten—oh, you've never met her. Kirsten Meier, she's an old friend. We've known each other since we were children. She's sweet—well, she's a little dull sometimes but it's not intentional. She's just not extremely imaginative. And Lino Cattaneo. He's—" She frowned and dodged, too late, around a large pothole. "He's sort of her fiancé."

"Sort of? I don't think you can 'sort of' be someone's fiancé."

"Well, everyone's assumed they'll get married for years and years. It's not, you know, they don't have to. But it's just expected that they will. Their families are such good friends and of course, there's a lot of money involved. It's just a matter of when they decide to get around to going through the whole ceremony."

"Oh."

"Does that seem odd to you?" She was smiling.

"It seems a little medieval," I said.

"It's not as if they don't like each other. They've known each other forever. No one would expect them to go through with it if they weren't compatible. And they are: intellectually, socially, sexually."

"Emotionally?"

"Oh, Lydia." She tapped her long fingers on the steering wheel. One of her rings was shaped like a honeybee, striped with citrine and jet, gold wings angled dangerously. "They're both quite good-looking."

The house was a long way out of town, and although it was hot, the road was too dry and dusty to have the windows more than cracked. When Anita brought the Duesenberg to a crashing halt outside the listing gate, I was glad to get out.

"A house," I breathed. The villa crouched like a tawny lioness in the wild garden, glowing with repose. "You said this was a *house*."

"That's what it is," she said and pulled the bell.

No one answered, not even when she pulled the bell again and again, not when she shook the gate and shouted. By then the first impression of the house had faded, and I began to feel uneasy staring down this obviously dilapidated building. I had imagined antique grandeur but also at least some modern comfort. The villa drowsing in the weeds appeared to offer neither, and the blue had begun to fade from the sky, bled out by a sickly silver haze.

"Is anyone there?" I asked. I sat in the car with the door open, fanning myself with my hat. I rather hoped we were locked out and would have to leave.

Anita, still in her hat and glasses and shawl and gloves, scowled and leaned savagely on the horn. "They're there." And then, with vicious satisfaction, "They're *there*."

From the shadows and overgrowth gathering about the gate, two figures emerged, young men about our own age. One of them, handsomely built and elegantly dressed if a bit rumpled, carried a wicker basket and a blanket. He had large, soft blue eyes that would, if someone else had looked out of them, been quite soulful. With his delicate mouth, they softened a rather patrician face. The other, his dark hair so long that for a moment I mistook him for a very tall girl, came to wrap his hands around the flaking coils of the gate.

"Where were you? I specifically told you that I was picking Lydia up and that you should keep an eye out for us."

"We had a picnic."

"Oh, a picnic," Anita snapped. "Dare I ask what's in the basket?"

"You daren't," the dark-haired man said. He reached up and began undoing what looked to be a complicated lock.

"You let me into my house this instant." I'd never seen Anita in such a petulant, demanding mood; there was something in her attitude to the man opening the gate that reminded me, unpleasantly, that she was probably much richer than anyone I'd ever met and used to determining how she treated people based on their position with regards to her. She kicked the gate. "Alec, you have no business locking the gate without my permission."

"Lino didn't want anyone just wandering in..."

"No one comes down here!"

He swung the gate in. "Welcome home, madam."

Lino, without asking permission, carried the blanket and basket to the car and climbed in the backseat. Anita gave a tense shrug, and Alec took that as his permission to join Lino. She pushed the gate open a little wider, and then we drove up the rutted remains of the drive. The nodding, feathery heads of the tall grass tapped against the sides of the car and bobbed in through the windows as we bumped up to the house. Anita pulled up just past the door, turned the car off, and held the keys out over her shoulder.

"Put Lydia's bags in the room next to mine."

As Lino and Alec unloaded my luggage, we climbed the few wide, shallow steps to the door. I was by that time tired from the long trip and savoring that anticipation of ease which is almost more delicious than the realization of it. It's almost possible to believe, at that stage, that even the meanest accommodations will do, if only there is a narrow bed and a hard chair and a basin of water; but the certainty that a more sumptuous comfort awaited me made the pleasure, and the pleasurable sense that I could be satisfied with so little, all the keener.

But Anita opened the door on a barren entrance hall: a dusty, dim room lit only well enough to show where faded frescoes were falling from the walls. There was a splintering chair in the corner by the door and beside that, a scarred deal table on which a blue and white porcelain vase had evidently sat undisturbed for many years. Electrical wires ran along the walls and ceiling, and from the center of the ceiling hung a bare bulb. The floor was scattered with bits of leaves and debris, and in several spots near the base of the wall this formed suspicious little forts that, I suspected, guarded the openings to extensive warrens.

Anita sighed as if in relief. She unwound her lace shawl and left it along with her hat and sunglasses on the dusty table. She shook her hair out, then took my hand and led me through a series of rooms, each as grubby and desolate as the first.

"Is it all like this?" I asked nervously.

"Yes." Anita smiled and cast a look of satisfaction around: no—she fairly beamed at the bare windows and the plaster crumbling from the walls. "Yes, you see, it's all like this."

At last, we entered a room that had been furnished for some limited use. There were two bookshelves crowded with books and curling newspapers that possibly antedated the Duesenberg by a few years. Opposite the shelves was a very old piano painted with a pretty pastoral scene. Several mismatched occasional tables and a heavy, iron-bound chest were posted along the walls. On one of the tables was a record player and on the floor beside it new, expensive stereo equipment and a crate of albums. The center of the room was covered by a threadbare Persian rug and on that was a massive, medieval-looking oak table deeply carved along the edge with a garland of leaves and fruit. A handful of old, high-backed chairs were set around it, and at the outer perimeter of the rug was a genuine Empire settee, the ancient fabric stained and splitting. A door opposite the one we'd come in was cracked open.

"Hello, we're back," Anita called. Then, to me, "Sit here, Lydia. Do you want a drink? We have ice but it's all the way over in the kitchen. I'll ask Alec to bring some in here."

She knelt to open the trunk and took out a bottle and a pair of heavy, greenish glasses. As she poured the wine, a woman walked in through the other door. She was about our age or a little older, very tanned and athletic, with dark hair in a long ponytail. She was wearing a loosely belted kimono and a pair of sandals and carried a scent of suntan oil and sunbaked greenery. She had a hard, cool face and an air of impatience tempered by boredom.

"Kirsten, darling, this is Lydia. Lydia, this is Kirsten."

"Hello," I said.

Kirsten gave me a quick assessing look, then glanced at Anita. "Hello, Lydia. I've heard so much about you. Do you like to swim?"

"Yes." I did not but I was too uncertain of her evaluation to risk disappointing her.

"That's too bad because there's nowhere to swim here. There was a pool but it's old and no one took care of it. Alec tried to fix it but it's just a big fish pond now, full of plants. It smells bad."

"What a shame."

"Yes."

"Kirsten likes to climb mountains," Anita said so lightly and cheerfully that I suspected she was making fun of her friend.

But Kirsten either ignored or disregarded her. "How did the Duesenberg drive?"

"Awful," Anita said. "I think something fell off on the way back. Do you want a drink, dear?"

Kirsten's impassive face was animated with alarm. "You shouldn't be *allowed*. Is it in the garage? Did you say anything to Alec? Where is he?"

"Bringing Lydia's luggage up with Lino."

She made an exasperated sound and strode out of the room. "Tell him to come to the garage when he's done."

"Isn't she nice," Anita said.

"Very." I hesitated. In the car, she had mentioned only Kirsten and Lino, not Alec. "Anita, who's Alec?"

She laughed. "Why, you just met him."

"No, I mean, is he staying here? Does he live around here? Does he work here?"

"I picked him up a few months ago," she said. "Do you like him? I like him. He's like modern art: beautiful junk. Don't give me that look. That's exactly how he described himself to me. He tunes that piano beautifully, though. Come on, let me show you to your room."

The bedrooms were up a worn stone stairwell and, like the rooms below, were connected by doors. Anita's was in the middle, Kirsten's at the far end and mine closest to the stairs. Lino's room was on the other side of the gallery, not directly connected to ours. I was prepared for the worst, but the room Anita let me into was clean and, if not the sumptuous boudoir I had imagined on the train, offered a romantically shabby luxury. There was a new mattress on the narrow, antique bed and an embroidered lace curtain to pull around it. The Gallé lamp on the inlaid table beside the bed had been fitted with a new cord and gave a mellow amber light. There was a cupboard inlaid with shell and ebony; my bags were already set neatly beside it. On the wall beside the cupboard was a mirror, heavily flyspecked and blurred with age, in an embroidered silk frame. I started to fix my hair but stopped.

"Anita, how old is this?"

She was fussing with the bedclothes. "What?"

"This mirror. The frame."

"Oh, it came with the house." I saw her turn around and come to stand behind me. She met my eyes in the mirror and bent a beautiful smile on me. "Almost everything here came with the house. I guess it's pretty old."

"I don't think you should have it out. It looks like it could crumble!"

"It's just old." She kissed the side of my neck and reached over my shoulder to brush her fingers over the silk frame. "They made things to last back then."

It was a pale silk, faded to an oyster color, and embroidered all over with a bewildering series of figures. There was a richly-dressed woman in a gown trimmed with seed pearls and, when I looked closely, what looked like the desiccated traces of feathers on her cloak. Owls with human faces crowded a tree and twining among roses and violets were nude women that transformed into snakes below the waist. Along the bottom was stitched a vast, rambling house or a city and on either side great, hooded figures each holding a cup and what looked like a club.

"How strange," I said faintly.

"I suppose." She kissed me again. A distortion in the glass blurred her eyes into a silvery haze. "Do you want a bath? You must be exhausted."

Anita led me out of the room and up a few steps set in an alcove to the most marvelous thing I'd seen since I had passed through the gate: a real, modern bathroom. It had been refurbished and updated quite recently and the plumbing worked beautifully.

I spent a long time luxuriating in the warm water and Anita's rose-scented soap. This, at last, was the ease I had longed for. I got out, reluctantly, only when the water chilled, and wrapped myself in the frayed silk robe Anita left for me.

Back in my room, I started to slowly unpack. The air was close but, rather than being warm, it was quite chilly, at an almost uncomfortable contrast with the beaming summer day I could see through my window. I got up to see if the window opened.

There was a latch but it was stuck; after several frustrating attempts to loosen it, I pressed my forehead to the glass, palpably warmer than my room, and looked out at the wild garden. There were more sculptures scattered in that wilderness. Most of them appeared, from my vantage, to be like those lining the drive, Neoclassical and Baroque: figures allegorical, historical, or divine. There were also several rather monstrous Mannerist forms, their bizarre proportions half-swallowed up by the anarchic vegetation. Here and there I picked out weathered forms so crude and strange they could have passed, like Alec, for modern art. There was one quite near the house, a grotesquely oversized head with an open mouth and protruding tongue. Standing beside it were Anita and Alec.

I could just see them if I craned my neck. Anita's back was to me; I saw her make a few impatient gestures as she spoke. Alec looked unhappy and reluctant but not contrite. Then he shook his head emphatically at something Anita said. She stepped closer, shaking a finger in his face. He shook his head again and turned away, but she caught his arm hard enough that I saw him wince. She said something that made his face freeze in a rigid, blank expression, then pushed him away so that he stumbled against the statue.

I backed away from the window, guilty, troubled, and colder than ever. I had never known Anita to be angry. When she'd snapped at Alec earlier, I thought that she was simply being impatient and then, as she ordered him about, wondered if she had hired him to help keep the aging villa in order for the summer. But there was an odd suggestion of intimacy in the exchange I'd just witnessed, some level of emotion that did not usually pass between employer and employee. I was almost jealous and more disturbed by that, I think, than by Anita's behavior.

Less than an hour later, Anita tapped at our connecting door and with the warmth and sincerity of her affection smothered my misgivings. When, later still, we went downstairs, hand-in-hand, I was so reassured and sated that it did not occur to me to wonder how she had guessed I required that attention.

"I know it's a funny old place," Anita said.

Our shoes echoed on the bare stone of the stairwell. She had insisted on dressing for dinner—"it's a rule in my house"—and she was wearing a pink, yellow, black, and blue dress that would have looked garish on anyone else, even in the heady atmosphere of 196—. She lowered her elaborately feathered eyes then lifted them to mine with an impish grin.

"It's such a funny place," she whispered and squeezed my hand, "but it's all mine. Do you see?"

"Then it suits you," I said. "You're a funny person—but you're all mine."

"If you like funny things..." We'd reached the bottom of the stairs but she turned away from where I expected her to go. "...Then I have something for you. It'll only take a moment. Kirsten's probably still setting the table."

She led me through another room to a narrow, dark door. It opened, with some difficulty, on darkness so complete that when we stepped inside and she let go of my hand, I gasped.

"Anita!"

"I'm here." Her voice sounded strange coming out of the darkness; I had the irrational thought that it was someone imitating her voice: someone farther away, someone with a slight, undefinable accent. Then hard light flooded the room from a naked bulb hanging precariously from a wire, and there was my Anita, the genuine article.

The room was small and crowded with flat, roughly rectangular or square objects covered in cloth. As Anita rummaged through them, I saw that they were paintings: very, very old paintings. None of them could have been earlier than the end of the 18th century and some of them were very much older.

"Here it is. Look!"

I leaned over Anita's shoulder to see the painting. It was a portrait of a woman, perhaps made near the end of the 17th century: she had an oval face and a long, narrow nose, a thin, disdainful mouth, and dark eyes.

"That's Letitia Tiepolo," Anita said. "She lived here. She was a witch. She killed her whole family. She poisoned her most distant relatives, you know, childless great uncles and people like that, but as she got closer the most horrible, absurd things would happen to them. Her cousin Carlo died here, right at the bottom of those stairs: he had just reached the top when something rose up from the floor, like fog, and then it turned into some absurd creature, a mule's head on a bear's body with a woman's breasts. And he was so startled that he went over backward, head over heels, down the stairs and broke his neck and most of the rest of his bones. Her brother, Jacopo, died in Venice. They had a fleet, and he was meeting with one of his captains to look over a ship. And right in the middle of the deck it just—gave way—like all the wood was rotten even though it was perfectly sound. They were doing some work below decks, some usual stuff, I guess, maybe that's why he was there. And, this is the funniest part, he fell right where someone had left all these great long nails and hammers and a saw. And, oh, he didn't die right away! He was just thrashing around like a crushed bug, all these nails and everything stuck in the back of his head. It took him at least a week to die. His people knew it was Letitia's fault because they found a little note from her stuck on the bottom of his shoe. And her father—"

"Why did she do it?" I asked. Letitia's oval face was as reserved and irreproachable as a Madonna's.

"Because she was a witch, dear, that's how these stories go. She was supposed to be very extravagant: lots of parties, lots of lovers, lots of spending. But her cousin Julia Tiepolo found out what she was doing. Julia was engaged to one of the brothers, you see, and suspected something unnatural in his death and his sister. There were rumors but no one who mattered believed them: this wasn't Germany, after all. But the locals got scared. They wouldn't come to the house, they wouldn't do her laundry, they warned off anyone she brought in. So, she started to punish them, and that was really her mistake. Julia told them how to get into her secret rooms. They killed Letitia, right here in the house. Julia and the rest of the Tiepolos died a few years later. It was one of those plagues they were always having but they found a note from Letitia on the bottom of Julia's foot when she died. Isn't that wonderful?"

"I'm not sure that's what I'd call it."

"My uncle told me," Anita continued, her eyes fairly glowing as she gazed at the portrait, "that they used to say Letitia was still here. Sometimes people go missing—travelers, strangers—and they say Letitia took them. She gets bored and lonely."

"Anita, they say everything's haunted in these little towns."

"I think it's so interesting." She dropped the cloth back over the painting. "Not that I'm saying I believe it or I don't. But it's so...delicious."

"You are funny, Anita."

"Oh, you're too much. Don't be frightened."

I hadn't been frightened by Anita's story until then. But at the word—*frightened*—I found myself filled with that black, choking fear as I'd felt when she'd let go of my hand and her voice had echoed strangely in the small room. It was not until we reached the room where Kirsten was arranging heavy candelabrum on the table and Lino and Alec were in deep conference over the crate of records that my throat loosened enough to speak.

"Is it so late already?" I managed. It was apropos of nothing Anita had been saying and my voice shook so that Kirsten looked up quizzically; but Anita gave no sign that she noticed.

"Late?" Kirsten said.

"Yes, it's dark already. I don't think it was dark when we came down."

"Lydia, dear, it was pitch dark. You must be dreaming. Who cooked? What did you make?"

Anita prattled on, bright as a brook in the sunlight. Lino put a record on, and as we served ourselves, an atmosphere of cozy normalcy established itself. Soon enough, my good mood was restored. The five of us made up a perfect party: in attitude and taste complementary enough to be amiable but diverse enough in experience and thought to fuel conversation. We spent a long time over dinner, longer over the wine. Eventually, Kirsten and Alec gathered up the dishes and carried them to the inconvenient kitchen in the barchessa. They returned with armfuls of wine—"The cellars are full of it," Kirsten said, rather reprovingly, as if the bounty of untouched wine offended her slightly.

Later...much later, I thought, than should have been possible, Anita put me to bed. It must have been almost dawn. I believe I told her that, considering; it was a bit pointless to go up to bed. She kissed my forehead and pulled the blanket over me. "You'll thank me in a few hours." Then she went through the connecting door to her own room.

I did sleep, I think, because it seemed that I slowly woke up. It was still dark. At first, I had only the impression that something had awakened me, then I realized it was the sound of the connecting door opening. I saw it, beside the mirror in the embroidered frame, swing shut, and I heard the resistant creak of its old hinges. Anita, wrapped in a long robe or a blanket, turned toward me; I could just make out her delicate features. I thought she would come to me, and I moved slightly to make room for her in the bed. She stood, looking at me, for a long time, until my pleasure at her visit sputtered into weariness and confusion. Why did she stand there, so still? Why did she stare at me that way? She looked so strange—she looked at me so strangely. As if my unease had touched her, she turned suddenly and opened the door.

"Anita!" My voice, worn down by the evening, was little more than a rasp. I held my arms out. "Anita!"

The door shut behind her. I fell asleep again, almost too baffled to be hurt. When I woke, Anita's strange behavior was still fresh in my mind and heart. I lay on the soft pillows, shrouded from the early afternoon by the bed curtains, and puzzled over her brief visit. I could hear her moving about in her own room, opening and closing cupboards. There was something strange about that, about how I heard her separated only by the wall beside my bed. There was something quite wrong about the sound because the door she had come in through last night was on the opposite wall, beside the mirror.

I sat up abruptly and dragged the curtains aside. The connecting door was just past the foot of my bed. There was no door beside my mirror, only a blank wall.

***

I said nothing about my dream. It was too absurd: how could I tell anyone that I'd been frightened by a dream that Anita had slipped into my room through a door that wasn't there? The particular point of horror for me, the locus of the sense of wrong that permeated my recollection, was that the connecting door was on the wrong side of the room. Yet what could be more natural, after a tiring journey and such a night, in a strange house, to mistake the layout of the room in a dream?

Nothing, except that I had the same dream again and again, any time, in fact, that I happened to sleep, even for a few hours, alone in my room. It happened even when I was certain that I had not fallen asleep, when I forced myself to stay awake after Anita left me, complaining that the beds were too narrow to hold more than one person with any comfort. Inevitably, I would hear the grate of the old hinges and she would enter my room. She, the dream Anita, never made any noise herself. Sometimes she would simply stand and look at me as she had the first night; sometimes she sat in the chair and, with folded hands, watched me. As the visitations, for that was how I thought of them, progressed, she came to stand over my bed, and, parting the curtains, stoop over me. Her face was often just visible in the gloom but never her eyes: no stray bit of light ever glinted in them, and when she leaned over me I saw only pools of utter darkness staring down at me.

After each of these visitations, I would fall into a strange haze. Not a languor—I didn't stumble and swoon on the terrace—but a kind of fugue state. I would find that days, or even, once, a week, had slipped by in what seemed to me the space of a single day. Or, it would seem to me that days had gone by and I would suddenly discover, like stumbling over a step, that it was not even a single day had passed. It was not that I didn't recall what had happened, it was as if there was some misalignment in time. But I inevitably convinced myself that the fault lay in me, or, rather, our lifestyle at the villa. It was no surprise, considering, that time should be distorted. Despite or because of our diversions, each day assumed a certain predictable routine. Late mornings and sunbathing on the terrace with Kirsten while Anita, who could take only enough of the sun to touch her cheeks with a gentle gold, lounged in hat and sunglasses on the terrace, and Lino and Alec drove into town for cigarettes, newspapers, gas, the novelty of the risk of exposure. The days, shortening toward the equinox but far too quickly, dwindled into the lengthening nights and we gathered, the kiss of the sun fading from our skin, to celebrate each night as if it were New Year's and we five the only people left in the world.

If I had told them that days and nights melted into each other, they would have had a laughing explanation ready at hand: we were all too stoned, too often, too wound in each other's embraces, to distinguish anything outside our narrowing world of leisure and pleasure.

Finally, something disturbed our rote revels. Over a second bottle of wine after dinner, Kirsten announced that she'd begun to find the routine a little dull.

"I suppose it's inevitable," Kirsten said. "It's already September."

"September?"

"Yes, Lydia, the month after August."

"But it's only...." It was often unseasonably cool in the villa, Anita attributed it to either an underground lake or a marvel of 17ᵗʰ century design, but the shock at hearing the date ran through me as hot as panic. I looked away from Anita's teasing smile and caught Alec staring at me over his shoulder, his expression so bland it could only be disguising something.

"I know how we should pass the time." Anita clapped her hands to command our attention. "We should have a séance."

"I'm not that bored," Kirsten protested.

"It'll be fun!"

"I don't know anything about séances," she said firmly. "I'm not going to sit around the table holding hands in the dark."

"Alec knows everything about séances." Anita was already moving chairs back into place around the table. "He's done it before."

"Oh." Kirsten turned and bent a look of severe suspicion on Alec. "Have you? I didn't know you went in for that kind of thing."

Alec sat back on his heels. While he and Lino had discussed the merits of *Aftermath* or *Otis Blue,* they'd lit a joint. Alec took a long, very deliberate drag before he responded. "I'm not in any condition. I'm drunk." But his voice and the look he gave Anita were so bracingly clear that I felt sobered myself.

"That's perfect." She smiled down at him. "You'll be so much more open to the spirits."

"Anita," I said. "Anita, I don't think that's such a good idea."

"It's just a game," she said, but she didn't look at me. Although she smiled pleasantly down on Alec, there was something subtle in her posture and her expression that reminded me of the quarrel I'd witnessed from my window that first day. As I had that day, I had the sense that this animosity described a connection between them, some history that Anita deliberately concealed from me. I should have felt sorry for Alec, pinned and passive beneath Anita's brazenly triumphant sneer, but I didn't.

Anita had her way, of course. Alec folded quite easily, and his acquiescence fed my suspicions. He must know her and her moods so well if he intuited when it was futile to resist. He was seated at the head of the table, Lino on his right, Kirsten beside Lino, then Anita, and finally I on Alec's right. His hand felt strange in mine: large, long-fingered, bony. I wondered if he could feel a faint rill of animosity running from my hand into his; I hoped he could.

Anita turned out the electric lights before we sat. Then, she and Kirsten blew out the candelabrum and shut us in darkness. I didn't close my eyes when Alec told us to—I was disinclined to obey him and no one could see my defiance anyway. We sat in silence for a long while; I thought I could feel Alec's breathing grow slower and deeper, as if he slept. His hand grew cold and the chill spread to me, icing my bare arm and then my whole body. Gradually, my eyes adjusted to the dark, and I could faintly see Lino and Kirsten across the table and Alec's profile.

"Are there any spirits with us tonight?" It was absurd: it was a corny slumber party game, a trick that had fooled no one since the Fox sisters confessed to cracking their joints. When Alec's voice, soft and a little husky, ventured the dark, I felt dread: smothering, towering over me like an antique colossus eclipsing the sun. I knew, before anything happened, that he would be answered.

In the moment of silence after his question, I glanced at Anita, hoping that she would have opened her eyes, that by some silent appeal I could convince her to stop this. Although I could feel her hand warm and soft in mine I saw nothing: where she should have sat beside me was only unrelieved darkness. There was a terrible pressure in my chest, as if my fear was a physical hand crushing my heart, and I opened my mouth, unable to scream or breathe.

Alec began to cough, softly at first, then harder. Something shuffled across the floor and banged hard on the table. Lino shouted. Alec's freezing hand clutched at mine as he wheezed and choked. There was a bang in the center of the table, and Kirsten's voice rose, demanding to know who was doing this. I couldn't see anything there, but, I realized, I should have. I should have seen the ghostly shape of the candelabra and Lino and Kirsten beyond that. Something was blocking them, some shape darker and denser than the night. Suddenly it seemed to pounce on Alec, knocking him to the floor and dragging me with him. My head cracked hard on the floor, and stars popped in the darkness.

Then a real starburst above me. Kirsten had switched on the overhead light, and I blinked flashing spots from my eyes. I rolled carefully onto my side and sat up.

Kirsten stood across the room, her hand still on the light switch, breathing hard and looking around the room. Lino bent over Alec, who was crumpled on his side, his hands at his neck.

"What happened? Let me see," Lino said, pushing Alec's hands aside. There were marks on his neck, scratches and the red impressions of fingers that were darkening to bruises. Lino drew in his breath. "Who was it?" He looked around, bewildered, at the rest of us. "Who did this?"

"Anita." Kirsten's voice was almost shrill. She was breathing hard. "Anita."

She was sitting, unruffled and composed, in her chair at the table. She opened her eyes and smiled. "Yes?"

The mood that had held all of us together those weeks, like sap thickening slowly, sweetly, to amber, was shattered. I recall, quite clearly, looking around the room as if I'd never seen it before, a barren, broken down, shabby place sliding day by day to ruin. I caught Kirsten's gaze for a moment, and we each flinched away. Lino took Alec, dazed and unsteady on his feet, to his room. Kirsten left without saying anything, and Anita and

I were alone. Finally roused, she got up and made what struck me as a show of looking me over, asking if I was hurt and how I felt. Then, gazing into my eyes, she declared that I'd had a scare and a bad knock on the head and should go right up to bed.

"But I'm not tired."

"It's best." She pulled me to my feet. "What you need is rest."

She saw me upstairs and into bed like a nurse but refused to stay when I asked her. "Your head, my dear, I don't want to crowd you in that narrow bed when you're hurt." She turned off the Gallé lamp and shut the connecting door behind her.

I lay awake for what felt like hours. I could hear Anita moving around her room at first, and the rustle and creak as she climbed into bed. Then silence, silence as deep and funereal as when a blizzard back home finally spent itself in the dead of the night. Silence drifting up like dunes of snow, burying the villa.

Gradually, I became aware of another lamp or a light burning across the room. I turned my head on the pillow to see; it was only the mirror reflecting light. But what light? There was none falling on it.

I was paralyzed, every muscle in my body drawn immobile by fear, my heart stuttering. I thought, wildly, of jumping out of bed and running into Anita's room. But like a child, I couldn't bear to expose myself to the terror in the dark. A moment of courage, a moment of awful fear, and then I would be safe in Anita's room. But I found no courage and, as I stared at that watery light reflected in the mirror, I thought of the darkness I'd found beside me at the séance. My imagination built de Quinceyian citadels of terrible speculation on that trick of perception, and I climbed every fantastic, torturous turret, leaping to heights of fantasy more awful and bold each moment. What if I should enter her room and hear her sweet soft breath but find on her bed nothing but shadow, and what if at that moment....

At that moment the hinges that were not there squeaked and grated as a door that could not possibly exist swung open. I wanted to look away, I meant to look away. I saw her more clearly than ever before by the light reflected in the mirror: the refined features, the fair hair that fell around her....far longer than Anita's hair. She was dressed strangely, in a kind of robe or loose gown, like nothing I'd ever seen Anita wear.

I'd known all along that this was not Anita, and I had known, without truly admitting it, that I did not dream these visitations. For weeks, I had stepped back from the precipice of what I felt was a terrible question that I did not want answered.

As she had on other nights, she crossed the small space of the room to my bed. Her face was in shadow now, and her hair was lit with a wavering halo. I dreaded that she might tilt her head enough for the light to strike her face. She bent over me, and I had the sudden impression that she was, for the first time, aware of my awareness of her, that perhaps on those other nights she had thought me sleeping. Now, it was as if our eyes met, and she drew closer. I could see that she was smiling although I could not see her eyes even as her face hung above mine. She touched my cheek, and her hand was, terribly, as warm and soft as Anita's—as were her lips.

I fainted. I remember a sudden darkness, then a feverish jumble of dream fragments, stumbling through passages within the walls of the villa, the sun rising and setting over the garden, a woman's voice ringing out over the cypresses and motley statues and shattering a sky that was burnished by haze and humidity to the blurred silver of an old mirror.

I woke at last to ordinary sunlight and the house so quiet around me that it seemed empty. I washed and dressed quickly. I hesitated at Anita's door but, my dreams still hanging over me like the haze over the marshes, I turned away and went downstairs.

It was quiet downstairs, too. I looked out on the terrace for Kirsten, but it was empty. I found only Alec in the large, furnished room, sitting at the table and reading a book.

"You're up." He set the book down. "How are you feeling? Better?"

"Yes, I'm fine. I was fine." I circled toward the table. There were still marks on his throat but they were very faint; I might not have seen them if I hadn't known to look.

He raised his eyebrows. "You could have fooled me. We wanted to call a doctor, but Anita wouldn't let us. I told her I was going to today if you weren't better."

"What are you talking about?" I laughed but I folded my arms to warm or protect myself. "You were the one who...well...you know. I just bumped my head a little."

Alec frowned and stubbed his cigarette out in the ashtray. "Lydia. You've been sick for a week."

"I have not," I said furiously.

"You have."

I could have slapped him, and I advanced a few steps, fists clenched. "I would know if I'd been sick! You're lying."

"Why would I lie about that?"

"Because you—you want to—you want to upset me because I keep getting so mixed up about the days." I was almost in tears, although I don't think, even in the grip of my panic, I believed what I accused him of.

"I didn't know that," he said quietly.

"Yes, you did!"

"Alright." His voice fell even softer. "Yes, I am lying about that. I did know. Because it's been happening to me, too, so I could tell."

"What?" I was almost startled by his admission, and my anger, which tended to smolder for days, blew out at once.

"But I'm not lying about you being sick."

"How long have you...it's been happening to you, too?"

"I don't know how long I've been here." His lighter was lying on the table; he picked it up and began turning it over in his fingers. "I think—since May at least. I was on my way to Tangier to stay with a friend. I met Anita at a concert. We went out afterward...and then...."

He looked lost and miserable, and I had the acute and uncomfortable sensation that I was seeing him—really seeing him—for the first time. In some way, I suppose, I had absorbed the prevailing attitude toward him: modern art, beautiful junk. My family was quite comfortable, but we were not clever aristocrats, hoarding wealth while ceding purely ceremonial power, with the cunning and privilege of generations at our disposal. To Anita, Lino, and Kirsten, Alec was merely what he appeared to be: a handsome drifter, handy with a car or a piano, dispensing an assured taste in music, art, and other diversions appealing to the young and idle. I had taken enough note of him to foster fits of jealousy, but not enough to note the shadows that gathered daily around his eyes or how he laughed less and less.

"Alec, I'm sorry."

He looked up, confused. "What for?"

I didn't answer. I should have. "Where's Anita?"

"Asleep, I guess. She said she had a headache and went upstairs."

"What about Kirsten and Lino?"

"In Venice," he said warily. He took another cigarette out of the package and lit it without looking away from me. "They left...a few days ago, I guess. They had some business to take care of."

When I first arrived, I had longed to be alone all summer with Anita. Yet now, being alone, even with Alec, with her in the moldering villa was dreadful. I felt ill, overwhelmed with a dense, poisonous fear like the night of the séance and the night Anita had, smiling, told me about the witch.

"Are you sure you're feeling alright?"

"Yes." I took a slow, unsteady breath. "Yes. I was just thinking—what an awful place this is. No wonder we're so spooked and out of it. Did Anita ever tell you that awful story about the woman they killed here? The one they said was a witch? It's so absurd. I just—I got a little spooked and then I remembered that and...."

Alec gave me such an odd look, not simply wary, but outright distrustful. His fingers twitched and a little shower of ash fell from his cigarette. "What are you talking about?"

"Didn't she tell you? She took me to see the portrait the first night." I laughed but it sounded awful, scared and too loud. Alec was staring at me as if he was prepared to bolt if I moved. "Can I have one of those cigarettes?"

"Sure." He pushed the package across the table. "She showed you that portrait?"

"Yes." I fumbled with the package, relieved to have an excuse to look at anything other than his face.

"And you're asking me....how did she manage to explain that?"

I struggled to light the cigarette. "Oh, Alec, I don't know. She didn't. It's just a stupid old story. What's got into you?"

"Lydia," he said, and then, very quickly he stood up and lunged across the table to grab my wrists. I yelled in surprise but he shook me, violently, his eyes blazing, and I was as furious as I was scared. "Who the hell are you? Who are you, really?"

"Lydia! Lydia! And if you don't let go of me, I'll scratch your eyes out!"

He pushed me away hard enough that I stumbled. I caught myself, then rushed around the table to slap him, hard, across the face. "How dare you!"

He touched his face, but he seemed oddly calm now, as if my action had reassured him somehow. "I think you should come with me."

"No."

"I want to show you something."

"I don't want to see it."

"Lydia." He spoke softly as if he was afraid of being overheard. "I want to know what you saw when you looked at that portrait."

"A woman."

"What did she look like?"

"I don't know. Dark hair, dark eyes. Dark dress."

"That was Julia Tiepolo?"

"No, Letitia Tiepolo."

He sat down again, but I remained standing, still angry at him and glad to have that vantage. "When I first got here, there was a kind of housekeeper. I was alone—Anita asked me to go on ahead of her. I don't know why I agreed. Anyway, the housekeeper was local. She didn't like me showing up, and I thought it was just because she didn't want Anita to find out she wasn't really doing any housekeeping. She came in one day and told me that Anita had called and dismissed her. She said I should leave, too, if I had any sense. I laughed at her because it still seemed like a great deal, hang out in some beautiful falling down villa and write music for a few weeks before I went down to Tangier. She called me some pretty nasty names, then she said she had a couple of things to show me about the house before she left. I thought she meant what to do if the stove blew up or something. She took me down to that room with all the portraits, and then I got interested. Some of those are very valuable. Veronese, Giorgione, Bellinis....so. She was lifting up the cloths, peeking at the paintings, and I was getting as good a look as I could over her shoulder. When she found the one she was looking for, she told me to take a good look."

He stopped and stared at me until I said, "Okay. And?"

"You really don't...It looked just like Anita. I mean, exactly. I can see you're thinking the same thing I did. So what? The old lady told me probably the same story you got: party girl, black magic. And then Letitia figured it out and that was that. She said it was a big mistake killing Julia here. She said they should have just sent her to Venice. She said Julia's body died, but she's still here and she takes people to keep her company, people she thinks will entertain her. Strangers, travelers...."

"Stop!" I hadn't meant to shout. "It's just a dumb story. They have to invent something interesting in these places or they'd all die of boredom. She was just trying to be mean to Anita. You said it; it's just a coincidence that she looks like the portrait."

He played with his cigarette for a moment and, then, not looking at me asked, "Do you sleep well at night, Lydia? If you're alone, do you sleep well?"

"Don't you dare!" I was shaking, and I could feel tears, absurdly, welling in my eyes. "You can't talk about that! How could you! You never said anything to me before!"

"Well, Jesus, Lydia, do you blame me? I think I'm going crazy half the time. Sometimes I think I'm still...You've got a bad temper, you know that?"

"Yes." I was still trembling, but I drew an easier breath. "Don't—I can't talk about that. It's too—terrible."

"I know," he said. It was no comfort that he did know. We had both known all along, both suffered, and neither of us had found the courage to break away.

"Show me the portrait." He looked up and frowned. "I want to see."

He hesitated for a moment, then he stood without another word. We walked, softly, excruciatingly aware of Anita—asleep?—in the room above us. He opened the door and, without setting foot in the room, searched along the wall for the switch. The element crackled when the light went on; we both froze, but there was no stirring above us.

Among the covered paintings that filled the room, I couldn't have picked out the one Anita showed to me. Alec didn't hesitate; he shifted one or two paintings slightly to the side to reveal a third. He beckoned to me.

"This is it," he said softly.

My emotions had cooled, and I was less certain that I wanted to see what lay beneath that dingy shroud. I ventured the room slowly, expecting I knew not what—I dared not, out of reach of the door, speculate. When I reached Alec's side, he lifted the cloth, and I clapped my hands over my mouth to stifle a cry.

Because it was Anita's face, her delicate features, her gray eyes, her fair hair. There is always an element of fiction in a portrait, deviations from the truth dictated by the sitter, the tastes of the time, the style of the painter. Yet there was no mistaking the likeness even down to that charming, mysterious expression, the particular way her lips bent in a slight smile and her eyes caught yours to share or create a secret. In her hands, she held a threaded needle and a piece of embroidered silk that was so faithfully reproduced that I recognized it at once. There were the human-faced owls, staring madly and the serpent-women with flushed nipples. There were the hooded figures and the house that, newly stitched, showed the details that marked it as this house. And the woman, that faded, frayed figure was as a queen in beads and silver threads and kingfisher feathers, a queenly figure with gray eyes and fair hair. It was her own image of herself: Anita, my love.

The ceiling creaked above us, and Alec, more quickly than I had seen anyone move, flipped the cloth back down, pulled me out of the room, turned off the light and closed the door. We stood, clinging to each other, but there was no other sound.

"It's her," I whispered. "It's her, it's been her all along. I have her mirror, Alec, it's been in my room."

"Listen," he said. "What do we do? I'm not crazy, am I, Lydia?"

"No," I said, and then the awful implication of that, if he and I were not going crazy and this was real, rose up above me like a tidal wave, dark and trembling and deadly. If this was real, what would happen to us? Who— what—had I kissed and caressed and confided in? In what had I laid all my hopes and plans? What slept in that room upstairs beside my own? Did she hear us? That wave fell over me, and I broke beneath it, my heart, my courage, shattered. I bowed my head.

"No, I don't believe it." I did; I spoke from the bottom of a well, from the depths of despair and fear. "It's not possible. That's not real, Alec."

"Okay," he said, just that, and even then I wondered that he didn't argue. Did he believe that we were already lost? Had he finally spoken about it only because he could no longer bear it alone?

"I want to see her." I wiped my eyes and lifted my face. "I'm going to see her."

I don't know what spurred me to that depth of desperation. I remember climbing the stairs, hearing Alec coming up behind me, but I recall nothing of what I felt or thought in those moments. I stood before her door, my hand on the knob, and I was aware of Alec's dread as he stood beside. I knew he did not want me to open that door. I turned the knob and pushed it open.

The bed curtains were pushed aside and the coverlet lay smooth and undisturbed. Anita was not there. Her absence was, to me, more terrible than anything else could have been. I slammed the door shut.

"Where is she? Did you see her leave?" Then, in a flood of panicked clarity, "Alec, we have to get out of here."

"Let's go," he said, with such obvious relief that I wondered why he had waited so long.

He started to move toward the stairs, but I caught his arm. "Wait! We can't just walk out! I need my passport—your passport—money."

He was incredulous. "Money? Passports?"

"We won't get very far without them. I wouldn't count on them lending us a phone in town."

"You're going to go in there..." He pointed at the door to my room. "...and get your passport?"

"Yes! And then we'll get yours." I had my door open before I remembered the mirror. I froze on the threshold.

"I don't even know where it is," he muttered, and then, "What is it?"

"Alec." I took a step in, looking very deliberately only at the little table with the Gallé lamp where I'd left my purse. It was a clear day but the room was full of pallid, grayish light. "Stay with me, please. Don't look at anything. Just look at me. Stay with me."

"I'm going to touch your shoulder," he said. I felt his hand settle lightly on me. "I'm here."

How I wanted to look at the mirror. How I wanted to know what I would see reflected in it. I picked my purse up, turned carefully so as not to face the mirror and walked out, my eyes fixed on the open door. Alec closed it behind us. I would be leaving everything else: I didn't care.

Alec wanted to leave right away, but I insisted, clinging to some sense of order and practicality, that he get his passport. I had never been to his room; in fact, I had no idea where it was. It was a small chamber with a bed as narrow as a nun's and a peeling shelf where he kept his clothes, very neatly folded. There was a pretty parlor guitar leaning against the shelf, the box of tools for tuning the piano, and a copy of *Der Tod des Vergil* with a bookmark holding a spot only a few pages from the end. He rummaged through the shelf, tense and silent, and finally came up with his passport. He glanced around the room and then, as if on impulse, snatched up the book.

I don't think I expected to make it to the garage. I didn't expect the Duesenberg to start either, but it did, reluctantly, coughing in protest. Alec paused at the gates. He let the car roll forward just enough to test the gates, and then, seeing they were unlocked, drove through them. The iron banged and shrieked against the sides of the car. I put my hands over my ears and hunched down in the seat, imagining Anita rising up from—wherever she had secreted herself. Then we were on the country road, dust rising around us. I watched the villa dwindle behind us, and when it was no more than a smudge, a trick of the eye, I laughed.

"We did it." I was jubilant. A shadow that had grown so slowly I hadn't even noticed it lifted all at once, and I was in the land of the living, enchanted with the texture of the seat under my hands, the long stretch of country road unspooling before us. "We did it, we're free!"

Alec only flashed the merest, tensest smile.

"How far until we get to town?"

"A while."

I thought of pressing him, thought better of it, and sat back. "If there's a train leaving, let's take it, wherever it's going."

"Sure."

"I'll call my aunts. They seem to know someone everywhere. Will you go on to Tangier?"

"I don't think so," he said. "I don't even know if my friend is still there."

"Oh. You could come to Venice with me."

"I could," he said.

He seemed to be growing more nervous, and I, certain of our escape, was baffled by his mood. I left off questioning him and looked out the window. Hypnotized by the unvarying expanse of the countryside and a voluptuous sense of relief, I dozed.

The next thing I was aware of was Alec shaking my shoulder and saying my name. The car was not moving.

"What happened?" I looked around, still groggy. Around us, the serene countryside still spread out. The sky was darkening to slate.

"We have to get out of the car," Alec said.

"But why? How far away are we?"

"We're not getting anywhere," he explained. "Look."

"No." I knew, and no knowledge has been so unwelcome before or since, that if I looked back I would see the villa, that darker smudge against the stormy sky, that trick of the eye that refused to completely blink away.

"It's her car," he said. "It was in there for so long. I don't know—I don't understand. We can try to walk. Do you want to try?"

I couldn't speak for a moment. I thought of Anita's story, of those travelers and strangers who passed through and never left. I thought of my aunts kissing me goodbye on the platform, a pair of elegant women who had so carefully attempted to instruct me in how to enjoy life. I thought of my father and my brothers, and of my mother looking for me, wearing the rest of her life out looking for someone who would never be found.

"We have to try."

We didn't get far before the sky broke above us. We walked hand-in-hand to keep track of each other in the dark and the blinding rain. I could hear the water rushing in the ditches by the road, and then the road began to sink into mud. We stumbled on for hours and I think, at one point, we would both have given up but for a sense of obligation to each other; it's one thing to abandon yourself but quite another if that means abandoning someone else as well.

We may have heard the voice at the same time but, like our despair and exhaustion, neither of us wanted to say anything to alarm the other. The voice, familiar, terrible, grew closer and clearer, until neither of us could doubt the other heard it.

"Do you see that?" Alec said, speaking almost in my ear so that I could hear him above the rain and Anita's voice. "Up there, that hedge?"

I squinted. I saw an irregularity in the darkness. "Yes?"

"I think we're getting somewhere. That's a house just outside of town. There's a big hedge and then a break where it was torn up during the war and never fixed. You can see the wall, right? That pale stone?"

"Yes."

"If we run, can you make it?"

I barely came up to Alec's shoulders. "Don't let go."

"I won't," he promised.

There follows a space of time, perhaps no more than fifteen minutes, for which I cannot fully account, like those moments before or after an accident. We ran, we made the gate: that voice, sweet and mocking, nearly at our shoulders. I'm certain we were together as we plunged through the tangled garden and the dark. I recall his voice as we pounded on the door and shouted. I remember his voice, so much lower and louder than mine which was lost in the hammering of the rain and our fists on the door and then the windows. He was there, I know he was there. But when they finally opened the door, it was only me they drew in, bedraggled and hysterical, and they shut the door only on the storm.

There were three people in the house, the old couple and their son who was visiting. I made him go out and look for Alec. I watched the beam of his flashlight move around the house and even swing up and down the road but he came in alone. The old woman took charge of me; she gave me something to drink, to which she must have added something to make me sleep, because in another moment my eyes were shutting. She gave me dry clothes to put on and helped me into a soft little bed. And then I slept, truly and deeply, for the first time in weeks.

When I woke, I was aware that some delicate web that had bound me was falling to pieces. Everything that had happened not just the day before but all those long strange weeks already seemed to belong to the distant past. The woman, Silvana, heard me up and brought me my clothes, already mostly dry. She insisted that I have something to eat and, by way of thanks, I answered her questions. When I said that, yes, I meant the Tiepolo villa, the three of them exchanged a look. I told them that I was going back to my friends, and Silvana, after failing to persuade me to go to town, ordered her son to drive me.

He left me at the gates. I stood for a long time staring up the drive as I had that first day. The villa resembled more than ever a forgotten ruin, faded and bleached in a bed of weeds. It seemed bled, too, of some animating vitality and personality, and although I was apprehensive I was not actually afraid as I opened the gate. I had waited a long time in the road, long enough to watch the shadows shift decently, in their proper time.

I found Lino and Kirsten in the large room downstairs. They had papers and envelopes out on the table, and they looked up sharply when they heard me.

"I told you she hadn't left," Kirsten said. "She wouldn't leave all her clothes."

"Is...Anita here?" It took some courage for me to say her name but I was safe; I felt very strongly that I was safe.

"No," Lino said.

"She left a note for us. She could have called." Kirsten looked at me and frowned. "But didn't you know? You were here."

"I...." She had noticed the slightly rumpled state of my clothes and my carelessly done hair. "Um. Is Alec back?"

"I haven't seen him. Have you?" she asked Lino.

"No," he said, turning back to the papers.

"Have you looked?"

"Why?"

"Well, what if—something happened?" It was hard to keep my voice steady. "If he left, wouldn't he have left a note, too?"

Lino looked up again, annoyed. "Why would he?"

"But you are leaving, too?" Kirsten asked. "We're not staying. We just came back to get our things and to tell Anita in person. But she'll just get a card, like my cousin Marta. I'll tell you, Lydia, since you're here. We're getting married."

"How wonderful. Congratulations."

"Hm, it was just a matter of tying some things up. But, as I was saying, we're leaving this afternoon. You weren't planning on staying here by yourself, especially with Alec gone and no one to keep the place up? Anita should have made you go first. Didn't you say your family has friends in Venice?"

"Yes...."

"We'll take you to the train. We're going the other way, and we're driving. Pack your things. You can call from the station."

The whole place was empty—empty in a way that I realized it hadn't been before. It was hard to climb those stairs, harder still to open the door to my room, but it was empty and solid and the mirror was merely fine old Venetian glass in a badly decayed embroidered frame. I packed my bags and brought them down, and then, because there was still time, I went to Alec's room. Everything was still there—except for the copy of *Der Tod des Vergil.*

He was gone, I knew, as Anita was gone. He would not be coming back for the clothes folded on the shelf or the notebook or the little parlor guitar. There was no door that would open where there should be a door to let him out. I took the notebook and the guitar.

I carried the guitar, the notebook tucked into the case, to Venice. But when it was time to go on to Cairo, I left them both, deliberately, at the house my aunts' friends rented.

I also left, in the high, shuttered room in the rented palazzo, any conviction that what I believed had happened had really happened. There were a hundred more plausible explanations. I tried them all. I have tried all of them and they are each as unreal as my memory.

A few days ago, when I was alone at home, the phone rang. I answered with some vague expectation that it would be Denise calling to tell me that there was more trouble with the electricians at the theater or my mother to ask forlornly whether I would come back to Detroit to visit soon. There was a moment of silence as I drew my breath to say hello—but not quite of silence. There was a faint crackle and a gentle rushing like the sea or the wind in the trees. It sounded as if someone spoke, but very badly distorted as if it was a bad connection to East Berlin.

"Hello?" I said.

"Lydia—"

I hung up. That voice—it came from very far away, across immeasurable distances, the hissing and crackling the natural sounds of some unnatural place—I knew that voice. It was daylight, and the guileless California sunlight flooded our pretty little living room with the windows facing the bay; yet every angle of the room, every mote of dust winking in the rich streams of sunlight was limned in terror as black and heavy as had closed in on Alec and me on the road.

I knew that voice then, but now, when I try to recall the sound, when I try to remember who I believed spoke to me, the line hissing with fire, I don't know who I thought it was.

Perhaps if I go back there, I will see the villa sprawled in an endless sleep behind the unlocked gates. Perhaps the door will be unlocked and there will be nothing inside but dust, and no ghost more terrible than my own fallible memory. Or perhaps, when I go there, I will find that I, too, never left.

LAND OF PROMISE
Dan Le Fever

"Ten more feet," he heard Greg yell beside him as they both ran for the trench. Jake felt like he was wading through molasses. A quick glance behind, and he could see the Germans advancing, their rifles aimed right at them. A loud bang and he heard Greg cry out. He turned back too late as he tripped over his best friend's body, losing his rifle. The gray mud filled his mouth and nose as he landed face first into the muck. Jake awoke suddenly, coughing and drenched in sweat. He reached for his rifle and came up with a pillow instead. He blinked in confusion. Looking down, he could see that he was in a bed, the blankets thrown on the floor. He realized that he wasn't still in the trench in France, he was back home in Oklahoma. *I'm on my farm, everything is okay*, he thought.

He reached for the glass of water on the nightstand and took a sip, quickly spitting it out as it was more mud than liquid. Looking around the room he could see that the night had brought a fresh coat of dust through the cracks in his ceiling. *I need to get up there and get that sealed or move to a different room*, he thought. *There are plenty of vacant rooms in the house now ever since that boy...ever since that boy...*He shook his head, clearing his thoughts. "No need to start the day on a bad note." His voice sounded hoarse as if he'd been shouting in his sleep again. He stood up and went to the one chair in the room and grabbed his overalls, slipped them on and then slid into his work boots.

Headed for the door, he stopped in front of the mirror that hung on the wall. "Morning Clara," he said to the mirror: the only thing left in the room that belonged to her. Memories came back of watching his wife brushing her hair in front of the mirror before bed. Even when she was getting sick, she found time to work the dirt and knots from her long brown hair. She said it was to keep a semblance of civility in these parts, but he knew she did it for him.

He appraised himself in the mirror, seeing a weary, haggard man staring back. His beard was five months too long, his face covered in dirt and cracked. *Clara would have a fit if she saw me in this state*, he thought meekly, a bit embarrassed standing in front of her mirror like this. He smiled to himself, knowing it was just an old mirror, but not being able to help himself he ran his fingers along the frame. His fingers left trails behind; the mirror was coated in the ever-present dirt. "Well, we'll have to get this mirror right clean after breakfast." He walked to the door and stepped through.

Out in the hallway, he could hear as Beth moved about the kitchen downstairs, already getting breakfast ready. He walked down the hallway past the empty rooms, remembering what it was like when he was young, living here with his parents, sister and four brothers. Then the war started in Europe. "The war to end all wars," they said. He and his brothers had all been conscripted back in '17. His father was proud to see his boys getting packed up and ready to serve their country. "You know," he had said, "your great-grandfather had served during the Southern rebellion, fought for our country and made a good name for himself too. He was able to come out west here and buy this land and build this house all because of that war. It was horrible, don't get me wrong, but fortune smiles on the victorious, don't forget that while you are over there. Make sure you come back home, I'm going to need you back here to work the fields sooner than later."

His father had been a proud man, never one to really show his emotions, but when Jake was the only one to return from the war, it had shaken him to the core. While he had never been a quiet man, Jake could see the loss had broken his father. What hurt most was when Jake would catch his father looking at him in disgust, as if he was the reason his brothers were killed. When the Spanish Flu hit their county in Oklahoma, it hit it hard. He lost his mother and sister in the span of two months. With just his father and himself on the farm, the work was harder than ever. They could hire the random passing traveler for a meal and a place to spend the night, but they were few and far between. Then his father came down with the flu; the doctor had left his nurse to make sure he would be comfortable in his last days. That's how he met Clara.

On the night his father had died, he had called him into his room. Clara was standing by his side as always with a cool cloth on his forehead. "Jake," he had said, "you have to promise me. Promise me to keep this farm going, no matter what. We worked for this, it's ours, don't let anyone take it from you."

"I promise," he said quietly, swallowing the lump forming in his throat.

"A man is only as good as his promise. Let me hear it again, promise that our family will always be here, this land is ours and no one can take it from us."

"I promise. I promise this is our land," he said in a stronger voice.

"Promise me!"

He shouted at his dying father, "I promise!"

And that was the last time they would ever speak together; his father died the following morning in his sleep. He left the large two-story farmhouse, the barn, and the hundred acres of land to Jake in his will. Clara had stayed on, first out of pity for the young man left alone with so much work to do, and later because they had grown in love. Their son was born just nine months after they were married in '19, and Beth came along just a year after that.

Jake walked down the stairs to the kitchen where Beth was flipping the plates over and wiping out glasses before pouring some milk in each. Jake just leaned against the door frame admiring his daughter; she looked so much like her mother it ached sometimes. Her brown hair cascaded over her shoulders, and she reached up to push it back past her ears. When she looked up her blue eyes brightened.

"Morning, Papa!"

"Morning, darling. Sleep well?"

"As about as well as can be expected, it's hard to sleep with that damn cloth around my face."

"Hey now, watch the language in this house. And that cloth is going to save you from the damn cough I woke up with this morning," he said with a smirk.

"Oh, whose turn is it now to watch their language?" she smiled.

He sat down for his breakfast of bread and butter, the only thing that could be found at the store in town these last few weeks. He could see how tired his daughter looked. She would never mention it, but he knew that when those dreams took him, his shouting would keep the family up the whole night. Clara once tried to wake him from such a dream and ended up with a black eye.

"Going to check the south field today to see if anything is sprouting, while I'm gone can you do some cleaning upstairs? Your ma's mirror is pretty dusty."

"Everything is pretty dusty, I could spend a year cleaning this house and I'd still find dust."

"Doesn't mean we shouldn't try, right? Someday this dirt will be gone, and we'll have a clean house again. For now, we have to do our best to keep it as clean as we can."

"What do you mean 'we'?" she muttered under her breath.

"What was that?" he gave her a sharp look.

"Nothing, Father, just a bit of frustration coming out, I didn't mean anything by it."

"I know, darling, I know it's hard. We just have to hold out a bit longer. My father told me about a drought they had in the '90s, it was hard, but they pulled through and we'll do the same. I promise."

Sighing, she replied, "I know, Papa, I just wish we had more help. If only Brian..." She then cringed as Jake stood and smashed his plate against the wall.

Beth shrank back in her seat, looking down and saying she was "sorry" over and over again. Jake sat back down and drank from his glass with a trembling hand. When he finished, he quietly stood and walked out of the kitchen. He heard Beth get up and the tinkling of the broken plate as she picked up the shards. *I need to get outside before I do anything else I'll regret this morning,* he thought. He walked to the front of the house and pulled his handkerchief out of his pocket, wrapping it around his mouth and nose. Before he stepped outside, he grabbed his goggles hanging from the hook by the door, and looking back toward the kitchen, he shook his head as he turned back to the front door and walked out.

Outside he saw the sprawling plains move off into the horizon. It was a quiet morning; the wind had settled down to a light breeze. The constant brown haze in the air had eased up a bit from yesterday. He walked towards his old Model A, which he was able to afford back when wheat was still worth growing. He remembered the first day he had brought it home; Clara was all giggles and smiles when he went flying down the road, with her holding onto his arm like she was going to fall out. Beth and Brian in the back seat egged him on to go faster. That had been a good day. *Not many of them now.* He stopped and shook his head vigorously. *What's gotten into you today? Nothing but wool-gathering when there's work to be done.* Determined, he opened the door to the car, slammed it, and started her up. He was soon on his way to the fields, hoping for some better luck.

Before he even came to a stop he could tell his luck would not get any better. It appeared that a dust blow had covered over his field. Swearing as he hit his steering wheel, he climbed out of the car. If anything was going to grow, he'd have to clear off this extra dirt and re-water these fields. He was going to need help for that, and more than just him and Beth. He turned back towards the house, barely able to make out its shape now that the wind had started to pick up, blowing more dirt into the air. He remembered what it used to look like, the fresh coat of white paint he had put on after Beth had been born, the green trim that Clara was so fond of. She used to come out here and just stare at the house, telling Jake how lucky she felt just to have a bit of earth to call her own. *What changed, Clara?* he thought.

Wiping the dust from the lenses of his goggles, he climbed back into the car. *Maybe I'll take Beth into town with me, make it up to her for this morning.* He drove back to the house and walked through the door.

"Beth, darling, we need to run into town," he called out. He heard her upstairs with the broom, a constant sound in the house for well over eight years now.

"I just started in the bedrooms, Papa, do we have to go right now?" she called down the stairs.

"South field is covered, going to need help getting it cleared. I'm hoping I can get some while in town, and hopefully, the store got a shipment of goods in since last week. I'm getting a bit tired of bread and butter, how about you?"

"Maybe Molly will be in town, I haven't seen her since her brother went out west," she said excitedly as she came down the stairs. "And I hear the theater might be reopening, wouldn't that be fun?"

"Now we don't have time to spend dawdling at the theater, that field is priority. I have a good feeling about that crop and I need to get it uncovered before it's too late."

Pouting, she said, "Oh fine, but if Molly is there I at least want a little time to catch up."

"That's fine, it might take me a little bit to find a farmhand anyways."

***

"Looks like the Henderson's farm is empty," Beth said, looking out the window as they drove along the road. Jake slowed down and looked where she was pointing. There was a small, one-story house with what had been a wide porch, but now all that was visible is just the railing on one side. A pile of dirt had blown and covered the whole front of the house.

"Guess some people just can't make it out here," he said as he continued down the road. "They came out here during the boom about twelve years ago. That Walter thought he was going to make it big and then head back east a rich man. I bet he went out west a poor man."

"Father! That's a right mean thing to say!" she exclaimed.

"I know, I'm sorry. Come to think of it, that's all I've been lately, sorry and mean. You understand I don't mean anything by it, right, darling?"

"I do, and I'm sorry for wishing things were different. It is what it is, and we must make the best of it. Just like you said this morning, we just have to hold on a bit longer." She looked at him. "We're all we've got left."

"Well, you are right about that. At least until we get you married, little girl."

"Papa!" she shrieked.

"I'm not saying it has to be today, but you should start considering your options. The farm is going to be yours when I'm gone, and you are going to need all the help you can get. Where's that Emit boy I used to catch sniffing around the farm been? He seemed rather fond of you."

"I've seen him in town a couple of times and he is always polite. He was working over at the McGregor's farm for a while. It's been at least a year since I've seen him."

"Old Tom McGregor knew a good hand when he saw one; let's see if we can't find that boy while we're in town. Maybe he can help me out a bit, and maybe you two can have lunch together."

"I don't need you playing matchmaker for me, Papa, but it would be nice to see him again," she said wistfully looking back out the window.

From the farm to town, the ride usually took two hours, but the going was slow with the visibility dropping. The previously well-traveled main road was now all but a dirt path, with dunes filling up the spaces along the sides of the road. It left very little room for two cars to even pass each other. They drove by a car stacked high with furniture stopped on the side of the road with no one inside, left to the elements, the front end covered in a newly formed mound of dirt.

As they drove past several more dust mounds, the realization hit Jake: *These are burial mounds of people's lives. Everything they were is under this dirt and grit, and they abandoned it all. Well, I'm not deserting my life or my family. That farm is who we are. Who we will always be.* He gripped the wheel tighter as he drove on. Suddenly a strong wind ripped through the air blowing a cloud in front of them so thick he couldn't make out the road. "Papa, slow down!" He pumped the brakes and the tires skidded over the loose gravel, sending them careening this way and that. Just then, a figure appeared on the road in front of them. Jake quickly turned the wheel to avoid hitting the person and managed to come to a stop before sliding off the road and into a dust-filled ditch. Both were breathing heavy, stunned by the quick turn of events. A knock on the driver's side window made them both jump. Someone was standing next to the car, wiping the dirt off the window with a handkerchief. When Jake could finally see through the window properly, and he saw a man in his mid-twenties in what was left of a suit. He must have lost his jacket somewhere. Around his face, covering his mouth, was the man's tie as well as a pair of broken glasses. Jake reached for the handle and opened the door.

"Everyone okay in there?" said the man's muffled voice.

"Yeah, we're fine. What were you doing in the middle of the road? We nearly killed you."

"Well, not much left to walk on besides the road, and I didn't want to get lost on my way back towards this town up ahead."

Jake looked the man up and down. His shoes were falling apart, and he looked sunburnt from head to toe. The man had been outside for some time and hadn't planned on it. "You in trouble or something, Mister...?"

"Erickson. Mister Robert Erickson," he replied, reaching for Jake's hand, weakly shaking it.

"I guess nice to meet you, Mr. Erickson. What are you doing out here by yourself? And on foot for that matter?"

"Well, I was on my way down the road here in my car when it broke down yesterday morning. I wasn't sure which way to go, but this was the last town I drove through, so I headed back this way to get some help.

Yours is the first car I've seen heading this way. Do you mind giving me a lift into town?"

"Not at all, climb in the back there."

They both got in the car. Beth looked back at the newcomer and they made introductions, as Jake straightened out the car and drove on towards town. "Sorry we don't have any water, but I'm sure you can get some when you are back in town. You sure look the worse for wear," she said.

"It looks worse than it is, but thank you for your consideration," he replied. "Things have been getting really bad out there. I'd sent my family out west while I finished up some loose ends up north."

"What do you do for work, Mr. Erickson?"

"I'm a lawyer, but there isn't much work when most of the people have up and left."

"Bunch of quitters if you ask me," chimed in Jake.

"When you have nothing left, and no way to make a living, finding some hope elsewhere isn't quitting."

"Yeah well, this will pass. Then they'll be back and someone else is going to have their land. Banks most likely. My family worked hard for what we have, we aren't going to just hand it over or walk away from it."

***

When they arrived in town, Jake could see more shuttered-up businesses and residences. It wasn't a big town, only about a thousand people had lived there during better times, but it was probably down to two hundred at most. Jake pulled up to the general store and turned to Beth. "Why don't you see if there's been a new shipment in the store? I'm going to head over to the bar, bound to be someone there to help with the field."

He then turned to Mr. Erickson, "Why don't you come along with me? I can introduce you to the mechanic in town. His shop is along the way."

Mr. Erickson nodded, "That'd be a great help."

All three climbed out of the car, and Beth waved at the two as they headed down the street and then disappeared into the store. The town was slowly being swallowed by the ever-changing dunes, empty shops half buried. The loose earth got caught up on fences with tumbleweeds piled high against them and quickly formed mounds of dirt. Not many people were left to clean them up, and those that were had more to worry about than appearances.

"Shaw's place is right around the corner here," Jake said as they came to the end of the street. When they rounded the corner, they saw a boarded-up pump station with a sign painted on it that simply stated "SORRY" in big black letters.

"Well shit," Mr. Erickson sighed. Turning to Jake he said, "Please tell me this town has two mechanics."

"Afraid not," replied Jake as he stared at the sign.

"I'm going to need a drink then, and more than just water. Where's this bar you were talking about?"

Jake pointed a couple of doors down, to where a woman was sweeping the dust off the sidewalk. "At least we know that place is still open. Bars will always get us through troubled times."

"I'll drink to that," Mr. Erickson chuckled.

They walked down towards the bar. "Margrett," Jake said to the woman with a nod. She responded with a polite nod and a weak smile. Jake could tell something was troubling her as he walked inside. The place was empty, save for the bartender who looked like he was asleep standing up with his head resting on his arms. "This day just keeps getting better," mumbled Jake.

They both walked up to the bar. Robert ordered a glass of water and after finishing it quickly, they both ordered a couple of shots of whiskey. Exchanging small talk, Jake learned that Robert was married and had two children who were living out with his mother in San Bernardino. He also learned that Robert had grown up on a farm, but since he was the youngest he wasn't going to inherit it, so he went off and got an education and was making a career for himself. While they were talking, Jake kept his eye on the door waiting for anyone to come in.

After a while, Jake's shoulders sagged, and he sat down, disappointment clearly showed on his face. The woman sweeping out front came in, and Jake asked where everyone was.

"Oh honey, they've mostly left."

"It's only been a week, Margrett, and last time I was here I didn't have any trouble finding some help."

"Well, most don't have your passion for farming, Jake," she said with a kind, but sad smile, "and with the way things are going, we aren't going to be able to keep this place open much longer either."

She then turned towards the bartender, once again with his head in his arms. "Besides, this isn't a good place to raise a daughter anymore, isn't that right, Frank?"

The bartender raised his head, looking weary and troubled. "Not with the school shutting down. Molly can't get the schooling she needs to become a nurse."

"Not Molly too!" came a cry.

All of them turned to the door as Beth walked in, removing her goggles and face mask with fresh tears filling her eyes. "First Emit, and now Molly," she wept and sat down at a table, putting her face into her hands. Jake stood and went to his daughter, placing an arm around her shoulders and pulling her close.

"What's this about Emit?"

"Emit left with the McGregor's. Billy, at the store, told me when I asked if he'd seen Emit around, that he left a few days back." Her body shook with a fresh bout of sobbing.

"I'm sorry, honey, I truly am," Margrett said, her lip quivering as she tried to hold back tears. "Molly's future is important, and we aren't farmers like you all are. With everyone gone, we just can't stay here any longer."

Frank muttered an apology and walked from behind the bar, heading through a door in the back. Margrett looked after him and sighed, and then she picked up her broom and headed back outside. "This place just can't stay clean."

Consoling his daughter, Jake felt a hand on his shoulder. He looked up and Mr. Erickson was looking down at him. "I know it isn't much, but I know how to use a shovel if you need some help at the farm. It's the least I can do for you two for giving me a ride."

Jake nodded, "Thanks, Mr. Erickson."

"Call me Robert."

After Beth had calmed down a bit, they walked back to the car. Climbing in, she was able to tell her father a bit of good news. The McGregor's had sold the store their last cow, so there was some meat for sale and she bought a bit. Not having had steak for a few months, this was the best news he had heard in a long time. "Oh, and I also picked up the mail," she said handing the bundle of letters tied together to her father.

"You didn't look through it?" he said, snatching the letters from her quickly.

"No, Papa," she replied.

Robert raised an eyebrow to this but kept quiet as they left the town behind.

***

They arrived back at the farm by mid-day, Jake remarking that they could still get in a good afternoon's work. As they entered the house, Robert remarked at how large it was.

"My family's been here for generations. We needed a lot of room to spread out."

"Now it's just you and Beth?"

"Yes, my wife died two years ago."

"I'm sorry to hear that. Was it that dust pneumonia?"

In response, Jake just walked up the stairs. He could hear Beth quickly apologize. "Papa doesn't like talking about what happened to my mother. She was sick for quite some time." Upstairs, Jake grabbed some clothes from one of the spare bedrooms and brought them down.

"Here, change into these." He handed him some overalls and a stiff cotton shirt. "There should also be an extra pair of boots in the closet down the hall there. You can change in the room upstairs, first door on the left."

When Robert went upstairs to change, Jake went through the mail, dropping the letters on the floor carelessly. "More bills. Always more bills. Why should I pay for this tractor when the damned thing doesn't even work? They can come and take it back for all I care."

Beth, picking them up after her father, chided, "Papa, please don't get in one of your moods again, not with a guest in the house, who volunteered to help. Don't drive him away."

He turned to her. "I'm sorry, darling, the trip to town just upset me a bit. I'll behave myself from here on in." He smiled and patted her arm.

Placing the pile of letters on the table in the kitchen, she could see that Jake was still holding onto one. "What's that?"

"Oh, nothing, it's nothing," he stammered and quickly placed it in his pocket. "Just another bill, don't worry about it."

Robert walked into the kitchen then, with his new clothes and boots. "I must say, I feel like a kid again," he said with a chuckle. Beth smiled and gave him an appraising look.

"Now don't we look just like a real farmer."

"Enough of this dilly-dallying, that field isn't going to work itself," Jake said sternly, then quickly gave Beth a look of apology. "Sorry. And sorry to you too, Robert, been a rough day."

"Don't worry about it, let's get to it."

They spent the afternoon out in the field, using shovels to remove the excess dirt that had blown in and uncovering the rows of planted wheat underneath. Robert started at one end and Jake at the other, and the plan was to meet in the middle. After five hours of hard work and shoveling, they were only a quarter of the way to clearing the field. Jake shouted over to Robert that it was quitting time and walked over to the irrigation pump. He turned it on to give some water to what was uncovered so far.

As Robert walked up, Jake turned off the pump, not wanting to waste too much water. "Looks like we have a couple more days' worth of work still ahead of us."

Jake nodded, "Seems that way. Feel like staying on?"

"I sure can. I should call my wife though to let her know I'll be longer than we planned."

"Sorry, but our phone hasn't worked since we stopped paying for it."

"Oh, well, I'm sure she'll understand. The kids will keep her busy anyways."

The two men made their way back towards the house in the car. "Need to make a pit stop before we can call it a night," said Jake as he turned toward the only tree on the property. He got out and walked along a flagstone path leading up to the tree, followed by Robert. "I always say goodnight to my wife and family."

Robert nodded, somberly. Jake stood before four headstones. Pointing at each one, "That's my mother, father, that there's my sister, and this is my wife, Clara." He placed his hand on her cross-shaped headstone. "Good night, darling." He then leaned forward and kissed the stone. Standing up, he turned back to the car and got inside.

"Where's the rest of your family buried? If you don't mind me asking."

"Most are in the town's graveyard; my brothers are in Europe. I buried them after they were killed, the war and all," Jake said, his eyes looking off in the distance.

"I was six when my father went over there. He never came home. I can't imagine what you went through, Jake. I'm sorry."

Jake coughed, and swallowed deeply as he started the engine. "Yeah, I just wish I could forget. Sorry about your father. I'm sure he did his best to get home. Some of us just had luck on our side." He drove the short distance back to the house and both men got out and made their way inside.

When they entered, Jake's mouth began salivating because he was welcomed by the smell of steak frying. Practically tearing his dirty boots off he ran to the kitchen with Robert, who followed quickly behind. Beth stood cooking on the stove. She had brought out a nice table cloth and placed it on the table. She turned and smiled at the two men, "I thought it was a special occasion, what with our guest and having steak after all."

"Yes, it is!" exclaimed Jake reaching for a chair but was quickly beaten back by a slap on the hand.

"No sitting till you've cleaned up, Papa. You both look filthy."

Making a show of it, Jake hung his head and walked slowly to the wash closet to clean up. When he was finished, he sent Robert to do the same. Then they all sat around the table and savored the meal. When they had finished, Jake pulled down a bottle of whiskey from the cupboard and poured a glass for himself and Robert.

"Looks like Robert will be staying on for a few days to help finish clearing the field."

"Oh, that's wonderful! This house gets so lonely sometimes, with just Father and me," Beth said excitedly.

"This is a lot of house for just the two of you. Have you ever considered selling? I'm sure you could get enough for this place and the land to start fresh out west."

"No, can't do that," Jake said simply.

"Why not?"

"Made a promise. This is always going to be our land. And I'm only as good as my word."

"Fair enough. Hey, can I ask a question? When I was changing earlier upstairs, I noticed a little height chart carved on the door frame. I saw one for you, Beth, and another for a Brian. Who..."

Jake slammed his whiskey glass down hard, and then threw it hard against the wall. Robert was taken aback and nearly dropped his own glass. "Papa, he doesn't know any better," Beth said quietly. Without looking at the two, Jake stood and walked out of the kitchen. He could hear them talking in the kitchen as he went down into the basement but couldn't make out what they were saying. *Beth's probably just apologizing for me. She's always been better with people,* he thought. In the basement, he grabbed some paint and a brush and walked back up. He walked by the kitchen and he could feel them both looking at him as he passed and heard Robert stammer out an apology for offending.

When he got upstairs to the spare bedroom, he looked at the door frame. He couldn't believe he had forgotten this was here. As he pried open the lid to the paint can he counted the tick marks for each child. Thirteen each for every year they measured their height. *I guess after thirteen years they stopped caring, or was it me?* He began painting over the frame, covering both of his children's charts. He could hear Beth downstairs once again sweeping up broken glass, the second time in one day.

"I'm sorry, Mr. Erickson, my father is usually a kind man. These days have just been hard on him and everyone in general."

"I'm just confused as to what I said to make him so angry," he responded, still sounding a bit shaken up.

"It has to do with my brother, Brian. We aren't supposed to talk about him anymore. My father and I made a promise to each other. But it's hard to keep when there are so many reminders of him."

"Oh, I'm sorry, did he pass away? Your father didn't mention anyone else in your family graveyard out there."

"No, he left..."

"That's enough of that," Jake shouted down the stairs.

"Papa, we can't keep acting like he doesn't exist. Look what it's doing to you!" Beth shouted up at him from the foot of the stairs. "I'm done cleaning after your messes, you break any more things around here and you'll have to do it yourself!"

"Hey now, everyone calm down," interrupted Robert, "I didn't mean to start a fight over this. Look, today has been a rough day for everyone. Let's all just get some sleep so we can get an early start tomorrow." He had walked halfway up the stairs and looked at both Beth downstairs and Jake upstairs, still kneeling with a paintbrush in his hand, his knuckles turning white. For a tense moment no one said anything, Robert just looked at both pleadingly. Jake eventually relaxed his grip on the paintbrush and went back to painting the door frame. Beth had crept up the stairs and was peeking her head up just past the landing to see her father.

"Well, Jake? Can we agree to this?"

"Let me finish my work," he grumbled in reply.

"Please, Papa, I'm sorry. I just can't stand seeing you so unhappy all the time," Beth said tearfully.

Putting the paintbrush back in the can, Jake looked up at the ceiling, almost imploringly. He rubbed his hands over his face, then turned to look back at them. Robert began to chuckle, and Beth started laughing outright. "What?"

Robert replied, "You might want to look in a mirror."

Jake got up and walked into his bedroom and looked in Clara's mirror. His face was streaked with white paint, and he looked down at his hands which were also covered. Walking back out into the hallway, he began to laugh at himself. Beth had come up with a damp cloth and handed it to him. "Alright, maybe just one more mess, Papa, but this is it." Everyone burst out laughing.

When they had all calmed down, Jake turned to Robert, "You must have been a hell of a lawyer back in Kansas."

Robert smiled, "Thanks, I did alright."

Nodding, Jake said, "I agree that we should all get to bed. There's lots to do tomorrow. You can sleep in the same room you changed in, there should be pillows in the closet. Keep the window closed, dust will keep you coughing all night otherwise." He then turned to Beth, "I'm sorry for acting up today, my thoughts have been in the past lately. I'll try harder, darling." He then leaned in and kissed her on the forehead. Blinking back tears, Beth smiled and nodded. She wished both men a good night and walked to her room at the end of the hall. The two men nodded to each other and went into their respective rooms.

As Jake changed into his bed clothes, he looked at his wife's mirror. The moon was behind the tree where his family was buried, and he could see its reflection in the mirror. It always felt that was a way of his family telling him good night. He brushed the dust off his pillow before he lay down and watched the shadows of the branches move across his ceiling as he faded into sleep.

***

The next morning, when he had woken up, Jake could hear conversation downstairs in the kitchen. He got dressed and walked out into the hallway. "He left about a year ago now. Papa didn't take it so well." Beth was talking, but quickly quieted down when she heard the floorboards under Jake's feet creak as he walked toward the stairs. *Behave yourself today*, Jake told himself. He walked into the kitchen where Robert was seated at the table with a book, and Beth was once again preparing breakfast.

"Morning," Jake said with a nod to both.

Looking relieved, Beth smiled. "Good morning, Papa."

"Morning, Jake," responded Robert, closing the book. "I hope you don't mind if I borrowed this? I found it in the closet and had a hard time sleeping last night."

Looking over at the book, he saw it was one of his boy's dime novels he used to collect. "Don't mind, got no use for them myself." He sat down and had breakfast with little conversation. He didn't trust himself to keep his cool so the little he spoke the better. Just get the field cleared and when he's gone life can return to normal. When they were finished, Robert thanked Beth for the meal and both men went out to work.

It had been a quiet night; the wind hadn't blown that much back onto the field, so they made better progress with the early start. By midday, it appeared that they were halfway through the field. Jake always liked to see hard work amount to something, and it put him in a good mood. He called to Robert to let him know it was break time and walked over to his car. He pulled out a lunch box and waited for Robert. When Robert arrived, he handed him a sandwich made with some of the leftover steak from dinner. The men sat in the car and ate their sandwiches out of the breeze. Both stared ahead at the field, and the house could be seen through the haze.

In the distance past the house, they could make out a dark swirling storm slowly moving their way. "That's all we need now, probably put us back a day's work when that hits," Jake grunted.

"It must be hard here, doing all this work by yourself," Robert said.

Jake responded with a grunt as his mouth was full.

"You know, it's not quitting if you leave and come back when things are better."

Jake said nothing, just kept chewing his sandwich.

"It must be hard for Beth too, seeing all her friends leaving but she has to stay here."

Swallowing, Jake spoke quietly, "It's hard on everyone, but we are all that's left, and this farm needs us."

"I'm not trying to pry, and if I am, then tell me, but what happened with Brian? I don't want to get Beth in trouble but this morning she told me he was her older brother and he just up and left last year."

"Not much to say, that's what happened. Are you finished eating? We have more work to do."

"Just about. Did something happen between you two? Is that why you get so angry?"

"You're prying."

Robert turned to him. "Sometimes it can help by talking, getting it out might ease some of that frustration."

"I don't need some college-educated boy telling me what I should do. Now get out there and shovel," Jake said as he got out of the car and slammed his door harder than necessary. He grabbed his shovel and started to walk back into the field when he felt a hand pull on his shoulder. "Get your hand off me," he said as he turned around taking a swing and stopping short of hitting Beth, who blinked from behind her goggles in shock.

Robert was just then getting out of the car and jogged over to the two.

"Damnit, Beth, what are you doing out here?"

"I-I came to tell you we have guests," she replied.

"Who?" Jake asked as he planted his shovel into the ground.

Robert stood beside Beth, "Everything okay here?"

"Everything's fine. Now, who's here, Beth?"

"Molly and her family, I think they are here to say good-bye."

"Okay, go and wait in the car, we'll drive back."

When Beth was in the car, Robert said, "That punch was meant for me, wasn't it?"

Jake looked at him. "That punch was to ease my frustration. Now get in so we can get this out of the way. All this is a distraction from getting the work done."

When they arrived back at the house, Jake could see Frank's pick-up truck piled high with furniture and boxes and covered by a tarp. The tarp did little to protect their belongings from the ever-present dirt in the air and driving through it had only made it worse. All three went inside, shaking off the dust and removing their protective coverings. "I had them wait in the living room while I went to get you," Beth mentioned as she went into the kitchen. Jake nodded and then walked down the hallway to see about the guests. Robert went upstairs as Jake passed him by.

"Frank," Jake said with a nod as he came into the room. He saw Frank and his wife were sitting in two hardwood chairs while Molly stood by the window looking outside.

"Jake," Frank responded.

"Margrett, Molly," he nodded to them in turn. "What brings you out here?"

"Well," Frank started, "remember our conversation yesterday? Well, we decided to head west, and we just wanted to let the girls say their farewells. I know this is going to be difficult on Beth."

"Yeah, I reckon it will be. But it isn't forever, you know that? Weather's bound to change sometime."

"We all don't have your conviction and faith, Jake." He turned to Molly, "Why don't you go say your good-byes to Beth, honey?"

Molly turned and looked at the group, and her green eyes rimmed with tears. She pushed her red hair back behind her ear, smudging dirt across her tear-streaked face. She nodded quietly, looking down as she walked past Jake. Margrett shook her head. "She hasn't been here since your boy..."

"Since he left," Jake finished, sitting down in a chair across from them. He pulled off his dusty hat and placed it on the coffee table between them. "I know she was sweet on him, and I figure he must have known."

"He sends her letters, Jake, telling her all about the places he's seen in California, about the people. He makes it out to be a paradise compared to here."

Jake sniffed in irritation.

"I know he wronged you, but you have to understand things from his perspective," Margrett said. "He wrote the other day that he's been sending you and Beth letters but neither of you has responded, he just wants to know you two are alright."

Just then they heard a crash by the door and looked up to see Beth standing over a tray with broken glasses at her feet. She glared hard at her father. "Beth, what are..." is all he could get out before she quickly ran up to him.

"Get up!" she shouted.

"What's gotten into you?"

"I said get up!" She tried to push the chair over with him in it.

Jake stood with his hands up defensively in front of him, trying to calm her down. "Beth, honey, what's wrong?"

She reached into his back pocket and pulled the letter he had tucked in there yesterday, looking at it before Jake could snatch it away. "This is addressed to me! He's been sending letters all this time and you've been keeping them from me? Why?"

"Darling, I-I," he stammered.

Beth pushed him hard, and he fell into the chair as she ran out of the room. Molly had been standing by the door and glared at him before she quickly turned to chase after Beth who could be heard running up the stairs. A door slammed above them, and they heard muffled yelling. Jake moved to get up, but Frank motioned for him to stay seated. "She's got to get it out. Let her and Molly be alone."

"Why've you been hiding the letters, Jake?" asked Margrett. Jake looked over at her, seeing the disdain on her face. He looked to Frank, who leaned forward and looked at Jake with an inquisitive tilt to his head. Jake breathed deeply, letting it out slowly. He leaned back in his chair and ran his palms along the armrests.

"He's been hiding something. More than just letters," said a voice from the doorway. Everyone looked up to see Robert leaning against the door frame with his arms crossed. He was sifting through the glass with the toe of his boot.

"What do you mean?" Margrett asked, looking back and forth between Robert and Jake, who was now sitting with his face in his hands. Robert reached into his back pocket and pulled out the dime novel he had been reading that morning and tossed it onto the table between them.

"Seems Brian used these for more than just entertainment. He also used the blank pages as a diary. This one is from four years ago."

Margrett picked the book up and flipped to the end. Frank leaned over to look as Margrett mouthed the words as she read them. When she finished, she looked at Jake. "Clara wanted to leave the farm? She wanted you all to leave?"

Frank stood and walked over to Jake; he looked down at him and placed a comforting hand on his shoulder. Jake lifted his head and looked at Margrett, who flinched in response. Jake's eyes were full of rage and fury, his voice, however, was quiet and controlled. "Who the hell do you people think you are?"

"Now, Jake," Frank began.

Jake forcefully brushed Frank's hand off his shoulder and stood, knocking his chair over. He pointed at Margrett and growled, "Get out of my house." He turned to Frank. "Both of you. Now." He then left the room and walked to the closet in the hallway. He pulled open the door and retrieved his old service rifle from the war. He kept it in working order as he had been trained to do all those years ago. Some habits were hard to break. He returned to the living room, but he didn't point it at anyone. He simply kept it slung over his shoulder.

"Jake, please, don't let our years of friendship end like this," Margrett begged. She ran to Frank who held her protectively.

"I said leave. Get Molly and go. Never come back here," Jake said, the frustration building in his voice.

Frank nodded, having always been a quiet man, and as he led Margrett from the room, he looked at Robert, who was staring pale-faced at Jake with the gun. Frank called up the stairs for Molly, letting her know that they were leaving. Jake took the rifle and hid it behind the door frame when Molly arrived and looked down the hallway at him. She said a cold farewell and hurried out with her family. No one moved until the sounds of the truck disappeared in the distance.

"Jake, I read it all. I know why he left," Robert said in a calm voice. "I know you probably blame yourself for everything, but we can talk about this."

Just then a large gust of wind shook the side of the house as the storm arrived. Both men looked at the window as the storm engulfed the farm, turning day into the darkest night. Robert looked back to see Jake walk out of the living room and head towards the front door. "Where are you going?"

"Storm shutters," Jake responded as he walked out into the swirling dust.

Coughing and half blind in a matter of seconds, Jake worked his way around the house and managed to get the shutters closed. On his way back, he heard a large crack and a crash over the wind some ways from the house. Looking in that direction, he was blindsided by a piece of fence that had been ripped loose by the wind and struck him in the head. Staggering and disoriented, Jake walked a distance before his foot was tangled in something. As he tried to pull it free he lost his balance, pitching forward. He landed on his knees, his palms scraping on the hard surface of a tree in front of him, on its side.

Realization came to him as he got back to his feet. *No, please, no,* is all he could think as he felt along the trunk and used it to guide him to the other side of the tree. He suddenly tripped over something hard, and fell, sprawling spread-eagle on the ground. His arms scrambled to raise himself when he felt wood, but not from the tree. This was finished wood, painstakingly crafted. He raised himself to his knees, moving his hands along the ground for guidance. He found the thing he had tripped over, a stone cross headstone. Crying now, Jake continued back along the ground. Knowing the truth before he even arrived, he felt the wood of the coffin he had placed his wife in. The tree had spread its roots among the graves, and when the storm uprooted it, the graves came with it.

Jake was openly wailing when he felt someone grab him from under his arms and pull him to his feet. He turned to see a Hun wearing a gas mask behind him. Jake began to choke. *Gas! They're using gas again!* His mind screamed at him to get his mask on. He looked around quickly, not finding one. Then he realized he could just take the one off the German. He ran forward, tackling the soldier to the ground. He knew he had to be quick, this is how his brothers had gone out, and he had to get home for his family. He straddled the soldier, trying to pry the mask off his face. The soldier was yelling at him, trying to keep his mask on.

I need to get home for Beth, she needs me, he thought. He paused in his struggle. *Who is Beth? Beth's my daughter.* He blinked and looked down, and he was able to make out a bloody-nosed Robert with his goggles and cloth mask torn away from his face. Robert looked up at him in fear and confusion.

"Jake! What's wrong?" shouted Robert.

Jake stood, and looked around as the storm quieted a bit. "I...I was back in the war," he said with a choke. He placed his hand on the fallen tree for support. "I'm on the farm, aren't I?" He looked to Robert who was getting up.

"Yes, yes you are. You've been out here for an hour. I was afraid you had gotten hurt or lost, so I came to find you," Jake adjusted his goggles, using the mask to wipe away the blood spilling from his nose.

"The tree. I heard it fall. My wife!" Jake quickly turned to the upheaval the tree had left behind. He saw three caskets sticking out of the ground, and his wife's casket had cracked down the middle. Her desiccated remains had spilled out of the top.

"Oh my god," said Robert, looking away.

Jake dropped to his knees, and cradled his wife's head in his arms. Tears streamed down his face. "I have to get her back in the ground. I have to get them all back in the ground," he looked at Robert. "Help me."

Jake nodded. "I will, we just have to wait for the storm to finish then we can set things right," he reached out to Jake. "Now come on, we have to get inside. Storm looks like it is gaining strength again."

"I can't just leave her!"

"You can't stay out here either," Robert said in a calm voice, "what if something happened to you?"

Reluctantly, Jake let his wife go. He stood and allowed himself to be led back to the house. The storm began whipping up more dirt, making the way difficult. Robert, with his goggles, was able to get them inside safely. Once inside, Jake sat at the kitchen table and cried into his hands. Huge, body-wracking sobs shook him. "This isn't what I wanted, this wasn't how this was supposed to be."

Robert, carefully placed a hand on his shoulder. "We don't always get to decide how things are, but we have to make the best of it."

"She was supposed to still be here. He was supposed to still be here. My brothers, my sister, my family!" Jake wailed. "I sacrificed so much already, how much more do I have to give up?"

In time Jake looked up from his hands. He hadn't heard Robert leave the kitchen. He looked at the window to see that it was still dark, and the storm was raging outside. He slowly stood up and walked out into the hallway. He climbed the stairs; he just wanted to lie down and forget. When he got to the top, he saw that Beth's door was still shut. He walked over to it and placed his hand on the door. "I'm sorry, darling." Not expecting a reply, he turned and walked toward his room, when he passed by Robert's door he heard his name called quietly.

"Jake, come in," Robert said from inside the room. Jake looked in to see Robert seated in a chair with, one of Brian's novels in his hands. "We need to talk."

"Just let me sleep," Jake croaked.

"Does Beth know? About your wife?"

"Know what?"

"How she really died," Robert said quietly, as if not to be heard from down the hall.

Jake walked into the room, and he turned to shut the door and rested his head against it. He breathed deeply. "No."

"Brian found her, that's what he wrote," Robert said, holding up the book. "How does Beth not know?"

Turned to face him, Jake said, "Beth only knew that her mother was sick. She was tired all the time, some days she wouldn't even get out of bed."

"Did you know there was a note?"

Jake looked at him sharply. "What note?"

"She had left a note. Brian kept it in his book." Robert opened to a page at the end of the book in his lap. He pulled out a carefully folded piece of paper and held it out to Jake. Shakily, he took it with both hands, which then fell into his lap as if the note weighed a hundred pounds.

"You read it?"

"Yes," Robert answered, closing the book again and placing it on the bed. "She only wanted to leave. There was nothing to keep you all here. The children would have had a better life if you would have only listened."

Jake's hands balled up in his lap, crushing the note. His gaze remained on the floor between them. Suddenly his shoulders dropped, and he nodded. "I wouldn't let her go. Everything we had was in this farm. My great-grandfather built this house." He pointed out the window. "For Christ's sake, my family is buried right out there. What was I going to do? Walk away from it all and let someone swoop in and take it all away?" He stood up and walked to the window, looking out into the maelstrom of swirling black dirt.

"And you blame yourself for your choice to stay. And if you left now, why couldn't you have left before while she was still alive?" Robert gave a low whistle. "The emotional turmoil here is worse than that storm out there." He stood and walked to the window with Jake, both men looking out the window. "I'm sorry for everything that's happened to you, but you have to start thinking about the family that is still alive. Living in the past often makes you lose sight of the here and now." Robert placed his hand on Jake's shoulder. "I said it before, you might want to consider talking to someone about these things."

Jake forcefully brushed the hand off his shoulder. "And what happens then? They throw me in an asylum? Beth is left on her own? I'm all she has!"

"I can help..."

"I'm not abandoning my family, and I'm not abandoning my farm!" Jake yelled. He pushed Robert roughly, making him stagger backward and fall over the chair in the middle of the room. He hit the ground hard.

"Jake, calm down. Please, relax." Robert slowly got back to his feet, keeping an eye on Jake the entire time. "There's no need for this." Suddenly Jake charged at him and slammed him into the wall, knocking the wind from his lungs. As he tried to regain his breath, Jake backed away from him. Drool was falling from Jake's mouth, face contorted in pure rage.

"You dug up the past! You!" he screamed. "You're destroying my family!"

Finally catching his breath, Robert shouted back, "I didn't make my wife hang herself!"

Jake reacted as if he had just been punched in the gut and bent over with his hands on his knees. They then heard a loud gasp from the other side of the door followed by someone running back down the hallway. "Beth..." Jake groaned.

Breathing heavily, Robert pushed off the wall, "I'll go talk to her..."

"You stay away from her!" Jake shouted as he charged him again, slamming him harder into the wall. Suddenly there was a crash in the next room. Jake's room.

"No...No," Jake hurried out to the hallway. He slammed the door to his room open and cried in grief as he saw the broken mirror on the floor. He slowly dropped to his knees, his body quaking as he wept. Barehanded, he began to scoop up the broken glass, cutting his hands and arms. "I'm so sorry, Clara, I'm so sorry." He hugged the broken shards to his chest, drawing blood.

"We have to leave now!" Beth's voice shouted from down the hall. Jake, in a half daze, listened to a commotion in the hallway and the sound of something heavy being dragged towards the stairs.

"Do you know where he keeps the keys to the car?" Robert said. "Leave the bag, we have to go quickly."

Jake, his body dripping in blood, let the pieces of glass fall to the ground and stood. At the sound of the glass falling, he heard Beth scream in fright. As he turned and walked out of the room, he saw Robert grab her hand and pull her. She turned and they both ran down the stairs. "You leave my daughter alone!" He screamed and ran after them. He tripped over the large duffle bag that Beth had been dragging in the hallway, smearing the floor with blood as his hands slid along the ground. Quickly he rose to his feet and ran down the stairs.

When he arrived on the first floor, he saw the front door open, the storm blowing it back and forth. He ran to catch up with them but stopped short as he spied his rifle by the side of the door. Nodding to himself, he quickly picked it up and ran full speed into the black abyss. The storm took him, he was once again blind and coughing, but determined. He brought his rifle up, aiming into the swirling dust. He stalked forward and listened. He heard a shout to his right, and he spun and fired a shot in that direction. He heard someone shouting behind him he turned, swinging his rifle like a club and hitting nothing. He almost lost the grip on his weapon, his hands slick with blood.

Damn, must have hit the barbwire a little too hard, he thought. *But when Sergeant says charge, you damn well charge.* He wished he still had his mask; the smoke was making it hard to see and breathe. He righted his weapon and slid his feet forward, not wanting to trip over anything. He heard another shout from behind him; he quickly spun around and made his way in that direction.

A loud roar and bright light greeted him. Scared, Jake started shooting. He then heard a woman scream in pain. "Oh my God," he heard a man shout. Still blinded by the light, Jake felt someone tackle him to the ground and rip the weapon from his hands. He made out the face of Robert above him, the rifle raised to club him. "You killed her!" Robert shouted at him.

His mind clearing, and realization coming to him, Jake asked, "Where's Beth?"

"You son of a bitch, you killed her." Robert looked down at him, his eyes filled with anger.

"What? I...the woman?" Jake stumbled over his words, tears welling up in his eyes. He shook his head and fought to push Robert off him. "Get off me! Let me see my daughter!" Robert stood up, and he held the rifle tightly, ready to hit Jake with it. He nodded toward the lights about ten feet away. Jake made his way slowly; he reached the lights and saw they were coming from the headlamps on his Model A.

He used the car for guidance, his hand sliding along the body. He felt the first bullet hole and the second, all in a line. He finally arrived at the passenger side door. "Beth?" Jake whimpered, and reached for the handle. He opened the door and cried. Slumped in the passenger seat with blood pouring out of her chest was Beth. The shot had gone clean through the window and hit her square on in the heart. He screamed in anguish and grabbed at her. Pulling her out of the car, he fell back with her onto the ground. "Oh, my baby girl," he cried repeatedly.

The storm soon died down, leaving a brown haze in the air. The sun was rising off in the distance, casting long shadows on the farm. As Jake heard Robert approach, he looked up through grief-stricken eyes. "Just leave," he croaked. He buried his face in Beth's hair and muffled a scream.

"I...I can't just walk away from this, Jake. I'm taking the car and getting the police," Robert said shakily.

His eyes closed tight, Jake nodded, resting his chin on the top of Beth's head. "Just give...just give me enough time."

"Enough time for what?"

He let Beth go and slid out from underneath her. He stood there quietly for a time and looked over his farm, tears still rolling down his cheeks, mixing with the blood on his chest. "Enough time for what, Jake?" Robert asked again.

"I have to bury my family," he nodded towards the fallen tree with the coffins uprooted from the ground.

Swallowing, Robert asked, "Do you need help?"

"No, I need to do this on my own."

Robert nodded, he looked down at Beth and tears soon welled up in his eyes. He looked away, breathing deeply. "You should have left me on the road, Jake."

"Don't dwell too much in the past, Robert. You'll lose sight of the here and now," Jake said in a hollow voice. "Can you do me another favor? I'm sorry to ask this of you..."

Robert walked to the driver's side door and threw the rifle into the back seat. He looked over the roof of the car at Jake. "What?"

Staring back at the house, Jake said, "Just make sure the farm goes to my boy," his voice hitching in his throat. "Don't...don't let them take it from him."

Both men stood there for a long time staring at the farm before Robert responded, "I promise, but, what are you leaving him? It's just dust and pain."

Looking up at the sky, Jake sighed and closed his eyes.

"It has to rain sometime."

THE HOUSE OF STAKES
Jaap Boekestein

I

The running and shouting figures looked like the denizens of Hell, drawn against the backdrop of the burning house and with a storm wind howling in the night.

With his two-day-old baby boy on one arm and reigns in his hands, the young man urged his steed on. As expected, the fire he had started had distracted the servants and the family. This was his chance to escape this place of madness and unholiness.

"Brother!" a voice called out. "In the Lord's name, stop! What are you doing?"

Two men came running: his in-laws, father and son. They were blocking his retreat.

The young man pulled out the flintlock pistol he had bought in London last year. He had meant it to be a precaution against robbers and highwaymen. He had never dreamt pointing it at the family of his wife.

But he did.

"Get out of my way, or I'll shoot. By God, I will!"

"Brother, please don't! I understand you are frightened, but we mean you no harm. There is no evil here," pleaded the brother-in-law. "I assure you—"

The young man did not listen, but spurred on his horse.

His brother-in-law jumped aside, but the old man tried to catch the horse's reigns.

A flare! A bang! Smoke! In a reflex, the young man had shot his father-in-law, point blank, through the chest.

The horse shrieked and the young man fought to keep it under control, dropping the pistol in the mud. His little boy cried at the top of his lungs.

For one moment it looked like the horse would throw its rider, but somehow the young man got the animal under control once more.

His brother-in-law was kneeling beside his father, holding the old man in his arms.

This was his chance to escape. The shouts and gunshot had attracted the attention of the servants and they came running from the house.

And then...

"William."

Her voice sung through the night. *Her* voice.

"William."

Like a specter she came from the darkness, golden-haired, fair skinned, still wearing the dress she had been buried in. She reached out, her frail hands begging. "William, come back! Don't leave, don't take our little boy!"

It started to rain. Cold and heavy, like the last reminder of the past winter.

The young man shook his head. For the last time, he looked at his dead wife and then he spurred on his horse and galloped away into the darkness.

"William!" he heard one last desperate cry.

II

Ten years after the final defeat of Little Boney, the Continent was relatively peaceful. But even in peaceful times, it took days for a letter to make it from London to Göttingen. By the time I received the letter of the solicitor, my father was already buried. William Hankins was dead, leaving me, his only child Xander, as the last of his line.

I decided to end my study of metaphilosophy at the University of Göttingen and return to London to settle my affairs, as the solicitor, Mr. Sullivan, urged me to. Father had made his fortune in buying and selling stocks, a trade I had no interest in at all. I decided to sell all his belongings and...

I have to confess I had no concrete plans for the future. Maybe I would try my hand at being an artist, or travel to the places of antiquity, or try to make my name in some distant, wild land. I didn't know. My studies weren't going anywhere and looking back I only had taken them up to be as far away as possible from my father, a man I hardly knew, but despised anyway. I felt little kinship with him once he had told me my mother died at my birth and he had refused to provide any further information. Most of my life I had spent in boarding schools abroad, seldom returning to London.

For all purposes my father, William Hankins, always had been a cold and distant figure. A stranger.

So why was I weeping then?

Maybe because now I was truly alone in the world. It certainly was not out of love.

I packed my belongings and returned to England, knowing little about my past, and nothing about my future.

***

"William Hankins is dead."

The words of the last son echoed through the huge cave and started to have an effect.

The freshest slumberers, from the last century or so, opened their eyes. The older ones just twisted, hanging from their stems. They could still hear and comprehend, but the will to engage had slowly faded throughout the ages.

"William Hankins, that damned arsonist and murderer?" asked Jacob. In his excitement, he moved his arms and legs, with little control: like a puppet with half of its strings cut. It had been over a decade since Jacob had walked. Even after all those years, the scars on his chest hadn't disappeared. They probably never would. The stems provided the slumber, but did not turn back age or decay. The mask of death was for all eternity.

The old man, who was Jacob's son, leaned on his stick, waving with the newspaper. The obituary about the London stockbroker was only a few lines. "Yes. He died after a short sick bed, it says."

Jacob grunted. William Hankins had what was coming to him: eternal death. He touched his chest.

"Does it say anything about my Xander?" a young woman's voice asked eagerly.

The old man looked at his sister. They were born with four years in between, but died over twenty years apart. During his life he had grown old quickly, plagued by rheumatism. She had remained forever young—an eternal beautiful maiden.

"It says nothing about your son," her brother answered. "But it mentions a solicitor handling William Hankins' affairs."

***

Mr. Sullivan was a middle-aged, balding man wearing thick reading glasses. After offering his condolences and explaining the will—my father left everything to me—the solicitor provided me a list of my father's estate. The sum was larger than I expected. I guess I was what one called 'well placed' but neither the words nor the numbers stirred any emotion. They were as empty as I felt inside.

"Your father is buried in Bunhill Fields," Mr. Sullivan told me. "In case you want to pay your respects."

I had no plans to visit the grave of my dead father, but I kept my peace.

"And there is this letter of your uncle, Mr. Todd Fairlane, Esq."

An uncle? Father had never mentioned an uncle, or any other relatives. I grunted and Mr. Sullivan explained, "The gentleman wrote me after learning of your father's death in the newspapers. Apparently, he is the brother of your late mother, Mary Fairlane. A sealed letter, for your eyes only, was enclosed."

The solicitor handed me a heavy letter, sealed with red lacquer, bearing some coat of arms. The thick lacquer obscured any meaningful details.

In a dreamlike state, like I was under the influence of hashish, I took the letter and put it away in my coat. *Mary.* My mother was called Mary. Mary Fairlane. Father had never told me her name. It felt like suddenly an old, locked door was thrown open to reveal a dusty, sun-drenched room. A room of secrets and laughter and warmth.

The rest of the meeting went by quickly. I signed some papers and gave Mr. Sullivan the authority to sell my father's belongings. There was nothing I wanted or needed.

What did I do afterwards? My memories are vague, but I must have gotten drunk.

I can't remember how I ended up at my father's grave in the Bunhill Fields Cemetery, but I did. Like so many cemeteries in the ever-expanding London, it was terribly overcrowded. There was hardly any room between the graves, and stories were told of people buried on top of each other. It was a dark and desolate place which fitted my mood perfectly.

"William Hankins, 1772-1825" read his tombstone. Nothing more. In death, my father was as cold and uninformative as he had been in life.

I looked at his grave, but I had spent all my tears back in Göttingen. I was empty.

Somehow, I remembered the letter from my new-found uncle. I broke the seal and started to read. *Dear nephew,* it started.

***

-- Advertisement in the Times *--*
WANTED by a Young Lady, a Useful Companion aged between 20 and 24.
She must be musical, a good reader, domesticated, industrious and can be well recommended.
References required. Apply by letter, postpaid, to T. Fairlane, Esq., Fairlane House, Bootle, Lancashire.

***

The journey from London to the Lake District was an uneventful one, except for maybe the last stretch. My uncle lived in Fairlane House on the coast of the Irish Sea, the same house where my mother was born and raised, he wrote. I was welcome to visit him and stay as long as I wished. He would love to meet his nephew which he had only seen as a babe.

I had no recollection of my uncle, or any other family for that matter, nor of a house at the coast. Still, his words evoked strong emotions and that's why I accepted his invitation. I wanted to visit the place my mother grew up and speak to the people who had known her. That part of my life had always been denied to me and I felt the urge to explore the past.

Maybe I was looking for a place to belong.

The trip up north was a succession of coaches and the last one would take me from the town of Kendal to a little village called Bootle, from where I planned to make my way to Fairlane House. I had sent word to my uncle about my travel plans and I hoped that in Bootle there would be a carriage waiting. If not, I would either rent a carriage or a horse to get to my destination. I was traveling light and money was the least of my concerns.

I discovered in Kendal that my last coach only had one other passenger, a young, plain-featured woman, dressed in a brown dress and a tartan traveling cloak with matching bonnet. She had reddish-brown curls, fair skin adorned with freckles, and quick, light brown eyes. I introduced myself and I learned her name was Miss Gissing, from Lincolnshire.

When the coach departed, Miss Gissing took a novel from her traveling bag and started to read. I entertained myself by watching the scenery of the Lake District. I pondered about my uncle I knew so little about. He was my mother's blood. Would I recognize something of myself in him, or would he be a stranger the same way my father had always been to me? I had never experienced a family life, and the thought of being confronted with relatives made me feel on edge. What if they didn't like me? Or if I didn't care for them? My life had been filled with strangers, those I knew how to handle. But blood? That was a foreign country to me.

At a stop at one of the toll charges, I asked the coach driver how far we still had to go before we arrived in Bootle.

With his thick local accent, he told me it would be at least another hour, and satisfied I returned to my seat.

"Excuse me, Sir," Miss Gissing said. She had put down her book and was looking at me. "Did I hear correctly that you will get out at Bootle?"

"I am, Miss. I am heading for Fairlane House."

"So am I! I am hired to be the Lady Companion to Miss Mary Fairlane. You know her?"

"I...my mother was Mary Fairlane," I confessed. *She cannot be alive, can she?* It was like I suddenly stood at the edge of an abyss. *Had my father lied?*

Miss Gissing must have noticed my confusion, because she said, "I understand the young lady is nineteen years old. She is the daughter of Todd Fairlane, Esq."

Of course. How silly of me. I smiled. "They are certainly not the same person."

Josephine Gissing smiled back. She seemed to consider something for a moment and then asked, "Sir, forgive me my forwardness, but do you know the Fairlane family, or the place? I know little, except what my employer, Mr. Fairlane, disclosed in his letter. I would like to be acquainted with the facts as well as possible, if you are willing."

"I am afraid I know even less than you," I confessed. "This is my first visit. I wasn't even aware my uncle had a daughter."

"Ah. Well, that makes us both explorers of the unknown."

For the next hour, we talked about all kind of things. Josephine Gissing was a quick-witted, intelligent, well-read young woman who, after the death of her widowed mother, had decided to make a living on her own. This was her first job, and although she didn't say, I could sense she was a bit anxious. I told her about the different places I had been on the continent. For some reason, Father had sent me to schools outside the United Kingdom, in several German states. I was fluent in English, German, and French, and I could at least understand some Italian, Polish, and Dutch.

We were both surprised when the coach came to a halt and the driver announced, "Lady and gentleman, we've arrived in Bootle."

Bootle was nothing more but a few houses, but a carriage with an elderly fellow was waiting for us. "Young Master Hankins? Miss Gissing? Welcome. My name is Jacob. I'm here to take you to Fairlane House."

***

A dozen tendrils pulling back—nay! *tearing*—from her flesh.

Kneeling on the wet cave floor, Mary panted. She knew a little blood trickled down her back. Waking up from the slumber itself did not hurt, but detaching oneself from the stem...it was a bit like giving birth, only much shorter.

And this birth restores my life instead of taking it away.

Mary looked at the empty spaces. She was late, as usual. Her father had left, as had her brother, and several others of the family who would function as servants. She had never seen so many empty stems. Everyone who could still walk was out there, blowing new life into the house.

As quick as possible Mary Fairlane got up. She had to hurry! Her face, her hair, her dress! She had to be presentable to welcome William and Miss Gissing.

A wave of little spasms ran through the other slumberers, their bodies swaying on their stems. They could sense her excitement.

Mary threw them a kiss and hurried to the stairs leading to the house.

***

How to describe the house where I was born? As a ruin? Yes, a substantial part was a ruin: black walls covered with dark green ivy-grow. Once a fire had gutted a whole wing of the mansion, but what remained still stood proud on the edge of the cliff: a three-story house of gray stone, surrounded by extensive gardens which were bordered by woodland. This was my mother's house and a deep feeling of coming *home* overwhelmed me when we rode down to the muddy road to the coast. The sun was shining and a playful wind blew holes in the blanket of white and gray clouds above the Irish Sea.

"What happened to the house?" I asked Jacob. The elderly man moved stiffly, like he was suffering from an old wound which had healed badly.

After inquiring if we had a good trip, he had been quiet, although he didn't seem a sullen soul. He appeared to observe me, no doubt curious about the long-lost relative visiting the house of his master.

"A fire, a long time ago," Jacob answered. "The whole house would have burned down, if it hadn't been for the rain. The family started living in the remainder of the house. My s—Master Fairlane had plans of restoring Fairlane House to its former glory. But money and manpower were lacking." Jacob shook his head. "Quite a shame. Once the Fairlanes were important in these parts, but those days are long past. Now it's only Master Todd Fairlane, and Miss Mary." The old man glanced at me. "She is Master Fairlane's daughter. Named after her aunt who died before she was born."

My mother.

Jacob shrugged. "They are the last. All the others are dead. Without new blood the Fairlane family will end soon. Nobody left to keep things running."

I didn't reply; I did not want the misfortune of my mother's family to ruin my good mood. The sun was shining and I was going to meet relatives I didn't know I had a month ago: Uncle Todd and his daughter Mary, who was named after my own mother.

It took us ten minutes to drive up to the house. By the time we had arrived at the sturdy front door, about half a dozen people were waiting for us. Most of them were servants, all rather old and looking a bit alike, like they were all part of the same family. Two people stood apart. One was a frail old man leaning on a stick, no doubt my uncle, Todd Fairlane Esquire. The other was like a fairytale creature: a young maiden, golden-haired, green-eyed, delicate features...an angel who had decided to visit the mortal realm. My cousin, Mary Fairlane. She was the most beautiful creature I had ever seen.

My uncle's eyes were lively and in spite of his frailty, he matched my grip when we shook hands.

"Xander, you are most welcome in my house! I am so glad you came. You look so much like your father. My condolences with your loss, dear boy."

"Thank you, Uncle. I'm honored to be here." There was a kindness to the old man, a genuine warmth I had little experience with. *Is this how true family feels?*

"And this is Mary, my daughter."

The touch of her hand was electrifying. She looked at me with her green eyes which somehow seemed so much older and wiser than her mere nineteen summers. Mary smiled when she said, "You are a handsome boy, Xander."

I felt my ears burn, not expecting such a frank remark. "You're very beautiful yourself," I blurted out before I could stop myself.

Mary's laugh was like sunlight, sparkling and warm. Suddenly she stepped forward and kissed me on the cheek. "Welcome home, Xander."

She left me dazed, unable to speak, to move, to breathe even. Meanwhile, Mary turned to Miss Josephine Gissing who stood in the back, a little bit lost. My sweet cousin took her hired companion's hands. "And welcome to you, Josephine. I hope you will be happy here at Fairlane House. I can imagine you feel a bit anxious. Please come in, you will be thirsty and hungry after all that traveling. There is tea in the salon."

Mary took Josephine and me by the arm, and walked us inside. Uncle Todd followed slowly.

***

"He looks a lot like his father," Jacob told his relatives.

The slumberers didn't reply, but they were listening. Listening and dreaming their eternal dreams. Their bodies hung motionless on the stems.

"And she is a decent lass, she is," Jacob continued. "Nature will take its course, I'm sure of it."

Still, the slumberers did not reply.

Jacob took off his shirt. Guided by the light of the single candle he walked up to his place. He felt bone tired, it was time to sleep. He offered the stem his bare back and waited with clenched teeth.

For a moment nothing happened, but then the huge, fleshy pillar struck like a viper.

A dozen or so thorn-like tendrils penetrated the flesh of the old man, finding the spine and arteries.

Jacob grunted, refusing to cry out.

After a handful of heartbeats, he relaxed and closed his eyes.

The stem lifted him up from the ground.

***

"This is your mother and me," Uncle Todd said, pointing with the stem of his long Dutch pipe at the painting above the hearth. We were sitting in the smoking room after dinner. Mary was showing Miss Gissing her rooms and I got acquainted with my eldest relative.

The painting, done about thirty years ago, to judge by the style of clothes, depicted a young man and woman, clearly brother and sister. Todd Fairlane must have been in his early twenties and he had been a proud, handsome fellow. Mary Fairlane, my mother, was about sixteen and beautiful with golden hair and green eyes.

"She...your daughter looks exactly like her," I said. The resemblance was uncanny. The Mary upstairs was the spitting image of the girl in the painting. A few years older, but the same build, the same face, the same hair.

Uncle Todd nodded. "We named her after Mary, my sister, and she grew up to be like her. Sometimes it is like seeing a ghost." My uncle looked at

180

me. "What do you know about your mother?"

"Nothing," I confessed. "Only at the solicitor's office in London, I learned about her and your existence. My father never mentioned her, or your family. We...he was a very private man who didn't discuss the past, ever. Until your letter, I had never heard the name Fairlane, or knew that I was born here."

"I see." Uncle Todd took a puff from his pipe before continuing the conversation. "Do you want to know what happened, between your father and my sister?" The old man looked at me from his chair. In spite of his age and condition, he was a strong man, but now his voice was soft.

"Please," I croaked. My mouth felt dry.

"Back then your father was a young lad, who already had made good money by investing his modest capital wisely in several ventures. He came from the south in search of investment options. My father owned a small mine but needed capital to exploit it properly. William Hankins stayed at Fairlane House, where he met Mary. They both liked each other from the moment they met, and after four weeks your father proposed. Our father gladly gave his permission and four weeks later Mary and William were married. We joked about the marriage having a royal flavor, because of their names."

Remembering the past, my uncle was quiet for a moment and took another puff. "Your father and mother stayed for the winter and you were born here in the spring."

"I...I understand she died giving birth to me?"

Uncle Todd nodded. "She did. My little sister. She could not stop bleeding after giving birth to you. There was no saving her."

"I'm so sorry."

"The earth took her gladly, my boy. And she left a beautiful baby, which was you."

We were both silent for a while, lost in thoughts. Finally, my uncle continued, "I think your father was overcome with grief and could not stand to remain in the place where he had loved, and lost. He took you with him and we never heard from him again."

"You had words?" Maybe it was an improper question, but I had to know.

"Yes." The old man nodded. "My father didn't want his grandchild to leave Fairlane and we pleaded with your father for us to raise you, to no avail."

I tried to imagine how my life would have been growing up in this house. Better, worse? At least I would have had the company of relatives. My father had denied me that.

"At least you got Mary," I said.

"I...yes, I did. That was a few years later. I lost my wife when Mary was still a child and I never had any other children. The Fairlane line will disappear, which weighs heavy on my heart. That was why I was delighted to receive your letter, dear boy. You're the last li...vital member of our line. The last male, I mean."

"I am glad to be here, Uncle, in spite of my father. I hope we can heal the old wounds and start afresh."

I think there were tears in the eyes of the old man. He took my hand and said, "I would like nothing better."

And so started my stay at Fairlane House.

***

It was one of the happiest summers Mary had ever experienced.

"I wonder how far that cave goes," Josephine said.

"Not very far, I'm afraid." Mary shook her head, which caused the wind to take hold of her hair and loosen her braids. Little flowers flew over the beach.

"I will get them!" Xander called out and while he was chasing flowers, both girls laughed. It was a wonderful, sunny day and they had decided to have a walk on the pebble beach at the foot of cliffs. They had spotted a small cave in the rock face, its entrance covered with slimy kelp.

"It looks very old," Josephine continued when Xander had finally returned with his booty. He had been able to save most flowers from the waves. "Think of it, ancient barbarians could have walked on this same beach and visited this cave. And Picts and Romans and Druids and Vikings!"

Mary laughed. "I think they were all disappointed. It is all slippery rocks and little pools, but come, I will show you. Father never wanted me to visit the cave, but we did nonetheless when we were kids."

"We?" asked Josephine.

"I...a few friends and I," Mary explained. "We have visited the cave quite a few times. But come, I will show you. It isn't very deep, but very, *very* wet!"

It was a summer of friendship, of hope.

And inevitably the summer ended.

***

Above the gray sea the storm released its anger, whipping the water with hail and rain making the dark clouds roll through the sky. I stood at the edge of the cliff watching the distant violence, seeking a release for the turbulent feelings inside me.

I was in love. I had been in love from the moment I laid eyes on Mary, now three months ago.

And now I knew my love went unanswered...

Oh, how golden had the summer been! Days filled with sunshine and laughter. Fairlane House was an old place, the current house built on the spot of an ancient fortress which already belonged to the Fairlanes until a time that was lost in the dawn of history. Mary showed me the house and surrounding lands. Her laugh was enchanting, her eyes and hair were magic. The three of us—Mary, her Lady Companion Josephine and myself—spent the days together, as far as possible. Mary's condition was delicate and in the afternoon she needed her rest, just like Uncle Todd. I usually went horse-riding, or passed the time reading in the company of Josephine.

There was a fondness between Mary and me, an attraction even. I was sure of it! How often did she take my hand without thinking? Countless times I caught her looking at me. When we were together she smiled and my heartbeat quickened. Soon I could think of nothing but Mary. Her voice, her looks, her smell, her little mannerisms. Mary! Mary! Mary!

For the first time in my life, I was in love and it was the effects of a heady wine: sweet, intoxicating, and with an undercurrent of madness.

Madness to fall in love with my own cousin? No, not that. There was no law, human or divine, which forbid such love. It was madness to instantly fall in love the moment I saw her. Madness, but surely destiny, fate. Mary! Mary! Mary!

I wanted her. I wanted her body and her soul, I wanted her to be my wife. I wanted her to be the mother of my children. I had dreams of Fairlane House full of the laughter of children and grandchildren. A family, a home.

Of course, I could have asked her father, dear Uncle Todd, for her hand, but I wanted to be sure. I wanted to consult Mary first. She would be my wife, but she would also be my equal. My life had been dictated by a distant father I hardly knew. I had sworn not to be such a husband. We would be together, the two of us. I wanted her to be happy.

This morning we sat in the walled garden, the three of us, Mary, Josephine, and I. Slowly the summer was changing into fall and the walls of the garden kept out the sea winds and held the heat of the sun.

I looked at Mary; she was so lovely.

"Miss Gissing," I spoke, "would you be so kind as to leave us alone for a while?"

Josephine glanced at Mary, and my angel nodded.

The young woman rose and left the garden.

It was like a little piece of paradise, caught in that garden. Sunshine, late-blooming flowers, the soft sounds of insects.

I took Mary's hands in mine and looked her in her wonderful green eyes.

"Mary, I want to ask you something. Something I've wanted to ask you for a long time."

Mary laughed gaily. "Oh Xander, do tell! You make me curious, with sending dear Josephine away! She is wondering what you are up to, as am I. She really likes you, you know."

Dear Mary, sweet Mary, always thinking of others and never of herself. That was one of the many reasons I loved her.

"I...I..." The speech I had rehearsed had vanished from my mind. Mary had me under her spell, without even knowing it herself.

"I love you," I blurted out. "I've loved you since the day we met. I want you to be my wife, sweet Mary. I want to marry you."

For the very first time, I saw utter horror on someone's face. And it had to be Mary's face, the woman I loved, after I confessed my love for her.

She pulled her hands away, like I was a leper. "Xander, no! Oh dear boy, how could...you are not supposed to fall in love with *me*. I...no, this is impossible! A nightmare!"

Every one of her words was like a dagger plunging into my heart. The pain was incredible. For the briefest of moments, I hoped she was joking; that she was toying with my feelings. But the look on her face convinced me her feelings were genuine. She was horrified by the idea of me marrying her, of my love for her.

"Don't you love me?" I managed to utter. It was a foolish question, but I was incapable of coherent thought.

"Of course, I love you," Mary cried out. "But not in *that* way. You are my...my cousin. We can't marry, we can't have children. I...I am bare, dear Xander. My...my condition. I can't give you children. It would mean the end of the Fairlane family."

"The future of the family be damned! I want you, Mary. I want you to be my wife. With or without children." I was shouting, out of despair and anger.

Mary rose. "We will never marry, Xander. Such a thing is impossible. Marry another girl, marry Josephine, and live here at Fairlane House. Be the new Master, fulfill the destiny your father walked away from. But we will never be man and wife. Love, lust, between us, is impossible."

"I don't want any other woman! I want you."

Tears filled Mary's eyes, she tried to take my hands. "You don't understand Xander. You don't know. I...it is impossible."

I did not want to understand, I did not want to know. I stormed off.

And now I was standing at the edge of the cliff. Considering how cruel fate could be—considering my future.

What future?

The love of my life was disgusted by me. Didn't want anything to do with me.

My mother had died giving birth to me, my father never wanted to know me, my love had scorned me. What future did I have?

The waves crashed on the rocky beach, deep down below. How would it be to fall, to fly for the briefest of moments and then...oblivion.

No more pain. No more bleak, meaningless years to live.

"Mister Hankins," a woman's voice called out.

I turned around. Josephine Gissing was approaching. The wind pulled at her dress and hair, with one hand she held a woolen wrap. She looked worried and determined at the same time.

"Miss Gissing," I replied shortly. I didn't want to see anyone, not even Josephine, who I had to come to consider something like a friend the last months.

"Can I have a word with you, Xander?" she asked. "Somewhere shielded from the wind, and prying eyes." The subtle nod with her head was in the direction of Fairlane House.

"If you want to." Only a few moments ago I had been willing to throw myself off the cliff. The desire had not disappeared completely, but I wouldn't commit suicide in front of Josephine.

We walked to a shallow vale closed off by man-high bushes on three sides. It was completely quiet in this little shelter.

"What is on your mind, Josephine?" I asked.

"I expect you to get angry at me," the brown-haired woman started, "And you got every right to be. But promise to hear me out. Promise me."

"I will," I said with a sullen voice. I wanted the conversation to be over as quickly as possible.

"Good." Josephine Gissing looked at me. "Xander Hankins, I know you love Mary, and I know she has refused you."

My face must have reddened and I said icily, "I don't see how this is any of your business, Miss Gissing." Had she been listening at the door of the garden? She must have.

"I told you, you would be angry, and you promised me to hear me out," she reminded me.

"Fine, I will."

"You have been in love with Mary almost from the start," Josephine continued. "It was plain to see. But I fear this love has also made you blind for the strange things that are going on in Fairlane House."

"I..." I started angrily, but after taking a deep breath asked, "What do you mean?"

"Xander, we've sat at numerous meals. Did you never notice how little Mary and her father eat? They nibble a little, but hardly touch their food."

"They have little appetite, some people can live on little," I said, while remembering our meals. Sure, neither Mary nor Uncle Todd ate much, but they didn't seem to be worse off.

"Granted, but there is more. Both of them rest for several hours during the daytime, but not in their beds. Once I had to ask Mary something very urgent, so I went up to her bedroom and after knocking a few times, I entered. She was not where I expected her to be. The bed was unslept, and covered with a thin layer of dust, like it hadn't been slept in for a long while."

I got angry once more. What was all this foolish talk? "You must be imagining things! This sounds to me you are spying on the one you are paid to keep company. Mary considers you a friend and trusts you!"

My words hurt Josephine, that much was clear, but she stood her ground. "I also consider Mary to be my friend. She is a kind and warm person. But something very odd is going on, Xander. And yes, I am spying on her. I've observed Mary, Mr. Fairlane, and even the servants. None of them seems to eat much and all of them disappear during the day for long stretches of time. I am not sure, but I believe the house has several secret underground exits, leading to some cave. I've found traces of loam on the floor after several re-appearances: the same kind of loam that can be found in the cave down at the beach. I believe this whole cliff is riddled with caves and Fairlane House is connected to them."

"A smugglers' cave? Maybe filled with old pirate's booty, or slaves imported to work in some secret mine?" I ridiculed her. "I am sure there are rational explanations for everything you've observed. The servants are an ancient lot. A carpet which isn't cleaned or a bedroom which isn't aired properly? You let your imagination get away with you, Josephine."

"It does not. I thought so myself many times, but I can't ignore what I see." Josephine sounded upset, but she would not budge.

I shrugged. "Think whatever you think, tomorrow I will leave Fairlane House."

"You are leaving? Where will you go?"

Once more I shrugged. I really didn't know. I had made my decision just then and I had no plans whatsoever, except to get away from Fairlane House and my lost love.

Just like my father, back then. Well, I will not be burdened by a son whose life I most probably would ruin.

Josephine's face was a battlefield of emotions. Finally, she said, "Please don't leave, Xander. Don't leave Mary, don't leave me."

"My mind has been made up, Miss Gissing. As promised I've heard you out. I won't mention anything to Mary or my uncle about your silly notions, but if you feel there are ghouls and boogiemen in Fairlane House, you might reconsider your sanity, or your employment."

The slap in my face was unexpected.

Too amazed to reply, I watched Josephine Gissing walk away without looking back.

Finally, I spat on the ground. Hurt by two women in one day, one with words and rejection, one with violence. I had my fill of cursed Fairlane House. Tomorrow I would take my belongings and leave, on foot if need be.

***

"He proposed," Todd repeated to his sister. "Oh my God, how could we have been so blind!"

"I did nothing to encourage him!" Mary cried. "I love him, he is my own flesh and blood. And he...he...he wants..." She could not make herself say the shameful words again.

The old man took his young sister's hand. "It is not your fault, dear Mary. How could a man refuse you? Josephine is a very nice girl, but compared to you she is a mere candle and you are the sun."

"I am afraid he will leave, just like William," Mary cried. "He will leave us, I am sure of it!"

Todd Fairlane shook his head. "We cannot have that. Our future depends on your son, Mary. We need the living to continue the family, to keep Fairlane House running. Xander has to stay here."

***

"You wanted to speak to me, dear boy?"

It was late in the afternoon and I was sitting with my uncle in the smoking room. The storm had finally made landfall and the howling wind was rattling the shutters of the windows.

"I do, Uncle," I said. "I am afraid I will be leaving for London tomorrow."

Uncle Todd raised his eyebrows. "This is most unexpected, dear nephew. Has this something to do with Mary's refusing your proposal for marriage?"

For one, two, three moments I didn't answer. It was too hard to admit, but it was the truth.

"Yes," I said, finally.

My uncle sighed. "I guess we should have seen it coming. Mary being who she is, so lovely, so sweet. She is very fond of you, Xander, but she can't marry you."

"She made that perfectly clear," I sulked. I wanted to be angry at my uncle, but it was impossible. He had welcomed me in his house and treated me like his own son.

"The Fairlane family is almost dead, Xander. None of us are able to have children, and we need a new generation to keep things running. You are born from Fairlane, which makes you one of us. I would want you to stay here, my dear boy, and become the new Master of Fairlane House. The only condition is that you marry a healthy woman and make sure there will be a next generation. Mary is barren and that is one of the reasons you two can't marry. One of several."

I leaned back in my seat. "With Mary as my wife, I would gladly have stayed here, dear Uncle. I am honored by your trust in me. But I can't live under the same roof with the woman who is the love of my life, but who does not answer those feelings. My mind is made up. Tomorrow I will leave your house. I'll have to find my way in the world." *Alone. Utterly alone.*

Slowly Uncle Todd nodded. "I understand. We will miss you dearly, Xander. Let us have a drink on your future. I have a special bottle of brandy which I've been saving. This occasion is as good as any other."

The old man poured two glasses from a dusty, brown bottle. Even in my chair, I smelled the potent spirit.

"Down the earth," Uncle Todd proposed.

"Down the earth." I repeated the quaint toast and threw back the drink in one go.

The last thing I remembered was my uncle watching me, his drink untouched in his hand.

***

Only three people were at the dinner table that night: Mary, her father, and Josephine.

"Xander is not feeling well and has excused himself," Todd Fairlane explained. "He, apparently, has come down with something."

Josephine glanced at Mary, who was playing without much enthusiasm with her food. Would she dare to ask if Xander had told Mary and her father he was leaving? She decided against it. Maybe Xander came to his senses, and it was not her place to speak for him. Besides, they hadn't parted on peaceful terms. No, she would not ask! Xander was a grown man, responsible for his own actions. *The blind, uncaring buffoon.*

"I hope he gets well soon," Josephine offered.

"As do I," Todd Fairlane said.

The rain battered against the windows and the storm wind haunted the room in the form of cold drafts and the oil lamps' dancing flames. Josephine tried to keep the conversation going, but somehow it sounded like she was a clueless actor performing in a bad play. Her gaiety felt forced and finally withered away. The meal went by slowly with large parts of it in silence.

Afterwards, the old man shook his head. "We are a somber lot today! I blame the weather. I think we need something to lift our spirits and I have the cure here right at hand."

He procured a dusty, dark brown bottle and poured three glasses of brandy.

"This will keep the chill from our bones," he said. He raised his glass and proposed a toast: "Down the earth."

"Down the earth," Mary and Josephine repeated.

Josephine drank from the brandy, which burned in her throat. Her mouth filled with the weirdest of tastes and the spirit went down like liquid fire. She coughed and blinked.

"Finish your drink, dear," the old man urged her. "You will feel better soon."

What a strange thing to say, thought Josephine.

It was her last coherent thought for the night. She wanted to say something, but the room began to spin.

Dreamlike images. Mary helping her upstairs to her room and out of her clothes.

"Where is your nightgown, dear? Ah, there it is."

"Am I drunk?" Josephine asked Mary. "I have never been drunk before!"

Mary shook her head. "You're beyond drunk. Your spirit is now free to follow your heart's desire."

"I am? It does?" Josephine laughed and kissed Mary on the cheek. She was such a lovely creature.

Now Mary, sweet Mary, beautiful Mary, golden-haired Mary, smiled. "Come, you are ready." She guided Josephine through the corridors of the house, carrying a single oil lamp.

Josephine held on to Mary's arm. The world was spinning and the dark was full of colors she had never noticed before. Things whispered and the portraits of the long dead Fairlanes winked and waved, or smiled. The young woman waved back, giggling silly.

Mary stopped at a certain door. "Your heart's desire is waiting for you in his room."

"Xander!" Josephine called out. It had to be Xander. Who else? All the men in Fairlane House were so *old*.

"You love him?" Mary asked. Her voice sounded strained, like everything depended on Josephine's answer.

"I do. But he loves you," Josephine pouted. She tried to kiss Mary again. If she could not love Xander, she could maybe love Mary. She was so sweet. Everyone loved Mary.

"He will love you," Mary promised. "You will see."

Mary unlocked the door. Josephine giggled, everything was so wonderfully weird.

"Shh, wait here and be quiet, my dear Josephine."

"Promised! Shh!" The girl leaned against the wall. Everything was spinning, the night sang to her. Wild songs. She felt her heart beat like a drum in her chest.

Mary stood in the door opening, holding the light up high. "Xander," she said. "Xander, my love? Here I am."

Josephine took a peep. Xander was lying in his bed. Naked as the day he was born. Which was *very* naked. Utmost naked. *Terribly* naked. With open mouth, she looked at him. She had never seen a naked man before. It was quite a sight. So that was...what a weird thing! A bit like a sausage. How weird and funny!

"Mary?" Xander called out from his bed. He sounded quite feverish. He tried to get up, but fell back halfway. "I want you, Mary. I love you!"

"Shh," Mary said. She killed the light, leaving all of them in utter darkness.

Mary took Josephine's hand. "Follow your heart's desire," she whispered and quickly kissed the girl. She led her into Xander's room.

"I am here, my love," Mary called out.

In the dark Josephine touched the bed, touched Xander. Hot flesh. A naked male body. She felt flustered and excited.

He took her in his arms. His mouth found hers. He started kissing.

For a few moments, Mary listened to the unmistakable sounds of two people in a passionate embrace. Silent tears ran down her face. Was it because of the betrayal of two people she loved dearly, or was it because of memories of long ago, when William had loved her in the same fashion? She didn't know herself.

Quietly she closed the door and left.

***

What have I done? What have I done? What *happened* last night?

I must have gotten drunk and...and...

She was still sleeping when I woke from my slumber, her warm body against mine. A bundle of brown hair, curled up like some little animal. Josephine, Miss Gissing. *Josephine*...Mary's companion.

I must have cried out, I must have moved.

She woke.

Her surprise and horror were as big as mine. Clutching the sheets to cover her nakedness, she veered back to the other end of the bed. Her eyes were big, her mouth was half open, frozen in a scream that got stuck in her throat.

A trail of red droplets colored the bed linen.

We both looked at the spilled blood. We both knew what it meant.

I tried to find words, but my mouth was full of ashes. I made a gesture, reached out for her.

With a feral snarl, Josephine slapped my hand away. Pulling at the sheet she got out of bed, grabbing her nightgown in the process.

"Josephine!" I managed to say, finally.

She fled from the room without looking back.

I...

I fled. I threw on some clothes and fled out of the house.

I was a beast, a coward. I had used that young woman and destroyed her, under my uncle's roof! I had sunken to lowest of the lowest. How could I have done this evil deed? I had not only shamed myself, but my family name in the process I had dragged an innocent woman down with me.

What would Mary think? What would Uncle Todd do?

I...

Deep down, at the foot of the cliff, the waves bashed against the rocks. Although the rains had stopped, the winds were still blowing in full force, whipping up waves.

Yesterday I had stood here, at this very same spot, with dark thoughts because the woman I loved had refused me.

This morning I was here again. Not only scorned by the love of my life, but also a man who had abandoned all morality and who had destroyed a young woman's life.

I looked down. The sea was calling.

I jumped.

***

They brought his broken body back to the house, those old, slow servants of Fairlane House.

"Can...can he be saved?" Mary asked. Her face was wet with tears.

"It will take time," Jacob, her father said. "Many months. The question is: does he deserve it?"

Todd stepped forward. "He is of our blood, father! We can't refuse him. No matter what his father did to you. He is your grandchild."

Jacob grunted. He knew his children were right. Xander Hankins was blood of his blood. He deserved to live forever. "So be it! Bring him to the cave."

Josephine grabbed Mary's arm. "What madness is this? Talking about saving him? He is dead, Mary! The fall broke the bones in his body, he drowned in the cold, dark sea. He cannot be saved!"

Mary held Josephine. Suddenly, the blond woman didn't seem to be so young anymore. "Josephine, dear Josephine. Sometimes death is not the end." Mary stroked Josephine's hair. "We did awful things to you. You deserve to know. Come with me. You don't have to be afraid. With Xander gone, it does not matter anymore. The family has ended with him. Everything will end."

Arm in arm the two women started to follow all the old Fairlanes, carrying the very last member of their line.

***

I woke up and for a moment I fell in almost complete darkness; the next moment pain shot through all my limbs. I'd landed on an uneven, wet, rocky floor. Sharp little stones scratched my knees and hands. I was bare breasted and barefooted, but still wore breeches.

I...I am Xander Hankins. The memory bore upon me like a silent ghost ship, emerging from thick fog. *Xander Hankins.* A million other memories were connected to that name. A life: *father.* Love: *Mary!* Loss, shame...death. *A fall, one moment of terrifying, ultimate freedom. And then...Then...*

I swallowed. Was I dead? Was this Hell? Or Limbo? Or any other place

191

in the afterlife?

Still kneeling I looked around. The darkness was not complete. I was in some cave, sloping down gently. At the beginning of the cave, or at least the most elevated end, burned an oil lamp which needed to be trimmed badly. It took a few heartbeats before my eyes had adjusted and I was able to perceive the remainder of the cave.

It was Hell.

As far as the eye could see stakes—nay, *stems*, like some demonic perversion of Earthly plants—grew from the cave floor. Hundreds of them, if not more. And every stake bore *a human body!*

Some of the bodies wore decaying clothes from days long gone by. Others were naked. Men, women, even children. The stem-*things* seemed to be connected to their back, somewhere between their shoulder blades. Thank God it did not emerge from their chest or mouth.

One of the devil plants stood a few yards from where I had landed. The stem was a sickly white, covered with blueish veins. It ended in a knot of tendrils, all with a crooked thorn at the end. What was this?

The realization struck me as a lightning bolt. Had I been hanging from this thing before I woke up and fell? Had I been *part* of this thing?

With a shout I crawled backward, watching the silent, evil growth. The black smudge at the tip of the thorns, was it blood? Was it *my* blood?

Left of me something moved.

It was the corpse of Jacob, the old servant. His body spasmed once more and he opened his eyes. The dead old man was looking at me and said, "You're awake, Xander Hankins. Good."

Everywhere in the cave bodies started to move. Eyes slowly opened, heads turned.

I screamed. I jumped up and fled. Upwards, upwards! Towards the single oil lamp.

My weak legs were barely able to carry me, but half falling, half running I managed to make my way up the slope. The oil lamp revealed a pair of stairs carved out in the rock. It was the only way out and I took it.

Fifty, maybe a hundred steps. I ended up in a room lit by another oil lamp. A passageway led both left and right, and there was another pair of steps going up.

At random, I took the right passageway and after ten steps I ended up at a small door.

Were those dead things in pursuit? Did I hear the sound of shuffling feet? I pushed the door open.

The smoking room was deserted. The little door was camouflaged as one of the wooden wall panels.

My uncle knows about the cave. Suddenly I remembered the words of Josephine, that afternoon Mary had refused me. She had talked about strange things going on, about secret passageways and caves. How right she had been!

*Mary, Josephine...*were they in danger? Would the evil cave things attack them?

Is Mary aware of the cave? Her father must certainly be...Uncle Todd. I had thought him a good, decent man. How wrong I had been! Everything I had called the truth, had been a lie. Suddenly my whole life felt like a farce. *Did Father discover the truth, all those years ago? Was that the reason he left Fairlane House and refused to ever talk about my mother's family?*

My eyes darted around. On one of the walls hung a set of old swords. I took one.

What to do next? I had to get away from this evil place, but I could not do so without Mary and Josephine. I had to find them and convince them to come with me.

I looked at myself. I was bloody and filthy, half-naked, with long unkempt hair and a sword in my hand. And...and...didn't they think me dead? How could I have survived the fall? How did I end up in the cave?

There was no time to consider those questions. I had to act!

Quietly I opened the door of the smoking room.

Down the hall from the salon, I heard voices. Female voices. They were too faint to make out words, but I recognized the voices nonetheless: Mary and Josephine!

Quickly I ran with bare feet towards the salon, leaving a trail of wet footsteps on the black and white squared tiles. I pushed open the door of the salon and slipped inside.

The two women were sitting at the window, utilizing the sunlight. Mary was sewing something and Josephine...Josephine was breastfeeding a babe.

Completely perplexed I stood there, watching them. *Josephine is with child? Impossible! She was a virgin only last...last...*It was like I was buried by a mountain. *Dear Lord, how long have I been asleep?*

They noticed me and Josephine cried out from surprise, clutching the baby against her breast, taking every doubt away it was her child. The little one started to cry, which drew Josephine's attention away from me.

"Xander! You are awake!" Mary said. "What are you doing with that sword?"

"I..." Somehow, I suddenly felt very silly. I wanted to say: "We must flee," but I really was questioning my own mind. Mary didn't seem to be surprised to see me, and neither did Josephine, apparently. Mary's friend had comforted her baby and once again looked at me. She said, "Hello Xander, please put down that weapon. You are frightening our son, William."

Our son, William.

I dropped the sword and started to laugh insanely.

***

We got married, Josephine and I, under common license in the St. Michael's Church in Bootle. Uncle Todd and Mary were present, as well as my grandfather Jacob, masquerading as a servant.

I am one of the slumberers now. My time away from the cave is limited, but I spend every minute with Josephine and my little boy, as does my mother.

I will die again next year, leaving Josephine a widow and Uncle Todd the guardian of little William. Of course, I will stay around, in the form of a gamekeeper or such, but it will give Josephine the opportunity to remarry and have a full, real life with someone who loves her and can give her more children. Alas, slumberers are infertile, men and women alike. That is the price of eternal life.

I have a son, I have a wife, and I have more relatives than I ever thought possible.

And I am dead.

But happy.

THE LUNATIC SONG
Callum McSorley

Her family had an illustrious name, so I took it when I married her. I signed away my old name on our wedding day and was glad that the past might be dead and buried, for at that time I no longer wanted anything to do with it and the man who owned it, called Charles Hale.

The wedding was at St. Paul's in town, the reception at the country estate owned by the bride's family—my family. The carriage-drivers wore top hats and bow ties, the horses were frocked in white, spattered with mud as they trotted through the unlaid road up the hill through Hampstead Village and on to Promontory House. Our first dance was to Schubert's 'Adagio in C,' played by a string quintet. There was no pianist to accompany. I hadn't requested this myself but Mr. Myerscough, the father of the bride, was a perceptive man, so there was no pianist. Our marriage proposal was something of a not-altogether-unpleasant surprise for him and, secretly, a relief. He knew more than he let on, I guessed. His daughter did not credit him this.

We danced, our cheeks brushed, I felt her lips touch my ear. She whispered, "Kiss me again, brother dearest, and this time try not to look so revolted."

Her cheek was soft and rouged and disgusted me like touching a moldy peach, but our relationship was nothing if not competitive so I replied, "You're the one who looks as if she's been made to kiss a trout, sis," and kissed her. The crowd around us cheered and then joined the dance.

The dancing went on. Then there was the meal, cutting the cake, and, worst of all, working our way around the room to be congratulated by each guest individually. I knew a few faces but most were strangers, friends of Mr. Myerscough. I could tell instantly the ones who had heard the rumors from Europe. Their teeth looked like knives when they smiled. I was almost waiting for one of them to get drunk and say something outright, but it didn't happen. It came close though. A man called Darnley, who had some connection to the church but was mostly just—like many of the guests—a rich man and nothing more, asked me, "And why are you not serenading us yourself tonight? Such a talent, why I can't remember the last time I heard you play! It would have been, let me see..." He made a great show of struggling to recall it. "...Before you went off to Europe. Where was it again? Paris? Berlin?"

"Both. And Amsterdam, Budapest, Prague, St. Petersburg, all over," I answered.

He smiled. The knives appeared. "St. Petersburg, how *interesting*. But you must let us hear you play again! Just one song, how about that?"

Mr. Myerscough rescued me. "Not on his wedding night, Arthur! If a man is allowed a night off it would be his wedding night!" He laughed just a little too loud as he pushed us away to the next guest. There would be no piano tonight. I hadn't played for some time.

Eventually, it was over, and the newly wedded couple made their way up the stairs to their newly prepared bedroom. The candles were lit, the bedsheets of the four-poster turned down, its curtains drawn aside, the handle of the brazier sticking out from within the sheets. Gilt-edged frames burned around thick oil paintings too dark and old to be properly seen by the light of the chandelier. The view from a grand bay window attested to the house's name; the drop into the valley below was almost sheer, the wild Heath stretched out beyond, the healing iron waters burbled along at the bottom which I could hear but couldn't see.

I had never been in this room before, though for all intents Promontory House had been my home for these past twenty years. Or if not home, then headquarters. I was ten when I came to live here under my patron, Mr. Myerscough, now my father-in-law. I boarded at the conservatoire in the city during term time, spent summers traveling and playing concerts. Charles Hale, child prodigy. A busy life for a teenager. But Christmas and Easter, those holidays were Promontory House and Hampstead Heath. And of course, sweet sister Lizzie.

Lizzie flopped down on the bed. "And so, what now? Are you going to ravish me? Take my virginal white lily and turn it into a red rose?"

I threw my jacket over a wingback chair and busied myself making drinks from an array of crystal decanters and jugs. "One of those flowers is poisonous and the other has thorns," I said. "Besides, I believe that maiden voyage has sailed."

Lizzie laughed. "And has well and truly sunk." She patted her belly, though there was not much to see yet. The short notice wedding was Lizzie's idea but it served both of us. It would put to bed the rumors that followed me back from the continent while providing an explanation for her condition. When I pointed out some simple arithmetic could undo her plot she answered, "The important thing is the numbers coincide with your return to London, if not the wedding. Father might think we jumped the gun, but we're married now, there is little scandal in that. We've known each other a long time, Charlie, and finally we are husband and wife, and he is to have a legitimate grandchild. That's what is important. Besides, he doesn't *want* to know so he won't do the sums." I felt this last was the truest. Mr. Myerscough had no illusions about his daughter, or his surrogate son. Which is not to say he wasn't loving or caring: he was both.

As children we quickly fitted into the role of rivals, each vying for their father's attention. I was a usurper, she was a spoilt brat. But like real siblings, there was love there too, buried deep—very deep. Now sham brother and sister had become sham husband and wife. "Not so very different from all the others," Lizzie said. That night we slept fitfully in our chaste marital bed, then thereafter went back to our own rooms in the house, as was proper.

***

Lizzie announced the pregnancy around five weeks later; she calculated she was close to three months pregnant by that time. Mr. Myerscough was a little too surprised, a little too merry when he proposed the toast. Lizzie didn't notice. She pulled me aside that day, into the deep shadow of the long gallery where the Myerscough ancestors kept watch, and said, "Try smiling, Charlie. You've recently found out you are to be a father for the first time. It's a *joyous* occasion. We're celebrating. Wedding night luck, eh? Look happy!" She pinched my cheek hard then headed for the main hall before quickly turning back and adding, "But not too happy!" As she walked away I noticed the way she was arching her back, her stomach thrust forward, her hand coming to rest on it, the bump yet barely visible. She was beginning to enjoy all this. I was beginning to realize my part wasn't over yet, wouldn't be for a long time.

She was right though. After the wedding I had returned to the folds of the black cloud that had plagued me since arriving home. I had not performed, nor sought out work of any kind. I had not even been seen in public, in fact, I had not traveled as far as Hampstead Village in all that time, the wedding ceremony being the one exception. I now hid under the guise of the happy honeymooner who couldn't bear to be away from his wife. It was a usefully polite way of turning down all would-be visitors and concerned friends and shameless gossips. The baby would make this alibi all the stronger, and that thought, in the end, made me smile.

It wasn't just a public retreat, though. The ebony Steinway in the parlor, where Mr. Beach had drilled me on Hanon's notorious exercises as a boy, remained untouched. It wasn't sheeted so it gathered dust, as did the vast music library Mr. Myerscough had curated for me. Even Lizzie, who was a fair player herself—many girls from such households learn to play the piano to increase their marriageability, God knows why—left it alone, as if it too was cast under my gloomy spell of silence. One might hit the key and hear nothing come out. I began to avoid the parlor altogether.

Instead, I took long walks on the Heath with the dogs, a miscreant pack of mongrels Mr. Myerscough had taken in one-by-one over the years. No gun dogs or working animals for him, his pets were rescues, each one found wanting on the street while Mr. Myerscough was on sojourn in London, and brought back, fed up and fattened, and made tame. I had an affinity for these animals—"Oh I do wonder why?" came Lizzie's sarcastic voice in my head—and their slobbering, boundless affection was a source of some comfort. There were even moments when I watched them bound among the hills and chase each other around the trees and splash through the filthy, freezing brooks and I would cry, "On, my boys, on!" and I would forget everything. The past was lost in the icy mist that hung in palls over the drab and dreaming landscape, and I felt, not happy, but free. It was always temporary. The Charles Hale I had hoped to bury under a new name always came back, just as bitter and ruined—buried alive, so it seemed.

I returned to the house from one such walk, intending to do nothing more strenuous with the rest of my day than clean the mud off my boots, to find I had been ambushed.

"He's been waiting for nearly an hour," said Mr. Myerscough, who had himself been lingering by the door.

"Then at least have Stevens fetch him a drink and a slice of cake before he leaves," I replied.

"He has had two already."

"Then it has not been a wasted journey."

"Charles, please." Mr. Myerscough did not raise his voice, he never did, but he had a certain way of speaking sometimes—a precise, stiff tone—that was terribly effective at getting a child to do as he or she was told. But I was no longer a child. "Just speak to the man. Just to say hello, just to turn him down in person, with a smile on your face. Introduce him to Elizabeth, tell him about the baby. All this moping around isn't good for you, and it's not good for your reputation either."

"My reputation?" We had never yet spoken directly about what happened in Europe, though Mr. Myerscough, ever the protective patron, had been instrumental in keeping me from official investigation. He had a name, he had money, he had influence. Pietre, on the other hand, had none of these. I was the lucky one, for all the luck we had been granted.

"And mine. You are a Myerscough, officially now. You are my son."

A child after all...The man was waiting in the parlor, scanning the volumes of music manuscript on the shelves, his back to the door, a glass of brandy cupped in his right hand. "Good afternoon, Mr....Danforth, was it?" I said.

"A remarkable collection," he said, not turning around. He pointed, "Ah! Bach's 'Goldberg Variations.' I do believe I saw you perform those one summer at Hanover Square. You must have been twelve years old. Quite remarkable!"

"For an Englishman," I replied. "In St. Petersburg they have children playing the 'Variations' before they are finished nursing."

"So I've heard!" He laughed and turned to face me. He had a healthy excess of chin and cheeks, and flabby white-haired brows which clashed cheerfully with his swollen, purple nose. "You have seen the Conservatory yourself?"

"Yes, I tutored there as a guest briefly. There was little I could teach." I recalled then a particularly precocious boy called Sergei who made my ten-year-old self, a proclaimed prodigy, seem a rank amateur. (I closed this line of thought for I knew it too led to Pietre.)

"I'm sure that is not true, sir!" Mr. Danforth said and drained his glass. "Will you join me in another?" He didn't wait for an answer before he started busying himself with the glasses and bottle left out on the hearth by Stevens.

"And to what do I owe the pleasure of your company, Mr. Danforth?"

Again, he seemed not to hear me. "I agree, though there does seem to be some kind of magic at work in that Russian school. They're turning out virtuosos by the hundred, all of them little Mozarts, child prodigies like yourself. One finds though that the sooner they start climbing, the sooner they reach the peak, don't you agree?" The challenge was in his eyes as well as his words. I looked away. It was true. Even before the disheartening visit to the St. Petersburg Conservatory I had begun to feel as if I was slowing, becoming mired in the increasingly frenetic cacophony of the sounds I created. Contemporaries intimated that I might be distracted, and maybe I was, but if love is a distraction then it is a worthy one.

I didn't have to reply. He continued: "How long have you been back in London now? Two months, three? I daresay I thought I'd have been seeing more of you. Not personally, but on the stage. I'm a big fan, you know. I go to every concert I can. I also happen to be, if I may say so, a generous donor to the conservatoire, as well as several other smaller music schools in England. You may have heard my name at some point, I don't doubt, for I am also a good friend of your benefactor and father-in-law, which is why he granted me audience with you while turning away so many others."

"Well, Mr. Danforth, I daresay you will know I have recently wedded and have been somewhat preoccupied—"

"Yes, I heard your wife was *enceinte*. Congratulations!" He lifted his glass in a toast then took a deep quaff. I held mine in hand, untasted.

"Thank you. Forgive my ignorance, Mr. Danforth, but did I meet you at the ceremony last month? There were many faces and good friends of Mr. Myerscough; I couldn't hope to remember all of them." I knew he had definitely not been at the service; I am actually better than most with faces. However, he ignored my barb so completely he might not have heard it at all.

"Mr. Hale, let me ask you something—"

"It is Myerscough now."

"Quite. Forgive me. Now let me ask you, Mr. Myerscough, what do you know of a man called Lawrence Roper?"

I smiled. "He is a fine pianist, an accomplished composer, and a mass murderer."

"You are familiar with the story then?"

"I recall what was in the press. How long ago? Eleven years?" The ghoulish story of the musician and madman Lawrence Roper was impressed firmly in my mind for two reasons. The first was the outlandish grotesquery of it, which shocked the public, myself included. The second was it coincided with my first studies abroad. I was a young Englishman with surprising talent and inventiveness as a pianist on the up in the tight circles of classical music, much as Roper had been at that time, which caused my new foreign compatriots to suggest—as a joke of course—that I too may be hiding a deadly secret. Pietre even took to calling me "Il Pazzo," particularly when astonished at some technical feat of playing I had impressed him with. I liked it. More so because it came from him.

"Let me refresh you on the details. Let me refresh myself also." He poured himself another glass of brandy. "They called them the Townhouse Supper Murders. Lawrence Roper, a musician who was becoming somewhat renowned, was invited to play at a private gathering hosted at the London home of a wealthy gentleman by the name of Catesbury—a man not unlike myself—with a small crowd of close friends, all genteel, all of a certain class, of course. What kind of money they paid him to perform such an intimate show I can only guess at."

"And what do you guess it at?" I was already beginning to see where this might be leading.

"All in good time. Now, this is where fact and speculation converge. Roper plays for them. He plays a particular song, a melody of his own invention, one that has never been committed to manuscript. Of that, I am sure, for I have done extensive research. This melody, as one version of the story goes, drove the crowd to commit barbarous acts upon each other, as if they were under some violent spell cast by the music. The other, mundane and likely true version, goes that two individuals known to Roper broke in during the performance and butchered Catesbury and his guests. These culprits, claiming to be disciples of Roper's music, came forward of their own will after Roper had been arrested. Their testimonies, however, differ in several key areas and are a source of contention to this day. The fact remains, though, that by morning Mr. Catesbury and ten others were found dead, having greatly suffered in their final moments. So far as I can tell, there are only three people living who have heard this final, mortal melody, all of whom are inmates of Bethlem Hospital."

"And I'm sensing you intend to make yourself the fourth."

"No, that honor will be reserved for you, if you agree to take the job. I will be your audience."

"My audience?"

"A select group of men and women, all music lovers, who are keen to hear this much-mythologized piece, this, shall we call it 'Lunatic Song'?"

"I fear this speaks more of morbid interest in the macabre than love of music, Mr. Danforth."

"We are dealing with a lost masterpiece, Mr. Hale. I cannot live with the idea of it."

"I bet it's been keeping you up all last week."

Danforth chuckled. "You have me skewered all right, Mr. Hale—"

"Myerscough."

"Silly old man with passing fancies and enough money to indulge them, am I correct? One week he's buying up art galleries, the next he is in his garden digging up bones. You may laugh at the codger, but it is such men that put bread on your plate, is it not?" He gestured to the piano and the shelf of music books, taking in the high ceilings and grand fireplace in the sweep of his hand. "I myself fund several music schools."

"So you said." I became aware of the glass frozen in my rigid hand.

"In England and elsewhere, some in Europe, even. How long did you live on the continent?"

"The last three years, but I've been coming and going for near twenty— concerts and tuition and the like." My voice was flat and dry. It didn't occur to me to drink the brandy.

"Not going back anytime soon though, eh?" He smiled, knives flashed. He drained his glass and set it down on the tray. "It is a lovely old building; I can see why you are reluctant to leave it. And the Heath, it must be wonderful for the dogs! Potentially dangerous for children though, no?"

"Well, it will be a while before we have to worry about that."

"Nature can be lonely sometimes."

"I find I actually quite like the solitude."

"Do you now?"

***

With every yard I descended into London, the air got blacker. The rotten stench of the Thames was on the wind, providing the only relief from the greasy coal smoke that settled above the streets like a cloud atop a mountain. The hansom's thin curtains weren't enough to stop it pervading the carriage and I soon felt suffocated. I held a handkerchief up to my face and I cursed myself for the weak-willed child I am. Of course, it was Mr. Myerscough who convinced me to consider the request in the end, though I doubt if he understood fully what Danforth required of me. I guessed he believed it to be little more than a private performance for some well-to-do types from the city. Provide some musical accompaniment to their supper. "It will be good for you, Charles, a way to get back into it, slowly," he said. We turned into a narrow, cobbled alley; from the window of the cab I observed a woman throw a pail of what I could only hope to be brown water into the street from the steps of a blackened tenement. I cursed my father-in-law, too.

Before long the horse was clattering down the Lambeth Road. We crossed the fetid river and passed the cathedral and the palace with its gloomy gatehouse and forbidding battlements. Watchmen were visible in the crenels, leering down at the street like gargoyles.

Not much further on we came to the gates of Bedlam, as the Londoners called it, and the carriage juddered to a stop. From its proud chapel dome and grand Corinthian columns holding up the porch, it could be mistaken for a museum. Hidden behind a shroud of oaks there appeared to be a fine garden. In fact, the only thing that attested to its true identity was the gate and fence itself, which stood twenty feet tall and was topped with black iron spikes like poisoned arrowheads. That and the mournful call of the wind, which I realized after a minute of contemplation was not the wind at all.

The driver had been instructed to wait for me there, and took nips from a flask to ward off the chill that seeped from the dying trees.

"Mr. Myerscough?" The man in a white uniform that awaited me looked more like a boxer than a nurse. He was every bit as broad and sturdy as the pillars on either side of the gate which supported the gaslights. "This way, please. Dr. Hill is waiting for you in the chapel. He prefers to receive guests there."

The orderly led me down the path through what was indeed a fine garden, if a little too neat to be called beautiful. The building loomed above; the wind blew. Of course, it wasn't the wind. The entranceway had a smell, a tang of carbolic and vinegar that rose from the floor in a vapor. The orderly must have seen my nose wrinkle as he said, "You get used to it. Better than the alternative."

"The alternative?"

"You'll understand when you get onto the ward."

He led me down the hallway, past other similarly hulking specimens in sweat-stained white tunics, and then we were under the grand dome. Light sliced down from the high windows, diffusing into a twilight hue by the time it reached the pews. Of the men on the walls, I recognized Saint Bartholomew and John the Baptist. All were beatific in their suffering. As proper Englishmen should be, they said—for they were surely drawn as Englishmen.

"Dr. Hill, Mr. Myerscough to see you," the orderly said.

A man stood up from the front row and turned towards us. He was thin and had a pallor to match his doctor's coat. From his dark hair, sprinkled with just a grain of gray here and there, I guessed he was only a little older than myself, but thick spectacles gave his face a distorting agelessness, his eyes grown huge and flat. I got the unnerving impression that if he took the spectacles off, there would be nothing underneath them.

"Mr. Myerscough, a pleasure." He held out a white hand. I shook it, keeping my gloves on.

"The pleasure is mine, Dr. Hill."

"The chapel is not the place for insincerity, sir," he replied, but he was smiling. "Though it is my aim that every visitor shall leave glad of their visit, however they arrive."

"Do you get many visitors?"

"Those gentlemen, and their ladies, who wish to become sponsors are encouraged to take a tour of the hospital."

"Sponsors? How much do they donate, a shilling a go?"

The doctor's smile paled. "People have a lot of preconceived notions about hospitals like this. My father was head practitioner here for near fifty years, and my grandfather was head practitioner before him. Things have changed a lot in that time. You will see."

"Well, I hope you understand I am not here for the tour, sir."

"Your good friend Mr. Danforth has explained at length the reason for your visit, and I would like you to know I am only in agreement because I believe it may benefit *my* patient. Mr. Roper hasn't played the piano since his arrest over a decade ago, and I have come to believe it may, in some way, be therapeutic for him."

"You are not worried about this song of his being played?"

Dr. Hill chuckled. "It was no song that butchered those men and women. The lady and gentleman who committed that atrocity are locked up right here."

"They are both mad?"

"Wouldn't you think so?"

"So then why is Lawrence Roper here if he didn't do anything?"

"Because regardless of his action or inaction, he is an unwell man. You will see."

He led me from the chapel, the pugilist orderly walking ahead with his keys on a large iron ring. These he used to open two sets of heavy doors that barred entry to the north wing. "For the criminally insane," Dr. Hill explained. "The east and west wings are for male patients and female patients, respectively. This, however, is a mixed ward."

As soon as the last door opened the smell hit. It overwhelmed the stinging chemical smell of the corridors and entranceway. Human waste, human sweat, moldering skin, and decaying teeth. Then came the noise, the wailing howl that had carried beyond the walls on the wind, now a frenetic baying and screeching. My heart battered against the constraint of my body around it. The wing had two tiers which stretched far to the back wall, lit by burning gasoliers that cast pale shadows across the floor in the shape of twisted, leafless trees. Slices of cold sunlight filtered through glass panels in the roof, revealing the grains of sawdust floating in the air. Scraggly, filthy faces pressed against the bars. Chains rattled. There was an air of expectation, the howling pitched up. It was the moment before the curtain was drawn...

We climbed a tight, spiral staircase—more like a ladder, really—and started down the right-hand landing. I kept well to the railing, away from the barred cells. "Rooms," Dr. Hill corrected me when I asked why the floors of some of the cells were covered in sawdust. "The sawdust is for those patients who are incontinent. It makes it easier to clean." It also added to the overall impression that I was in some kind of zoo. Most of the men and women we passed were in some way manacled, often pinned to the brick wall by a long chain that took in their wrists and ankles. Some wore braces around their necks and torsos and others bore devices that looked fit for a trap pony.

We came to the last cell. "I will give you some privacy, Mr. Myerscough, but Price will wait here to escort you back." The orderly leaned against the railing. "I will see you back in the chapel."

The man behind the bars was sitting on a stiff-looking bed bolted to the brick wall. Unlike the others I had seen, he was not chained or hobbled in any way. He could move freely around his "room" but he did not, and remained sitting on the narrow bed with his back straight, watching me. Though his hair and beard were long and streaked with gray, they were not unkempt, nor did he have the bedraggled and unwashed look of self-disregard shared by the mad. What was visible of his face had a gaunt handsomeness to it rather than emaciation, and his clothes—though thin and gray from boil-washing like the bedsheets—were not sweat-stained or befouled by the various excretions whose stink polluted the air. Books were piled neatly on the floor.

"Mr. Roper?" I almost felt I should stick my hand through the gap in the bars.

"I wouldn't have recognized you," he said. "The man looks nothing like the child. Not even the eyes are the same."

"You know me?"

"I saw you play. Charles Hale, the Mozart of Whitechapel."

"Nobody has called me that in a while." I smiled but then wasn't sure why.

"Hanover Square, just after Myerscough bought you up. Danforth informs me you're a real member of the family now."

"In the eyes of the law, at least. You have met Mr. Danforth?"

"Just the once. He paid a lot of money for the ticket."

"So you know why I'm here?"

"He wants me to teach you the song." He leaned forward and brought his hands together, clasping them on his lap. His fingers were long and fine-boned, the nails short and clean, an instrument in themselves.

"He wants me to play it for him. At some sort of supper party."

Roper smiled without showing his teeth. It conveyed no emotion, neither smirking disdain nor genuine happiness.

"Might be good for the old career, eh? Something bold and risqué to relight the fires."

"Did Danforth give you that idea?"

"I still keep up with the arts section." His head motioned to a bundle of newspapers among the books.

I'd had enough with shuffling my feet and conceding nervous smiles. "I'm not sure what it is Mr. Danforth expects me to say to convince you to take part in this charade, so I will just say that merely by showing my face here I feel my part to be well and truly done and I'd just as soon not—"

"Oh, I have already agreed. The purpose of this interview is to convince you."

***

And it did, because of something Roper said as I was readying to leave. He began to chuckle. It seemed every person I spoke to found mirth in my obvious irritation, behind every smile was hidden something they knew which I did not. "Why are you laughing?" I snapped.

"I was just thinking it might easily have been me outside those bars, and you in here."

"And how do you figure that? I'm no murderer."

"Nor am I, and yet..." He indicated the windowless walls of his cell. "Anything they can't understand is deemed madness. Even love. It would be nice to have a cellmate for a while."

As we drove back out of London the smog didn't choke me, nor the smells distract me or the traffic frustrate me. An image stood clear in my head of Roper's cell, but Roper was not in it. Instead, on the bed, sat Pietre. I closed my eyes and bid the horrific image to leave me, but instead, I joined him there on the bed, his cellmate. I felt sick, and it had nothing to do with the foul city or the rocking carriage that bid me away from it.

The fog over Hampstead Heath was lonely. A man could disappear in there. It tempted and appalled me. I was glad to be out of the hansom and closing the door of Promontory House behind me.

"Stevens?" I called out the butler's name, who shortly arrived laden with a silver tray, a decanter and a glass shining in the light of the sconces.

"Yes, sir?"

"Where can I find Mr. Danforth?" Danforth had stayed the night upon Mr. Myerscough's insistence. He accepted as if his arm had been twisted up behind his back.

"He is in the parlor, sir, I was just on my way to attend him."

"Let me." I snatched the tray from Stevens's hands before he could protest, his calls of "Please, sir!" following me down the hall.

I heard the piano keys plonking from outside the door, fat fingers picking away at 'Au Clair de la Lune.' Danforth, red-faced and bleary-eyed, was bent over the ivory teeth, squinting at his stupid fingers as they probed the instrument with robust carelessness, a keen but fumbling virgin. "I do say this thing may require tuning," he said. An empty glass rested on the lid. I lifted it and pushed it into his hand, filling it up again, near to the brim, from the decanter. I poured a slosh in the other glass and lifted it to his.

"I am accepting your offer. Now I want to know the details."

He smiled. He had crooked teeth. The knives were out in his eyes too now, slightly dulled by drink. His voice slurred. "I'm so glad to hear that, boy. They'll be ever so pleased. Your father-in-law too."

"Leave him out of this."

"You've made the right decision, you really have."

"When is this concert of yours to be held?"

"You will have three months to prepare. In that time Dr. Hill has ensured me you will have complete access to Roper. I'll have a piano sent over there and—"

"In his cell?"

"Well, that will be up to Dr. Hill and his staff."

"And you want the piece transcribed?"

"Now, see, this is where things get a bit delicate." Danforth took a long pull at his brandy. "Part of the deal I have made with Roper is that the song shall not be put down on paper, but—"

"And what is the rest of the deal? Why has he so keenly agreed to this?"

"I'd guess because he respects you as a fellow musician; he admires your talent and thinks you worthy to carry on his legacy."

Now it was my turn to smile a crooked smile. "He agreed before he even knew I was going to be a part of it, he said as much himself. What is he getting?"

"Very well. If he goes along with us, he will be moved to a small, private psychiatric hospital out of the city, one funded by myself and a few friends."

"Friends who will be in the audience at this supper of yours?"

"Yes. You've seen the conditions at Bedlam. It's not a place you'd want to stay the night, is it?" I felt the implicit threat. The brandy had made him less guarded.

"And how does Dr. Hill feel about it?"

"Dr. Hill is not for you to worry about. All *you* need to worry about..." He slurped his drink. "...Is getting some practice." He ran his fingers across the keys in a jarring glissando, the weights and hammers clunking like the wheels of a steam engine.

"Good day, Mr. Danforth." I drank my brandy down in one and turned to leave.

"You know, I wasn't being totally untruthful," he called out. "He really does have an interest in you."

***

Danforth left before dinner: "So as not to impose." Stevens laid out our meal in the dining hall. Mr. Myerscough congratulated me on accepting the job. "It will be good for you," he said again.

"But will it be good for Lizzie and the baby, me being away all day at that horrid place?" I tried to steer the conversation away.

"You're away all day anyway, dear, with those mutts," Lizzie said. "Besides, you call it horrid but isn't the madhouse awfully interesting?"

"Elizabeth, please, don't be so crass," Mr. Myerscough chided.

Lizzie was exactly the kind of person who would find a lunatic asylum interesting; I almost recommended she take Dr. Hill's tour. "It's a human menagerie," I said. "I could get you a room, if you like?"

"Listen to you both bickering away like...like an old married couple, after barely a month," Mr. Myerscough said. *Like children, like siblings.* What he didn't say, what he might have said, hung over the table and we finished our meal to the sound of silver scraping on china.

After Stevens cleared the table, I retired to the parlor. I did not have to ask not to be disturbed. A candle in hand, I ran the tip of my finger across the thin spines of the manuscript books. Mozart? Bach? Liszt? I came away empty handed and sat down on the bench. Danforth's glass had left a ring on the lid of the piano. I wiped at it, then let my fingers run over the ivory of the keys. Mendelssohn? Beethoven? In the end, I played not a note that night and lay in bed with my eyes open in the dark for a long time, listening to the river, the iron water, burbling away at the bottom of the hill.

In the morning, I resolved to tackle it in a practical manner, and so sat down at the piano with Hanon's 'The Virtuoso Pianist in 60 Exercises' spread out on the music stand. I then proceeded to torture myself for hours at a time. After three days of this, I was having fun. On the fourth morning I made the return trip to Bedlam. Again, I was met at the gate by that brute of an orderly and led through the trim garden and into the museum of mania.

"Welcome back, Mr. Myerscough," said Dr. Hill, who shook my hand under the great domed roof of the chapel. "I would like you to meet our chaplain, Reverend Kent."

"How do you do, sir?" said the reverend, a squat, balding man of sixty who took my hand in turn. The skin of his hand was soft, and reminded me of my cheek brushing Lizzie's during our first dance. It repelled me with a force equal to the asylum smell, to which I had not acclimatized and feared I would not ever. The drab cloth that shrouded him stood in stark contrast to the grand and colorful surroundings of the chapel. "I understand you are here to speak with Mr. Roper."

"I am here to take piano lessons from him, actually," I replied.

"And I am here to warn you against it. Are there no teachers among the righteous that walk outside these forsaken walls?"

"Forsaken? You don't think highly of your congregation, sir."

The doctor attempted to butt in: "What Reverend Kent means to say is that—"

"It is my mission to bring as many of these unfortunates to God as I can, sir, but some are irredeemably damned, in this life and the afterlife."

"Lawrence Roper, for example?"

"A devil, sir."

"He claims innocence. You don't believe him?"

"He will tell you many, pretty lies, Mr. Myerscough, I pray you do not heed them. He is a conjurer, a—"

"Kent!" Dr. Hill put his hand on the man's chest. "Now, Mr. Myerscough, come this way." He led me once more through the heavy doors and drafty corridors to the criminally insane ward, followed by the orderly called Price. "Forgive him, but Roper winds people up. He does it for fun, and the good reverend is an easy target. It was my father who appointed Kent, having overseen the construction of the chapel itself during his tenure."

"And I gather you believe the funds could have been better spent elsewhere?"

"I believe in the healing power of God, Mr. Myerscough, make no mistake, but practically I could do with a few more beds."

"A donation from our mutual friend Danforth could help with that. Not to mention the one vacated by Roper." Hill spun round, and for a moment I was trapped between his glare and the monstrous body of the orderly pressing up behind me.

"Price here had to haul that damn piano up to the second floor. He'll be keeping you company today."

I bowed my head in thanks at the glowering Price and we continued up to the cells. The stink of human waste was heavy in the air. Wild and wasted figures screamed out from behind barred doors. Chains rattled. The blue light of the gasoliers painted them as ghosts.

A cottage piano had been wedged into Roper's cell. He sat on the stool, his ankles lashed to its legs. He wore heavy-looking cuffs on his wrists which were also bolted to the sides of the stool, the chain with just enough play so he could reach the keyboard. "Welcome, friends," he said. "Please do come in."

Price rattled through a hoop of keys until he found the right one and turned it in the lock which sang of rusty cogs and infernal mechanics. "I'm afraid the door will have to be locked again once you are inside, sir," Dr. Hill explained, "but Price will be waiting right outside with the key ready, should anything happen. Not that it will." He forced a smile, which I returned.

Only once inside, with the door shut, the lock tumblers turned, did I feel how truly thick and sturdy those bars were. Roper's room smelled of damp book paper and urine from the chamber-pot kept under the bed, in some bizarre semblance of decorum. "Come, sit down," he said, with that flat smile, as if laughing at an inside joke. There was little space on the stool. Our shoulders and thighs touched. *A smiling murderer*, I thought, *just waiting to get his chains around my neck!* I dared not put my hands on the keys first for fear they would shake.

"How would you like to begin?" I asked.

"Tell me what you have been playing."

"Truthfully, I've been going over Hanon's exercises."

"That rusty, eh?" With a flourish that rattled the chains and made me jump, he brought his fingers into position and rattled up and down a hasty variation of 'Exercise 47.' "Me too, so it seems. It's been, oh, a decade or so since I've touched a piano."

"Over three months," I said, and played a near-perfect imitation of the exercise from memory. The room was cold, the keys were cold. My fingers trembled. The sound, within the low and narrow stone confines of the cell, was crashing and jarring. Every slight vibration of dissonance and minute problems with tuning were amplified and exposed in ugly, echoing waves.

"Bravo." As the sound dissipated I could hear the moans coming from beyond the bars, that fell wind. "We both need a little practice then. What is in your bag?"

I lifted the bag, containing several scores I'd picked from the Myerscough library, onto my knee. When I opened the clasp, Roper immediately thrust his hands in and snatched the papers out, making me jump for a second time. From the corner of my eye I saw Price move towards the door, just a fraction, a reflex, then stop. Roper acted as if he didn't notice either of us twitch. He flipped through the pages of manuscript, licking the tip of his index finger to separate them, every so often making a humming noise or a grunt. His eyes flickered back and forth across the paper. He read the way a starving man eats. "How about this?" He spread the music out on the stand: Mozart, 'The Rake Punished.' I squinted; it was hard to see in the dim light of the cell.

"Well?" he said, but before I could begin he started playing himself. The stone walls meant we might have been in a cave, everything came out loud and breathless, the intonations and dynamics lost in the endless reverberation. The high end came out as smashing crystal, the low as battlefield noise. Under it was the moaning, which turned to screaming and wordless, incomprehensible yelling and soon overtook even the thunderous hammers of the piano, the same in my chest. Chains rattled, spirits wailed. A chamber-pot hit the bars of the cell next door with a dull *thunk*, stewed piss crashing in a wave over the floor and onto Price's shoes. "Stop!" He clung to the bars, sticking his face between them. "Stop!" But Roper kept playing, and the screaming continued until Hill and Kent came charging down the corridor, shoes soaking and slipping, and ordered Price to open the door.

The music stopped; the howling continued. The reverend's face and bald head were red. There were tears in his eyes. "The song! He's trying to tear the place apart with his devil's song! I told you! I told you he would—"

"That is not the song, Reverend!" I shouted over him. "That is just Mozart." Roper began to laugh then, a deep, handsome rumble. He smiled, a real smile. It was beautiful and horrible. I looked away.

I stepped out, carrying the sheet music in a bundle, and Price locked the door behind me. Hill began to usher us back down the ward to the spiral stairs and the door at the far end.

"Hale!" Roper called. I looked back. "I want to hear something new!"

***

On the way home I was light-headed and giddy and afraid. The noise of the screaming prisoners followed me. *It might easily have been me outside those bars, and you in here.* He wanted to hear something new. I smiled as I pulled music from the shelves that night, flipping through and compiling. "New" could be just about anything scored in the last decade, but I was meticulous, I was searching for something, something just...I wanted to impress him. The realization thumped down into my stomach like an anchor from a ship. A sickness rose in me again.

"It's a bit late for practice, Charlie," Lizzie said, coming into the parlor. "Father is in bed already, you know." She was right. I was working purely by candlelight.

"It's okay, I'm not planning on playing, just preparing."

"Preparing for your madhouse concert?"

"The concert won't be in the madhouse, and anyway, what do you know of it?"

"Only what little Father does, and the crumbs you've deigned to give your wife." I couldn't decide if I had heard the expected sarcasm in her voice or not.

"My wife..." She had her hand on her belly. "How...how are you feeling, Lizzie?" She rolled her eyes and said goodnight.

It was nearly a week later when I managed to return to the asylum; Danforth and Hill had to go through another bout before the "experiment" continued. Partly this was due to the reverend's implacable fury that Hill wanted further practice sessions held in the chapel, away from the other patients. Indeed, as I opened the doors to the hallowed place where the mad worshipped, Reverend Kent blew out the other direction in a tempest, his head and face a remarkable shade of puce, as if his entire skull were a blood vessel ready to burst.

Unlike Roper's rigid patience upon our first meeting, as I entered he was mulling away at the keys, playing a bagatelle whose bouncing and chirpy notes echoed cheerfully up and down the great church dome above. The acoustics were much more pleasing than the cave of the cell. It struck me then, the restraint he must have shown in waiting for me the day before. I remembered his starving eyes devouring the black notes of the music.

Roper spotted me and finished the piece with a music hall flourish. "Good morning, Mr. Hale! Come, take a pew." He shifted over on the piano bench. He was chained to it as he had been the week before. "What have you got for me?"

I sat down on the edge of the seat, once again painfully aware of the closeness of our bodies. It was with a schoolboy's delicate pride that I laid out the piece on the stand. After days of agonizing, (Why was it so difficult?) I had chosen a piece from Dvořák's second series of piano duets, 'Op. 72.' The Bohemian composer created unique "four-hands" pieces, that is to say, songs played on one piano by two players. Perfect for our situation. I estimated Dvořák's first book of Slavonic Dances to have been created around the time of Roper's incarceration, so I selected the second book to be on the safe side. I was immensely pleased with this choice and waited to hear what he would say. "Funny," he said.

We began to fumble through the piece together. "Cheat! You've had a go at this already!" Roper accused, smiling, as he hit another wrong note. The cuffs and chains got in the way of his movement and more than once we tripped over each other as our hands strayed into the middle ground of the keyboard.

"That one was mine!" I said, when his little finger landed atop my own on C#. He began to do it deliberately after that, keeping up only a rudimentary semblance of the lower melody. Every so often he would miss, his hand stayed by the cuffs fixing him to the stool.

When Dr. Hill called time on our second lesson I asked Roper when we would get to learning his song. He simply replied, "That was fun. Let's have more fun." I urged the driver on to Promontory House as quickly as possible, eager to tear through the shelves of music again. Then, eating dinner across from the quiet and sober faces of my adopted family, I reminded myself of what Roper had done. Allegedly done. And I reminded myself of Pietre.

Yet, we continued to have fun. I visited twice a week, a limitation stipulated by Dr. Hill following the second round of discussions, which gave me some twenty-odd practice sessions before the final recital. We worked away at various pieces but often returned to Dvořák's modern folk music. Roper was fast and intuitive, his long, thin fingers exquisitely expressive, and there was something else, something people can recognize but can't describe, that thing which marks an individual out—he's talented, he's *special*. Such whispers follow a performer as they rise up. We played and laughed but talked little of anything but music. Our tastes and opinions complemented, even where they differed or outright contradicted. Arguments were playful and teasing. In this way, ten lessons passed and we had still not come around to his song. I asked when we would properly begin.

"Properly?" I was becoming used to his blank, handsome smile. "Let me ask you, Charles, are you worried?"

"Worried?"

"If we sit down next time and I play you my song, are you not worried it will make me kill you?" He clanked the chains on his arms and legs. "Or you kill me?"

"No, I don't believe it will. Nor does Dr. Hill."

"Okay then...next time."

Price the orderly, who was stationed outside the chapel doors, came in and took Roper back to his room. Reverend Kent caught me as I was leaving. I hadn't seen much of the man in all this time, no more than a skulking, disapproving shadow. The idea came to me then that he had been keeping Price company.

"Enjoying the music?" I asked.

"I want you to speak to someone. Follow me." As if I had no business of my own to attend to. He led me to the east wing, an unfamiliar orderly taking us through the doors. The east wing, reserved for male patients, was near identical to the other ward, except its fixtures were much older, the bars rotten and steps bowed. The smells of human decay were accompanied by the damp of the decaying building itself. It had been over a month since I'd last had to tread the ward and the smell assaulted me as if for the first time. I gagged and put my handkerchief to my face. Most of the cells were occupied by two, three or even, in some cases, four men who lived in soiled sawdust and overflowing chamber-pots. For every one that raged and chewed the skin from the bones of their fingers was one that was silent and staring, fixed in place.

The man we came to see had a room to himself. "He was supposed to be on the criminally insane ward but Dr. Hill wanted the three of them kept separate," the reverend explained. "This is Mr. Archibald McGowan, who confessed to committing the Townhouse Supper Murders at the behest of Lawrence Roper. Mr. McGowan, tell Mr. Myerscough here what you have told me."

McGowan was a wretch. Toothless gums sucked at filthy fingers. His eyes rolled deep in their hollow sockets. He spoke in a stuttering, slurring manner like a drunk. "I—I didn't d-do it. I s-said I did but I...I wasn't there, s-sir. Honest."

"But you said you were. You said you took a knife to at least six of the men and women yourself."

"I-I didn't. I didn't!"

"You said it in court."

"The song made me do it! Th-that's what I said."

"No, you just said you weren't there."

"I-I-I..."

I turned on Reverend Kent. "This man is mad, he's changing his mind minute by minute."

"There was no evidence that Mr. McGowan was at the scene of these crimes," Kent said, "only his statement. And as you said yourself, he is mad. It is the same story for Lucy Bremen, the other confessor."

"And she is here too? Can I speak to her?"

"Hill didn't tell you then?" There was a hint of a smirk on his fat face.

"Tell me what?"

"Lucy Bremen hanged herself in her cell the day the piano arrived."

***

The next lesson, Roper was due to show me this song of his, and I approached those black gates with trepidation, the reverend's gurning face following me wherever I went. I couldn't sleep these past nights for imagining some woman swinging by her neck. Those awful chains, clinking, haunted me, and I smelled sawdust on the wind over the Heath. Pietre called to me, wherever he was...

As with my first visit, he was waiting patiently on the piano stool, his hands folded in his lap, pleasant-bland smile on his lips. I saw it immediately as mock solemnity; beyond the stiff back was the playful and boyishly enthusiastic pianist I had come to know over the weeks. Unlike previous visits, I couldn't return this sentiment.

"I want you to tell me what happened," I said.

"You've been speaking to Mr. McGowan?" He might have guessed, or maybe Price had informed him.

"He is a confused man, his version of the story isn't, well…"

"Dr. Hill believes it," he pointed out.

"Does he? I struggle to understand what Dr. Hill believes. He keeps you chained up after all."

"But he's willing to let me play my song, is he not?"

"Yes, I rather thought he'd be here with us today, actually."

"Part of the deal, I expect. No interruptions."

"Are you going to tell me your version of the story?"

"Sit down." He pointed me to the front row pew, rather than shifting over on the stool. I obeyed. "Listen carefully now." He smiled, not blank or pleasant this time; there was something behind it. Mischief, maybe. It made him appear more handsome than ever. Younger too.

He began his tune, a soft, plinking melody accompanied by the rattle of his cuffs. It birthed into something light and sad, low notes hanging, the melancholy air reeking of autumnal rot, sawdust…Robust melody was subverted by contrapuntal movements, off-kilter and dizzying, becoming jarring and sickening, the lingering after-taste of that sad sweetness and soil…Rhythmic stabs, joyous progression…It was a folktale and an epic, love and loss and death writ large and lived small…It was a dance, it was diving into a roiling cauldron to be destroyed or purified…It was, ultimately, nothing I had heard before. Hints here and there of the famous dead composers, pickpocketing from the living, I imagined even a hint of Dvořák, certainly there were sections where the sprawling, shuddering, swiftness of the melody seemed to require four hands to play. On the shallow level of immediate thought, I realized truly how difficult this task would be, somewhere deeper I knew I had been changed by this music, a feeling I hadn't felt since…I remembered Pietre playing 'Moonlight Sonata' in a practice room of the Paris Conservatoire three years ago, long after hours. I hid out of sight and he pretended not to notice me watching. The same scene repeated in St. Petersburg years later, where someone else watched too, out of sight.

"Tell me, what do you think?" He asked.

My mouth was dry. I attempted to stutter out some answer but instead came out with, "We better get started."

So together we began playing the 'Lunatic Song.' Roper would not permit me to take down any notes, so I was forced to memorize it beginning to end. Like mechanics, we broke down the beautiful music and laid it out, piece by piece, end on end. For the first time since returning to London I was brimming with thoughts of performances and applause and, more than that, creativity, life itself.

At home, I practiced with little fear of what the song may do to the household. Indeed, it seemed to have little effect, except that Lizzie began to hover around the parlor to listen in. She found the opening sections pleasing but the later ones: "Ghastly...I can see why they locked him up! What happened to music being pretty?"

"What happened to you being pretty?" I retorted. I was aiming for the teasing banter of our childhood but she seemed genuinely hurt instead and sulked around refusing to speak to me for days after. Mr. Myerscough even went as far as to mention this to me—he usually made an effort not to notice the chaste distance between myself and Lizzie—and gave me a good dressing down. Was this not *her* idea after all? *Her* scam? I wanted to scream that it wasn't even my child! That I wasn't a Myerscough! I wanted to let the dogs loose on the hills and chase down the wild animals myself. But the rage passed, and I had work to do.

The weeks went by and soon enough we reached the final lesson before the performance. When I entered the chapel I found that Price had chained Roper to a pew, where he was seated rather than at the piano. "Now it is your turn to perform it for me," he said. I played the whole thing, start to finish, and to my mind dropped not a note or beat.

It was my turn to ask: "What do you think?"

"Perfect. Perfect and perfunctory." There was no teasing smile to his criticism. It cut through me. I was a boy again. I wanted to scream, or cry.

"And what was wrong with it?" I asked, trying hard to keep my voice steady.

"You've lost something, Mr. Hale."

I scoffed and rolled my eyes, in imitation of my dear wife. "Spoken like an inarticulate hack," I spat. "And it's not Hale, it's Myerscough." Indeed, I'd heard this lame accusation before, usually from critics who lack the language of music and can find no constructive comment to make, or no particular foible to pick out. They say it about everyone eventually.

"You've lost something, Mr. Hale. Tell me what you've lost."

I stood up and grabbed my coat and my bag and my hat.

"Tell me what you've lost."

"Good day, Mr. Roper," I said. "Enjoy the rest of your stay." As I strode past he grabbed hold of my wrist. Those fine, bony fingers were as tight as the manacles he wore. A jolt of fear lit the hairs on my neck, and I almost called out for Price to free me.

"Tell me, Charles." His voice was soft now, his face kind, eyes pleading. I sat down next to him and I began to cry. I told him about Pietre. I told him about how I fell in love with him, and how he had fallen in love with me. I told him about how we were discovered, and how Mr. Myerscough bought me out of any trouble and brought me home to the safety of Promontory House. While Pietre...Shame washed over me and I began to cry hard again. I had pushed him from my mind all this time while I brooded in my self-confinement and attempted to bury myself, and him, and the past. The truth was I didn't know where he was now. Maybe he was chained up somewhere just like this, like a madman, because he loved me..."Il Pazzo."

Roper pressed his cheek to mine. My tears ran down his face.

"I didn't lose anything," I said. "They took it from me."

"Then take it back," he said, and kissed me on the mouth.

***

It was the night of the concert. A carriage arrived outside and took me to the city in the dark. Mr. Myerscough wished me good luck, Lizzie waved from an upstairs window. I kept the curtains shut to the trundling world outside and played Roper's melody in my head, fingers twitching, taking deep breaths. It had been some time since I had been this nervous before a performance. I was a twelve-year-old boy waiting behind the heavy stage curtain. We stopped at the bottom of the lawn of a Georgian townhouse, the building resplendent in its classical simplicity, warm candle-light spilling from tall, handsome sash windows.

Danforth himself answered the door, his cheeks already flushed red. "Welcome, Mr. Myerscough—"

"Hale."

"—I am so very pleased to see you. Come in, come in."

The hall was empty, the murmuring of voices coming from a lighted doorway ahead. I hung my traveling cloak and hat on the wall with the others and followed Danforth towards the sound of ladies laughing and the smell of pipe smoke. Danforth made the introductions and I nodded politely, shook hands, kissed cheeks that made me think of rotten peaches. He fetched me a glass of brandy which I smelled but did not drink. The men, in formal coattails, would give me a roguish wink; the ladies, in bustling skirts and exposing Bertha necklines, likewise fluttered their eyelashes. There was an air of the illicit, a secret fire that crackles between those who *know*. I felt as if I had entered some kind of masquerade ball, though the deformity of privilege was not hidden here.

The furniture was ghastly in its frou-frou patterns and fussy arrangement, and it was while admiring the ostentatiousness of a breakfront cabinet replete with untouched china I realized that while the house may belong to Mr. Danforth, the furniture did not. A large woven rug covered most of the hardwood floor and seemed out of place. He must have bought the house for a song...So this was where it actually happened—the Townhouse Supper Murders—where those fine ladies and gentlemen were driven to murder each other in some violent orgy. Or were victims of others, depending on your belief. And what did I believe? As I sat down to the piano, I was ready to find out.

There were fifteen people including Danforth. They arranged themselves close around the piano—a surprisingly plain, functional thing for such a room—creaking down to the floor like schoolchildren.

Danforth spoke: "Welcome all, to the home of the late Nicholas Catesbury. Twelve years ago this night, Mr. Catesbury and his guests sat down to a once-in-a-lifetime performance by a dangerous and dazzling young musician called Lawrence Roper. What happened during this performance has become a great mystery, though in the morning Mr. Catesbury and his friends were found having suffered violent deaths. From various policemen I have heard how Catesbury's ears were found tucked into his wife's bodice, who herself had her intestines forcibly removed. I have heard how a lady's nails were found buried deep in the eye sockets of another." The guests were nervous but smiling too. I could see fear, I could see enjoyment. "But what caused all this violence? Did they do this to themselves? Did Roper do it? Was it self-confessed accomplices Archibald McGowan and Lucy Bremen? Tonight, we may find out..." Danforth allowed himself a grin and some of the men chuckled. "Sit quietly, and hold your breath, while we listen to Lawrence Roper's 'Lunatic Song,' performed by Mr. Charles Hale."

I closed my eyes to the hungry faces and began to play. Could I have played them something else? Fooled them? Probably, but I didn't. My fingers quivered over the tremulous, opening notes and climbed up and up into the dancing maelstrom of Roper's imagination. Eyes tight shut, I felt again the exquisite pain, the longing in the drawn-out, hanging chords, the power they granted me. I crashed through the thunderous middle sections, the jarring, jangling counterpoints and discords—a tritone shivered through me like rubbing velvet the wrong way. I bit my tongue, tasted blood. I almost lost my way among the foundering coda, washing up in a tangled maze of near-impossible melodic runs. I saw Pietre's face, his outstretched hand. I played all the way to the end. I made it. My eyes were still closed when the last note rang out. I waited, breath held. Silence. I imagined the blood soaking into the rug, the last wheezing, choking splutters of life dribbling from the lips of ugly, fat men...Then the applause began.

***

That's how Charles Hale came back from the dead. There were more performances, I traveled up and down the country. Two months later I had even arranged a small tour in Europe, playing the song to small houses in the big cities. When I told Mr. Myerscough of this last, he sat me down for a serious talk about getting on with work and minding my business and how it was, "Marvelous, simply marvelous," that I had found my love of the piano again. He did not mention Pietre by name, but he was certainly warning me not to go looking. After all, I still did not know what had become of him, and maybe I never would. "It won't be long until the baby arrives either, don't stay away too long. If you miss the birth of your first child Lizzie will never forgive you, nor will you forgive yourself. Trust me as a father."

Lizzie's belly had grown massive. Her arched back and slow waddle were no longer just for show. She implored me to be there for her. I wanted to remind her that I was her husband in name only—where was the real father anyway?—but something about Mr. Myerscough's speech had stayed with me. After all, he wasn't my father, and yet...

However, there were concerts to be played first. And another thing, Mr. Danforth had asked me to visit with Roper in his new countryside abode. A new deal was made. Roper had agreed to let his song be recorded onto wax cylinder, the stipulation being that he played it, not myself. He was also keen to meet with me again—and, truthfully, I him—so it was that I elected to accompany the Volta gramophone (a quite ridiculous yet compelling-looking thing with its great horn bell and needle that looked like some torture instrument) out to Sussex in Danforth's carriage.

This asylum was little more than a small country estate with some stout bars over the windows of the clean, aristocratic house. The staff, including orderlies, had the look of gentlemen and were casually dressed. I was led upstairs into a bedroom where Roper, unchained, sat in a deep leather wingback at a window that looked out over the fields. Well-fed and living in comfort, he seemed altogether less gray. The same cottage piano we had practiced together on was against one wall of the room.

"Lovely day, Hale, good to see you again."

"Good to see you too, Mr. Roper. I had hoped to come sooner, but—"

"You were too busy having your back slapped?" He grinned.

"Something like that."

"I'm glad everything has went so well for you."

"For you too." I motioned to the airy, high-ceilinged room with its piano and bookshelf and comfortable-looking bed.

"A cage is a cage, Charlie, something you should do well to remember. It could just as easily be you sitting here and me heading off to Europe..."

I thanked him then, for the song, for teaching me. Two orderlies humphed the Volta up the stairs and into the room. We chatted a little, but we didn't play the piano and I found myself stretching for an excuse to leave.

"I will come and visit again, when I get back," I said.

"Goodbye, Charles." He blew me a kiss; I felt my face flush. I remembered that kiss, his lips wet from my tears.

Two days later it was in the papers: a violent bloodbath at a private insane asylum out in the countryside in Sussex. The inmates, orderlies, and doctors had been butchered. Possibly, they had butchered each other. Lawrence Roper was missing. Danforth kept his own name out of the papers, Mr. Myerscough kept mine out of them too. Naturally, the police came calling at Promontory House and I told them everything, everything but the kiss.

A week went by with no sign of Roper. Two weeks. I stayed at home, tried to muster up excitement about the imminent arrival of Lizzie's child, *my* child. Guilt nagged at me. Pietre haunted me. Was he not alive somewhere? In what condition? *A cage is a cage.* Was respectability also a cage? What about a loveless marriage?

Then a parcel arrived. Inside was a wax cylinder. I knew what was on there. The real 'Lunatic Song,' not the one he'd taught me, which was just some invention he'd cooked up and fed me. (I really had heard a hint of Dvořák in there after all.) Yet, what I had felt about that song—the pain, the sorrow, the relief, the power—was that real? I wondered.

I walked out onto the Heath, leaving the dogs at home. I walked for a long time, in loping circles, taking random changes in direction until I was sure I was lost in the wild and the fog. Then I buried the cylinder in the ground next to a knotted old tree. With the blade of the trowel, I carved a cross into its trunk.

I found my way back home eventually. It was dark by then. A shrill cry came from upstairs. I followed the growing sound and the smell of sweat and blood and excrement, those madhouse smells, into Lizzie's bedroom. It was a boy.

GOBLINS, GHOULIES, AND GHOSTIES
Cody D. Grady

Jennifer woke to the all-too-familiar sensation of massive hands wrapped around her throat, crushing her windpipe between thick, sweating digits. Struggling to breathe, she tasted bitter bile and copper rising up from the back of her throat. *This wasn't real. I didn't do that. I couldn't have.* The constriction increased as invisible hands clenched tighter. Whatever slight, cool breath that made its way into her lungs stopped suddenly. The slowly escaping air was soon replaced by a burning sensation that grew as Jennifer lost herself in the darkness. She needed to stop before it was too late. Panicking like this was the opposite of what the doctors had always told her to do. Jennifer grew lightheaded, dizzy...something had to be done, now. Before she lost consciousness. *No goblins, no ghoulies, no ghosts,* she thought, while attempting to slow her racing heart. *No goblins, no ghoulies, no ghosts. No goblins, no ghoulies, no ghosts.* She repeated the singsong mantra over and over. Her shallow, arrhythmic breaths deepened and then slowed. Those terrifying, clammy hands of death relaxed until she no longer felt their nightmarish fingers pressed into her throat. Jennifer realized she was smiling and for a moment was horrified at this discovery. Before she could focus on why, understanding slipped from her like drifting smoke as the dream receded from her mind.

Rain bounced softly on the window panes and the wind rustled the leaves on their branches. Somewhere in the woods a bird cried out, closely followed by an explosion of flapping wings as its flock took flight in the dead of night, heeding the watchman's warning of impending danger...spooked by something unseen. Jennifer still wasn't used to the sounds of nature being so close, having lived in the city for most of her life. The two-story farmhouse didn't put her at ease, either. The decades-old building came alive in the night, creaking and groaning in the dark as if it too suffered from night terrors. Pulling herself from sweat-sodden sheets, Jennifer struggled to sit upright and then climb out of bed, wincing slightly as her feet touched the cool, hardwood floor. Her skin was clammy with cold sweat, and her hands trembled uncontrollably. These nights when Steve was away for work were the worst. Jennifer longed to curl up against his chest, a crushing comfort that would warm her icy goose flesh and push the horrors away. Her husband was a thousand miles away though, and the only comfort to be found in bed was thick down pillows she had arranged in his general shape. It was a trite and childish reaction to the situation, but this practice had helped her sleep most nights. Except for ones like these.

Stepping into the master bathroom, her numb feet found the thick bath mat, which Jennifer happily gripped with tingling toes. Running lukewarm water from the silver tap, she splashed several handfuls across her sweaty brow, hoping to chill the fever brought on by the nightmare. As she massaged the soothing liquid into tensing flesh, Jennifer imagined she could wipe away the night terror and the lingering fear its images had left in their wake. She wanted to be washed clean of these horrors that visited her; stealing restful slumber with visions of violence, rape, and death. A ridiculous and childish wish, perhaps, but one she wanted more than anything else. Jennifer had suffered from night terrors since she was a small girl, survived imaginary violence and horrors well beyond the boogeyman under the bed. Pills hadn't helped, and the psychotherapy had only taken the edge off. Stephen had been the true difference; he had taken the time to understand, to console, and to love her, regardless of the sleepless nights they had both experienced. This was before the move, of course, and the promotion that sent him across the country once or twice a month.

The sweat running down her spine was frigid now, having cooled shortly after Jennifer left the warm dampness of the comforter. She reached blindly for a nearby hook, grabbing the familiar plush material and then wrapping her nearly nude body in the soft pink bathrobe. On nights when the dreams were this bad, Steve would slide out of bed as well, waiting patiently as she washed away the violence. He would then hold her in silence, stroking her long, frazzled hair as she burrowed her face into his muscular shoulder. Some nights she would cry out, screaming at the shadowy, retreating tendrils that had frightened her. On others Jennifer would weep uncontrollably over the blood she saw every time she closed her eyes. Steve would guide her back to the bed and lay her head in his lap. Saying nothing, her husband would hold her tight while focusing on taking long, deep breaths. With each exhalation he pulled her closer and held her tighter against the rhythmic rise and fall of his chest. The hypnotic motion always soothed her frayed nerves, rocking the hysteria out of Jennifer. After many long minutes she would slumber once more, pacified by his calm demeanor and the solemn, meditative routine that accompanied it.

Steve had explained his breathing technique as one of the methods he used to alleviate stress. It was how her husband had learned to cope with high-pressure situations. She had watched him teach it to Charlie when the boy complained to them about his nightmares. Jennifer had been in awe of how Steve took deep breaths with the boy, instructing their child that repeating a ridiculous *magic phrase* would keep monsters out of his closet and banish them from under his bed. Where had he been when she was a child? Perhaps Jennifer wouldn't have suffered all these years. The phrase worked well; the boy's late night outbursts had been silenced, thank God.

Maintaining composure was a valuable asset, Steve always said. Without focus, one couldn't have direction in life and would wander aimlessly every day of their lives. *Her night terrors only controlled her because she allowed them to do so*; Jennifer could hear his baritone voice lecturing her as they shared coffee each morning. *She must always be in control.* But saying the words and living them were two entirely different things, Jennifer had discovered.

Steve knew what he was talking about, though she resented him for it just a little bit. His executive boardroom abilities had bought them this beautiful country house away from the world, had kept her from having to work, and had allowed them to invest greatly in their son's future. Jennifer still remembered touring the home months before, running her hand across the smooth, wooden bannister that was a hundred years old if it were a day. The tall, vibrant green trees that encircled the property had swayed beautifully in the summer's breeze, causing the picturesque landscape to come alive with motion. Yet, with the passing of fall, the land had turned harsh and unforgiving, losing its vibrancy day by day until nature inevitably acquiesced to winter's icy grasp. The once beautiful trees now slouched like twisted creatures in the stormy night, their long limbs stretching out towards the home. The surrounding land was a dead, nightmarish wasteland in comparison to those lush country fields she had fallen in love with so long ago. So too had their lives changed; the three of them had enjoyed family time together in the woods around the house, taking long walks and grilling under the stars after they first moved into the place. Now Steve was away arranging the big merger, while she, Charlie, and the house stood together in the elements, aging and withering away in the cold of a late fall night.

A nearby howl broke Jennifer from the maudlin thoughts, and she rushed to the window, expecting to see a large, gray wolf with glowing Baskerville-esque eyes upon the lawn. Instead, she saw a wet animal with hay colored fur loping about the property; its tail drooped behind the beast as it retreated to a small shack near the barn. Rufus had been another one of Steve's ideas in an effort to put his wife's worries at ease. Her first major attack had been the weekend Steve had gone to Chicago. Jennifer awoke and found herself on the bathroom floor late Friday night, shaking in terror.

All about her, the old farmhouse creaked and groaned as the ceilings stretched away and the entire room warped to a single point where glowing red eyes and gnashing, bloody teeth stalked her. Jennifer had called him in a panic when she had finally been able to move at dawn, and she didn't sleep until his tall form walked through the door Sunday evening. Behind him trailed a golden retriever, the dog's movements hesitant as brown eyes cast uncertain glances at the new surroundings. Charlie had fallen in love with the hairy mutt immediately, rushing up to the animal and crushing it in the biggest hug the four-year-old could muster. For the first time all weekend, Jennifer felt herself smile. She looked up into her husband's smiling face. He reassured her that this was a good idea; that she'd feel safer with Rufus around. And for a while, that worked.

Jennifer watched the dog shake itself several times in a vain attempt to find comfort in the increasing downpour. Turning around twice, Rufus entered the recently built house, slouching down in the muck with his muzzle laid upon his front paws. As she watched, the golden retriever cocked its head slightly as Rufus turned to stare up at the bedroom window. At her. Teeth bared in a vicious growl, it accused Jennifer from across the yard. His judge and his jailer.

Rufus had enjoyed his run of the house for a time. The next weekend Steve left, Rufus had leapt into bed to comfort Jennifer. She hadn't insisted the retriever return to the floor as she had when the retriever had tried this before. Instead, she lay against the dog, finding comfort in his shaggy, musky warmth. That night, sleep had been easy...and the next had as well. Upon returning home Steve was pleased, though he made Rufus sleep on the floor until the next business trip. The unconditional love of a dog was to be expected, but Rufus provided what she had needed to make the bad nights go away. At least until the green, summer leaves began to lose their color.

Then one autumnal evening Jennifer awoke with that same familiar catch in her throat...felt claws tearing through her vulnerable, soft insides. Panicked, she reached for the warm ball of fluff that had eased her nerves for many nights only to find an empty space beside her; the sheets still warm and smelling of dog. Struggling for breath, she scanned the dark bedroom for her canine companion, spotting a dog shaped mound on the floor near the foot of the bed. Looking for solace, she snapped for him. After several seconds, Jennifer whistled for the dog, calling his name softly. Rufus had always been responsive to commands. When he still didn't move, she feared the worst.

Crawling across the bed she stretched her delicate right hand over the edge beyond her limited vision. Inches out of sight Jennifer's fingers contacted the smooth, warm fur, feeling heat radiate off the dog's flesh. With slow repetition his body moved, and she felt the horror that constricted her every thought ease slightly. Rufus was fine, simply sleeping at the foot of the bed. Hoping to push away the remnants of the dream she began stroking the long, lean body absentmindedly. In response, she felt the muscles beneath her fingers tense as the dog's hair began to stand on end. A moment later, Rufus moved out of reach; his objective plain...the bedroom door. In the near-perfect blackness, Jennifer watched as the dog stopped and turned back to face the bed. Deep within the beast's belly it began to rumble, a warning growl that promised violence and bloodshed. Fear gripped her once more.

Perhaps what had woken her was not a tired, familiar nightmare, but something far worse. Rufus was warning her; of that Jennifer was convinced. Fighting back the horror-induced paralysis, she walked towards the door. Though blind in the blackness she strained to uncover what had provoked the angry response from the dog. Burglars, a fire, Charlie...that final thought pushed back the terror for good as Jennifer strode towards the closed door where she was met by fur and teeth.

The growl turned into a snarl as Rufus leapt at her with surprising speed, the thing's jaw snapping closed inches from her face. Throwing her hands up, Jennifer blocked the salivating muzzle with her forearms, the canine's sharp incisors slashing deeply into flesh. She cried out, attempting to knock the dog from her. Rufus persisted, throwing his full weight against her chest. The sudden impact of force knocked her to the floor, the blow stunning her. The beast pounced upon her prone figure; hungry, salivating. Again and again the teeth snapped together, inches from Jennifer's face. Just like the nightmares. She was going to die.

Fear transformed into violent rage as she struck out against the terrifying monster, dealing it an unexpected blow to the head. Staggered, the thing whimpered as Jennifer struck it again, falling from atop her chest to beside her on the floor. Never again, she promised herself, kicking the beast in its soft underbelly. She felt a satisfactory crunch beneath her foot as the thing yelped in agonizing pain. No more night terrors, she thought. Now this ends.

Sudden, brilliant illumination stunned her, shining white light on the violent, crimson scene. Rufus lay cowed upon the carpeted floor in a growing pool of blood, whimpering as he struggled for breath. A soft cry drew Jennifer's attention from the dog, and she turned to stare into the blinding hallway light. The small silhouette of Charlie stood in the doorframe, quaking with fright. His little head turned from mother to beloved dog, unable to comprehend the grisly tableau before him. Tears fell down rosy cheeks as the toddler began to cry. Heart breaking, Jennifer moved towards the boy, but only managed a step in her son's direction.

Blindsided by the canine once more she tumbled into the wall, her head bouncing painfully off of the old, hard plaster. The animal's bulk rested atop her crumpled form, pinning her to the floor. But deep within Jennifer the white-hot fire of anger still raged. She cast off the beast, and stood to look down upon it. The leap seemed to have done more damage to it than it had to her. Unable to stand, it now lay pathetically before her; a shuddering, whining, vulnerable thing. One last strike to the thing's bowed head would end the threat. Striding toward the beast, Jennifer's pulse raced as she raised a closed fist.

A second small cry issued from outside her vision, and the little boy's body collapsed upon his beloved pet, chest heaving as he cried into the retriever's golden coat. Jennifer stopped cold, doused in the realization of what she had nearly done. She dropped to her knees beside her son, who turned to stare at her accusingly through tear-filled eyes. The rest of that night had been a blur of dream-like memories highlighted only by major events that appeared like blinding flashes of a camera...frozen moments of crystal clarity. Carrying the shallow breathing dog to the car. Driving through the night at top speed as Charlie bawled in his car seat. Hauling the dog into an emergency clinic, stammering as the vets asked what happened. Having no answer. Sitting in shame as judgmental eyes glared at her. The clock ticking by with no word. Carrying first the mended, sedated dog into the house in the pre-dawn light, followed by her dozing son.

Steve had come home later that night. It didn't take him long to notice the deep scratches on her face and arms, nor did he fail to note that Rufus kept his distance. He didn't need to ask anything, her husband just stared and waited until Jennifer broke the silence. She wept while confessing to him what had transpired, but through it all Steve held her...calmed her. *It had been the night terrors*, he was sure. Jennifer wasn't a violent psychopath. Nor was she a killer. Once she finished crying, he told her stories of how he would wake up in the middle of the night to find her beating on him, attacking her sleeping husband in an effort to fight back against the shadows that tormented her. She would be fine, Rufus would be fine. They would both get along. Steve's words soothed Jennifer's feelings, just as they always did.

Her husband had been partly right. Though it scared her to know she had been violent in response to the dreams before, Jennifer soon found that she forgot the rage that had gripped her so strongly. The dog, however, did not forgive. When Steve was present Rufus was calm, but he became aggressive towards her whenever the alpha male wasn't in the house. For the first few weeks, Jennifer was able to handle the heightened aggression...but then the retriever began to bare his teeth and growl whenever she approached Charlie without Steve in the room. Eventually, they came to the realization that the dog needed to stay outside, particularly on nights when her husband wasn't around.

Staring at the mud-covered coat that trembled slightly in the howling wind, Jennifer felt deep regret at what had transpired. No creature deserved to be outside in this horrible weather, to be treated so poorly. She stood there watching Rufus for several moments while she contemplated grabbing some towels and bringing him into the house. Perhaps compassion in this moment would change the dog's attitude towards her.

Without warning a series of lightning strikes played across the sky, blinding Jennifer. The light must have illuminated her form at the window, and in response the animal began to bark harshly towards the house, straining at the chain that kept him within several feet of the old, rotted building. Sighing, Jennifer pulled the drapes closed and walked back to bed.

Returning to the shadowy bedroom, Jennifer found that the dream still haunted her. She could feel the claws latching on to the deepest recesses of her memory, threatening to drag her back down into a bloody nightmare as soon as her head rested upon the pillow. Images of teeth gnashing raw flesh kept Jennifer from lying back down. Instead, she sat on the edge of the bed waiting for the visions to disappear. But she was not alone in the bedroom. Something else drifted in the dream space between sleep and waking. And it bothered her; beyond the fear, violence, and madness...something was wrong.

The sky went white and the world shook with a roar of violence. Jennifer cried out as panic took hold. As the rumble petered out, the room became a cave of complete blackness. Lightning strike...a close one; it must have struck the house or the power lines nearby. The darkness was all encompassing now. Deep breaths. *One. Two.* Jennifer felt strange yet familiar arms wrapping around her body from behind, restricting her movements in a clammy, rough embrace. Dragging her back to bed, to the dreams. To the teeth.

Their touch chilled Jennifer to the bone. She stood abruptly to brush off the phantasmal, roving hands. Still blinded by lightning, her eyes were slow to adjust to the vast emptiness of the house. There were no lights, no hope in sight. She heard the rain increase, beating a rapid tattoo against the windows while the wind shrieked as it passed around the home. Jennifer fought the urge to dive under her covers and hide from the storm. Besides, her dreams resided in that space between comforter and mattress. The bloody mouth smiled at her in the dark night as it read Jennifer's thoughts; it would be pleased immensely if she lay back down.

Lightning strobed the room again, an accompanying peal of thunder echoing in an unending call and response of the terrible storm. Jennifer was paralyzed by these unseen hands, rouge colored teeth, and an unspoken promise of being flayed slowly for the enjoyment of her tormentor. She had to get up, to leave the room, to find a source of light. This stormy night belonged to the thing that stalked her dreams, not to living, fleshy, vulnerable people. If she expected to survive, Jennifer needed to get moving. Direction did not matter, but her body needed the perpetual motion to gain ground on whatever horrible things lurked within her bedroom.

Blindness consumed her once more as the last cacophonous rumble and brilliant flash faded into the distance. Shadows made the old farmhouse unfamiliar. Darkness swallowed up open doorways, twisting them into unending caverns. Family photos full of smiling faces turned sinister, their evil faces displaying wicked intentions. Jennifer felt herself swirling down a paralytic drain, headed for the belly that lay beyond the gnashing teeth. Needing light, she fumbled across the top of the bedside table, knocking off her alarm clock and nearly upending the lamp as well. Struggling, she grasped the familiar handheld object, disconnected the charging cord, and pushed the 'on' button.

The phone's soft glow only teased vision, giving Jennifer a small halo of light one step in front of her. But she found if she focused on that dime-sized spot of hope, Jennifer could move. One step at a time she passed through the literal sea of awful, crawling darkness that washed about the room. *No goblins, no ghoulies, no ghosts.* After a lifetime of shuffling, she saw the wall before her. Not taking her eyes off the dim guiding light, Jennifer grasped for the knob and opened the door. From behind, the roar of a thousand feet echoed against the woodwork, the sound of slathering jaws snapping at the chance at a fresh meal. In childish terror she jumped across the threshold, slamming the bedroom door shut behind her.

Happy to be alive, Jennifer collapsed against the hallway wall, panting. Tonight it seemed, her dreams were real...either that or she was going mad. *No goblins, no ghoulies, no ghosts.* The magic phrase was meaningless now, but she held on to the words like a doomed man wraps himself in prayer, seeking salvation. *No goblins, no ghoulies, no ghosts.* She needed some other comfort in this trying time, and only one thing had ever provided that for her before. One person. She needed him. Now. There was no other solution. Jennifer fumbled with the phone, flicking her thumb across the screen and touching his image. Just seeing Steve's face warmed her inside, knowing his voice was moments away. She brought the phone to her ear expecting to hear ringing; but there was only static, then silence.

Pulling the device away from her, Jennifer saw the phone had no reception and that the battery was barely charged. Cursing silently, she stared at his picture for several moments, hoping Steve might somehow emerge through the screen. Perhaps it would become a magic portal that delivered her knight in shining armor, bringing warm light radiating from his dazzling smile into the pitch-black hallway that Jennifer lay in, hiding. Instead, the phone buzzed once and the screen darkened to conserve its one percent. There were only a few precious moments of illumination left. Behind the closed bedroom door, sharp talons scratched at paneling furiously. A low rumble echoed. *It's laughing at me*, Jennifer realized. It would be patient, as it always had been. The nightmares knew she had only a few minutes of relief. Then it could tear into her throat, just as it always whispered to her that it would.

A series of lightning strikes brightened the upstairs hallway turned cavern, the light bouncing from one side of the hall to the other and then down the wooden staircase. As each flash subsided the shadows twisted once more, reaching into the surprising brilliance to pull the house back into darkness again. But for just one second the heavens had illuminated the path to safety...she had to get downstairs. Steve had shown her how the old fuse box worked in case of emergency. Perhaps a breaker had been tripped and lifesaving power could be restored at the flick of a switch. Slowly Jennifer inched her way across the smooth hardwood floor towards the staircase, doing her best to ignore the catcalls that softly echoed from behind her bedroom door.

This won't be like last time, she told herself. *He will have to understand. I need his help.* A series of memories rose up unbidden from within her mind; white-hot flashes of anger, the feel of cool tears running down her face, her husband looking down at her, angry. This sudden swelling of emotions overtook Jennifer, and she collapsed to the floor, trembling from fright.

Keep going. She couldn't stop, not now. The monster with the blood-soaked teeth would feast upon Jennifer's flesh as she lay there helpless on the floor, a prisoner of her own horrible memories. Yet, no matter how much her mind pleaded, the memories rushed over her in a torrent of emotion and she found herself lost once again in a half-remembered dream. *No goblins, no ghoulies, no ghosts. No goblins, no ghoulies, no ghosts.*

Steve had always been so understanding before. The real change began when he had come home one Sunday and discovered Jennifer in bed where she had lain since his departure two days before. Charlie had been crying for a day or longer, unable to care for himself. She hadn't heard. Hadn't known that he had messed himself several times, or that he had tried futilely to get his mother out of bed. The floor had become a pit of blackness, and Jennifer wasn't able to step on it, lest she fall into an eternity of nothing. *This was different*, she had tried to tell him. For so many years the nightmares had wanted her to leap out of bed; now they laid traps for that eventuality. She refused to give in to their ploys. Steve had calmed down eventually, though he started sleeping on the couch after that weekend trip. The bed had been so much colder, but Jennifer knew her husband was just downstairs if needed. A single cry would bring him running to her rescue. That thought warmed her heart.

Steve didn't leave the farmhouse for a long time after the incident, and Jennifer felt her world return to normal. Daily life became like it had been earlier that summer, and the cold grip of death seemed to disappear into thin air. With it, the night terrors receded back into the depths of Jennifer's unconscious, so much so that she thought she might finally be free of a life of constant shadows. Then, one Friday morning, a strange woman knocked on the door and asked to see Steve. The three of them sat down over mugs of untouched coffee as her husband attempted to explain to Jennifer that Anna was here to help, just in case she should have an episode again. It all sounded very rational as Steve's voice droned on, but inside the creeping voices warned her that Steve believed she was crazy. His words became muffled and unintelligible, their meaning senseless. Her body grew numb as this thought became pervasive and all-encompassing. Jennifer could only nod over and over as the slowly cooling mug that she held tightly between her hands trembled. She nearly spilled its contents with each repetitive nod of acceptance. And with repetition, realization finally dawned. Perhaps Steve was right after all; Charlie needed someone here for him.

That first night had been awkward; Anna had prepared food for the three of them, and she made sure that Jennifer and Charlie were resting comfortably in their beds before retiring to the guest bedroom down the hall. The following day was considerably more pleasant. Having a helping hand around to care for her son alleviated the daily pressure of mothering, just as the two had assured her the day before. Perhaps this was the solution that she and Steve had sought for so long. After bidding goodnight to Anna, Jennifer drifted off into a peaceful sleep with happy thoughts of her husband returning tomorrow evening.

Noises woke her in the middle of the night, an unknown and repetitive squeaking sound. At first she panicked. *No Goblins, no Ghoulies, no Ghosts. There are no such things as monsters. Use logic to fight fear and illuminate the terrifying darkness.* Though the words were in her own head, Steve's booming bass voice filled her with warmth. Confidence renewed, Jennifer pulled herself up from the covers to confront the unknown.

Ears straining, Jennifer struggled to place the noise, but after a moment's concentration she discerned its location: down the hall, in the guest bedroom. The sound continued, unabated. Then, as the noise increased steadily in volume and rhythm, Jennifer raised her hand to her mouth to stifle the oncoming cry. A squeaking sound escaped her lips, though her mouth was tightly covered by interlocked fingers. Instead, the house seemed to scream at her as the high-pitched, repetitive squeaking was suddenly accompanied by a rhythmic thump against the wall.

Steve must have come home in the middle of the night, sneaking in to prevent waking the rest of the slumbering household. He must be lonely; Jennifer knew she was. If he felt even a fraction of the emotion that she did, then her husband missed the soft touch of another human being, of a special connection to another's soul. They hadn't slept in the same bed for weeks now, and Jennifer had always wondered if he might have been finding comfort in the arms of another. The idea bothered her, but she could push it from her mind easily during the day by focusing on other things. To hear him, now, in their house...waves of nausea, anger, and sadness crashed against her over and over without end. Each surge was stronger than the last, threatening to drown her as the increasing tempo of emotions kept pace with the slamming of the guest bed against the wall.

She could picture them together...that was the worst. Jennifer had been married to Steve for a long time, knew what it took to curl his toes and cause him to cry out in ecstasy. Each change in the sounds from within the guest bedroom came with an accompanying mental image. Yet, the pleasurable turned profane as she realized that it was Anna in there with her husband, not her. The nerve of this woman and Steve, with their son down the hall? The awkward, excessive noises, both inanimate and human, grew louder. Struggling to not listen, Jennifer covered her ears, biting the pillow beneath her. *No goblins, no ghoulies, no ghosts.* But the mantra didn't stifle the crescendo of desire she heard, nor did it stop their cries of passion. The two must be nearing completion, she realized. And that thought made her scream. A long, painful cry escaped Jennifer's lips as she howled like the wounded thing she had become. In one guttural screech of agony she tried to push the horrible emotions and gut-wrenching pain from within her, to cast off and expel the building rage.

Moments later the bedroom door flew open, the hallway light outlining the individual standing there...a shadow of a person. But the lithe frame, shapely curves, and long, beautiful hair told Jennifer who stood in the entrance to the master bedroom. Anna's voice called into the darkness of the room, asking if everything was okay. The other woman adjusted her nightgown slightly to better cover her exposed skin. *Harlot.* She asked if it was okay to enter, or if she could get Jennifer anything. Anna said she had been hearing Jennifer toss and turn for some time but hadn't wanted to disturb her unless necessary.

Replying with a wry laugh, she had accused the other woman of infidelity, releasing a tidal wave of anger and obscenities at Anna. The woman at the door listened for several moments, reassuring her that Steve was not here, that everything was a terrible dream. Jennifer considered this for a long moment...perhaps Anna was correct. Maybe the noises were caused by the night terrors laying another trap for her, like when they made the floor disappear. They had been known to show up in all forms of psychological torture. Jennifer admitted this to Anna with a sheepish apology, feeling ridiculous for her prior accusation. Anna shook her head as if it were nothing, then smiled in response to show that no harm had been done.

Jennifer recoiled in horror and began to scream. Anna's mouth opened too wide to reveal a mouthful of silver, metallic teeth, the hallway light reflecting off their dazzling surfaces. The incisors were thin, pointed, and serrated; the type of teeth that had always desired to tear into her soft innards. Still, the thing's mouth opened wider beyond the human limits of facial structure and bone. A soft, red tongue licked the silver teeth expectantly. Some of the back ones were still coated in blood from a previous kill. The only question was Steve, or Charlie?

Jennifer flew at the approaching thing that was not a woman, pummeling it with all her might. She felt the blows land again and again on the monster, its blood coating her rapidly bruising knuckles. The creature beneath her struggled and wailed, but Jennifer refused to let it go. This thing had killed her husband or her child, maybe both. She refused to play victim. Yet, the beast would not be defeated. With a vicious blow to the back of her head, Jennifer saw stars. She felt her body, now weightless, fly across the room; striking the wall with enough force to knock the wind out of her. Gasping for breath, the shadowed monster with glowing eyes and sharp, bloody teeth stood over her as the world faded into darkness. She was dead.

Waking up had been a pleasant surprise for Jennifer. She lay in bed, and Steve leaned in over her. Looking about frantically, she saw her son in the corner, staring at her with fear in his eyes. At first she felt relief. They were all alive. Then Steve began to talk at length about what had transpired.

His version of the story was different, as it always was. The elderly Anna had discovered her in the throes of a night terror and had attempted to wake Jennifer. Lashing out against the nightmares, she had, apparently, tackled and punched the other woman repeatedly. The most horrifying fact, in Steve's opinion, was that Anna was only able to escape because Charlie had struck his mother in the back of the head with a toy bat. Jennifer didn't hear his words then, couldn't hear them. She was too happy. Her family was safe.

Steve grew more distant after that, rarely speaking to Jennifer at all. The supposed assault charge was dropped, and Anna never entered the house again. When he did start a conversation, Steve attempted to discuss doctors and treatment with her. Jennifer refused to engage with him. These solutions hadn't been helpful in the past when she was a child, and they wouldn't help her now. Besides, the monster had finally made its intentions clear, and they went beyond torturing her in the dead of night. The thing intended to murder her whole family, and Charlie and Steve needed Jennifer's protection.

Remembering this promise, she drew herself up on her elbows and began crawling towards the stairs once more. More memories rose up in her mind; images of Steve packing his bag extra full the last time she had seen him...leaving the house with tears in his eyes. But these were twisted ploys of the monster, she realized. To stop her resistance. They weren't real. Steve would never leave her. Jennifer had to protect her family.

Behind her, the door groaned on its hinges. A pitiful cry escaped Jennifer's lips; she had waited too long. Sharp nails clicked on the wooden floor, followed by heavy footfalls. Jennifer could hear the beast panting, salivating as it towered over its latest meal. Face down, she could feel the dribbles of wet saliva drop lightly on her neck and then run down the line of her collar to the front before dripping off her throat to the hardwood floor. Like an animal sprawled for live field dressing, she lay prostrate before the terror she could not see nor bear to face. Jennifer knew its red eyes must be glowing as they regarded her, heard the sharp metal teeth clink together in joyous anticipation inches from her ear. She felt its hot breath and caressing talons exploring her body.

Jennifer shuddered as the thing searched her slowly, like the touch of a teasing lover. It would not stop, she knew. It fed on her fright, taking extreme, visceral pleasure at the pain it has caused for years. If this was the end, she was determined not to give it the sadistic pleasure that it craved. In the last moments of her life, she would face this thing, as Steve would have wanted her to. Even if, after all this, he still didn't believe. *No goblins, no ghoulies, no ghosts. No goblins, no ghoulies, no ghosts.* Repeating the lifeline phrase, she rolled over to face her attacker.

Jennifer stared up into the empty darkness. No drooling monster awaited her, no red eyes glared at her with bared, silvery teeth. The thing was tricking her, she assumed. The nightmare was hiding for one last, impactful moment of terror before slitting her throat with its claws and devouring her soft insides. She waited, staring intently at the bland, drywall ceiling. One heartbeat, then two. At ten she strained to see the back of the hallway without raising her head. At thirty a lightning strike illuminated an empty hall, the door to the master bedroom swinging slightly in the breeze as the house exhaled. It was a trap, had to be. She lay down, expecting it to strike any time. After a hundred, she lost count. Then she heard a scream from farther down the hall. *Charlie.*

No longer were her muscles useless from terror, nor her mind terrified with fear. Protecting her child, her baby, was the only thought she had. Rage built within Jennifer. This thing had terrorized her for years, and now it sought to do the same to her son. She wouldn't let it, she decided, three steps from the door. No matter what the horror wanted, no matter what the beast did, she would not let it have her child.

From around the corner she saw the door to Charlie's room was open, the inside deep in shadow. *A nightlight should be on,* she thought. *Or did he have it turned off tonight? Had he been a brave boy?* The terror struck her brain like a sickness tonight, rotting memory from the inside outward. She needed to take a deep breath. Another. Three. *No goblins, no ghoulies, no ghosts.* Jennifer peered into the blackness, terror quashing the bravery induced by rage. In truth, she expected to see gore, violent dismemberment, or something worse. Memories of dreamy violence came to her mind, and she reeled from nausea. Gazing into the room, Jennifer saw something unexpected.

The room lay untouched, as perfect as it had been when she had laid Charlie down for the night. His sheets were still tucked around his little body, covers thrown over his head. Stepping in, she looked around but could detect no creatures lurking in the corners, no horrors hovering over his bed, and no predator waiting to pounce. She moved swiftly to the bed, laying a soft hand on his body. Jennifer would shake him awake, would take him to the barn and have Rufus protect him. Or better yet, if she could get the keys off the dining room table, the three of them might escape this nightmare if they drove fast enough. As her hand touched the sleeping form its shape compressed before her. He was cold and soft...as her fingers rested there, Jennifer felt no rise and fall of the boy's chest. In a panic, she tore the sheets back.

An oversized child's doll lay there before her. Roughly the same size and shape as Charlie, its plastic eyes bore into her. No blinking interrupted its harsh, critical gaze. The painted smile seemed amused at her mortal concern; life is just one big game when you're a doll. *Perhaps she would like to play?* Again Jennifer began to tremble. Perhaps the terror from her dreams already had her son, then? Was it mocking her? Slowly her head swiveled around the small boy's bedroom, looking for any sign of where Charlie might have gone.

Everything seemed in place according to her mental checklist. Charlie was a well-mannered young boy and would put up his toys without being asked. All books were on their plastic, primary-colored little shelf, and the two Fisher Price chairs were tucked neatly under his little table. All drawing paper was stacked on top of the two-tiered drawer that contained crayons and markers. Everything seemed in place, but something still nagged at Jennifer. She searched the room again for any minor irregularity. The closet door wasn't quite shut, though its interior was an even deeper pit of blackness than the rest of the room. But that still wasn't what bothered her, wasn't the source of this nagging feeling. It was...

...his bat. Turning to face the bedside table once more, she noticed his foam Lil' Slugger wasn't beside the bed. Ever since discovering his mother and Rufus, Charlie had been determined to protect everyone in the house from bad dreams. Steve, upon realizing his mantra was no longer enough, had told his son to keep the bat nearby. The soft foam would keep the kid from breaking things (or bones, for that matter), and the bat seemed to comfort the boy. She had rested it against the headboard as part of his nightly routine when she had lain him down earlier this evening. But the bat wasn't there, which meant...

"Charlie?" she asked, her words dry and raspy like those from a forty-year-old chain smoker. It surprised her, almost as if a stranger's voice echoed from her mouth. The emotion was too much, and it had caused her question to crackle and break as it passed her lips. Convinced her son was still in this room and prepared to battle her monsters, she summoned the courage to speak out again.

"Charlie?" Closer to her normal voice this time, though the words broke again. She took a step towards the closet door, but paused as it began to move on its own. A small hand reached out, pushing it to the side. In his footie PJ's, the four-year-old stood before her, the handle of the sixteen-inch foam bat gripped tightly between his tiny fingers. Charlie stared up at her, cocking his head slightly in wonder.

"Mommy?" he asked, unsure. Feeling her heart melt, she began to rush towards her son. He raised one of his pudgy hands up, palm outward, encouraging her to stop. "Mommy, there are monsters here."

"I know baby, Mommy is so sorry. We have to go." Jennifer held her arms out expectantly, hoping the young boy would run and jump into them, gripping her around the throat in a tight bear hug.

"It was just here, where did it go?" The boy's frantic searching unnerved her. His head twisted this way and that, looking in each dark pool of blackness in the room. The two of them would be safe together, Jennifer was sure of it. But they needed to go. Now.

"Come on Charlie, let's go." She moved towards her son, but he shuffled back from her outstretched arms, huddling deeper into the closet. His eyes grew wide, staring at her.

"Mommy, what are you doing?"

"What do you mean, Charlie? We need to go."

"Your face..." he replied, staring at her. Jennifer paused, and she noticed the muscle tension across her cheekbones.

"I'm smiling, honey. I was so worried that something had happened to you. I'm glad you're safe. But we need to go now, Charlie." The words were choked, broken. Hard to get out.

"But, but...your teeth, Mommy." As the soft, stammering words left the young boy's throat, terror gripped her. She leaned back and turned towards the large mirror that sat above the double dresser. Lightning flashed, and for the first time tonight, Jennifer truly looked at herself.

The specter looking back at her was close...an almost perfect duplicate. But monsters always get the details wrong. The uncanny valley made the thing's mistakes obvious. Human eyes don't glow, but the ones in her reflection did...a soft red. And the monsters' mouths, they always open too wide...impossibly wide. Lightning flashed again outside as the room roared with accompanying thunder, and the glow flickered off of her sharp, jagged, metallic teeth. Teeth made for tearing into the soft innards of prey. The smile in the reflection grew wider, jawbone unhinging to reveal a slithering red tongue. Its mouth ached from the strain; stomach rumbled from the hunger.

But it would feast well this night. Turning back to the boy, a horrendous scream warbled from within as it dove into the closest. It wasted no time diving in after the meal, knocking clothing and shelving away with a single swipe of a powerful hand. The boy, in tears, huddled against the back wall; weak and helpless. Snatching him up with long sharp claws, it tore into the mewling thing's flesh playfully as the spawn cried out again and again for his mother, begging her to stop. It ignored the pitiful cries, but the sharpness annoyed the thing. Meals should not make noise. With a single talon, it simply tore across the throat, and the screams became a delightfully soft gurgle, each cry causing the blood to bubble up splendidly. With an unhinged smile, its tongue lapped up the warm liquid, the nails tearing...

...tearing at something constricting her body. She couldn't get loose of it all; the blood, the screams, the viscera. Jennifer fought against it sightless, until, finally, the force that held her down was released. Throwing the sheet back from her face, cool night air rushed over her. Outside lightning struck, and the light from its impact played across the ceiling of her bedroom. *This wasn't real. I didn't do that. I couldn't have.* Yet, the blood, the taste of copper in her throat, felt all too right. But all that was gone now, the remnants of a night terror. She had returned to reality.

But the screaming hadn't stopped, she realized. A child's soft cries echoed down the hall, along with the squeals of something else. Horrified, Jennifer began to rise, but as she did so, she felt something hot and wet run across her chin. She touched two fingers to her face, felt a substance that was sticky and smelled of copper. Jennifer felt that her cheek muscles had tightened into a rigorous grimace, and as Jennifer continued exploring her own visage, she realized her teeth felt sharp and unnatural.

No goblins, no ghoulies, no ghosts, she said, throwing herself back into bed. Jennifer pulled the covers over her own head, not so much to hide from Charlie's screams, which had become softer and less pronounced, but to hide herself from whatever might be coming down the hallway to her room next. *No goblins, no ghoulies, no ghosts. No goblins, no ghoulies, no ghosts.*

Charlie no longer screamed, and the soft gurgling noise that had replaced the screams became inaudible. *No goblins, no ghoulies, no ghosts. No goblins, no ghoulies, no ghosts.* Jennifer closed her eyes, repeating the phase in her head as the bedroom door creaked open, and the house groaned as it yielded to heavy footfalls. *No goblins, no ghoulies, no ghosts. No goblins, no ghoulies,   no   ghosts.*

GODS OF THE SOUTHERN HORIZON
Christopher Stanley

Clouds move fast against the oily sky, chasing the sun below the horizon like vast and unforgiving gods. Rain falls in sheets and the moon is absent but for a distant, blue-green glow on the water. It's impossible not to feel vulnerable in this dark and elemental place. If life is more than finite, if there are shadows that linger after death, now is their time.

Somewhere on the coastal road, a rented, three-door hatchback struggles up the side of the cliff, tires sloshing through puddles, windscreen wipers shuffling from side to side.

The driver, Daniel, leans forward for a better view of the road ahead. Caught between a boy and a man, his youthful face is home to tired eyes and wisps of unruly facial hair. His knuckles are white because he's squeezing the steering wheel so hard.

"It says here," says Jeremy, "that eighty percent of recorded sightings are auditory." Jeremy's in the passenger seat, using a pen torch to read a book the size of a tombstone. "Four in every five ghost encounters are nothing more than creaking doors and dripping taps." Jeremy has one eye rounder than the other and a permanent half-smile on his lips—what his mum calls an "absence of facial symmetry." He squints through the rain-smeared passenger window and says, "Shouldn't the sea be on the other side of the car?"

"Auditory *sightings*?" asks Daniel.

Jeremy smacks Daniel playfully on the leg. "I can't believe you're scared of ghosts."

The road narrows around a bend, taking them close enough to kiss the cliff edge. Two feet of tarmac and a twisted metal guardrail are all that stand between them and the boiling sea below. A badger lies dead on the center line, intestines erupting from its fur like meat squeezed from a sausage.

"I hope our tent will survive this storm," says Jeremy.

"I just hope we make it back," says Daniel.

They've been in Ireland for three days, sharing their tent with a crate of cheap beer and a creeping sense of boredom. Their friends have gone to Ibiza for a week of nightclubs, booze, and women, in an attempt to prove they're men more than boys. Daniel couldn't get the money together in time and Jeremy didn't even try. The camping trip was Jeremy's idea. He assured Daniel they'd come back with tales of misadventure to rival those of their sun-soaked, sleep-deprived friends.

He might have been exaggerating.

It's rained non-stop since they arrived and the only member of the opposite sex they've spoken to is the owner of the campsite—an intimidating, middle-aged woman called Sheenagh, with painted fingernails and a permanent scowl. They found Sheenagh sitting behind a small desk in the campsite's reception hut, busy typing on a computer, her fingernails clacking against the keys. When Jeremy asked what there was to do in the area, she carried on typing with one hand and pointed to the rack of brochures with the other, saying, "Take your pick."

Jeremy shook his head. "We're after something that isn't in the guidebook."

Sheenagh stopped typing and turned to face them. For a moment, she just stared, as if appraising their appearance. Then she asked how they felt about ghosts.

On the coastal road, Daniel tries to focus but he's tired and part-hypnotized by the sleepy beat of the wiper blades. He's barely concentrating when the car's headlights pick out the figure of a young woman up ahead, bronze haired and bare-legged, her yellow plastic raincoat puffed up like a windsock. He steps on the brakes and the tires lose their traction, the car slewing towards the guardrail and the drop beyond. Time seems to slow down, taking on a surreal quality, and Daniel's aware of everything—raindrops reflecting in the car's headlights, Jeremy's hand on his arm, the book of ghosts sliding into the footwell of the car. The car scrapes the guardrail, metal against metal, and slows down enough for Daniel to steer them away from the edge.

"Fuck," he says, as the car comes to rest.

Ashen-faced and shaking, Jeremy opens his door and vomits onto the verge. "There goes our deposit," he says, wiping his lips on the back of his hand.

"The girl," says Daniel. "Do you think she's okay?"

"Don't," says Jeremy.

"Don't what?"

"Don't go back for her."

"Why not?"

"We're in the middle of nowhere. There's no phone signal. We don't know who she is or what she's doing out here—in this storm, miles from the nearest town. We don't know anything about her."

Daniel slips the car into reverse. "We know she's miles from the nearest town." He adjusts the rear-view mirror and carefully reverses down the slope. The young woman waits for them, wet hair pasted in ringlets against her cheeks, her raincoat billowing in the wind. As they draw near, her white skin glows in the car lights and her lips twitch towards a smile. Daniel feels a tingle of excitement. At last, a story he can imagine sharing with his friends when he gets home. And the night isn't over yet.

"Why are you doing this?" asks Jeremy, trying to dislodge his book from the footwell. "I thought we were going to see the ghosts?"

"We can drop her at the next village," says Daniel. "It won't be far."

"I don't like it," says Jeremy. "What's she doing out here?"

Daniel lifts the handbrake and unclips his seatbelt. "Let's find out."

***

In the back of the car, sitting in the middle seat, the young woman peels back her hood to reveal green eyes, round cheeks and a mass of curly red hair. She doesn't seem threatened by the storm or the strangers she's hitching a ride with, and her presence in the car chases Daniel's fears back into their dark corners.

She says her name's Ellen. She's a few years older than they are; a student at Trinity College in Dublin. She was out hiking and lost track of the time. When the weather turned, she took shelter in the ruined chapel. "No signal out here," she says, waving her phone. "Where are you headed?"

"Coastguard's Cottage," says Jeremy.

"The haunted one?" asks Ellen. "I've heard stories."

"What stories?"

"Something about a baby crying and a woman in a bedroom window."

Daniel glances in the rear-view mirror. He hates the thought of ghosts but when Ellen talks about them, with her soulful voice and lilting accent, they almost sound appealing. "Do you want to come with us?" he asks, hurrying the sentence in an effort to hide his nervousness. He doesn't need to look at Jeremy to feel his friend's disappointment.

***

They approach the cottage from the rear with their heads down and hoods up. A security lamp pops on, illuminating a small courtyard guarded by a barn and a high stone wall. Rain drums against the barn's corrugated roof and animals murmur indistinct, guttural warnings from within its timber walls. *Probably just goats and pigs*, thinks Daniel. *Nothing sinister.*

There are stories here: in the crooked trees and missing roof tiles, the peeling paintwork and patchy roughcast. Stories the animals would tell if they could. A single upstairs window is lit. Daniel is reluctant to look but his eyes are drawn upwards, expecting to see a devilish silhouette or moonlit face staring back at him.

The room appears to be empty.

He's trying to stay calm when something rushes at him from the side, appearing out of nowhere, waist-high and growling fiercely. He jumps backwards in surprise, his instincts telling him to flee. The creature stops suddenly, and its growl rises to a heart-stopping howl.

Ellen steps forward, crouching until she's face to face with their would-be attacker, clicking her tongue and stroking its head like an old friend.

"It's just a dog," says Jeremy. "A dog on a leash."

Daniel takes a deep breath. "I hate this place."

They follow the path to the front of the cottage where it forks, one half curling around to the main entrance and the other continuing for twenty meters or so before disappearing over the cliff edge. It looks like there used to be other cottages—three or four of them in a row—but the rest have fallen into the sea. All that's left are fragments of wall and exposed foundations.

Coastguard's Cottage sits on the edge of the cliff the way death row inmates perch on their bunks. Waiting. From the front, it looks like a child's drawing with arched windows, a steep roof and twin chimneys like the horns of the devil. Looking at the cottage, Daniel can't shake the feeling that there's more to it than simple bricks and mortar. That it's somehow an extension of the cliffs on which it sits.

They crowd for shelter under the porch and Daniel hooks his fingers around the cast-iron knocker. He's convinced he isn't going to knock, that he'll leave it for another time—next month or year, maybe, when the weather is warmer and memories of this night are nothing more than whispers in his dreams. Then Ellen steps forward to press the doorbell and Jeremy laughs until Daniel elbows him in the ribs.

They all fall silent when the door shudders in its frame.

Moments later, it swings open to reveal an old man in a midnight blue cardigan, with white hair ruffled like flames and eyes loaded with suspicion. Around his neck, he wears a pendant on a sturdy, silver chain. It isn't a cross or St Christopher like Daniel's father sometimes wears. Instead it seems to be a fish—a manta ray, maybe—with a thin, whip-like tail and giant fins on each side of its head. The old man squeezes Jeremy's jaw in his hand and says, "Do I know you?" Jeremy's mouth moves but no words come out. "What do you want?"

"We've come to see the ghosts," says Daniel.

"Gods?" asks the old man.

"*Ghosts.*"

The old man waves them away, telling them they've come to the wrong place.

"We're not trouble-makers," says Jeremy, massaging his jaw. "The lady at the campsite sent us. Sheenagh."

Something changes when Jeremy says this. The old man relaxes. He steps back into the shadows and invites them in, introducing himself as Thomas Marley.

Daniel follows Ellen and Jeremy into the small hallway. As Marley locks the door behind them, Daniel wonders if they're making a terrible mistake.

***

The sitting room at the front of the cottage has a small, box-shaped television and an even smaller coal fire, which burns wearily in the grate. The ceiling creaks like footsteps and rain patters against the window. Marley takes their coats to the utility room at the back of the cottage and they wait for his return with their hands in their pockets, too nervous to sit down.

"Didn't he offer to take your coat, too?" Daniel asks Ellen.

"It's okay," she says. "I prefer to keep it on."

Above the fireplace, there's a brass-on-wood plaque that says, "I seem to have been only like a boy playing on the seashore and diverting myself now and then in finding a smoother pebble or a prettier shell than the ordinary, whilst the great ocean of truth lay all undiscovered before me." Daniel steps forward to read the name underneath the quote.

Sir Isaac Newton.

"Pretty special last words, don't you think?" says Ellen.

Daniel nods. He likes that Ellen knows they're Newton's last words when the plaque doesn't say so. He wonders if he'll be able to come up with something as eloquent and philosophical on his deathbed. Right now, the best he can think of is *Stay away from haunted houses.*

Before he took their coats, Marley explained that the neighbors' cottages had fallen into the sea after years of cliff erosion. For three of them, it had been a slow process, the owners having packed up and moved long before their cottages disappeared. The fourth cottage went suddenly one night, plunging into the water while the family were asleep. Marley said he heard them screaming as they fell. By the time he reached the window to look, the cottage was already gone.

Standing at the window, watching the storm play out on the horizon, Jeremy says, "What if tonight's the night?"

Daniel hears the footsteps again, creaking across the ceiling.

"What do you mean?" asks Ellen.

"What if tonight is the night this cottage falls into the sea?"

"Let's hope that doesn't happen," says Ellen.

"I don't know," says Jeremy. He turns to face Daniel. "I reckon if you have to die, it's better to die in good company."

Daniel hears his friend, but he isn't really listening. There's someone standing in the room above his head. He's sure of it. He's about to mention it when Marley returns to the room, saying, "Right, who wants to see some ghosts?"

***

They follow Marley up the clop and squeal of the wooden staircase, Daniel's fingers carving trails in the dust on the banister. Behind him, Ellen rustles in her waterproof jacket, and he wonders again why Marley didn't offer to take it. He feels Ellen's arm brush against his as she squeezes alongside him at the top of the stairs. Their hands meet, fleetingly, and the touch of her knuckles makes his heart flutter. Daniel wonders if she feels the same.

"How come you haven't moved?" asks Jeremy.

"I've lost too much already to worry about such things," says Marley. "But don't worry. The cottage isn't going to fall into the sea anytime soon. I promise you."

The light catches Marley's eyes when he says this and Daniel sees a glint of something—something the old man isn't telling them.

"Do you believe in life after death?" asks Marley.

"Only if I can see it," says Jeremy.

"What about life beyond the southern horizon? You can't see that, can you?"

"You can if you go there," says Jeremy.

"Maybe the same is true for life after death."

As Marley says this, the landing light flickers and dies. Daniel waits for his eyes to adjust but the darkness on the landing seems to be more than just a sudden absence of illumination. It's a thing that's seeped out of the walls, spreading, watching.

Breathing.

Marley flicks the switch a few times without success. "I guess some things don't want to come back," he says with a chuckle. Then he reaches into the bathroom and tugs on the pull cord, the resulting light chasing the shadows back into the walls.

Daniel blinks a few times, relieved to be able to see again. The landing carpet is a deep, dusty orange with a swirling, irregular pattern in blacks and browns. It reminds him of the shadow of a tree cast by a streetlamp, and he can almost imagine the branches swaying in the breeze. There are photos on the wall, black and white portraits of a family who were unable to muster a single smile between them. The photo in the center is of a mother and baby. The mother, hunched over, is looking down at the floor, as if she's just been scolded. Something about her expression seems vaguely familiar. In her arms, the baby's eyes are shut and its little mouth is open in a wail that will last forever. Why would anyone take such a photo? And why would Marley hang it on the wall?

"Does your family live here with you?" asks Daniel, remembering the footsteps on the ceiling.

Marley shakes his head but doesn't answer straight away. Then he says "These days there's nobody here but me. Nobody alive, at any rate."

Daniel tells himself that the noises he heard must have been the timbers creaking in the wind: just the normal noises of any old building in a storm. But Jeremy's book claimed that auditory encounters with ghosts were more common than actual sightings. Daniel wishes he'd said something about the creaking ceiling while they were downstairs. He'd feel much happier if he knew his friends had heard the footsteps, too.

Marley points to the bedroom at the end of the landing, the roll and tumble of an unmade bed just about visible at the furthest reaches of the bathroom light. "That's my room," he says. "There's nothing to see in there except dirty clothes and an old man's bookcase." He pulls the door closed anyway.

Ellen moves closer to Daniel. "I want to take some photos with my phone," she whispers, "but I left my handbag in your car. Can I borrow your keys?"

"Sure," he says. "Want me to come with you?"

"You'd better stay here to keep Jeremy out of trouble."

Daniel watches Ellen creak back downstairs. He's known her for less than an hour and already the sight of her leaving makes him anxious. When the night is over, will she want to stay in touch? Will they ever see her again? When he turns back towards the landing, Jeremy is staring at him with an expression he can't read. Is it possible that Jeremy has feelings for Ellen, too?

"Right," says Marley, "who wants to see inside the nursery? There are ghosts in here, for sure."

***

Daniel expected the nursery to smell of baby lotion. That's how nurseries are supposed to smell. Baby lotion with notes of wet nappy.

The nursery in Coastguard's Cottage smells of damp and decay.

The wardrobe leans sideways against the wall. One of the doors is dented like it's been hit with a cricket bat and the other is missing. Inside, the wardrobe is full of baby clothes—bodysuits and jumpers in pinks and grays—falling from hangers or crumpled up on the bottom shelf.

There's a rocking chair in front of the window, looking out towards the sea. Daniel's wondering what the view would be like during daytime when lightning skitters across horizon, illuminating a vast expanse of black, lumpy water.

In the far corner of the nursery, there's a cot—a flimsy, rickety thing decorated with splinters and mold. A tattered mobile of cardboard birds and cobwebs hangs above it. The duvet is missing and there's a dark brown flower blossoming in the middle of the sheet that might—though surely not—be dried blood.

"What happened in here?" asks Jeremy.

"My wife," says Marley. A shadow falls across his face. "We didn't know. She didn't know."

"Didn't know what?"

"This history of this room. The murders that have happened here over the years. The way they linger. The way they get under your skin." Marley stops speaking and pins Daniel to the wall with his stare. Daniel tries to step back further, willing himself to be absorbed by the plaster and brickwork.

Jeremy steps in front of him, shielding him from Marley's glare. "Murders?" he asks.

"It was a night like this a couple of decades ago," says Marley. "My wife was in here nursing our little girl when the banging started. All I could hear were these terrible, soul-shaking thumps, over and over. At first my daughter was screaming but then she went silent. I rushed in, of course, but I was too late."

Daniel swallows. He'd assumed that any ghosts in the property belonged to the distant, unknowable past. Dead, if not buried. He never imagined they'd still be alive in the old man's memories.

"My wife was in here," says Marley, "swinging our daughter like a club."

Silence haunts the nursery until Jeremy says, "What happened to your wife?"

Marley doesn't answer; he just shakes his head and looks at the floor. His wife is gone. Probably dead. Daniel searches for tears in Marley's eyes but the old man just seems lost, as though his soul has left his body.

And then someone walks past the nursery door.

Daniel turns quickly, hoping to see Ellen returning from the car. But it can't be; she hasn't been gone long enough and he'd have heard her on the stairs. His skin prickling, he steps out onto the landing. The air is cold and tastes like trouble, but there's no one there.

"What did you see?" asks Jeremy.

"I don't know," says Daniel. "Someone walked past the nursery. A woman, I think."

"A ghost?" asks Jeremy, standing at his shoulder.

Marley grins. "Isn't that what you came for?"

It's then Daniel notices the door to the spare bedroom. It's wide open.

***

In the light of a naked bulb, the spare bedroom looks even more haggard than the nursery. The peach and cream wallpaper has been torn off in wild, jagged strips. There's a built-in wardrobe, padlocked on the outside, and a metal bed frame that's missing a mattress. On the mantel piece above the boarded-up fireplace, there's a cracked mirror and three candles burned down to nothing. And that's it.

Daniel doesn't know how the old man can live in such a sad, decrepit place. Forget about the ghosts, the rooms alone would keep Daniel from sleeping at night. A splash of paint and some new furniture would surely exorcise every last trace of the past.

"Where did she go?" asks Daniel.

"It's your wife, isn't it?" says Jeremy to Marley. "She's still here."

Marley stuffs his hands in his pockets and shrugs. "Could be," he says. "No one ever really leaves this place."

Yesterday, ghosts were the creatures of overactive and immature imaginations. Now, Daniel doesn't know what to think.

"Can we look in the wardrobe?" asks Jeremy.

"I wouldn't recommend that."

"Why not?" asks Jeremy.

Marley leans against the wall and sighs for all the centuries. "This cottage has many stories," he says. "But the wardrobe?" He frowns and rubs his forehead. "Before we moved in, another family lived here. They had two daughters and a son on the way. Unfortunately, there were complications during the birth and the boy's brain was starved of oxygen. He was born severely handicapped—mentally and physically.

"Maybe it's this place," continues Marley, "or maybe the parents just didn't know how to cope. Whatever the reason, on his third birthday, they locked their son in that wardrobe."

Daniel imagines the boy's father fitting the hasp and staple to the wardrobe door. The mother fastening the padlock after she'd condemned her son to darkness. Surely no one locks children in dark spaces outside of horror movies.

And why the hell would Marley keep the wardrobe?

"The boy was in there for over a year. Shunned by his family. Sitting in the stench of his excrement. Banging his head against the wardrobe door and howling for attention. In the end, he died of blood poisoning. But like everything in this cottage, he's never really left."

"We want to look inside," says Jeremy. "Don't we, Daniel?"

Daniel steps away from the wardrobe. Through the window, he can see trees being buffeted by the wind and he can just make out the roof of the barn. Somewhere beyond the courtyard, his car is waiting, ready to take them away from this awful place.

Except Ellen hasn't come back yet.

"Are you sure you want to see inside?" asks Marley, slipping a small key from his cardigan pocket. "Sometimes people get ...stuck."

"I'm going to look for Ellen," says Daniel. "I want to make sure she's okay."

"Who's Ellen?" asks Marley.

"The woman we arrived with," says Daniel.

Marley shakes his head, looking confused.

"In the yellow raincoat," says Jeremy.

"I have no idea what you're talking about," says Marley.

***

Standing in the courtyard, squinting into the rain, Daniel shouts Ellen's name over and over again. He replays the evening in his mind, trying to remember every little detail. The first time they saw her, opposite the ruined church, with the wind tugging at her raincoat. Then later, when she calmed Marley's dog in the courtyard. Daniel's sure she's not a ghost—he felt her brush past him on the stairs—so why would Marley suggest otherwise?

"You don't think she fell off the cliff, do you?" asks Jeremy.

"I promise I didn't see her," says Marley.

"She's out here somewhere," says Daniel. "She might be in trouble. We should phone the police."

"My landline's been out of service since the storm started," says Marley. "The nearest phone is in the next village, a few miles away. I doubt you'll find a mobile signal before then."

"Damn it," says Daniel. "I gave Ellen my car keys."

"Let's go back inside," says Marley. "I'll check the phone again and see if I can find some torches. I don't much care for this weather." Without waiting for a reply, the old man turns back towards the cottage, leaving Daniel and Jeremy alone in the courtyard.

"You know she was real, right?" says Daniel.

"I don't know what to think," replies Jeremy. "If you say she's not a ghost, that's good enough for me. But why would Marley say he couldn't see her?"

"I don't know. But I don't trust him."

Jeremy rests a hand on Daniel's shoulder. "We wanted a big adventure, didn't we? This is it. This is the story we're going to tell everyone when we get home. And we're going to get through this. You and me. I ...I love you, Daniel. I won't let anything bad happen to us, okay?"

"I don't want to go back to the cottage."

"We can't stay out here. We need torches and coats. The phone might be working again. If not, maybe Marley will give us a lift in his truck. What choice do we have?"

"If we go back to the cottage, I'm afraid we'll never come out again. What was it he said? 'No one ever really leaves this place?' I think he was talking about us."

"Then why don't you stay here?" says Jeremy. "Take shelter by the barn. I'll go back and ask Marley for a lift to the nearest village."

"What if he says no?"

"We'll borrow his truck. The keys are on the table by the front door. He doesn't need to know."

"And what if you don't come back?"

"I'm not going to leave you," says Jeremy. "But if I don't come back, you start running. Don't come looking for me. You promise?"

As Jeremy heads back to the cottage, Daniel brushes the wet hair from his forehead and folds his arms across his chest for warmth. Behind him, the barn creaks in the wind. Above him, the powerlines hiss. There are so many shadowy corners in the courtyard, and so many acres of fields on the other side of the road, Ellen could be anywhere. There's no way they'll find her before daybreak.

If they find her at all.

Daniel wonders how it came to this. Why isn't he in Ibiza with the rest of his friends, drinking until sunrise, dancing in nightclubs and throwing himself at every half-dressed, half-pretty young woman who returns his gaze? Why does his life have to be so different to everyone else's?

And then he sees something on the side of the cottage, barely visible in the dark. He steps forward, squinting, trying to work out if his eyes are deceiving him. But they aren't.

There's an external staircase.

Maybe the woman he saw walking past the nursery didn't go down the stairs to the hallway. Maybe she came down outside the cottage. She could have been in Marley's room when they arrived. That would explain the footsteps on the ceiling.

Daniel can feel his chest growing tight. Something is amiss but he can't quite see what it is. And then the security lamp clicks off and the courtyard rushes to darkness.

He looks up and there's someone standing in the spare bedroom window.

A woman.

Before he can react, the shadows in front of him start moving and something is coming for him, bleeding out of the darkness. He knows it isn't the dog this time, so he doesn't stop to think about where he's going, he just runs. Past the barn. Past the kennel. Around the side of the cottage. Towards Jeremy, the one person on this whole island he can trust, who is—

Wait.

What?

Jeremy and Marley are standing at the end of the lane, overlooking the drop. Something below them is glowing blue-green in the darkness, bright enough to bathe the two of them in its light. Daniel can't see what it is but Marley is pointing and Jeremy is leaning.

"Jeremy?" calls Daniel.

As Jeremy turns around, Marley shoves him towards the cliff edge.

Jeremy is wrong-footed. He steps backwards and backwards again, eyes wide in surprise, arms flapping like some ridiculous bird, his feet searching for balance. When he steps back a third time, his foot finds nothing at all.

Time slows down like it did when their car hit the guardrail. Daniel notices the rain bouncing up off the paving stones; Marley's silver pendant glowing blue-green like the light beyond the cliff; and Jeremy, his eyes wide in shock, his mouth already moving to a scream, his arms flailing as he falls.

And then all that remains of Jeremy is a long and rapidly diminishing shriek, which sounds a lot like "Daniel."

***

Daniel's heart is beating so hard he thinks it'll explode. His thoughts are white water, tumbling and crashing without form or meaning. He tells himself murder is the stuff of tabloid newspapers and late-night television shows. It doesn't happen in real life. Not to people he knows.

And yet, Jeremy is gone.

He runs because he doesn't know what else to do. He twists away from the cliff edge and sprints towards the courtyard, expecting to feel Marley's hand on his shoulder, pulling him back. But it isn't the old man who stops him.

It's Sheenagh. The woman from the campsite.

Daniel slips and nearly falls in his effort to stop running. Sheenagh's standing at the end of the path, blocking his route to the courtyard.

"Help me," he says, shouting to be heard over the wind. "We have to get away from here."

And then he remembers-

It was Sheenagh who sent them to the cottage.

With Marley behind him and Sheenagh in front, Daniel's only other option is to return to the cottage. He might be able to lock the door behind him, giving him time to...what? Maybe Marley was lying about his landline being out of service or maybe Daniel will find a phone signal upstairs. If nothing else, he'll have time.

Time to come up with a plan.

Time to find a weapon.

Time to be alive.

He reaches the front door and realizes it's closed. He pushes against it but the door won't budge. Tears fill his eyes as he thumps against the wood with his fists.

And then it opens.

"Ellen?" he says.

In blue jeans and a smart leather biker jacket, Ellen stands in the doorway, drying her hair with a towel. Somehow, she seems taller. And older.

"You're okay!" says Daniel. "Where have you been? What are you...?"

He stops speaking. How could he have been so stupid? Ellen was the woman in the spare bedroom window. Around her neck, she wears a silver necklace with the same fish pendant as Marley. And like Marley's, it's glowing. It was Ellen he saw in the spare bedroom window and Sheenagh who came at him in the courtyard. "What's going on, Ellen?" he asks. Even as the words come out of his mouth, he knows he won't like the answer.

Ellen drops the towel to the floor and looks past him, saying "Haven't you dealt with him yet? I've dried my hair already."

Daniel steps away from the cottage, shaking his head. "Let me have my car keys and I'll go," he says. "I don't want any trouble. I won't say anything."

Ellen looks at him but with none of the warmth she had before. "Your car's going the same way as your boyfriend," she says.

"What?"

Daniel is beaten. He's going to die. This wretched place with this awful weather will be the last thing he knows. If only he'd gone to Ibiza. If only Jeremy had settled for one of the brochure destinations instead of the cottage.

"Why are you doing this?" he asks.

"To protect our home," says Ellen.

"The cottage should have fallen into the sea years ago," explains Marley. "But we learned of a way to save it. Our neighbors refused to believe and look what happened to them."

"The Gods of the Southern Horizon demand a sacrifice," says Sheenagh. "Two lives a year to prevent further erosion of the cliffs."

"Two lives a year," repeats Daniel, realizing what this means.

"There are always travelers passing through the campsite," says Sheenagh.

"You're the woman in the photos on the landing," says Daniel. "You're his wife."

"And Ellen's mother," she says.

"But your daughter died when she was a baby. You killed her."

"You didn't believe all that crap, did you?" asks Ellen.

"You wanted ghosts," says Marley. "We gave you ghosts."

"But it's not the ghosts you should be afraid of," says Sheenagh. "Not out here."

"Are you going to kill me?"

"Not us," says Marley.

"Then let me go."

Marley wipes the rain from his brow. "I'm afraid we can't do that. You heard Ellen. We're not going to kill you, but you still have to die."

"One sacrifice to wake the beast," says Sheenagh.

"And another to appease the Gods," says Ellen.

As they say this, something large and wet smacks Daniel in the stomach. He's jolted backwards, grunting in surprise. An arm—no, a tentacle—has wrapped around him, pinning his arms and squeezing the air from his lungs. Its skin is oily and covered in scales. It lifts him backwards off the cliff as if he were no heavier than an insect. He tries to slip free but its grip is too tight. He tries to call for help but the air is gone from his lungs.

Marley, Sheenagh, and Ellen huddle together in the rain, bowing their heads as though in prayer. All three of them wear glowing pendants around their necks.

Daniel screams with his eyes.

In the blue-green glow, he can see the craggy rocks of the cliff face. He can see the crashing white waves. He must be a hundred meters up, maybe more, and the lack of oxygen is making his head feel light. Black spots appear in his vision. Below him, the water is rising, pushed upwards by what looks like thousands of glowing blue-green eels. And then something breaks the surface, like a submarine but many times bigger. It's not thousands of eels but one giant creature with skin that glows in wild streaks. It has teeth and gills, and a mouth as wide as a football pitch. Enormous, scaly tentacles snake upwards from its chin like the beard of Medusa. It rolls sideways until Daniel can see a single black eye staring up at him.

Daniel doesn't want to die. Not like this. And yet, as the tentacle lowers him towards its open mouth, he begins to feel calm. Maybe it's the lack of oxygen or maybe it's because he's powerless to fight. Whatever the reason, he doesn't feel afraid anymore.

Jeremy is already down there somewhere. Tangled up with the beast. And no doubt he has a plan. Whatever Daniel's fate is to be, he won't have to face it alone.

As he descends, Newton's last words come rushing back to him.

...whilst the great ocean of truth lay all undiscovered before me.

There are so many things Daniel's never seen or done. So many adventures he never had and lessons he never learned.

But he'll always know that he was chosen.

And unlike Newton, his last words don't need to be eloquent or philosophical.

He's discovered the truth of the great ocean.

And it's staring right at him.

THE NIGHTMARE OF NIK THE NECROPHELIAC
David Kotok

The Guard: The mynah birds stop their chatter. The prisoner stabs his spade into the red earth and spits out a mango stone. The birds flinch, ready to fly, but the grubs fleeing the cut soil give them courage to stay, their yellow eyes fixed on his hands and the engraving needles in his belt. Nik takes a steel point from its sheath, peels the dirt from his fingernails and digs the nib into his teeth, curling a lip and growling as he fiddles.

"There be something there," he says, slobbering on his thumb. "Something I eats not yet gone."

Nik does not speak to me. He speaks to the breeze tugging his ropes of gray hair, to the mynahs fretting on the wires, to the ants crawling over his shovel, to the bloody halves of a worm squirming either side of the blade. He sucks loud draughts of spittle and drags the morsel from his jagged teeth.

"Ah, it be gone," he shouts, and pretends to fling the dart at the mynahs, "I eats it!"

The birds scatter, the white on their wings flashing in flight. They circle and resettle, hopping over mourning tinsel and knotted plastic body bags strung amongst the graves, cackling at what may happen next. I cradle my rifle close and engage the stock. I make sure Nik is watching as I grip the trigger.

The Necrophiliac: I digs a hole and lies them in. I scoops out mud with a swab of sweat by morning light and rest whilst priest or *kiyai* say grief words and them as bereaved (some serious, some not so serious, all in for the purse) trickle a pinch of gravel on the coffin. Maybe them toss in a posy of white flowers; lilies for rich, when once I buries them packing full wallets, and frangipani, plucked from near-side bushes for them poor bastards as never left a tip for same.

So it be in days past when Nik be a free man with pick and trowel and a pack of dry tinder. In days gone when I keeps a careful watch over Sleepers under the turf, them whom I did choose to tuck in gentle for slumber. In days before I be shackled as a man of dark wisdom and distasteful truths.

In days gone, before I has the learning, Nik be wed with handsome wife and beautiful daughter; a man proud as any other, if not more so besides. Mine graveyard skills be appreciated and I be paid fair. Mine wife also, for she polish one building of concrete and glass from floor to floor to roof, a giant sarcophagus riven with marble and steel. We lives comfortable, and mine child attend class in the *kampong,* and I be blind to signs of infidelity until one White Horse gallop from that edifice with mine wife and ride her for pleasure in the pastures of Kemang. Him teach her many foreign trick and fill her head with arrogance and greed. She learn to covet gleaming stones and dress like a fancy Madam. I says to curious neighbors I has thrown her out, but truth be told she walk away with mine child, whom she steal and pervert. Mine demeanor did change. I becomes a man of hate and suspicion and afflicted with a darkness thick and sour, until one other day Mister White Horse discard mine wife as horse-wank. She ask one time to come home but I have no forgiveness, rage only, and she show spite and take up with shamans and wizards and paint her face and push up her titties and loiter in bars filled with rainbow stars and lie in the beds of Euro-man and Asia-man and mine neighbor, if him pay. She put mine daughter in Old Supandi Fellatio School and them work at night together, or so I dares to think. Mine mind be unclear in them days, fat-fat with jealousy and full of filth, and with the hammer of wickedness I cleans them of vice, mother and child. One sin begat sin and for that I has no pride, but such be the shame brought upon mine wretched soul.

In days long past I knows not of life beyond its passing. I be ignorant of how a soft burial may tempt the Black Moon to labor and give birth. Had I the understanding, I might have brought mine family back from slaughter, and begged forgiveness and given pardon also. In them times I thinks only of how not to be caught, so I sets a funeral pyre and places them, wife and daughter, into caskets with men they be unacquainted and I thinks it apt bedding. I light the sticks and watch them burn, mine head bowed with them gentlemen's relatives, as in official respect, but I has mine own reasons to watch the flames flicker and become embers and ash. In them days I bears no guilt. I sees mine deed as a reflection on life as in death.

Today I curses mine dalliance with evil and the ignorance which cause a man to act on impulse and fury, and to seek the avoidance of consequence. Today I faces justice with this guard, digging trenches for fellow prisoners to lie within, but this be not the reason for mine incarceration. Sir Judge know nothing of the deed of familial murder, him be ignorant of mine original sin. Him know only of Nik's modern works with Sleepers, which him pronounce as 'nefarious' and set sentence without end because I practices a secret truth. I be captive for learning what must be unlearned.

The Guard: Nik gestures for me to come closer. I nod but, like the birds, I keep a steady watch on his movements. He turns slowly, his way of assurance, and passes me the long staff of the spade.

"You hold the iron which cut the ground," he says. "I stamps it."

He starts a curious shuffle over the freshly turned earth. His feet patter in light steps, delicate and deft for a thick-set man, a dainty jig. I swallow a smile at his prancing, hands fluttering by his thighs, tresses bouncing like the mane of a show-pony. He raises his head to the swirling clouds and whistles as the mound reduces, smoothing under the patter of his toes, and when he stops, with a flourish and a bow before the headstone, the grave holds the shape of a bed and pillow, as if the boy he has buried is tucked up snug under a blanket of loam.

"Is this how you put them under, prisoner? Soft and loose, so they are easy to dig up?"

"Sleepers need comfort," he says. "Him will yearn to stretch after the long dreaming, and has need to know him shall be cared for when waking under the darkest of our dark nights."

Nik turns and kneels, resting his brow on the stone and muttering low so I cannot hear. His eyes are focused, as though he uses the veins in the rock to path his sight, down into the earth to the face of the entombed child.

"Are you talking to the boy?" I ask. "Are you making promises you cannot fulfil?"

He ignores me and continues his whispers. I want to lean closer, to catch his words, but it might be a dangerous thing. He may be playing a trick, waiting to snatch my throat and use his tools to render me as lifeless as the boy, another of his breathless toys.

The Necrophiliac: This guard tell of the deception which turn the locks by which I be caged. The keys on him belt ensure mine sermon of rebirth be mute. Yet, him have mine motivation wrong. I does not care to dig up Sleepers. There be no need. I sets them down gentle so a coverlet might be shaken aside by limbs weak with death. Sleepers cannot climb from a nest too deep, or even shallow if clay be packed firm. Them have not the strength of folk blessed with beating hearts and flowing blood but be frail infants, feeble of will and able only to meekly claw and mew. Them be in need of nurture and shelter to grow strong on special evenings, such as this very night as creeps into dusk. Them as dead shall surface with the Black Moon but need protection, and quick, for them be prey of Scavengers as haunt our dark skies.

I speaks of Demons of Sleep, imps with leather wings, set loose by our devious gods to butcher them as wriggle free of soil. Monsters which not be commanded by instinct but by men who share mine insight, but more devious. Men whose purpose be to ensure fragile norms do not fracture. Them Demons feast not just to fill empty bellies, but to protect the myth of eternal rest.

Mine task be to receive them resurrected and create a field for safe celebration. Them shall dance with joy. Them shall dance with love for I be their guardian.

The Guard: The gravedigger grins, scars across his mouth tug over smashed teeth.

"What be him name?" he asks.

I unfurl the document. The type-face is poor, barely visible, although the typist has forced the keys hard to punch holes through the paper.

"I am not sure. There was little ink on the ribbon."

"It be ever so," he says, his hands together as in prayer. "It be for even and ever. Amen."

"You should not taunt the Lord," I say. "He has punishment enough for you."

Nik's neck twists and he thrusts toward me, lips thin and angry. He takes an etching pin from his belt and holds the steel tip forward like a dagger. The mynahs flee in a flurry of shrieks as I step back, levelling my weapon at the veins on his head. He stares into the muzzle, squinting into the recesses, as if he might check for the bullet, should the sergeant have failed to load it.

The convicted know there are not cartridges to fill guns. Each time a gun is fired is one pellet less. There is not ink to wet type-writer ribbons and not candles to light the dark. We collect sticks to burn, and lava rock to scrub skin and clothing clean. Rice porridge is watered and dumplings are rich in paper fibers more than suet. There are not caskets for the deceased, who lie wrapped in their rags. There are not chains for the insane and not padlocks for the desperate. We guards are posted promissory notes by dint of wages and live precarious by the wavering threat of a bullet.

Nik knows this well: a game of chance to subdue dangerous men. Only the destitute gambler, tired of parasitic hope, might take the wager, but such a man wants to lose and has no plan if the chamber is empty.

Nik is no risk-taker. He wants to live. He may love the dear departed but not death. He must know what awaits him beyond the last breath. Men of terrible deeds can be certain of worse to endure, and for an eternity longer than to age in our crumbling jail. If I were to gamble, this penury is not so different from his toil beyond these walls. Nik is still the digger of pits and custodian of the Dead.

The Necrophiliac: Was one time gone, under a sky lit only with stars, when

I first hears the scratch of them interned by a hard crust. Curiosity, not faith, took mine shovel and steered it to release a couple from incarceration; one old lady, flesh in stinking ribbons, and a man with snapped back and cracked skull. O, how confusion turned to relief as air touched fester! Them lift from the crush of soil and twist in deformity, but without the pain of fracture and the agony of being. We dances through to dawn, and mine presence keep all them circling marauders at distance, as if I be a shield, until the sun blues the sky and them devils fly away hungry. Then I helps them pair of dancing dead lie back for sleep, and I covers them lightly with soil so as not to scare the ignorant and, yes, to allow them to rise again.

This be mine schooling. I learns to place folk down gentle. I learns a hole dug deeper than one average man be but a sly prescription to silence the drums of our bondage. If a crypt be a skim of mud them as dead shall return, and them which live shall be free in the knowledge the fatal be naught but a short and sharp pain. I learns the decreed depth of interment be the dungeon of them deceased, described in law to secrete the truth of immortality and keep man and woman fearful on pain of purgatory. I learns the truth of life marching onward after our demise, and without agony or regret, if it be allowed.

This I knows not when Nik sparks the tender to him family, wife and daughter, embraced with strangers in fiery coffins. Had the perception of passing and return been with me in such days, I would not choose the flame but the soil, and them would be with me now, on nights as this, risen from their bed and sharing our bonds. That be a sourness to taste year on year but give me reason to share mine wisdom, for the benefit of all others.

For this I vows to speak the unspeakable truth, though such words threaten them who hold the chains of our obedience. So here I be, incarcerated for repugnant deeds as falsified by the tongues and pens of them servants of our scheming Masters. Them same men as release Scavengers to forage for Sleepers whom escape the proscribed depths of burial, as might lie in shallow pits or fields or forests, or float on nearside tides.

Mine hymn, should ears listen, be of restoration; a song to exult a second coming for all. We shall walk again, less the hurt which grabs the throat and stifles life. The drapes hung to veil our minds shall be discarded and our bindings severed.

This be my work also.

The Guard: Nik turns a chisel to the granite. The sound is harsh and his cuts cause the slightest tingle in my jaw. This is the depth of my feeling, as scant as makes no difference. If not my teeth, Nik hopes to make my ears wince by the angle of his chisel, as the frustration under his dripping brow tells, but I hear no more irritant than the whine of a hungry mosquito. He digs and studies my reaction but I perceive only his intent.

"Write the words less angry," I say, to humor him.

"The stone be brittle. I angles the nib should it crack. The stone be too thin."

This is not so. He has carved many a time in a way less sour. All memorials are as thin, or thinner, than this one. The sear of his effort may not afflict my ears, but the mynahs have flown. They hop in the boughs of the mango tree, hiding their heads under their wings. A puff of smoke works from the tip of Nik's busy steel and curls a frail noose about his neck. It is tempting to wish it a garrotte to tighten with each cleave of his fingers.

Then he stops.

"I needs a name, I needs an age," he says. "And it be done."

"It may be Santoso," I say as I struggle to read the paper. "Hendra Santoso, seventeen years and a thief."

Nik starts again, deftly nicking at the rock, drawing a spider-like script. The screech of his art is subtler somehow, as if he digs softer in reverence for the boy who has a name and, by the word 'thief,' a sense of being.

The mynahs are emboldened and return to perch on the wire, an audience waiting for the theatre to close. Nik blows the powder from his work and runs his nails over the curves of the letters he has etched, 'Rest In What Peace Thee May Find'.

What sacrilege is this?" I ask. "Additional words, a phrase unasked for and scrawled by a sinner for a sinner who must meet his Maker? Or do you make trivia of this little death to argue with me?"

A mynah springs for the tatters of the worm as it rears from the soil, and is pierced by a needle flicked from Nik's fist. The thin blade protrudes from the bird's eye and through the back of its head, sunk to the bamboo hilt. A slither of pink mucus sways from the point as the bird twitches on its legs, choking as it swallows the worm. It falls, feathers aquiver, and stills.

"Him last supper," says Nik, and I look to see if his lips wear amusement.

My finger plays on the trigger. If he laughs, if he smiles, I will take my chance to remove his twisted soul to Hell. As the Judge might have done by a hangman's knot, rather than pander to the needs of our rising prison mortalities through Nik's repute as a digger of tombs. Yet I know I cannot, for if the barrel proves wanting I will fall, a hail of engraving pins in my heart. All that keeps either one of us alive is the lie of a bullet.

"Do you like your work, prisoner?" I ask, deciding the verbal barb of mockery will suffice.

"I loves it," he says, leering, returning a dart of his own.

The Necrophiliac: Mine guard be innocent. All them guards equally so. Ignorance be their custodian. Them know not the rules of men be drawn to set down Sleepers in trenches and under rock so that we might ask no questions of our gods, so the preaching of snarling priests and cheating presidents and greedy ministers and men of commerce be beyond doubt. The measurement of burial, if not written, be set in tradition, to ensure our necks be bowed and our Will be compliant. The Rule of Law demand the perpetuation of pretense, for what would become if life after bereavement be proven? Not as a dream-world of clouds where angels pluck harps, cherubs sooth the ache of servitude, maidens offer teats for suckling and the genitalia of men be gold-plated, but a cracked mirror of what we once had, empty of breath yet life once more and without the burden of pain to prickle the soul. In such fashion we might live long and long, in slow decay it be likely true, yet all but immortal.

I prays not to clemency but for the hot oils of candor to spill. O, what will come to pass if mine hymn pour from pulpits and minarets, applauded by a Choir of Death? What world might emerge from the chaos born of long-hidden truths at once revealed? A land of peace and contentment, without fear of our demise and where all be possible. This I predict.

I be the Priest of Unholy Verity.

The Guard: The sun drops behind the fire mountain, as dormant as the bodies Nik sets down in light toppings of earth under stones erased of the name of those who had lain before them. In turn, their names will be cleansed, their bones removed and memorials re-ground, once a period of false mourning is spent. Dignity in death is discarded, all expense removed to keep the governor and his accountants munching on *ristafel* dainties and their plump wives in silk robes. And to spoon thin coconut broth into the mouths of convicts and warders, enough sustenance to muster strength to wake and realize our roles, prisoner and guard, and return to our beds in a cycle of mundanity. Often I think this way and it worries me to be aimless.

I have no memory of life before this work as a shepherd of vile men. I lie awake in the silent hours and look deep into my head but there is only darkness. No feeling of sadness or joy, or warmth or pain. No images of childhood, of school or other work I might have done. No field or beach or lake, no river or jungle or mountain. No parent, no sibling, no friend, no partner, no enemy. No faces beyond my treacherous charges and my listless and introvert colleagues. I lie in my bed in my hut, in my uniform, which is over-large and faded and frayed, and see nothing but the moment of existence. I watch the ceiling and the *chic-chaks* as they chase gnats, and the spiders stalking flies and spinning webs, and the scurry of rats, and I understand when I must rise and where I must go and how I must collect my gun from the Captain. I know I will be passed keys for the cells of those I must watch over that day, but I don't remember who taught me this, so how do I know? I eat what I am given and do what I'm told, and if I ever sleep I don't know it. Yes, it worries me to have no memory and, so it seems, no future to speculate. Just the moments that fade one into the other. I am indeed aimless.

Yet, as I watch Nik clean his implements and fold his cloths, I see the necessity of my role in monitoring the miscreant, however hollow I am within. I see the result of unfettered belief, of deed without restraint, of heinous fantasy realized, of evil unleashed by the collapse of Faith.

It is told Nik would venture under a moonless night and dig up bodies he had previous laid to rest and play ghoulish games. It is said he would place the Dead in immodest poses and hold them in his arms and waltz and pour toddy down their throats, though they cannot drink and cannot dance and, of course, cannot protest. Even, it is rumored, he may make love to them, woman or man, girl or boy, each corpse violated for his satisfaction. I must not give a thought to this horror for the revulsion in me is strong but, as I watch him carve stone, I am tortured by the depravity. He shines with perspiration, surveying his task, his spade strung across his back, the tool of his fetish. I am appalled by his very form before me.

The mynahs have gone, leaving the remains of their brother on the soil. Nik wipes his brow and picks up the bird and draws his needle from the skull, wiping it clean on his tongue. He tosses the frail carcass onto Santoso's grave.

"Would mine guard prefer flowers?" he says as he turns to face the sun, a fire-ball balanced on the shoulder of the volcano.

His face is flushed crimson like the sky, his hair whips of flame, his skin blood-soaked.

"Let us stay here this dusk," he says. "The sun will not begat a moon. What we sees in this field shall make a charade of prayer."

For the first time I can remember, I feel anger as a physical manifestation in my chest. A rock, cold and sharp, thumps my ribs and my finger itches on the trigger.

The Necrophiliac: I sees hesitation and distress and I believes mine guard harbors a doubt. Perhaps I be quick to judge him as guard. Him stand upright in uniform and cap, clasping gun and keys, but I sees questions in him sallow face and sterile eyes. I senses the rot in him soul, turning faith to dust. Mine guard will be swayed if we may witness a rebirth together, should we dares to confront them winged parasites as warriors, and them as risen shall donate love to us. Them shall give in gratitude and in celebration of the passing of solitude. Them shall express joy in generosity and mute wonder. Them shall give with the innocence and trust of new-born babes, but delivered a second time.

Mine Sleepers shall embrace them as be so brave to watch their parade and keep them winged predators at bay. The Dead shall adore more-so them who share in the Dance of Resurrection, as has been mine pleasure.

As I has done.

The Guard: I will not answer his mischief but do my duty and return him to his hut, and turn the chains about the door and fasten the padlock. My thumb flicks the rifle's safety catch and I motion with the barrel it is time to go. Nik turns and ambles around the burial, a final inspection. I maintain my distance, the gun sight trained on the small of his back; a shot to render a man immobile.

As he skips under the shade of the mango tree, as sunset sparkles rubies in the leaves, a swollen fruit falls and splits over the nearest headstone, spilling flesh and dribbling juice. Nik crouches, his hands wavering by his belt.

"Sleepers stir," he says. "Them would be among us and we must protect the risen."

"Nonsense, Nik," I say, addressing him by his name for the first time, which I am oddly comfortable with. "It is fallen crop, not offerings."

"You be wrong. The stirrings of them below shake the roots and drop the fruit. I says there shall be romps and elation this night, and so there shall, if I be able to protect mine Sleepers from them hell-born horde as wait hungry in the mountain."

Nik talks of legend, of winged monsters swooping from caves to feast on the living in their beds. This is fable he has altered to his fancy. The *Orang Bati* slaughter those in slumber, not the deceased in their boxes or the criminal in his pit. Bats begat of men fly on the darkest evenings to chew on the soft tissue of dreamers, to strip meat as store for when the moon is too bright for saucer eyes. The prisoners are full of such stories, once told to them as children to horrify and to force manners, threats to instill good behavior and learning. Does he allude to these tales to scare, to bend me to his whim as a child cows to a mother, or the meek to a bully? This may be his ruse, but as shadows weave the branches of the tree into the claws of witches, I am unnerved. The cemetery is a place I do not wish to be. The silence of the charnel yard is brittle, taut to snap and scatter shards of devilment across the world.

I do not wish to be in the company of the digger and his trickery. Even now he goads me, assuming a bent gait and prancing light-foot, arms spread, the shovel on his spine a horn above his head and a tail between his legs, trailing like a beast loping in the bushes.

It would be better to be in my room, on my bed of damp straw, with the door secured against this terrible night.

The Necrophiliac: The lessons I learns among thieves and murderers and holy bombers cast into this festering camp can sway a man to kill, but mine be not to snuff out life. Not nowadays, whatever be done in mine history. If I ever takes life, it be to restore same when right to do so, not to destroy. Mine be to bring life forth. Yet, such deed be condemned as fiendish and magic.

Ha! How can this be when them I assists do walk and play and make love as them who live? This be purity, this be good, this be the work of gods. Within this hour them as buried shall emerge to resume a presence in the world, if I be permitted to offer protection from hordes of winged beasts greedy to gather flesh and who, with efficient butchery, abet our Keepers maintain their fiction. Sleepers be frail and bewildered and easy larder for *Orang Bati* with their hollow teeth and claws like knives. Demons will feast if I cannot defend them as seek to festival in divine renaissance.

This I swears to do.

The Guard: Nik talks to himself as he watches the sky, a batik of purple and gold. We have not moved, despite my order. He wastes time as ink seeps into the heavens and the stars shine their spite. He challenges my authority and it angers me, and makes me nervous also.

"It is time to leave," I say, but he does not move, other than to nod at the volcano.

"See, them creatures come to set a path, to search fresh dug graves and listen for movement under mud and grit, as birds hunt worms."

A thin plume streams from the mountain, spreading like smoke against the fading light, the flight of bats from their caverns. It is the same each night, when the flying fox and lesser cousins soar as one to feed, but a vision of monsters clad in cloaks of stitched human hide settle amongst my thoughts. Anxiety quivers in my chest as the flock advances upon us. It is as though I have felt this threat before, as though the darkest nights lean down to swallow me and ingest.

"*Ayo*, Nik! Pick up your tools. Let us go," I say, and there is a shake in my voice.

"When them creatures fly, *Orang Bati* follow," he says, waving at the advancing swarm, and I note a tremble in his voice too, as if he were also afraid. "Them know pickings await as ripe fruit this night."

I shout again for him to move, but he ignores me and unties the sheaths of his pointers.

"I protects Sleepers," he says. "This be my task."

He arranges a set of needles between his fingers, to dress his clenched fist with a glove of sharpened steel. He slips the spade from his back and holds it in his other hand like a spear, aimed at my chest. Sweat glints in his reddened brow and drips from his nose, from his neck, his arms, his chest. Sweat drenches his body.

"What waters your skin?" I ask, and my throat is dry and my bravado a whisper. "Does fear of this night cause you to tremble?"

I wipe my brow but it is dry. I do not perspire. I am not able. Though the air is hot and the humidity wretched and dread walks cold on my back.

"Leave," Nik says, "or I shall slay you and bring you about once more, with a heart as chill as stone. Your death be nothing but a brief passing and you shall be one of mine children."

I stroke the trigger and a panic shivers in my belly, as if a spark of memory tells me I have never shot at a living being before. I have never killed. I carry a rifle but have never fired a gun. I tap the trigger more forcefully.

The Necrophiliac: Mine guard prevents me from mine duty. Him pray for a bullet but it will be a prayer unanswered. Only corrupt and avaricious men own bullets; lawyers and seated officials and men of commerce and big-big crime, all turned to cash in their wallets and pastries in their taut bellies. My watcher prays only for the possibility of a bullet. The firearm shall shout as him finger close on the firing pin, a noise to scare toads from the paddies and make the captive flinch, but it be no more than bright discharge and a whiff of cordite. It saddens me some that mine rifflers shall strike him down. I has held hope him ears might listen to the voice of him whispering doubt and the fright on him tongue. I has wished for him to witness the wondrous events this night and become mine disciple, but he decline the invitation and it be a disappointment, even if it also a matter of small consequence. The blemishes mine quills cause shall be minor yet fatal, but him shall live again and, in reincarnation, be mine to instruct. Not as a follower to spread holy subversion and widen mine audience, that be a sad pinch of true, but led by mine Will nonetheless.

Him shall be one more child I cares for, alongside all others coming unto me this hour. Him shall be one of mine family.

The Guard: The rifle barks and knocks me back and Nik's chest shatters in a plume of scarlet, slick with pearls of grease and bone. His mouth gapes with surprise and he gasps and shrieks for, I am sure, he did not imagine the weapon loaded. He sinks backward, spraying innards as lava from the volcano, writhing, legs kicking, arms beating. I should help my victim but I don't know how, and I have spilled the rifle and the recoil has broken my arm. I look at the curious curve of my snapped elbow as Nik garbles and froths and flays his barbs and wheels his spade.

I am not in pain but a little dizzied as his darts strike, at my face, my neck, my breast. I fall into the shovel's blade and it shaves off my cheek, from chin to ear. I am on my knees as Nik shivers on the dug earth. I tug at the spikes which made their mark and my left eye sucks out and my face will not stick back but flops like a rag. I tear it off and, in my dislocated eye, I see my scalped jaw, pale and bloodless like a cut of pig, swinging in my hand. I see Nik also, twitching under the mango tree, soaking the mud, head bouncing against a gravestone.

I want to ask how it is possible to see in two directions at once, but the eye which swings makes me confused and my tongue slips through the bone where my cheek is missing, and there are no words, and no one to ask even if there were. When I turn the world sways wildly in kaleidoscope patterns. This is maddening but there is no hurt and when I catch a glimpse of my wounds they gape gray and sallow, as if marbled by emersion in water. They do not bleed but weep a thin sap.

The mynahs have returned, shrieking as they scurry over Nik's foaming lacerations, taking a drink or tugging a thread of sinew. His protests are a mere shiver, and the birds flutter and return, to sip and bite again.

I force my eyeball back into the socket but see only black, the inside of my skull, whilst the other regards the pit-digger's life washing away on the beaks of starlings. His mouth opens and closes but no words slip out.

The Necrophiliac: O, mine guard, look upon your sliced face, your disregard of mine thorns! You be one of mine children and I does not see it! Time has given you strength to make a second life without the need of slumber between moonless nights. Who could tell you are wanting of beating heart? Who might suppose pus stagnates in your veins? Not I, carer of the dead. I wagers not even you know this of yourself! As them living cannot recall birth, so it be for them reborn. Tell me it be so!

I would rejoice, but rejoicing be tempered by more than this hole you carve inside me. I sees mine family imprison their father and I glimpses inky fingers tugging at mine strings. I and, yes, us both, we be puppets in a shadow play but I be one big-big fool. Mine toil be naught but manipulation. This naïve father begets a cohort of guards to watch over them who be penned under sentence. I delivers a legion of slaves to control, and if them suffer it be of no consequence for them already been killed. For what else might mine children be of use to a Puppet Master? As soldiers to be slaughtered in battle, to rise and be slaughtered once more, over and over until them be no more than remnants crawling faithfully towards the enemy? As laborers digging roads and quarries and setting burning tar with bare hands, or collecting sulphur in wicker baskets from the hearts of smoking volcanoes, or felling forests teeming with poison snake and insect and plant, or scooping sand and blasting coral from the ocean floor, or stealing tern eggs and swiftlet nests for soup from sheer cliffs, and pellets of shit from the arses of enraged *musang* for the coffee cups of them rich, over and over until them limbs melt and them fingers be severed and them choke and drown and scald and fall and be splatter, over and over and over. Amen.

The hands on mine trowel and mine spindles be not mine but the dexterous fingers of them Puppet Masters. Mine truth be their deceit as much as this lie of mortality. Directors of this theatre collect mine children for toil and I be their guide to endless supply, the merchant of misery.

Tonight, them who dominate this wretched world did act to preserve silence, to hush the anthem I would roar across land and ocean. Our Masters saved one bullet for a sky barren of celestial light, so as to render the Gravedigger as fodder for Scavengers, now them learn how to bring about Sleepers most fit and able to perform them bidding and build infinite profit.

How much cruelty to endure? O, mine child, pray pity. Death be a matter worse for me, should I be cast deep to lie for eternity, or buried light so as to be flayed by Demons from the fire mountain. How might I climb through packed earth the height of a man? How can I ascend to the dance macabre when scattered as harvest in a cave? And if the *Orang Bati* be commanded to spare me from them jaws, shall I be commanded in turn? To follow instruction as a flunkey, a thrall to march into war or the belly of a cave or the bottom of the sea, or to parade a prison with an empty gun. Or, for cruel amusement, as a vassal to dig ditches, deep or shallow, to lie a cadaver dependent upon use, so who rises and who sleeps shall no longer be mine choice but for them. This be my nightmare.

O child, I hears the wings, I sees the shadows cross the clouds. Mine choice be barbaric, but I chooses life however despicable. Cover me in dirt before them feast on mine remains. Keep them fiends from me, I begs of you. Stay until I be risen and dawn seeps into the dim heavens. Let us walk together from this field as them which be resurrected. I be pleading, do this for mine sake, for I be your father.

Mine throat boils with blood-iron and lung-fat and I fear mine words ring only in mine head.

The Guard: The slain bird is touched by the prisoner's sap pooled on the turf. I pick the puny body up, it hangs limp, of little weight, a discarded rag devoid of the life that pumped through veins, pulsing energy and instinct. What can be life starved of a throbbing heart, other than listless and futile, empty of terror and bereft of love? To be reborn solely to act upon the bidding of other men, in toil they would not do for themselves. To accept a task without complaint and lacking the will to be free. Whether a warder of terrible men or an obedient servant for the indulgence of others.

I am a creature who has learnt the gift of flight but sees no merit in it, no joy in the feel of a breeze through my feathers, under my wings. I have returned to be a soldier of toil in a distasteful task. Is it better to be alive but not really so, or to be dead as dead, catching what peace we may find?

I scoop out a patch of mud and lay the mynah down, dressing it in a shower of grit. Tonight this bird will fly if given but a kiss, a petting, a touch of love. I do not know if this is a good thing or bad.

See, the feet flex, weakly clawing the air. The wings tremble and shake off the dirt.

The stars are full now, peppering the bowl of Heaven. Are they a silver dust of God's light or pin-pricks made by the Devil's needles, peep-holes to glimpse through? I do not know this either. I do not know if it matters.

There is a shudder on the wind, like a catch of celestial breath, as if an army sighs. The air is alive with the flapping of wings and the hissing of snakes and the shrieks of vampires. Around me, the ground moves and turns in ripples like water. I pick up my discarded fold of skin and press it to my cheek and I know I will sew it back, though it seems a task of futility. I place my cracked limb against a headstone and lean upon it until the bones snap into place. I flex my fingers and they curl and I lever myself up. I must leave. I tuck my rifle into the crook of my elbow where it rests warm, puffing a milky smoke.

The bird rises, ruffles his feathers and flies clumsy from the soil stirring beneath its feet. Pale fingers, thin and soft, claw through Santoso's tomb, pushing, wavering in the cool air, feeling for the night as the carcass of the Necrophiliac is dissected by the *Orang Bati*. I do not see them. I do not turn. I do not wait for them to notice a Sleeper walking from this dormitory of death with an empty rifle. I hear their fangs gnaw and their talons slash and the rustle of wings as the earth splits and the Dead arise to their fate.

FRUITING BODY
D. R. Bartlette

July 20, 1920: Here I am in Eureka Springs, Arkansas, a world away from the wide plains and open skies of the Midwest. Though it has only been a few short days, it already seems months ago (how time behaves so oddly when traveling!) that I stepped from the platform in Chicago, teaching diploma clutched proudly in hand. I waved good-bye to Mother, dear little Sylvia, and Father—who has made it clear how he disapproves of my "rash" and "dangerous" decision to make a career for myself instead of rushing into marriage. He doesn't understand that it's a new era, and I'm a New Woman.

Yet I shall dearly miss the intellectual life of college, and my chums there: Mary, Winnie, Margaret, and the rest. I must remember to send them postcards when I arrive. It shouldn't be hard to find a scenic one: the Ozark Mountains are deep and lush, miles of primeval forests interrupted only by green pastures and fat cows. Here and there are sparkling rivers bounded by tall, pale cliffs. The air here is clear and fresh, despite the heat—a welcome change from the miasma of Chicago's clogged streets.

The trip hasn't been all lovely scenery, however. The ESNA railway is an appallingly run-down line that should be shut down. Dust billows from every thread-bare cushion, wooden beams show the unmistakable scars of decay, and the springs creak and squeal so I fear they will snap at any moment, sending us crashing down into the steep ravines below. Between the odor of mildew and the twisting route—always up and down, turning this way and that—my stomach threatened revolt.

As I stared out the window, I began to see signs of human habitation in this wilderness. The countryside is punctuated with such scenes of poverty and deprivation that I am taken aback. Flimsy, leaning shacks barely cling to the steep hillsides, surrounded by wretched, barefoot children clothed only in dirty rags, their little faces gaunt with hunger. I have never seen such terrible want, though I know that until now, I have lived a sheltered and protected life. I steel myself with the firm conviction that I'm coming here to make a difference, for nothing vanquishes poverty like education, hard work, and discipline—the value of which I intend to instill in every one of my pupils.

I now sit at the Eureka Springs station, awaiting my escort to take me to Mr. Winchester, the superintendent of schools, and to find lodging.

July 21, 1920: What an ordeal! I must have sat in that crowded station for an hour before Mr. W's driver arrived. A kindly fellow traveler shared some peppermint candies with me and we chatted a bit. She explained she was visiting Eureka to "take the waters," which she insists have miraculous healing powers. I don't believe such hokum, of course, but I politely held my tongue. However, I will admit that a long soak would do wonders for my aching backside!

The town of Eureka Springs is quite a contrast to the countryside: both sides of the street are packed with strolling tourists—apparently drawn to the "miraculous healing waters," all dressed finely despite the cloying heat.

Finally, the driver arrived, but he spoke in such a sleepy, slushy dialect I could not understand a word. I politely asked him to repeat himself, and though he spoke more slowly and loudly, I was still as perplexed as before. I surrendered all hope of reciprocal communication and asked to be taken back to Mr. W's house. On a whim, I told him to take me by a scenic route. I might as well orient myself a bit while I'm out, I reasoned. He responded with something that sounded like, "Ite, ten," but I had to assume by his tone that it was more or less affirmative.

The man drove at a frightening speed and disregard for pedestrians. The roads here are the narrowest in Christendom, barely wide enough to accommodate the car's wheels. And steep! One side of nearly every road is walled in by colossal limestone bluffs, layered like bolts of gray fabric stacked upon one another, the whole edifice curved as if smoothed by a river's flow. But one can't crane the neck to stare for long; the downhill side of the road is barely intact, crumbling away abruptly mere inches from the wheel's edge, with neither curbing nor guardrail to slow down a plunge into the valley below.

Once he maneuvered the car through the chaos of downtown, and through many hair-pin turns, we found ourselves on a pleasantly uncrowded dirt lane with the most darling Victorians and a few newer Craftsman bungalows. Then, in a rather uninhabited section of town, I spotted something: a lovely wrought-iron gate with a rusted chain wrapped around it. Hanging askew, a small sign with paint so faded it was scarcely legible: "FOR SALE: Inquire at Citizen's First Bank, Main St." Peering through the gate, I saw the most magnificent Queen Anne mansion, with a wide, curving porch; bay windows; and a tall round tower rising above the gables. Though the windows were boarded over and the porch adrift in dead leaves, I could tell it was still beautiful, a stately home simply in need of maintenance and occupation. But soon we were past it, on the way to the Winchesters'.

The Winchesters are quite the odd couple: Mr. W. is a corpulent, red-faced man with full dark hair, yet Mrs. W. is as pale and thin as a birch switch. They were quite surprised to see me, as the letter containing my arrival date had never arrived. They were, nonetheless, extremely hospitable, ushering me into their cool parlor for refreshments.

"My dear, we weren't expecting you so soon," Mr. W. explained, sipping his iced tea. "I don't know where we shall put you up. Nearly every hotel and boarding house is full—summer tourists, you know..."

Mrs. W. interjected. "We have our own sons here, home from college, or else we'd gladly offer you accommodations."

"I see," I said, unsure how to react. Was I to sleep on the street?

Then I recalled the empty Victorian we'd passed. I had no illusions I could afford to purchase it, but thought perhaps the owners would be willing to rent it for a reasonable sum.

July 23, 1920: Arkansas is a different world indeed—as primitive as darkest Africa. But all is not doom and gloom. The school where I will be teaching, a three-story brick structure, is relatively new, still in decent repair. And most importantly, I have secured the most incredible new home, a sprawling 13-room mansion. It has an enormous parlor with a chandelier, a stately formal dining room, a cavernous kitchen, and best of all, an impressive library filled with books!

It's a bit of a tale about how I came to possess it. The bank had taken over the property, which had previously belonged to a Dr. Hanover, a retired professor of botany at the nearby University, and his wife, who both died in some horrible accident there almost forty years ago, according to the realtor. Since they died without any heirs or next of kin, the property went neglected for many years before eventually being foreclosed upon. I was able to buy it for a shockingly small sum (which, nonetheless, still mortally wounded my modest account).

In all those years, it has been surprisingly untouched by vandals. Every stick of furniture remains—hand-carved bookcases and tables, mottled mirrors with their rich gilt frames, and elegant antique chairs—all cloaked in a thick layer of dust. The linens are still folded neatly in their closet, the dishes stacked in their cupboards and the silverware in its drawers. Even the larder is fully stocked—albeit with rusted tins and moldy preserves! Tomorrow, when I go into town to post my letters home, I shall have to hire some cleaning ladies to help blow the dust out of this place and see about getting the antiquated gas-lights turned on.

I shall also have to hire a groundskeeper or two—the garden has gone to rack and ruin for decades. I imagine that once, it must have been a veritable Eden, but now it is completely buried beneath the choking weeds and aggressive kudzu. Even the greenhouse, which must have been impressive in its day, is barely visible above the tangle.

July 24, 1920: A strange encounter in town. After dropping off my letters at the post office, I stopped near the back entrance of one of the resort hotels, where I saw a few women in maids' uniforms dumping trash. I introduced myself and told them I was looking for two or three women to help me clean and organize my new house. The women seemed interested, but when I wrote the address on a slip of paper, their interest disappeared, and they refused to even touch the paper! After trying to convince them to at least consider the offer, to no avail, I bid them good day and tried again at another establishment, with the same results. I finally resorted to writing up a few handbills and posting them on lamp-posts. As I was doing so, I saw some people making a strange gesture at me, like a fist with the index and pinkie fingers extended. What a superstitious and fearful people!

It was the same at the local grocer. The clerk informed me that he would not, under any circumstances, deliver to the Hanover house. Now I know why it was so cheaply gotten...regardless, I couldn't begin to drag all the provisions I'd purchased all the way back on foot, and in this terrible heat. Near tears with frustration, I used the shopkeeper's phone and called Mr. W, who sent his man to pick me up again.

Since I have no means of cooking until the gas comes on (not for another three days, I'm informed), I dined on sardines and crackers. The light was nearly gone by the time I finished, and it's no use trying to clean in the dark. I write now by candlelight, sitting at the great dining-room table. It is a titanic maple thing, designed for entertaining at least a dozen people. I feel small and inadequate sitting here by myself, like a little girl playing at being an adult. I loathe to admit it, but I have no desire to venture into the other dark rooms. I don't want to think the villagers' superstitions have rubbed off on me, but the dark beyond my meager candlelight fairly presses in, claustrophobic despite the spacious surroundings.

I distract myself with the view: the French doors leading out to the veranda frame the garden, now a dark jungle barely touched by moonlight. I can just make out the delicate greenhouse roof, its glass dimmed like cataracts by time and neglect.

July 26, 1920: I awoke this morning (after a night of vague and disquieting dreams) to a most unexpected sound: a knock on the door. I hastily donned a dressing gown and answered it, fearing the worst. But there on my doorstep was not some torch-wielding mob, but a stout, plain-faced woman who introduced herself as Bessie O'Connor, answering my request for housekeepers.

I could have hugged her! It's a dispiriting thing, to be shunned as a pariah by the whole town. I ushered her in, apologizing for my disheveled appearance.

Relieved beyond all logic, I began to take her through the house to show her what needed to be done. However, it seemed to me she already knew which room I referred to before we set foot in it. When I asked her, she simply said, "Yes'm, I've been in this house before." When pressed, she explained that her mother had been Dr. and Mrs. Hanover's housekeeper, and she had been allowed to accompany her mother frequently. "They was the kindest people," she explained. "Treated me and my mama just like fambly, they did." I was exceedingly curious to hear more about the former owners, but there was much work to be done, and I didn't want to frighten her away with too many questions.

While Bessie cleaned the kitchen and put the larder in order, I ascended the spiral staircase to the library, which sits in the uppermost (and, therefore, hottest) room in the tower. It's an impressive room, the expensive cherry-wood and leather furnishings attesting to their former owner's distinguished position.

I sat down in a puff of dust at the enormous desk, its deep color still rich beneath the years of grime. Its surface was neat as a pin; the blotter, though stained by flyspeck and mildew, showed no sign of ink. The oil lamp and inkwell were quite dry, but in their proper places. Everything seemed in perfect order...except one small wooden box, placed crookedly near the lamp.

I snatched it up, eager to discover its secrets. Not much bigger than a matchbox, it was carved rather crudely, and appeared to have no finish. I tried to open it; to my surprise, it held fast. I could hear something hard rattling around inside it, and my curiosity overcame me.

Hoping for better light, I took it downstairs and onto the second-floor balcony. Even in full daylight, I couldn't for the life of me decipher how it was fastened. I could make out no lock or hinge. Figuring it must simply be stuck, I rapped it on the railing. Success! The box popped open as if on a spring...but my celebration was cut short nearly as quickly as it had begun, for whatever was inside the box instantly fell out. I caught but a glimpse of it—something round and dark, like a peppercorn—before it rolled off the balcony and down to the veranda below. I strained over the railing, only to see it bounce off the veranda's wooden decking, through its railing, and land in the tangle of weeds beyond.

A curse escaped my lips as I was about to toss the box after it in frustration. But something caught my eye and stayed my hand. Within the box was wedged a small bone chit, like a domino or mahjong tile. Only instead of a series of dots or Chinese characters, the chit had a strange, pagan symbol carved upon it, a complex arrangement of lines and crosses.

Just at that moment, Bessie called me down for lunch. I showed her the box and asked if she had ever seen it, but she merely shook her head.

July 29, 1920: Bessie makes great progress on the house—the main rooms are now positively gleaming—while I busy myself settling into the library. Today, somewhat sheepishly, I began going through the heavy desk drawers, sorting through old receipts and letters, but found nothing of interest. However, in one drawer, I found a false bottom, firmly locked. I tore through the remaining drawers looking for the key, to no avail, until Bessie called me down for lunch.

Over a welcome meal of egg-salad sandwiches and sweet tea, we chatted a bit. Dear Bessie, hearing of my troubles getting groceries delivered, has agreed to have things delivered to her home, and to bring them with her when she arrives for work. Bless her! She spoke about the Hanovers some; she paints a picture of a most generous and benevolent family: "Mrs. Hanover jus' doted on me so, give me candies and bows for my hair. For Christmas and Easter she'd even give me a new dress and a new pair of shoes." She also revealed that she suspects the reason they tolerated and spoiled her so was because they never had children of their own. I felt sad for them, even though I'm not sure if I will ever want children myself. Messy, loud creatures, and they spoil your figure besides!

I asked her if that was why she'd come to offer her services, when no one else would. "Well, truth is," she said, "I was just plain curious. It's been almost forty years since I seen the inside of this house, and, well, I jus' wanted to see how it looked."

"How does it look?" I asked.

"Just as it did then," she said. Her voice dropped to nearly a whisper, as though she were speaking more to herself than me: "I didn't know what to expect, but it wa'n't this..." Her face flushed and she quickly rose and began clearing the dishes, leaving me with my questions.

Before I left for the library again, I asked if she might know where the key to the desk drawer was. She didn't; I have my work cut out for me.

July 30, 1920: Last night a great storm blew in, so drenching I feared the roof wouldn't hold. But this house, as neglected as it is, held stoutly.

The rain continued all day today, blessedly cool and refreshing. This allowed me to spend the entire day searching through the dusty library for that key. Even so, I haven't gone through half of the late Doctor's collection. Expectedly, a great number of them are botanical in nature—

gardening treatises, scientific textbooks, even seed catalogs—but I also stumbled across several titles dealing with the occult, alchemy, and Voodoo. At first, I was shocked that a man of learning would deal in such nonsense. But on further reflection, I reasoned that he would likely take an interest in the historical uses of all kinds of plants, and this would include primitive witchcraft and herbal superstitions.

Yet, for all my searching, Dr. Hanover's key remains hidden—or lost.

I should venture back into town soon...I really must find some men to clear the garden. I can see through the French doors, there is another great weed sprouting near the veranda.

August 1, 1920: This morning I met with Mr. W. and toured the tiny school. The textbooks are, sadly, quite out of date—the geography textbook doesn't yet show New Mexico or Arizona as states!

This afternoon, as I sat at the table fighting to breathe in the sauna-like humidity, I looked out and saw something odd: the weed I saw yesterday, which was barely peeking over the decking, is now a full hand-span above it. It's like nothing else in the garden—thick stemmed with wide, jagged leaves, all darkest violet—so I assume it must be from that strange seed I dropped.

I know it must be some rare specimen, probably prized by the late Doctor, but in all truth it is hideous. Tomorrow, in the light, I will get rid of it.

August 2, 1920: First thing after breakfast, I tried pulling the thing up by the roots, but its stem was slick, almost greasy, so I couldn't get a firm enough grip on it. Next, I went inside and found a large knife, but succeeded in doing more than bruising the thick, fibrous stalk and sending a bright red, stinking sap flowing over my hand.

It was clear that I needed a tool more suited to the job, and that tool would most likely be found in the greenhouse. There was something about its brooding, decaying presence that repelled me...or perhaps it was the look in Bessie's eyes when I said I was going to the greenhouse. The look was like fear, but she said nothing. Still, if I was to dispatch the ugly weed, I had to screw up my courage and forge ahead. So forge I did; I trudged through the weed-choked yard, crashing through aggressive briars and vines as thick as my wrist.

The whole edifice showed the effects of decay: the iron lattice-work now rusted, the glass gone milky and iridescent with age. Dark vines crawled up the walls, nearly covering them, as if the earth itself were reclaiming it. Looking within was like looking into the depths of the sea, everything within half-glimpsed, dark and distorted.

As I stepped onto the threshold, my boot crunched on broken glass. I thought it odd that the shards had fallen outside the structure; stones thrown by vandals would have landed the shards inside.

Still perplexed, I ducked inside so as to avoid touching the glass. Inside, the air was thick with heat. The whole thing was like an over-exposed photograph, all color washed out by decades of sun. Along the walls, spindly shelves held rows and rows of clay pots in all sizes, some overturned, some upright, their contents long shriveled to dust. Insects crawled among them; how they thrived among the curtains of cobwebs, I do not know.

Sweat dripped into my eyes; it was broiling inside, like trying to breathe through wet cotton. I wanted nothing more than to find some blade or hacksaw and get out. As I scanned the shelves, my eyes came upon an enormous plant near the back of the greenhouse. It was long dead, of course, but its twisted, woody stalks remained, dark as ebony. The few remaining leaves, though long-dead and curled into dry husks, looked exactly like the very plant I was going to dispatch.

When I stepped toward it for a closer look, my boot kicked something like a giant curled-up leaf, and it crumbled into gray dust and a few tangles of dried veins. Then I saw something, like a mark, on the floor. I stooped down and brushed the brittle leaves and insect husks away. Indeed, there was a thick white mark there, like chalk. I dropped to my hands and knees, flinging away more and more of the dirt, until it was fully uncovered.

There, on the polished cement floor, was the outline of two human beings, one curled up on its side, the other, on its back or stomach, one arm flung out. The floor beneath both was stained dark brown from what could only be blood.

I won't say I ran screaming from the greenhouse—I am an educated woman, after all—but neither did I tarry to find a blade.

Bessie, seeing my state, rushed to soothe me with a cool rag for my forehead and a tall glass of water. "It's my fault, ma'am, I should have told you," she clucked. I feebly tried to dismiss her guilt, but she was insistent. "I'll take care of the cursed plant, ma'am, you just sit here and rest yourself."

With that, she went inside and fetched a can of kerosene and a pail of water. Standing next to the plant (which has grown nearly half again in size just since yesterday), she poured the kerosene over it, lit a match from her apron pocket, and tossed it into the dark foliage. It caught fire instantly, crackling and popping like a fourth of July display, sending up clouds of thick, oily smoke.

Seeing it curl and blacken into ash, I did finally feel relieved. Now it can vex me no more (& how silly that it did!).

August 3, 1920: Bessie has nearly finished polishing the house; I've gone through most of the Doctor's library searching for that damned key, with no luck.

One (other) happy result of yesterday's adventure is that Bessie seems to have opened up to me more about the Hanovers. Over lunch, she described them as not only very kindly, but well-traveled. Apparently, the Doctor had gone to nearly every continent to study and collect specimens, and Mrs. H often accompanied him.

"They must have been very happy people," I judged.

"Oh, mostly," she sighed. "Except for not having any chil'ren. That was the one thing they always wanted, and never could have." I waited, sensing she would continue if I didn't prod.

"They tried everything," she finally said. "I overheard Mrs. Hanover speaking to my mother often of it. They moved here specifically for the waters, you know."

I was tempted to respond rather unkindly—a doctor and his wife, taken with such primitive nonsense—but kept my tongue.

"Before they moved here, the Dr. and Mrs. Hanover had gone to see special doctors all over the country," she continued. "But they didn't help one bit. When the waters here didn't fix the problem, they traveled to the Battle Creek Sanitarium all the way up in Michigan, but it didn't help either. My mama, rest her soul, lit a candle and said a prayer for the two of them every Sabbath." She shook her head and began clearing the dishes, and the subject was done.

Tomorrow I think I shall visit the town library and dig through the newspaper archives, just to see for myself what happened to them. It's such a tragic tale; I should know it more fully.

August 4, 1920: The good thing about a tourist town is that I can, with relative ease, blend into the crowds. I made my way to the library to find out more about what had happened to the Hanovers. The interior was blessedly cool and quiet. I did the calculation quickly, and asked the librarian for the newspaper archives from 1880. The first item with the name "Hanover" was under "Talk About Town," an apparent gossip column:

It has come to our attention that the Dr. and Mrs. Hanover, formerly of Fayetteville, have departed for a short trip to New Orleans. We could not find out the reason for the trip, but were assured they would return soon, perhaps with good news.

A month later, another "Talk About Town" mention:

It seems the Hanovers have been very secretive about their recent trip to New Orleans. Now, Mrs. Hanover is no longer receiving guests. Dare we anticipate a long-awaited announcement??

I flipped through the brittle pages, scanning for more about the

Hanovers. There was nothing for several weeks, until, on the front page of the *Times Echo:*

HANOVER FAMILY MAULED TO DEATH IN OWN GREENHOUSE

Bloody Scene Greets Investigators

To-day the town of Eureka Springs was shocked to learn one of its prominent families was killed in a most gruesome fashion. Retired professor Dr. James Hanover and his wife, Marcella Hanover, were found by his hired man early Monday morning.

The hired man, Euell Jenkins, describes a horrific scene, wherein the Dr. and his wife were found, deceased inside their greenhouse, disemboweled and covered in blood.

Dr. Edwin Toomey, Lovely County Coroner, stated that he was certain the cause of death was not foul play. "No human hand could have done this," he said. "The two adults had a series of bite-marks resembling a fanged predator, such as a wolf or mountain lion. That, coupled with the missing viscera, leads me to believe this was, quite simply, an animal attack."

Services will be held Saturday at the First Church of Christ.

The chalk outlines on the floor of the greenhouse floated behind my eyes, and for a moment, I felt queasy. After taking a moment to collect myself, I continued scanning the papers. The next day was a small item on the front page:

SHERIFF OFFERS $1,000 REWARD FOR CAPTURE OF DEADLY BOBCAT

A week later, a photo of five men holding bobcat carcasses up like trophies; at their feet, several more carcasses are posed. *Bobcats destroyed by local hunters*, the caption read. *Citizens can now sleep safely at night.*

I closed the volume carefully. Something about this official story didn't hang together properly: the glass had been outside the greenhouse, like something had broken out, not in. And if indeed a wild animal had attacked the couple, why was the greenhouse still in such good order? Wouldn't there have been a tremendous fight, leaving the delicate shelves and clay pots in more disarray? I rubbed my temples, trying to make it add up, but it just didn't.

August 5, 1920: When Bessie arrived this morning, I couldn't wait to question her about the Hanovers' trip to New Orleans mentioned in the paper—perhaps it might hold some clue as to what happened to them.

"I suppose desperate people will try desperate measures," she shrugged.

"What do you mean?"

"By the time she passed, Mrs. Hanover was at an age, not puttin' too fine a point on it, where her childbearing years was likely behind her, rest her soul. I knew they was willing to try just about anything to have a baby, but I never understood what happened on that last trip. It was just vexing. That's the word: vexing."

"What was vexing?"

"That they went all the way to New Orleans, supposedly to adopt," she said, hand on her wide hip. "Like there ain't plenty of poor orphans right here in Arkansas. And what's stranger, they didn't come back with no baby. I know; I was right there--" she pointed toward the front door, "next to my mama to greet 'em when they returned. In fact, they never had no baby that I saw. The only thing different I saw was Dr. Hanover spent nearly all his time out in the greenhouse and Mrs. Hanover was jus' sick as a dog. I jus' don't know," she sighed. "I jus' don't know."

I offered my condolences, weak as they were, and started upstairs to continue dusting and searching for the key.

Later- The damned plant has returned, more prolific than before. Where previously there was but one thick stalk with many leaves and branches, now there are five stems, crooked and grasping, like some skeletal hand reaching out of the earth.

August 6, 1920: The gas is finally on, and the house is set in order, so I can truly start settling in and making it my home.

Feeling like the queen of my own castle at last, I sat down at the table to work on my lesson plan. Outside, I could see the Plant, its tallest branch just below the veranda's railing. I worked for a few hours, then went into the kitchen to make myself a snack.

When I returned, what I saw outside the French doors stopped me in my tracks; I dropped my plate in dumbfounded shock. *The Plant was now above the railing by almost a foot!* The branches seemed almost to grasp the handrail, curling around it; it looked like nothing so much as a bony black imp climbing over the rail. As I stood staring, the leaves bobbed and rustled, though there was no hint of wind. It was as if the Plant were looking back at me, laughing cruelly. I begin to wonder if it's possible that the stress of travel, and this awful heat, are taking a toll on my mind.

August 7, 1920: I write later than usual to-night, and I fear my penmanship suffers from my evening's adventures.

When the sun dropped below the hills and the sky darkened, I went to close the French doors for the night and could not help but see what lay beyond. The Plant (grown even more sizable as to block out the view of the greenhouse) had blossomed with massive, pale flowers. The scent nearly overcame me. It is very hard to describe, that scent. It is deep and sweet, like jasmine, with an almost musky undertone reminiscent of civet. Despite my hatred of the plant, I found the scent utterly compelling, so that before

I knew it, my feet had taken me through the doors and down the steps!

As I approached it, I could more closely inspect the saucer-sized blooms. They are much like orchids: thick, almost meaty, pink petals with bright crimson veins, shaped—I blush to even think it—like the feminine sex organs, yet with a slick red pistil jutting out. The entire effect is, dare I say, obscene.

I think the odor of those flowers must also have some opiate qualities, for as I stood there inhaling it, I began to hear laughter—children's laughter. Thinking some of the town's children were having sport of me, I looked around, but the movement of my head made me dizzy. The world spun; I felt as though I were drowning. And as I looked at them, the flowers seemed to transform themselves into the faces of babes—smiling, laughing babes. In my stupor, I reached out to pluck one, and a nasty thorn pricked my finger quite deeply, causing it to bleed. I ran back inside and bandaged the wound straightaway.

Tomorrow I shall purchase a strong herbicide—let's see how that thing stands up to the wonders of modern chemistry!

August 8, 1920: I fear that noxious weed has poisoned me. Though I run no fever, my stomach is cramped with hunger; all morning, I could think only of food. I consumed a full plate of eggs and toast, and still, I wanted more. All day I found myself walking back and forth between the larder and the table, always eating, eating anything I could lay my hands on.

But there was one welcome sight this morning: the hated blossoms have all withered and dropped, leaving behind a putrid odor not unlike rotten fruit. Perhaps this will be the last of the foul thing, after all. Good riddance!

August 10, 1920: Today I sent Bessie into town to order the pesticide. Unfortunately, she informs me it will take anywhere from two to three weeks before it arrives. I'm sure I'll be able to tolerate the sight of it until then.

School starts in one month, yet I cannot keep my mind on my lesson plans. The heat has sapped me all of my strength; I now have to take naps during the hottest part of the day, my hunger is nearly constant, and this gluttony causes my waist to grow larger by the day.

Thank goodness for dear, level-headed Bessie. After making me a nice chicken soup to calm my nerves, she made the suggestion that I salt the earth around the Plant to kill it. Only it was not as easy as it might seem. Other than the dropped blooms, the wicked weed shows no sign of decline. In fact, it has begun to fruit—a single, ebon sphere, about the size and apparent hardness as a Czech marble. So, strengthened by her soup, I approached it to apply the salt near the roots. Though I tried to remain steady in my determination, each step closer to that Plant made me feel more and more hopeless. The twisting branches seemed to reach toward me, intent on pricking me with their thorns or strangling me like a snake squeezes the life out of a mouse.

Bessie must have seen the fear on my face, because without my realizing it, she was there beside me. "Ma'am, are you all right?"

I shook my head to clear it. "Why, yes, I am...just...afraid to get too close to those thorns."

Bessie squinted at the Plant. "I don't see no thorns," she declared. "But then, my eyesight ain't so good anymore. Here, let me do that."

I started to protest—more out of obligation than anything—but she insisted, taking the tin of salt from me and striding up to the thing. She poured the salt in nearly a ring around it—missing only what she couldn't reach under the veranda—and walked back, as pretty as you please. "Now let's water that in, and that should take care of it."

August 13, 1920: I am still eating everything in sight. I've gone through nearly a week's worth of groceries in a day.

The salt has done nothing to staunch the Plant's unholy vigor. Indeed, the fruit has grown to the size of a fat, ruffled tomato, and from the dining room, appears to have lightened from black to a dark crimson color. I don't wish to give in to the thought, but something about that fruit calls to me; for all the world, I want to eat it, to feel its smooth skin and taste its soft flesh.

August 14, 1920: Last night, I was awakened by painful pangs of hunger, so I started downstairs and into the dining room. Blessed cool breezes lifted the curtains gently, and bright silver moonlight flooded my untidy heaps of textbooks and notebooks strewn across the table. But for the singing of crickets, the night was silent and still. I looked to the French doors, and there, illuminated by moonlight, the Plant twisted and moved, as if by its own design.

That is not what frightened me so; I have seen the way the Plant seems to move on its own before. No, that is not the end of last night's observations. For no other reason than to get a better view, I opened the doors and stood upon the threshold, gazing at the twisting, bobbing Plant. And there, among its dark stalks, my gaze fell upon its fruit—now nearly as big as a melon! I stepped closer, for the moonlight and shifting shadows seemed to be creating some optical illusion—the fruit seemed to be glowing red. Closer I stepped, my bare feet upon the creaking veranda, bending down to eye the thing straight on. I came very close to it and saw something within that strange fruit *moving*, fluttering like an unborn chick within an egg. Its branches were twining around me, as if it were to devour me...

I must have fallen into some kind of trance, because when I came to my senses, the fruit, the terrible fruit, was gone, only a hollow, rubbery shell left, the dark and stinking juices splashed across the veranda. Out of instinct, I raised my hands to my mouth, and felt something wet. Staring at my hands, they were covered in that same dark juice, looking like nothing so much as blood.

I ran shrieking from it, stopping only to bolt the French doors firmly behind me, leaving a trail of crimson smears like a murderer.

I know not what to do—I fear I have eaten the poison fruit!

August 17, 1920: I fear I may be in the throes of some heat-induced madness. Only a few weeks until the term begins, and still I cannot concentrate. I cannot sleep at night, only twist and turn, the sound of children's laughter like screaming in my ears. During the day, I am exhausted and weak, only able to pay attention for short periods of time before having to lie down and rest. I have gained so much weight, I feel so heavy, as though sandbags have been strapped to me, around my limbs and torso. And the heat! The humidity threatens to drown me if I but take a deep breath.

In my unbalanced state, it seems as though the Plant plays tricks on my mind. I find myself drawn to it; it radiates a sense of relief from the crushing fatigue. I know this is foolishness, some delusion of fever or poisoning. I want to write to Mother and ask her to send our old physician, Dr. Moore (no doctor here will come near this house to see me). But I know that Father will read the letter, and will use it as an excuse to whisk me away back home, smug in his victory over my frivolous will. I will never leave his house if he has to come rescue me now. So I will wait this out; I'm sure my strong constitution will prevail, eventually.

August 19, 1920: Last night, I dreamt I held a baby in my arms, a sweet little girl with big eyes and tiny pink fists. I could smell her downy head, feel the soft skin of her rosy cheek beneath my finger. As I bent closer to kiss her, she opened her mouth. It was full of fangs, long and sharp as needles!

I was still shaking this nightmare from my head when Bessie arrived with good news. The key is found! She found it when she was clearing out the closets in one of the guest rooms. The key was on a ring with two others in a shoe-box on a high shelf. One of the keys had the bank's logo on it; no doubt it unlocks a safe-deposit box. Of the two remaining keys, the first didn't fit in the lock at all. The second slid into the lock promisingly, but I couldn't get it to turn inside the chamber. I was about to give up in frustration when, almost of its own accord, the key turned and the wooden plate popped up.

At first glance, the compartment seemed empty. I reached inside nonetheless. At that moment, a great brown spider, nearly as large as a chicken egg, scurried from within and up my arm! I squealed in terror, flapping this way and that, trying to dislodge the monster. Dear Bessie saved me, using a rolled-up paper to swat it away.

After taking a moment to collect myself, I returned my attention to the hidden chamber. More cautiously now, I reached inside. The tips of my fingers touched something, so I pulled it toward me. It was an envelope, yellow and brittle, nearly weightless, and drawn upon it was that strange symbol I saw in the box.

By this time, the sun was low in the sky. So, both for want of more light and fresh air, I took the envelope out to the veranda. I settled myself into one of the rusty chairs, lifted the flap, and withdrew the thin, onion-skin leaf, holding it gently between my thumb and middle finger for fear of tearing the delicate thing. It has been some time since my last French lesson, but I could make out most of the text, which I shall endeavor to record here:

"You must water it when you see the first slice of the Moon in the Western sky.

You must water it with water that has never been through a pipe.

Pick not a single flower! When it begins to bear fruit, you must place nine iron nails at the roots, in a circle, and sacrifice a black rooster.

Do not eat the fruit, or touch it—though it will want you to! When the fruit ripens, you must give it a pure white goat to quell its hunger.

For this, James & Marcella Hanover, you give $500 and (here a word I cannot make out)."

Beneath, the signatures of Dr. J. Hanover, Mrs. J. Hanover, and M. LeVeau.

I sat for a moment in the gathering dark, the din of crickets in my ears, contemplating the queer document. I suppose Dr. Hanover often went to exotic places in search of rare plants to add to his garden, but why the secrecy, hiding it in a locked drawer? Perhaps he was afraid a colleague might steal his discovery? But why was his wife included in the transaction?

The more I learn about this wicked plant, the more I want it gone.

August 23, 1920: The cursed plant has indeed infected me. I can scarcely get out of bed anymore. I am swollen as a balloon, gasping with fatigue; my head spins at the slightest movement. My ankles are so swollen I can't put on any of my shoes; I've grown so much I'm only able to cover myself with my dressing gown (and even then, just barely). Bessie gives me sidelong glances and drops comments about my "state." When I questioned her about what was on her mind, she sat near me on the divan and looked me in the eyes. "It's none of my business, I know, but if you're in ..." here she paused and fidgeted, "any sort of trouble...well, I know of a way out. It's just a bitter tea, nothing dangerous."

It took me a moment to understand what she was saying. "Why, you think I'm pregnant!" I finally realized. Her face flushed deeply, but she didn't deny it. "Bessie, my dear, that is just not possible. I can absolutely assure you!"

Bessie retreated, furiously apologetic. I am no untarnished virgin, to be sure, but Harry and I always used precautions, and besides, it has been far too many months...

But maybe Bessie isn't entirely off-base. I have heard there are diseases, cancers, that can appear to the untrained eye as a pregnancy. I really must see a doctor...though I don't know who will dare set foot on this accursed property...

Sept. 1, 1920: Oh, how I do wish for some relief. The fatigue and hunger continue. I know it is foolish and irrational, but I swear I see my stomach moving, as if there is something inside waiting to get out, and I am filled with the most overwhelming dread and panic.

Sept. 5, 1920: It grows within me, I know it. My stomach is distended with its size, and I feel it stirring within, flutters of movement, sometimes delicate, sometimes sharp enough to send me collapsing to the floor. I am consumed with hunger...I have eaten nearly everything in the larder, including stale bread and moldy cheese! I fear I shall start gnawing on the furniture if Bessie doesn't bring me some good red meat soon...

Sept. 6, 1920: Am in agony...swollen and bloated, now and then I am seized with the most intense stomach cramps I have ever experienced. It feels almost like something is inside me, trying to get out...

The only relief I get is when I step out onto the veranda and hold onto the stalk of the Plant, letting it support my great ponderous weight.

This will end soon, it must, but I know not what the end will bring, if I should fear or welcome it.

Sept 1920: The sharp pains have worsened to the point of agony. It feels like needles, razorblades slicing me from the inside! Ah, but here comes another *[here an unintelligible scratch of ink]*

Too much to bear. I cannot resist it any longer. I must I must Must get it out of me before it destroys me

From the pen of Bessie O'Connor:
Nov. 10, 1920
Dear Rosey,
Sorry so long since Ive writin you. You know you and David are always

in my thoughts and praers.

So I guess you've herd about what happened at the old Hanover house. Its so sad it must be curst for sure. That poor woman, chewed to death, just like Hanover's was. I was the one found her, just like Uncle Euell found the Hanover's. She was on the back porch, just covered in blood, her belly split open like she'd been gutshot. I dint get too close just ran down the street to a naibor's and got the police. Maybe now they'll tare that place down for good.

I feel kina gillty because I was there for both fambly's, but I never seen any bobcat's nor wolves nor anything else like that. Thou now there's been talk of goats and dogs and such gone missing from the naibor's.

I only seen a bunch of growed-up weeds, no tracks or nothing. Which reminds me: one day I went into that garden to try and help that woman get rid of a bush she dint like. I don't know why, it was real pretty like a Caster bean.

Anyways, when I got home, I seen I had a seed that had fell into my apron pocket. I dint think much of it, but when I herd you had moved into a new house, I thought you might like to plant a garden of your own. So I am sending it to you, a rare and egsotic plant strait from the Dr's collection. I hope you enjoy tending it, it grows real big and hardy.

I will keep you in my praers, that God Almighty will bless you both with a baby soon. Allways remember He works in misterious ways so don't loose faith.

Your friend,
Bessie

DURANT & ELI
Joanna Logan-Costello

Durant was a man wise beyond his years. Naturally clever and studious, his academic achievements throughout his young life had provided him with a solid career and the foundational beginnings of a traditionally comfortable life. Mother-son talks had matured from work and managing finances to topics of love interests and grandchildren. It was clear that his parents expected him to generate another nuclear family soon. But Durant's interest in children or settling down hadn't been piqued yet. The fruits of his labors afforded him time and resources he never previously had.

All aspects of his life had come together providing a window of opportunity for self-exploration which the millennial generation all seem to need at some point. A new professional camera sat on his marble countertop revealing a desire for new passions. Plans of visiting museums and botanical gardens were made for both leisure and a snapshot or two for various social media accounts. There were restaurants to try, wines for tasting, and many interesting conversations to be had with friends old and new.

It was at one of those dinners that Durant met Eli and became infatuated with him against a backdrop of bohemian tapestries, twinkling yellow garden lights, and the sounds of raga rock. Eli's eyes were rimmed with coal-colored eye shadow blended outward and fringed by feathery black lashes, making it difficult to discern whether his gaze was intense or sultry. The group of friends conversed across a sea of spiced cauliflower, vibrantly colored curries, and fragrant rice. Durant had always found both men and women attractive and acknowledged that he hadn't ever contemplated the logic there. He was presently warmed by a deep and heady red wine, marveling at Eli's porcelain skin, where not a blemish or crease existed. It was as if his skin had been airbrushed, glowing at all the right angles. The gray-blue pair of eyes would float knowingly over to Durant without fear of detection and, in their silent language, smile.

Over the course of dinner, the two men established a connection, each becoming so intrigued by the other, that neither was willing to part. When the evening began winding down, Eli privately pointed out to Durant that he was in no position to drive home and, since his house was just a short walk away, he was welcome to sleep the wine off there. As the other guests coordinated rides home, a mutual friend named Pō excitedly suggested an after party at Eli's which the man dismissed with a wave of his hand—there'd be no after party invites that night.

After saying their goodbyes, the couple began their stroll along crumbling red brick sidewalks. They passed dive bars and lounges whose shuttered doors opened to the glistening streets allowing lonely brass jazz to float out into the night. An elderly man with skin like leather sat perched on a wooden stool staring off into the ether outside another club. His face was obscured by a shadow cast by the fedora hat he wore so that only the white stubble on his bronze chin was visible. He sucked heavily on a cigar, exhaling the fragrant smell of tobacco smoke which surrounded the two as they passed. The last of the neon lights pooled on the ground and the pair walked on in darkness. Moonlight glowed behind a canopy of sprawling live oak and the Spanish moss that hung from its black, crooked branches. "This is going to sound weird, but I feel like I've known you for years." Durant finally broke the silence.

"If that's weird, Durant, this'll sound a lot weirder...I nearly cried when you walked into the restaurant. I don't know why I was so happy when I saw you. That's not something you're supposed to tell someone you've just met, right? I mean, I felt like I'd missed you for ages. I would've never known I could feel that way about anyone if I hadn't met you tonight," Eli confided.

"It's strange..." Durant paused apprehensively. Eli lowered his head afraid of what might be said next. "You took the words right out of my mouth. I would've said something similar except I'm having trouble articulating any thoughts or feelings right now." There was another pause. "I'm at a loss for words. I guess I'm just so happy to see you again, Eli." Eli raised his head and smiled a smile Durant could feel even though the darkness stole it from his eyes. The exchange that occurred between them felt both liberating and frightening as they'd never met before and were unsure of what drove each man's need for the other.

Durant followed Eli through the gate of a beautifully detailed cast iron fence. In front of them stood a dark colored two-story, double gallery home whose presence loomed against the night sky. It was a structure representing another era complete with columns and three openings on each floor which he'd later learn was the signature of its architectural style. Three shuttered windows opened to a gallery on the second floor while two shuttered windows and the front door opened to a gallery on the ground floor. Eli jerked at the handle of the front door for a moment then thrust his shoulder into it causing it to open with a *boff* sound.

Inside the house, it was warm. The ambiance of the room Durant found himself in was so regal that he moved around almost at a tiptoe. The entire first floor boasted dark moldings covered in gold rosettes. The drapes and tapestries were all variants of deep reds ornamented with gold. Eli motioned for him to take his pick of the intricately carved oak chairs. Although the house was elegantly furnished, the floors creaked and groaned without reserve as if it pained to be walked on. Something about the home caused uneasiness, like it possessed some horrible secret one would never want to learn. Durant observed that the warmth and light in the room were created by a low burning fire in the fireplace. Had the fire been left unattended while Eli was out? Did anyone else live here?

As they took their seats across from each other, a plume of dust arose. Durant coughed and swatted at the air a bit. In the firelight, Eli studied Durant's face, unbothered by his surroundings. He longed to run his fingers along Durant's strong, squared jaw and olive skin. He wanted to gaze at his dark features uninterrupted but thought it best to fight intimate impulses that night. His priority was becoming reacquainted with his guest and deciphering their cryptic connection. They exchanged mundane details about one another—schools attended, occupations held, and similar interests but could not establish any links. Durant found himself distracted part way through the conversation by the faint shuffle of fabric heard from the hall behind him. The noise was comparable to the sound clothing makes on a person when they move—but no one was present behind him. "Maybe we knew each other in another life" Durant suggested after eyeing the hallway.

"Maybe," Eli responded thoughtfully.

"How did you end up with this house anyway? Do you own it?"

"No, but I had a hunch that this would be the best place for us to chat. Do you believe in past lives?" Eli asked.

"I'm kind of forced to believe in its possibility...because of what's happening tonight. How else would I know your face, Eli?" Durant felt a sudden surge of knowledge flowing into his consciousness, and he began to recite the information coming from some unknown source to Eli. "How would I know that you're dramatic and too honest for your own good? Or know that you're passionate about what you believe in and about the people you keep in your pocket?" He stood from his seat and walked towards the hall. Dust and soot dirtied the back of his black jeans and the leather vest he wore over his olive hoodie. "You're aggressive, abrasive, and pompous—you're the worst friend I've ever had!" He turned towards Eli softening his voice. "...And the best. To know all these things about a person you've never met and speak them as fact is just crazy to me. And why do I have this nagging feeling that you owe me something or that you have something I want?" Just as Durant had finished speaking, he heard strange noises coming from the second floor. Murmurs with the rising and falling qualities of speech drifted into the living area—the distinct *thup* of footsteps echoing afterward as they disappeared into dark unknown corners. "What is going on in this house? Who else lives with you?" Durant demanded as he performed an about-face, heading up the wine-colored carpet covering the staircase. As his black work boots clomped their way up to the second floor, the unexpected ricketiness of the stairs caught him off guard. He had to lighten his stride releasing the grand, albeit unsteady, banister—it felt like it would collapse onto the hall below.

Durant reached the second floor landing and peered down the corridor. It was dark and there were no light switches visible. It was quiet except for his footsteps advancing down the carpeted hall and the horrid creak that followed each thereafter. "This house is more like a museum than a place to live!" he hollered down to Eli and as he did, a faint but feminine voice came from behind one of the doors. He thought it asked: *who is there?* Durant came to a halt—his growing apprehension towards the house began to awaken fear and adrenaline within him. He turned the doorknob quickly giving a push on the door to the room he thought the voice might have come from, but it wouldn't budge. Remembering the flashlight function on his cell phone, he cast its light on the varnished door and found that nothing was wrong with it. Following Eli's example, Durant shouldered his way into the room hearing the splintering of wood overhead but not seeing any damage done.

The room was lit by kerosene lamps which glowed softly upon the many colored pillows blanketing the floor of the room. Some pillows were embroidered with intricate designs, some tasseled, and others were beaded. But there was no one else in the room, nothing capable of creating a sound, and the realization was unsettling. With senses heightened he heard Eli's hard-soled leather shoes approaching and entering. "Wow, look at this," Eli said in wonderment as he regarded the room. "It's very opium den-esque." Durant snorted in agreement. They studied the woven wall hangings together observing a procession of mythical beasts around the room, all with teeth and claws bared and tongues lolling out of their snouts. "Charming, let's hang around in here for a bit," Eli suggested, throwing himself onto the pillowed floor. "Be careful when you sit. They look much more comfortable than they actually are," he warned before coughing on the stale air.

"Who are you really? Seems like you might have a better understanding of what's happening here. I don't mean to sound melodramatic but I need to know what significance you have in my life," Durant asked earnestly. He was growing increasingly conscious of the hours that slipped away. "Prolonging this could make it awkward between us. Don't you think?"

Eli nodded. "My understanding of what's happening isn't much better than yours. I'm just sort of talking it through with you and grasping at whatever straws of information possible. Clues come to me sporadically but I couldn't tell you where they're coming from. I *can* tell you that everything you said downstairs was true. I'd add irresponsible, apathetic, reckless, and vain to your description of me. Call me the quintessential trust fund baby because I am. I'm addiction prone, Durant, whether its drugs, partying, men, or vanity—I'm the seven deadly sins incarnate." He looked away. Durant pulled a tangle of cobwebs from Eli's architectural designer shirt and from the frosted tips of his unnatural jet black coif. "We both know that you reveal only what you want others to see," Durant reminded. Eli fiddled with the tassel of a pillow beneath him then said, "You're the only one to have ever seen through my deception and I can't tell you how I know that."

Somewhere in the house, a door was shut in as ordinary a manner as someone retiring to their room for the night but neither man rose to investigate. Like the specters that roamed it, they too felt as though they conducted their own supernatural business made possible by the secretive house. As the veil of night began to wane, the air in the room grew heavier with a musk that seeped from the tapestries. A sense of urgency impressed upon the two and the warmth of the room fed a stupor that caused their eyelids to become heavy. Eli lay across from the beautiful stranger he had met earlier that night and mustered whatever energy he maintained from the horrible sloth that increased its siege upon them to take his hand. "They say ghosts are allowed to come back if they have unfinished business." His words were slurred. "After you left, I discovered that life wasn't worth living without you. Please forgive me for betraying you—I need to hear you say it. You have to know that I love you, Durant. I'm so sorry." But it was too late. In the midst of Eli's tearful confession, Durant had fallen into a peaceful sleep, succumbing to the asphyxiation of the room.

Durant's recollection of his trip home the next morning would reveal itself in snippets. He found that his hands, even under his fingernails, were filthy with dirt. His clothes and boots were caked with ash and cobwebs. As he showered he remembered stumbling down the staircase of the eerie house calling out for Eli. Most of his concentration had gone towards keeping his eyes open and keeping the world from spinning. He recalled heaving the heavy cast iron gate open, hearing it groan, and wiping mossy residue onto his jeans. There was a nagging dissatisfaction with the way the previous night had unfolded. The hangover he suffered was horrendous—he barely had the energy to feed himself. The funny thing was that he didn't remember drinking enough to be punished with the earthquake of a headache and the energy drain he wrestled. Illicit drugs were out of the question—it wasn't his thing. Questions about the couple's connection had gone unanswered and worse still, there'd been no word from Eli all morning. Durant felt used and a little lonely and decided to confide in their friend Pō, hoping to discover a little more about Eli. Pō could be heard on the other end of the line after what sounded like a scramble for the phone. "Hello? Hello?" He sounded upset.

"Hey, you okay?" Durant asked.

"Hey, I texted you a few times last night and this morning to see if you made it home safe. Why didn't you text back?"

"I'm sorry. I slept in. I'm not feeling very well this morning."

"I wish you'd have texted." Pō's voice quavered. Durant could hear the crinkle of tissue and a sniffle.

"What's going on?"

"Do you remember Eli? He was at dinner last night?" Pō reminded.

"Of course I remember him. Actually, I wanted to ask you—" but he was quickly interrupted by Pō.

"They found him dead this morning in his loft downtown," he began to sob. "He overdosed on heroin." He tried to stifle his crying. "The needle was still in his arm."

Durant reeled as the information raced through his brain. The news was shared without warning like gossip one just assumes everyone else wants to hear. Learning of heroin and needles felt like an assault on a man he thought he understood—a man he had just discovered he might love. "No," he said scoffing in disbelief. "His loft? What loft?" He couldn't understand.

"I know, I know," Pō replied, mistaking Durant's confusion for disbelief towards the passing of someone they had just spent time with. "You hadn't had the chance to see the loft his parents bought him. His taste was so mod. You'd have loved it, Durant. I know you and Eli were the last to head home last night. After finding out about Eli, I worried about whether you made it home safe." Durant realized that nobody knew they left together. "Oh!" Pō blurted. "I've got to take this call. Come over to my place if you feel up to it. It'd be nice to be surrounded by friends right now," he said before clicking over to the other line.

Durant sat on his couch, stunned for a few moments, unwilling to accept that, in under the course of 24 hours, he'd found and then lost his soul mate. It was a selfish way for Eli to leave him. He had gotten himself caught in the undertow of one of his addictions. As a result, Durant questioned how much he could have actually meant to him since the need for a high far outweighed his desire to be together. He had to face that with Eli went any chance of learning the reasons for their reunion. Though fate had dealt the two a merciless blow, Durant wasn't ready to let go. He wasn't ready to give up on the riddle, and longed to be close to Eli somehow. He made the decision to return to the site that appeared to stitch the fabric of time together with feeble threads.

Outside, the sky was gray and the rain fell to the earth as a ghostly mist. Durant was grateful for the rain that helped to hide his grief and the tears streaming down his face from the strangers he passed on the street. He headed in the direction he suspected the house would be based off scraps of memory—a distinct outdoor café overhang, a familiar street name, stately houses, and the overall look of the area in relation to the distance from the restaurant they had dined at last night. It wasn't until he happened upon a cracked portion of sidewalk covered in sticks and leafy debris that he noticed the sprawling branches above and tangles of Spanish moss. Anyone else would have rejoiced at the validation the twisted branches offered: it meant he had reached the handsome home where he spent a single surreal night with a phantom from his past.

Instead, Durant found himself seized in horror at the sight of a structure in ruins. All that could be seen from beyond an overgrown yard turned sinister jungle was the second floor gallery whose rotted floorboards jutted out in different angles. He drew closer observing a house riddled with flecks of chipping paint and the bare wood exposed beneath as if it were afflicted by a disease causing the decay of its outer layers. Dumfounded, Durant entered the rusted gates stepping carefully over lumber and trash littering the paved path towards the front door. He realized Eli's trouble had not been his fumbling with the key in the lock. The trouble was the decaying wood of the front door was swollen due to recent rains.

What Durant observed upon entering the house made his skin crawl. To think that any part of he and Eli had come into contact with what he discovered prompted an urge to be doused in scalding hot water. The floor of the old house was covered in a layer of dirt, soot, and animal droppings; drifts of which had built up in every corner. A dark, gaping cavity in the parlor ceiling was visible from the hall and was likely responsible for the mold, dirt, and decomposition indoors. Water trickled and dripped all around allowing vegetation to feed and invade from beneath the weakened floorboards—this explained why the ground groaned in agony the night before. Food wrappers, used tissues, even drug paraphernalia was strewn about suggesting junkies and squatters frequented the house. Could that have explained the voices and movement they heard? They may have been in the company of real life fiends instead of the ghostly things he had previously suspected.

Durant was under the impression the house was haunted because of its ambiance, sounds, and phantom voices. Now he wondered if two people could be haunted or perhaps haunt each other to the extent that they shared supernatural delusion. In place of opulent wallpaper and embellishments, plaster from the walls had completely crumbled exposing wood lath ribs like the decaying corpse of some once lovely debutante. The emptiness of the parlor was jarring in contrast to the guise of comfort the room offered earlier—the lavish furniture probably removed long ago. Large impressions were left on the ground where they must have both sat in the dirt deep in conversation along with footprints of work boots and hard soled shoes. It explained why mud fell in clumps from his clothes when he took them off in his bathroom at home. Tears swelled in his eyes as he crouched down closer to examine Eli's shoe prints. Seeing traces of his companion was an affirmation of his experiences—he'd begun to doubt his sanity. Eli had really existed and the thought of the two of them lounging around oblivious to the skittering bugs and filth was disturbing. Had Eli seen the house in its glory or as the condemned shell witnessed now? They had been so vulnerable and exposed during their psychosis somehow managing to avoid opportunities for accidents or attack by unknown lurking persons. Despite the timeless sensation that permeated the fabrics and furniture they believed they had lounged on, whether or not their circumstances involved the otherworldly had yet to be seen. He didn't know how much more of the truth he could take.

Before he could leave, there was one last place Durant had to see. It was the opium den room that Eli admired. Up the treacherous staircase, he went towards the door which now brandished splintered spears of wood where Durant had destroyed it in the night as if to say *you did this*. Inside, the room was empty. There were no tapestries hanging on the walls and, instead of pillows, an old grungy cloth was spread out on the ground which he assumed had been used by many and for what purposes he never wanted to know. This was the place where he had lain with the man he hoped, in time, would prove both their instincts right—together they would prove they were meant for each other. Maybe it was why he'd never settled down with anyone before. Now he would never know if they could have built a life together. The last thing he remembered was Eli's piercing eyes and whispers of what he assumed were sweet nothings as a death like draught of sleep took hold of him. On his way out, Durant kicked the door of the opium room in anger. There were no answers to be found only more confusion, upsetting memories, and the feeling that the house watched him, amused.

Under a cloud of grief and bewilderment, Durant lumbered through the streets with his head down. Slender residential concrete sidewalks grew wider and more gum-riddled until he reached red brick and realized he was near the area where the bars and restaurants were. Up ahead he recognized a faded green sign that read *Vortex Lounge*. The building was old; its green paint had begun to mellow. Inside, the lounge was dark, with the exception of the glowing lights hanging from the bar and the neon beer placards on the far walls. A man in a white cabana shirt and beige slacks sat perched on a stool under the lounge's green awning—the support beams of which were termite eaten. It was the tan, leathery old man he and Eli had passed the night before on their way to the mystery house. He sucked on another cigar eyeing him knowingly—a grin bloomed across his face. "I remember you," he said to Durant.

Durant kept moving. "No, you don't."

"Sure I do. I rememba' you and yah man friend with the makeup on. Two of you reminded me of a tale they use to tell when I was a young boy. It's an unfortunate story—you won' want to hear it." The man sneered at Durant, almost as if he knew there was no way to resist the telling of his tale.

Intrigued by the man's certainty and feeling a bit confrontational in light of recent events, Durant challenged him. "I'm listening."

He pointed at himself "Dulac" and then flicked the brim of his fedora. "You should know that I love a good ghost story. My big sistah used to tell the tale I'm gonna share with you because it gave us such a fright. Not like the tales of the *rougarou*, the werewolf, who hunts for bad lil' children wanderin' the bayou so he could rip 'em apart or put a curse on 'em. Nah, this one kept a kid up at night thinkin' 'bout the mysteries of time and wetha' every ghost has reasons for coming back. I used to wundah if you asked a ghost what they wanted, even the nastiest ones, if maybe they'd tell yah." He stared into Durant's eyes intently for a moment as if willing him to react but Durant just shrugged—if the man was hinting at something, he didn't understand it. Dulac continued in his bayou drawl, "Usually the grown folk would smoke in the evenin' and chitty chat, or maybe my mutha' would scrub pots off the side of the tiny porch of our shotgun house. But when my sistah told this pa'ticular tale, everyone would hush...you know, do their chores a lil' more quiet like they was listenin' to the misfortunes of someone they knew. It was about forbidden love and a curse the dandy son of a rich French aristocrat family suffered as punishment. That man loved to strut around all in velvet and frills and gloves like a proud ol' roostah' going to parties night after night and sleeping all during the day." He shook his head chuckling. "Liquor and taking remedies was his true love, really. Remedies and medicines was really just opium and morphine back then—people didn't know no bettah'. During a night out he met a free man of color and grew fond of him. Nowadays those things don't matter but back then it did, especially for the Frenchman. He was high society. If his family found out, whoop! There goes his whiskey, his money, his fancy clothes and jewels, his fancy friends, and worst of all his drugs." Dulac sucked on his cigar studying Durant's face as he exhaled its sweet earthen perfume. "Yup, he couldn't have that. So, he saw his man friend in secret in the home that his father bought for him. That free man was smart and made a good life for hisself." He tut-tutted. "But he was a tortured man my sistah explained. He never had a desire to take a wife, good lookin' as she said he was. I don't think that man had enough time here on earth to find his true self or find out that his true love would not be a woman. Rumors made its way to the Frenchman's father who threatened to have his lover killed if he kept on with him. But the Frenchman was too arrogant and spoiled to believe his father would make good on his threats. That is until some fishermen pulled the free man's rotted body from the swamp. People said whoever done it had it out for him because the body had been butchered like a beast. Body parts were missin' an' all."

"And your sister told this story to you before bedtime?" Durant asked. "That's pretty disturbing."

"What? Like the rougarou eatin' children in the swamps was any bettah'," the old man spat back. "These stories was meant to keep children from playing in the swamps or messin' around in ol' houses you ain't supposed to be in." When the signs of realization showed upon Durant's face, a wide, evil smile appeared on the face of Dulac, revealing yellow diseased teeth caked with plaque. A delighted, bombastic laugh erupted from the hard old man. Durant scooped the old man off his stool by his shirt collar and hissed, "Who in the hell are you?!"

"Get your goddamn hands off me!" Dulac yelled as he ripped Durant's hand from his shirt and gave him a shove with such unexpected force that he tumbled back onto the wet street. Durant rose slowly from the ground with his hands out in front of him, showing his surrender. "So you knew we were in that house, huh? I just want to know what was in there with us."

"*You* were in that house."

"I wish you'd stop with the riddles, old man. You must see that I'm not following."

The man now seemed to tower over him. It was as if the jig was up on his loose skin and skeletal frame. An otherworldly air of strength and all-knowingness escaped him. "If yah hadn't been so damn rude you'd have let me finish my tale and you might be understandin' a little bettah."

"Please, I apologize, continue."

Dulac shook his head. "You know, every generation gets needier and ruder. You got to spell everything out for them—y'all don't have no goddamn common sense." He sighed in frustration deciding to continue on, narrating. "When the Frenchman found out about what happened to his lover he lost his mind. He went out and had hisself the last party he'd ever have. People said he prowled the streets that night goin' to his friends' parties. He ripped the jewels from women's necks and cussed at 'em. They said he snatched hats off men's heads and stomped on 'em, broke their canes in half on his knee, spat in their faces, all the while screaming out for his lover. The Frenchman was untouchable because of who he was so there was nothin' to be done not even by the authorities. He pulled at his hair and tore at his clothes sayin' they looked ridiculous—he said he'd give all his money and his jewels to have his other half back. He swore to everyone that he'd defy God and defy time to see him again. An apology was owed for not actin' on his father's threats which led to the murder of his twin soul. They found him dead in his father's house the next day. All the life drained from his stiff corpse—he'd done too much drugs." He tapped at his cigar letting the ashes fall to the ground. "The thing is my sistah never told this ghost tale until after they pulled me from the mud. Her stories about the swamp monsters never kept me out of the swamp in the end huh?" Dulac laughed. "I've got me some serious unfinished business to straighten out."

"You're the free man."

"I am."

"Are you a ghost?" Durant asked.

"I am a ghost to everyone 'cept you. I am something a lil' different to you." The old man paused. "Elijah is dead, huh?"

"Yes, sir. He died the same way you described in your tale."

"He always does," Dulac said as he sat back down on the stool outside the Vortex Lounge in resignation. "There are rules, laws if you will, by which I must work. Spirits must always be mindful of the risks taken when messin' with time. We can't interfere too much. I have to believe Eli's out there doing the same as me or else why do I keep coming back? The songs of the birds and insects could lure me back to the still waters of the swamp in a heartbeat. What I wouldn't give to slip back into that dark eternity. True soul mates get as many chances as they need to get it right even in death. I'll rise from the mud's embrace to confront him over and over again as long as he's willing to keep seeking me out. Well, take care of yourself Durant—work on those manners." Dulac rose from the stool, walked past Durant, and disappeared into the mists of rain that blustered through the street.

Durant sat at home for days afterward, overwhelmed and exhausted, contemplating the entire experience and the mysteries of the world just as Dulac said he did as a kid. It made him feel vulnerable to the unknown. He'd retrace Dulac's face and features in his mind as he lay in bed at night noticing they were a lot like his own. Was it possible to cross the path of your previous self? Because, he believed, he hadn't just crossed paths with his past life...he had conversed with it. The events had him theorizing whether ghosts are souls possessing enough emotional energy to compel the past to run laterally to the present. This meant haunts were intentional and it was a sobering thought. How many messages were out there like beacons shining in the night waiting for someone to behold them and bring closure? How many of them were malicious and waiting for someone to unleash its wickedness and vengeance upon? Dulac could have been one of them, a soul scorned, scratching, burning, or sitting atop the chest of his victims and robbing them of their last breaths as in other legends. He was grateful that the latter had not been the case.

Durant became more and more certain that if haunted places, people, and things were filled with intent, then it meant he hadn't dreamt up the antique splendor of the house in which he and Eli bonded in—he saw it for a reason. Thoughts of the grotesque tapestries hanging in the room Eli dubbed the opium room drifted into his consciousness from time to time. Beasts with bulging oversized eyes and necks poised ready to snap were seen chasing its victims. Scaled monsters with wings outspread and fangs bared guarded treasures. Was it an omen foretelling the consequences of the evils of vanity and avarice? Praising and devouring beautiful people, in the case of the freeman, without a care for their welfare. Or the need to flaunt material things to an almost spiritual level as in the case of the dandy culture in which Eli partook. Had those tapestries always existed in the house or were they meant as a clue, revealing the lessons to be learned from Eli's actions and Durant's violent death in the past? He knew that Eli hadn't presently lived in the home but was convinced they were connected to it somehow—it'd be worth looking into the homes date of origin. Durant had been taking research slow. He couldn't help but harbor awkward feelings toward everything that happened. The squeamishness he felt when he tried revisiting the strange and emotional experience made discoveries difficult to digest. For instance, the shock of discovering that the surname of his early ancestors had been Du Lac had kept him indoors for days.

Old man Dulac had mentioned that the generations grew needier and maybe even less clever. With this in mind, Durant placed some efforts towards aiding and abetting their haunting—he crafted meaningful clues with plans to leave them at the old house, the Vortex Lounge, and on the gnarled oak in an effort to help increase the odds of a successful reunion. He wasn't sure their future reincarnations would run parallel to these places again but thought it wise to have them covered just in case. Perhaps the unlimited chances at reunion soul mates are granted in the afterlife turn curse when one causes evil towards the other.

Durant never had to suffer the fate of his predecessor Dulac for reasons unknown. Nonetheless, he often wondered whether death would have been a kinder fate. He never married and never fathered any children to his family's disappointment. Instead, he spent his life traveling in search of the sanctimonious and transcendent sensation abandoned places offered. The sensation was similar to that upon entering towering and majestic Gothic cathedrals and similar to what was felt in the abandoned house which had resurrected itself to its former glory for a single night. Trips resulted in haunting photographs admired by many. His recent photo of a roadside diner in the desert, the screen door of which he captured hanging from its hinges in the corner of the shot, had a very positive reception on social media. While on the road, he would tell the tragic tale of the two soul mates gifted and cursed with the ability to bend space and time to find each other. Not only did the telling of the tale help to perpetuate its existence in the future, but it also helped Durant feel closer to his soul mate, Eli. He told of the pain the tormented Frenchman's ghost carried, hauling the weight of his guilt for over a century—too vain to have professed his love and devotion to his partner before his murder. He spoke of the loneliness and confusion the ghost of the free man suffered while roaming the swamps, disappearing in and out of its mist, awaiting an explanation and apology for his partner's betrayal. Where scholarship failed in its study of the paranormal, Durant became a part of that company of renegade researchers, riders atop their beasts, crossing the endless dunes and shifting sands of time in search of answers to be found in damaged spaces where the years left indications of its aftermath. Despite the many extraordinary and confirmatory things he experienced and discovered in those places, Durant would never find Eli again in his lifetime.

RAVENGLASS
E. F. Sweetman

Hours after the eleven o'clock BBC news broadcast her as a cat burglar, Lady Katherine Bryce-Howard Floriel snuck into the back door of her home on King's Road in the wealthy neighborhood of Kensington, London. Her ancestors would not have been scandalized that she crept in back instead of making a proper entrance through the front; her title no longer had money or power behind it, and she had been sneaking in and out for years. Besides, she came from a long line of ancestors who built their legacies on their own versions of scandal or shame.

Kitty, she had never been a Katherine, was nearly invisible in the dark kitchen because she was dressed head-to-toe in black. The townhouse was silent except for a comforting tick of the radiators on the cold November night. As her eyes adjusted, she unzipped her leather jacket and pulled off the tight black knit hood that covered her head and face. The jacket was expensive, and she had no business with it, but like almost everything in her possession, it was hers because she stole it. Swiped from the dressing room at Impereo London while she waited for her friend Kath to get measured for a dress. To think her uncle Henry wondered what she saw in that crowd.

Kitty sat on the stepstool to unbuckle her boots, trying not to make too much noise with the heavy buckles. She carefully set them on the mat, and tiptoed toward the back stairs.

"I hope it was worth it."

Sir Henry Bryce-Howard turned on the kitchen light just as his niece reached the bottom step. Kitty whirled in surprise to see him leaning against the wall near the light switch with a cold cup of tea.

"Henry!" she gasped.

"Give me your backpack, and go to bed," he said.

"What?" She looked genuinely astonished. Her green eyes were wide open, and her short black hair stood on end from pulling off the tight hood.

"Don't do this, Kitty, please. I don't have the energy."

"Wait, I can explain..."

"Stop. Just...stop," Henry looked exhausted. His green eyes were bloodshot; his face was pale and ravaged. Like Kitty, he was small and slender, but hunched down in his rumpled bathrobe; he looked years older than his actual age.

"I'm just too tired to get into this. Go to bed, your *own* bed. Whatever you do, do not disturb Gregory. I'll deal with you in the morning..." he glanced at the kitchen clock, then added, "when it's light."

"What...why...what happened?" she whispered.

"You were the lead story on the eleven o'clock news."

Despite Henry's warning to leave Gregory alone, Kitty crept to the one spot she could fall to sleep since she was adopted by her uncles: at the foot of their king size bed. It was a habit she could not break, because it was the only place she felt safe. She drifted off to sleep before she could think of a plausible story for whatever Henry thought he saw on the news.

Kitty woke to her Uncle Gregory's raspy voice, "Do you *ever* sleep in your own bed?" She smiled. It was a question both uncles asked when they found her curled up at their feet, a tiny orphan child, undisciplined, unmanageable. They always followed up with a big bear hug from both of them.

She got up to hug Gregory, making sure she was careful. Gregory deWeyne, was her tall, dark, strong, and most energetic uncle, up until a month ago when he nearly died from pneumocystis pneumonia. He had been HIV positive for years, but managed well until, for some unknown reason, his body rejected the medications that kept the virus at bay.

They had no warning of how seriously ill he was when he woke with a cough. He ended up on a ventilator by the end of that October day. He fought hard, and was finally home after weeks in hospital, reduced to what he referred to himself as "a wheezing bag of bones." As Kitty hugged him, she listened to his breathing. It was still ragged but getting better.

"Do you want me to bring up your tea?" she asked.

"No, luv, I want to sleep." It was Gregory's way of saying he wanted to be left alone.

Kitty was about to go to her room when she heard voices coming up from the living room. She tiptoed to the top of the staircase to listen.

"...look, Henry, you're at the end of your rope. Let me help out. Good Lord, you've got enough to worry about, what with almost losing Gregory."

Morris Cuthbert! That weasel, Kitty thought when she recognized the voice.

He was one of Henry's distant cousins, which meant he was also somehow related to her. Short, fat and prissy, Morris drifted in and out depending on his need for money, or level of boredom. He was a lurker. He tried to hide his lust for drama as familial concern, and seemed to take an unnatural interest in Kitty. She could almost smell the peppermint Altoids he was constantly sucking on to disguise his stinking breath.

"I appreciate that Morris," Henry's voice was muffled. Kitty knew her uncle was sitting with his elbows on his knees, and his face in his hands. "But I worry about sending her so far away...she's a lot to handle."

"She's proven again and again that she can't stay out of trouble in London!"

Kitty tiptoed halfway down the stairway, and crouched to hear more of the conversation.

"She is disobedient, she breaks all your rules, and after everything you've given her. You should remind her that she could have been left to rot in an orphanage if it weren't for you and Gregory! She is Fiona all over again! Creating all sorts of problems, bringing nothing but worry and shame. Odds are she'll end up just like her too—"

"You are out of line Morris," Henry said sharply, cutting him off.

Kitty gasped then held her breath because the room went silent. She wanted Henry to throw Morris out of the house. Fiona Bryce-Howard was Kitty's mother and Henry's twin sister. There was always an implication that she was the wild twin and Henry was the responsible one. Fiona died, along with Kitty's father, in a plane crash when Kitty was five years old.

After several moments Morris said, "I apologize, it was never my intention to speak poorly of Fiona. What I *meant* to say was Kitty is on a dangerous path. She won't go to school, she won't work, and I don't think things will change if she stays in London. It's too easy for her here. She's making a mockery of you, and keeps getting into more trouble. I'm sure it's not cheap, and before you know it, she'll drain you of every penny!" Kitty rolled her eyes.

"Please Morris, just stop. This isn't about money, it's about what she is becoming. You would think her parole officer would rein her in, yet there she is on the eleven o'clock news..."

"Did they identify her?" There it was—Morris was greedy for the dirty details.

"Oh heavens no," Henry said, "it was a blurry security film from Harrods jewelry room...they called her a cat burglar, almost like it was funny. *I* know it was Kitty, especially when I saw she wasn't in her room. I can't figure out why she does these things!"

"You know what you need to do, Henry," Morris said, "Ravenglass is just the place. I need the help; I promise she'll work hard, and learn to obey. It's the right thing."

Ravenglass! Morris's latest project, a decrepit country manor in the northern Lake District of Cumbria he had revived as a resort hunting lodge. He had been badgering Henry and Gregory to send Kitty up to work for him for the past year, but they declined, and often joked between themselves that Morris was looking for slave labor.

"I don't know what else to do," Henry said. "I can't take care of Gregory when I'm constantly worrying about Kitty..."

"You won't need to worry about her up there, I promise Henry. She will have nothing but fresh air, hard work, and miles of open country. It is the best thing for everyone and you'll be able to focus on Gregory."

There was a long silence. Kitty was tired of their conversation, and sick of Morris. She stood to go to her room when she heard Henry say, "I hope you're right Morris."

Kitty froze. Had Henry just agreed to send her away?

"What will I tell Gregory? He loves her more than anything in this world. She has been so good for him, despite the chaos she causes."

Kitty didn't wait for him to finish the thought. She was crushed. She wanted to run down the stairs to defend herself, but held back because this time she knew it would play perfectly into Morris's hand. She crept back up the stairs into her room, and began to sob.

Henry called her down to his study after Morris left. It was a formality; Kitty could see that he had made up his mind the moment she saw his face, and her heart broke.

"Morris! It would be better if you sent me to Siberia!" she wailed.

Henry steeled himself to stick with his decision, although he could never bear to see Kitty cry. "You have left me no choice. No one is offering to put up with your antics in Siberia, so either you go to Ravenglass, or we show your parole officer the tape."

He waited. She stopped crying, but would not answer.

"Kitty, I've given you too many chances, and you've only gotten worse. I warned you the last time that I'm done. I won't lie for you, I won't cover for you, and I can't lose another night of sleep because you're a top story on the eleven o'clock news!"

She glared at him, testing his resolve. She knew how much she looked like her mother.

"You know all this! You know that I need to focus on Gregory, how much I needed your help, and you've just thrown it in my face," Henry continued. "You won't stop. And I cannot do this anymore. I can't take care of Gregory while I'm constantly worrying about you."

"I never asked you for anything," Kitty snarled. "It wasn't my choice to come here! I didn't make my parents die!"

Kitty could be cruel when she was cornered, but this time Henry was unmoved.

"You have no right to send me away!" She burst into tears again.

"I have every right," he finally snapped at her, "I am your guardian, and the sole conservator of your trust *if-or-when* you make it to twenty-five, which means you have six years to go until you're done with me. You will do exactly what I decide. You've pushed me to the limit, Kitty, despite all the chances you've been given. You won't go to university, you won't work at the foundation...and you can't keep up with those rich, spoiled brats you've fallen in with because you do not have their kind of money! Is that what it was all about? You're breaking into Harrods because you want to impress some rich idiot named *Devon*? You're going to work at Ravenglass, and if you refuse, I show the tape to your parole officer. Now go up and pack."

Henry called Morris to say Kitty would be ready by noon, which gave her less than an hour. It was easier than drawing out the hours where he might relent. He told Kitty not to take much, and whatever she brought should be warm, otherwise she would freeze in the drafts of the huge house. As she was stuffing a small duffle bag with her warmest black workout gear, Gregory rolled his enormous Louis Vuitton suitcase into her room. Typical, Kitty thought and couldn't help but smile.

"Too much?" he asked.

"You're not supposed to know what's going on," she said.

"Honestly, luv, I'd really have to be dead to not know," he said, sitting on the case.

"I can't believe he's sending me away, he—"

"Kitty, stop," Gregory interrupted, "you got yourself into this mess. Don't blame Henry. He's been through so much, and you haven't given him a moment of peace."

"But he's sending me with Morris? To *Ravenglass*?"

"Give it a couple of weeks. I'll convince him that we need you back," Gregory paused and gave her a serious look, "*but* you have to be on your best behavior! You can't make trouble up there Kitty, promise me."

"I won't go, I can't," she said.

"Kitty, you have to. I've never seen Henry like this. He's going to have a breakdown. I promise I'll get you back." said Gregory as he hugged her, and let her cry until she could speak again.

"Two weeks? Do you swear?"

"I'll do my best. You make sure you do the same."

"Then what, reform school?" She could not relent; she was gutted.

"Why not try going to university? If not, my cousin Bruce might be able to put up with you in New York City. I don't know, Kitty. You have to stop getting into trouble! And do something with yourself."

When she finished packing, Kitty waited alone with Henry in the living room. Despite her anger, she could see his pain. She wished, not for the first time, she could somehow stop adding to his worry. She reached for his hand, but Henry pulled her into a tight hug.

"I know you're never going to forgive me for this, Kitty," he whispered. A car horn sounded. She broke away, grabbed her bags, and ran down the front steps to where Morris was waiting in his Land Rover.

He grinned at Kitty as she climbed into the front passenger seat, and said, "I hope you've been to the loo, we're driving straight through, no stops," then he winked and said, "wouldn't want to take a chance at losing you at along the way, now would I?" She gave him a withering look, and curled up on her seat, leaning as far away from him as possible.

The rain in London turned to sleet in Liverpool, then heavy wet snow in Endmoor. Morris pulled off the highway at Blackpool to put the Land Rover into four-wheel drive. Radio and mobile phone reception faded out after Oxenholme.

When it was clear that Kitty was pretending to sleep to avoid listening to Morris drone on about Ravenglass, he filled the silence by sucking on Altoids and humming show tunes just to annoy her. Kitty watched out her window, trying to memorize every sign along the way.

Six hours after leaving Kensington, Morris said, "Nearly there."

Kitty did not answer. She swore she would not say a word for the entire drive. She could not stand being in the same car with Morris, let alone sitting so close to him, but she had no option because he had removed the back seats, inside door handles, and installed a heavy mesh barrier to separate the front from the back of his SUV. It was creepy, and very much in line with what Kitty thought about Morris Cuthbert.

"Thank you for making the long drive feel endless. It says an awful lot about what you really are," he said in a conversational tone.

Kitty stared ahead and said nothing.

"Aren't you special, what, with your uncles wrapped around your little finger, catering to your every whim. But you have never fooled me, not for a minute. So, let's get things straight Kitty, if you don't do what is expected, if you stray, even the slightest, you will be punished."

That was too much. "What on earth are you talking about?" she demanded.

"Oh my! She can speak! Even when it's not all sunshine and fairy dust!"

"What exactly are you saying, *Morris*?"

"Oh, that's right! Always making a point of calling me *Morris* after I asked you to call me 'uncle,' as if you would fawn over me the way you do with those two pouffes," and he chuckled and rattled the tin of mints on the dash.

"What I'm saying, *Kitty*, is that you're in for quite a wake-up, and it's too bad when you don't like it. You're hundreds of miles from anywhere. No *Uncle* Henry or *Uncle* Gregory to bail you out, or cover up for your nasty, thieving ways. So, make sure you do exactly what is asked of you, or..."

"Or what?"

"Do as you're told!" he roared at her. Beneath all those Altoids, his breath was rotten. "For the first time in your spoiled life, you will do as you're told."

Kitty pressed her face against the car window. She would not give him the benefit of seeing her cry. Morris laughed, knowing he hit the mark. An hour after pulling off the highway, he took a sharp turn down a private road and stopped at the tall stone perimeter. He turned off the headlights and they sat in the cold darkness, listening to the wind moan across the moor.

"This is what you'll get if you decide to run away," Morris said. "There is nothing for miles, and I mean nothing. Except things that you don't want to know about. Things that will hurt you."

He switched the headlights back on, and they drove up a long drive, past a newly paved rectangular parking area full of cars, to a circular flagstone court. Ravenglass was a sprawling three-story stone manor, many years in disrepair. At one time it was a regal country manor home, now it looked sinister in its dilapidated state. There was no warmth: no light glowed from the dozens of windows, some of them shuttered. The slate roof was steeply pitched, and was missing many shingles. Several chimneys were crumbling. The sharp eaves silhouetted at irregular intervals in the dark sky enhanced the ragged appearance. Nothing about Ravenglass was welcoming to Kitty.

"Grab your things," Morris ordered, "and get used to it. From now on you're the help."

He walked briskly up cracked marble steps to an oak door which opened into the dim foyer. Kitty hurried behind him to get out of the cutting wind. A very tall man dressed as a butler, and a woman in a long red dress who was nearly the same height made a formidable welcoming committee. There was heavy metal music and sounds of a raucous party coming from somewhere inside the manor.

"Madam Vernay, Egon, may I introduce your new house girl, *Miss* Katherine Floriel," Morris said, taunting Kitty by not using her title.

"Does she not speak?" Madam Vernay said with a harsh French accent. Her face was pinched and tiny, and her close-set eyes made her head look abnormally small on her large frame.

"Oh she does," Morris said airily, "she is quite free with her words when she wants."

"Do not tell me she is trouble," Madam Vernay snapped at him, "you know we cannot tolerate disobedience Mr. Cuthbert."

"Madam Vernay, I assure you, she understands her place," Morris said soothingly. "And how was the hunt? This snow should have made it easy, did they get both?"

"It was a total failure," Vernay said. Morris's nonchalant demeanor changed immediately as he said, "What!"

"You mistook our guest's enthusiasm for ability, Morris," Madam Vernay said in a flat tone. "They woke late, and according to Denny, they got too cold to be out for very long."

Morris did not answer; he walked quickly through the main hall to the back. Egon reached out his large square hand for Kitty's bags, but Madam Vernay slapped him away. "Imbecile! What are you doing? This is not a guest."

She stepped close and spoke to Kitty as if Egon was not there, "I have seen the likes of you before. You think you're better than any of this...Rest assured, you're not. Morris has told me all about you, and I promise, none of your little schemes will work at Ravenglass. You will do exactly what I say, or you will be punished. Now!" She clapped her hands, and Kitty jumped. "Egon, take her upstairs. The day begins at five o'clock, report to the kitchen ready to work."

Kitty was too shocked to answer. She followed Egon up to the top floor. Her room was tiny, with only a narrow bed and an iron garment rack. A shapeless gray dress and white apron hung off one of the hangers. Egon watched her from the doorway.

"Do we all sleep up here?"

"No. Just you and the other girl. The guests breakfast at ten." Egon said in a slow, measured cadence, as if he had to think carefully about what he said.

"How am I to know to get up?" she asked.

"You will hear a bell," he said as he trudged down the stairs. Kitty went to the end of the narrow hallway, past closed doors, into the bathroom. She sighed with relief to finally pee after hours in the car. Back in her room, she tried to open the one tiny window, but it was painted shut, so she just looked out. She could make out the grounds, a large barn, and the vast lands beyond the perimeter wall. Morris was not lying; there was nothing but wind and low-lying grassland. Running away would not be her best option. As she crawled into the cold, narrow bed, she thought of Gregory's promise, and all she had to do was be good for two weeks.

Kitty's quasi-sleep was shattered by an ear-splitting clanging. She bolted up in the dark room, petrified. When the racket finally ceased, the silence made her feel deaf until she heard a door slam and rapid footsteps going down the stairs. As she pulled on the large, shapeless gray dress and tied the apron tight around her small waist, she was committed to appear obedient.

Madam Vernay, still wearing the long red dress, watched her come down the stairs. Kitty's first thought was that she stood there day and night. In daylight, Kitty saw that her small eyes were the same mud brown as her hair.

"Next time use the back stairs," Madam Vernay ordered, "you are not to be anywhere in the guest areas unless you are cleaning them," then directed her into the kitchen. Two older, heavy-set women were busy rolling out a pastry and slicing a very dark cut of meat. A scrawny young woman dressed exactly as Kitty was filling silver carafes from a tall coffee maker, but instead of fresh bread and coffee, there was an odor of rotten food.

"Berthe and Eunice, my cooks. Nancy is my other housekeeper," announced Madam Vernay. None of the women acknowledged the introduction or looked up from their tasks.

"Begin with last night's dinner dishes," Madam Vernay ordered, pointing at the scullery, then went out to the dining room.

The stench was overpowering in the tiny space. A pile of greasy dishes covered with gravy and food bits were in the sink. Cheap wine glasses stained with a thick, dark red wine stood on the drainboard. Kitty's stomach lurched at the sight and smell. She covered her nose with her apron and backed away. Berthe and Eunice glanced over quickly while Nancy stared openly. No one offered any explanation or support, so Kitty gave herself a moment, held her breath and returned to the fetid pile. *Two weeks*, she reminded herself as she filled the sink with hot water and began scrubbing.

At ten o'clock, a small bell chimed twice from the dining room. Berthe and Eunice carried chafing dishes loaded with scrambled eggs and sliced meat to a long buffet in the dining room. Berthe nodded to two platters of breads and croissants for Kitty to take out. As she set the platters down, the guests began to arrive, or more accurately, stagger in.

They were a young group, not more than thirty years old, yet instead of appearing fit and ready to hunt, they were all overweight, and wretched. They lurched through the dining room, hanging onto the backs of the chairs as they found their seats. Egon escorted two unsteady women to their places. All eyes were bloodshot, all smiles were thinly veiled grimaces, and their laughter sounded like groans. The wild party from the night before must have gone on for hours.

Kitty stood next to Nancy near the kitchen door. She did not know what to make of Ravenglass. It was far removed from luxurious, and the guests were nothing like the hearty English hunters she expected. The idea that this wretched group could hang on to galloping horses for hours was absurd. As she lost herself in her thoughts, the fetid stench that permeated the kitchen overwhelmed the dining room. It was worse than the scullery and she tried not to retch.

"Put a smile on your face right now," Madam Vernay hissed, glaring at her, but Kitty rushed through the kitchen and flung open the back door. The air was cold and sharp; it was a beautiful sunny day. Kitty took several deep breaths, hoping not to vomit.

"Don't worry, you get used to it," a tiny voice piped from behind her. Kitty turned to find mousy little Nancy holding out a cup of black coffee.

She took it gratefully. After a few sips, she smiled at her. Nancy had a scar from her lip to her nose, probably a badly corrected hairlip. Her simple face was empty of any expression. She waited with Kitty on the back step.

"What is that horrid smell?" Kitty asked.

"It's the feral pig, I reckon. That's what they eat out here. Gives off a powerful stink, cooked or raw. This crowd's been eating the leftovers from last month 'cause they ain't been able to kill anything. Denny says they're a bunch of grotty berks, and can't shoot their way out of a bag. Madam says for you to get back to the dining room."

"A bunch of what?" Kitty asked, but Nancy had already gone back to the dining room. It took two cups of coffee before she was able to return. The lodgers appeared to have revived as well. Madam Vernay shot Kitty a death glare, then smiled politely at the young man at the head of the table. Morris had arrived in her absence and was serving brandy. He smirked at Kitty as if he knew all, then stabbed a slice of meat off the platter with the serving fork and popped it into his mouth.

Ravenglass staff had breakfast in the kitchen while the guests prepared for the hunt. It was a quick meal. Berthe brought a pot of oatmeal to the table and began filling bowls, and Eunice carried in plates loaded with eggs and shredded meat scrambled together. Two skin-headed men trooped in the back door. They looked like hooligans, rough and strong in dirty work clothes and heavy work boots. They grabbed plates and spoons and began eating without a word.

"That's Denny and Bilton," Nancy said, "they help with the things that need to be done outside."

Denny stopped shoveling food into his mouth to give Kitty a look that made her glad she wore a dress shaped like a potato sack.

"Check the new bird, Bilt-o," he said poking Bilton in the side with his elbow.

Bilton gave her a long-tooth smile with his mouth full, and said, "Ol' Morris is picking 'em better, ain't he Denn-o?"

Madam Vernay clapped her hands at them, and then pushed a plate to Kitty.

"Do not expect a formal announcement for your meal, and you better learn to eat quickly."

That rotten odor wafted up from the eggs and Kitty instantly pushed it away. The kitchen fell silent as they stared at her.

"Excuse me," Madam Vernay was furious, "is our food not refined enough for you?"

Denny and Bilton guffawed, punching each other on the shoulder while Egon snorted. Kitty felt faint. She could not remember her last meal, but knew she would have to be near death to eat those eggs. She was ready to lash out and shove the plate off the table, but she stopped herself. She reached for a bowl of oatmeal instead, and said, "Oh, Morris didn't tell you? I don't eat meat."

Kitty held herself together until she was alone in the scullery with another pile of greasy, befouled dishes. She burst into tears as hot water poured over the fetid mess. She did not know if she could keep her promise. And what if Gregory was unable to convince Henry? Or worse, what if he got sick again? She cried until she noticed the sink was about to overflow, and turned off the water. She sighed as she began washing, and managed to reign in her misery by the time the dishes were done.

Madam Vernay gave her a bucket and a mop, and sent her to clean the dining room floor. After one look at the filthy, scratched and gouged hardwood, she thought, *why bother?* She pulled open the dusty curtains to let sunlight into the dark room. Through the tall windows, she watched the guests file out to the courtyard. She was surprised to see they were all dressed in warm but decidedly urban-style clothing, and the women wore high heeled leather boots. They piled into two military jeeps. Further down the drive, Denny, Bilton, and Morris stood beside a beat up pickup truck holding shotguns. Two barking German shepherds were chained in the back. Morris looked to be giving instructions, then he turned and gave a big congenial wave to the guests. She watched as the jeeps followed the pickup down the long drive.

"Not your traditional hunt," Morris was standing in the dining room doorway. Kitty was startled that he had managed to sneak up behind her.

"Nothing about this place seems traditional," she answered, not wanting to engage him in more nonsense about Ravenglass. The place was a dump.

"Precisely, and that's what draws them," he grinned at her and continued, "My goal was to make it feel like a video game, it's what they all want. And I have found there are some very wealthy young people with money to burn who would rather play a real-life video game, using rifles and jeeps. And parties every night. Fast and exciting, less work than riding horses. Much more fun."

"Unless you're the pig," Kitty said flatly.

"Oh...yes, right." Morris was silent for a few moments, and then laughed unexpectedly. "Unless you're the pig." He covered his mouth and giggled. Kitty looked at him, confused. He took a deep breath to compose himself then said,

"And suddenly you're a vegetarian?" he asked her.

"I am if that's what passes for food around here. Morris, it's disgusting. You're giving English hunting food a bad name, which is saying a lot. The whole place smells bad."

"It's an acquired taste," again he suppressed his laughter. Kitty wondered if he was drunk. She watched warily as he paced the room while rubbing his hands together.

"Ravenglass is special, Kitty. You haven't given it half a chance."

"That's not fair! I'm trying, I'm doing everything I'm asked, and it hasn't even been one day." Kitty was afraid that Morris would tell her uncles she was not cooperating.

"I can tell you're *trying* to behave," he said slowly, "but you're not *trying* to like it. If you did, I believe you would come to appreciate Ravenglass. Who knows, you might even develop a taste for the hunt."

"I'm here to work hard and learn my lesson," Kitty said evenly. She was uneasy with the way he spoke to her, but did not want to provoke a fight. He snapped back to his usual self, and answered, "What a relief. I'd hate to think of hosting the likes of you as my *guest*," as he left the room.

Madam Vernay kept Kitty downstairs washing, sweeping, and dusting the main rooms. Ravenglass was shabbier on the inside than on the outside. The fireplaces were all blackened and full of soot, large patches of wallpaper had peeled off throughout the downstairs, and where paintings had once hung, pale rectangles marked their absence on the walls. The furniture was scratched, worn, and threadbare. Persian rugs scattered throughout the main rooms and central passageway were so faded and stained that it was impossible to see any of the original designs.

Kitty spent the long day by herself, and suspected Madam Vernay wanted to keep her away from Nancy. It was late afternoon when she heard the jeeps roar into the courtyard as she was sweeping the drawing room. There were yells and howls over the sound of the engines, so she hurried out to the front hall to the commotion. Morris stood in the front doorway with his arms raised in the air.

"Hail to the triumphant huntsmen! And women! Let us not forget this is a co-ed operation," he called out.

A guest jumped out of the first jeep yelling, "We did it! It was incredible! We actually cut out the heart and ate it the field!" Kitty saw in the fading daylight that his face and chest were covered in blood.

"Just one? Just one! You didn't catch two?" Morris bellowed as they climbed out of their jeeps.

"We only caught one," answered a heavy woman with flaming red hair and bloodied hands. "We were too worn out after the first kill to go on."

The pickup truck pulled up the drive and parked behind the jeeps. The dogs were in a frenzy inside the cab, and Kitty could just make out something wrapped in a tarp in the truck bed. It looked longer and thinner than a regular sized pig.

"What are you doing here? Come away from that door now," snapped Madam Vernay as she grabbed Kitty by the arm and pulled her away out of the foyer. "Finish the floors then report to the kitchen."

Kitty was angry, and sick of being a servant. She swept the big pile of dust into the fireplace then shoved the heavy screen back in place. She did not think she could go along with this treatment for the rest of the day, let alone two weeks. She believed Henry never would have agreed to send her if he really knew what it was like at Ravenglass. She wanted to find a way to call him, but had not been able to find a landline.

Kitty waited for the noisy guests to parade through to the foyer before she crossed into the back parlor with her mop and broom. She would not have bothered, except for one last hope of finding a phone. Instead of cleaning, she searched the corners, shelves, and closet without luck. She threw herself onto a dusty velvet settee in disgust and began to formulate a plan to befriend one of the guests. She was uncertain who she should approach. Of the five men and three women, no one stood out as particularly kind, or interested in her. They were such an odd bunch, she thought, stuck together at all times. As she pondered, she heard the pickup truck drive around to the back of the house. Through a narrow set of French doors, she watched Denny, Bilton, and Morris climb out while the dogs barked and jumped around the inside of the cab. Eager for her chance to spy, Kitty tiptoed to the windows.

"Shut it!" Bilton yelled at the dogs, their voices carried easily through the panes of glass.

"What happened!?" Morris demanded. He sounded furious.

"What'd you think happened," Denny shot back, "sending a bunch of fuckwits out like that? They're useless."

"Where is the other one?" Morris said each word slowly.

"How the hell do I know? It was bad enough getting them to stay with us; they kept veering off, wanting to stop for snacks. That's quite the lot of dimmos you have on your hands, Morrie."

"You imbeciles! There's still one on the loose! Get those dogs back on the trail now!" Morris shouted. Although it was dark in the room, Kitty tucked into the heavy curtain to avoid being seen.

"We ain't going nowhere," said Bilton. "Besides, anything out there will freeze to death after two nights in this cold."

"Listen Morrie, for the last time, these aren't hunting dogs, they don't track, they guard and attack," Denny said.

"Oh for God's sake, shut up both of you," Morris ran his hands through his thinning hair, then said, "Get back out there. Do not come back until you have the second one. That is an order."

The calm in Morris's voice made her feel more uneasy than when he was yelling. Kitty backed away from the window, gathered up her mop, broom, and bucket and went to the kitchen. Nancy was sitting alone at the work table with a cup of tea. "Where is everyone?" Kitty asked.

"Egon is napping. He doesn't do much anyway. Just stands around wherever the guests are," Nancy answered. "Berthe and Eunice went out to the barn to start butchering,"

Kitty made a face and said, "I am honestly considering becoming a vegetarian now. Madam Vernay kept me busy washing floors,"

"I did the guest rooms," Nancy told her, "though to tell the truth, I'd rather scrub floors. There's all sorts of nasty stuff in their rooms. I hate to touch it."

Kitty made another face. Everything about Ravenglass seemed perverted and depraved. Nancy listened to the racket coming from the guest rooms. It sounded like they were all shouting at the same time.

"Get ready, they all go nutty after they make a kill, then they make such awful messes, worse than dirty rooms. Disgusting. I hate cleaning up after big feasts."

"Then don't. What can they do?" Kitty asked.

"They lock you in the abattoir," Nancy answered in a hollow voice.

"No! Not really!" Kitty was stunned. "There is something wrong with this place! Did they actually lock you up?"

She gave Kitty that empty look which confirmed that Nancy was simple, or damaged, or both.

"How long have you been here?" Kitty asked.

"Oh, I don't know," Nancy answered, "I came along with Denny, he's my only brother. Mr. Morris promised him work when he got out of Belmarsh. I don't have anyone else, so I went with him too."

"Belmarsh? The prison?" Kitty asked. Nancy nodded.

"Did the other one, Bilton, come from prison too?" It made sense to Kitty that Denny and Bilton met in jail.

"Oh no," Nancy said. "Well, wait, yes, sort of. Bilton is Denny's best mate. He did his time in Doncaster because he raped a little girl."

"He...*what?*" Kitty was aghast.

Nancy did not answer because Madam Vernay burst into the kitchen.

"What are you two up to?" Madam Vernay demanded. She turned to Nancy with, "Have you been telling your lies again? Did I not warn you about that?"

"No ma'am, we were just..." Nancy could not continue.

"We were waiting for you to tell us what to do," Kitty cut in.

"Oh, is that right? How lovely, with the tea and all," Madam Vernay sneered, then pointed to Nancy, "You! Go downstairs and bring up the Medoc."

Nancy did not move until Madam Vernay stomped her foot, then she ran to the basement. Madam Vernay turned on Kitty.

"And *you*, set the table. Make sure the cloth is removed or you'll spend the night scrubbing the stains out of it. Now!"

Tension had risen throughout Ravenglass; Kitty felt it as she set the table with the same ordinary heavy, chipped plates and dull flatware as breakfast. She heard several loud thumps, then a scream from upstairs while Madam Vernay slammed cabinets and drawers in the kitchen. By the noise they made, the guests seemed to be escalating into a frenzy, and Kitty did not want to be alone in the dining room when they descended for their final dinner. She tested the edge of one of the butter knives. It was too cheap and dull to inflict any damage. She left it, and hurried back to the kitchen where Madam Vernay was berating Nancy for bringing up the wrong wine.

"Are you an imbecile, or are you deaf? Don't bother to answer, I know you are too stupid to read M-E-D-O-C..."

Nancy's blank expression crumpled and she began to cry. Madam Vernay slapped her hard and sent her upstairs.

"Go wash your stupid face, you filthy girl. I am sick of looking at you!"

She turned on Kitty with, "Bring up the bottles of Medoc. The wine cellar is at the back of the basement."

Kitty ran down the basement stairs, furious that Nancy was mocked and punished for her low intelligence. Her anger disappeared at the bottom step because it was dark, and like the rest of Ravenglass, it smelled rank. She found a light panel and flicked up all the switches. Unlike the rest of Ravenglass, it was neat and organized. A wooden workbench ran along one wall. Above it, neatly coiled rope hung from hooks next to a pegboard with sets of hacksaws and chisels. Metal shelves held folded tarps, rolls of tape, and large empty glass bottles on the other side of the workbench. Four box freezers lined up along the opposite wall. The wine racks stood at the dark end of the long room.

Not wanting to spend any time down there, Kitty quickly found four bottles of Medoc on the top rack and stepped lightly back up the stairs, but stopped shortly before she reached the top. She overheard Morris and Madam Vernay speaking in low, urgent voices from the back hall.

"...well if Denny doesn't think anyone could survive two nights in this weather, what are you worried about?" said Madam Vernay.

"There is no sign of him. Nothing! And they caught the first one miles farther than we ever imagined anyone could run in bare feet," Morris answered.

Kitty felt as if her blood drained from her body as she realized they were not talking about hunting pigs.

"You sent them back out with the dogs I hope, yes?"

"Yes...Denny tried to say they had to deal with the body, but I sent them right out. He tried to blame me because the guests bungled the hunt, and riled up his dogs, but Good Lord Maude, do you realize what a mess we're in if we don't find the other one—"

"Denny is right, Morris," Madam Vernay interrupted, "these people are fools! I have never seen such behavior...ever...you *never* should have promised them two, they were lucky they managed to catch one...Hush!

Here comes the imbecile."

Nancy must have come down the back stairs after washing her face.

"Now where is this new girl?" Madam Vernay said, exasperated. "I sent her downstairs for wine, and she has disappeared. These girls are useless Morris, I have to do everything myself!"

Kitty's heart stopped as she heard Madam Vernay walk toward the basement door. She leapt back down, taking three steps at a time, and ran to the back of the basement, terrified of what she overheard, and more afraid she was caught listening.

"You! New girl!" Madam Vernay called out as she came down the basement steps, "what is taking you so long!"

Kitty took a deep breath before she answered, "What was it you wanted? The Medoc?"

"Are you a bigger idiot than Nancy? Yes! The Medoc!" Madam Vernay shouted as she marched toward her. She looked furious until she saw Kitty's face. Her expression changed from anger to suspicion. Kitty tried to appear calm and stopped herself from shaking by pressing her knees together.

"What are you doing," Madam Vernay almost growled, her eyes narrowed, "why did you take so long?"

"I forgot what kind of wine you wanted," Kitty answered. Madam Vernay's hard gaze did not waver.

"You have been down here the whole time?" Madam Vernay said as she stepped closer.

"Yes." Kitty's heart was hammering so hard she felt it in her throat. Madam Vernay grabbed one of the bottles Kitty clutched to her chest.

She studied the label, and then looked at Kitty, "Upstairs. Now," she ordered.

They brought the wine into the dining room. Kitty arranged the bottles on the buffet until Madam Vernay stomped back down for more, then she went into the kitchen, and began to gasp.

"What's wrong? Did she hit you too?" Nancy was at the table, peeling parsnips.

"Nancy," Kitty whispered, "Oh my God, what kind of place is this? Tell me the truth, what is going on here?"

Nancy looked at Kitty with her unreadable expression. "I'm not allowed to tell," she said.

They heard Madam Vernay climbing the stairs, and they stared at each other, stricken with fright. "Here," Nancy shoved some parsnips at her, "start chopping."

Kitty grabbed a small knife from the counter. Her hands were shaking badly, and she did not notice the parsnips were unpeeled.

"My goodness, you two are quite a pair," Madam Vernay commented, carrying two more bottles into the dining room. Neither girl stopped working. Kitty watched, making sure she did not come right back, and whispered to Nancy, "Are all the guest's rooms locked?"

"What?" Nancy asked in a regular voice. Kitty shook her head furiously, then leaned over and whispered even lower, "Do all the guests lock their doors?"

"Sure they do."

"Do you have a key? One that opens all the rooms?"

Nancy reached down the front of her baggy dress and drew out a large key hanging from a long chain.

"You mean like this?" she whispered loudly.

Kitty shushed her, whispering very softly, "Does it open all the doors? Don't say anything, just nod yes or no." At first, it looked like Nancy did not understand, but after a moment she nodded enthusiastically. Kitty smiled and nodded back. She was about to ask for it when Madam Vernay returned with Morris. They both looked worried.

"Ah, yes. Kitty, I want a word with you," he said.

Kitty felt a wave of terror but willed herself to stay calm as she reached for another parsnip. She answered in a disinterested tone, "Yes?"

"In private," Morris said. "Follow me."

Crushing dread replaced her terror as Morris led her into the butler's pantry, which he used as his office. He rattled his tin of Altoids, popped one into his mouth, and sat heavily on the cracked leather chair behind a big banker's desk. Kitty stood because there was no place else to sit in the small room. She scanned for a phone or a wall jack, but saw nothing.

"Madam Vernay is concerned you may have overheard our conversation," he said looking at her very carefully.

Kitty shrugged.

"You honestly don't know what I'm talking about?"

Morris would not take his eyes off her face. He was watching for her to give something away, to break, to confess. Kitty felt as if her life hung by a thread. The edges of the room began to close in as a deep roar filled her ears. Then she thought of her uncles, how much they loved her, and that she must return to them. It gave her strength. Kitty took a deep breath and answered, "No Morris, I honestly don't know what you are talking about."

"Madam Vernay thought you took too long in the basement, and that maybe you were already at the top of the stairs listening?" he said as he tapped his tented fingers against his weak chin.

"I forgot what she asked for," Kitty answered.

"That is not what Madam Vernay believes...and neither do I. You remember *everything*, Kitty. It's just one of your many annoying quirks. In fact, Henry often complained it was how you made grades without cracking open a single book."

Kitty felt the sick panic rise again. She forced herself to think. If he did not accept that she forgot the name of the wine, what would he accept? *Think!* A tiny smile danced at the corners of his mouth as Morris watched her, and despite her will to survive, her fear rose...her fear...that was it.

"I'm afraid of her. I didn't listen carefully. I wasn't sure if she said Medoc or Merlot," she confessed quietly.

Morris dropped his hands onto the desk and said, "What?"

"She is so mean! And she talks too fast, I had no idea what she said, and I didn't want to go back up just to get yelled at. She was so angry at Nancy that she slapped her! Did you even know that Morris?"

He waved it away, "So you didn't overhear our conversation?"

"I told you *no* Morris, why do you keep asking me?" Kitty whined, certain that he could tolerate it. "Why are you acting like I'm not doing everything single thing you ask—"

"Stop wasting my time. Get back to the kitchen."

Kitty could not get away fast enough. She would get the key from Nancy. Her plan was to sneak into one of the guest's rooms while they were in the dining room, steal a set of car keys, and then steal a car. That was it, nothing more than to drive as fast and far as she could. Except that once she was safe, Morris would pay for bringing her to Ravenglass.

Both Eunice and Berthe were preparing dinner. Kitty stopped at the doorway, horrified as she watched Berthe place a dark red cut of meat into a large skillet and slam it onto the iron stove. Eunice was seasoning something that looked like gizzards in a big wooden bowl. The kitchen reeked with a raw, metallic stench. Nancy was still at the table, now chopping potatoes, her face a picture of pure misery.

"Get in here and make yourself useful," ordered Madam Vernay when she saw Kitty. She slammed two loaves of bread onto the table. "Slice these, then whip the butter. We have less than an hour to get this on the table," she barked out, furious. "I am not expecting anything spectacular, Berthe, and I don't think they care much either," and she stormed into the dining room.

As if on cue, the guests came down the front stairway with whoops and yells and trooped into the drawing room. Loud music blasted from tiny speakers wired to an iPod. Egon pushed in a loaded drink cart. The party had begun.

Kitty willed herself to go into the kitchen. She skirted past Eunice holding her breath, grabbed a loaf and brought it next to Nancy. She tried to catch her eye as she sliced the bread, but Nancy only looked miserably at the pile of potatoes.

"Are you alright?" Kitty whispered, feeling it was safe to do so, given the racket that was going on in the drawing room.

"Madam says I can't be friends with you," Nancy whispered back.

"Why? What did she tell you?"

"That you're a nasty girl, and you would be mean to me."

"Nancy, I'd never be mean to you. *She's* the one who's mean," Kitty whispered.

"You're bad, and you steal things. I'm not going to be friends with you." Nancy said.

Kitty's heart sank.

Dinner was ready within the hour. Egon rang the bell as Berthe and Eunice carried revolting platters of fried slices of flesh and diced organ meat to the center of the dining room table. Nancy followed with a bowl of mashed potatoes and parsnips. Kitty brought in the sliced bread, then backed against the wall near the door. Candles and a small fire in the fireplace were the only light source, which made the room feel like a dungeon.

Unfortunately, the guests were oblivious that their final feast was waiting on the table. They jumped and danced about the drawing room to an unrelenting dissonance of electric guitars and banging drums at top volume. They yelled, howled, and screamed at one another. Egon rang again, which was useless in the pandemonium. Madam Vernay shook her head, stalked into the middle of the mayhem and held up her arms to stop the nonsense. When the noise stopped, she announced, "Dinner is served."

Kitty was disgusted by their absurdity as they paraded into the dining room in full masquerade. The men wore dinner jackets and bow ties; the women wore long gowns and gloves. They all wore grotesque half-masks. It was ludicrous for eight people to carry on in masquerade, acting as if they had no idea who their friends were.

Kitty's mind was reeling from shock to fury to fear. She wanted to make them suffer more than the tremendous suffering they inflicted. They deserved to rot in hell for their evil. Her rage began to consume her, and she reminded herself to stay calm. She could do nothing until she escaped.

Escape. There would be no revenge if she did not make it out of Ravenglass. Kitty believed Morris never planned to let her go back to London. She almost sobbed at that thought, and held her breath in order to compose herself. She must not give herself away; her only hope was that neither Morris nor Madam Vernay suspected what she knew of their atrocities.

Yet, her mind continued to race. Why her? Whatever did Morris see in her to think she would take part in such abomination? Did he find her so corrupt that this was always part of his grand scheme? And how could Henry and Gregory not know of the evil that burned inside Morris? And just let her go? Kitty's eyes began to swim with tears. She blinked rapidly to prevent them from spilling over, and hoped the gloom provided some disguise to her sudden anguish.

The uproar of the guests brought her back. Kitty watched in disgust as they grabbed the cooked flesh with bare hands, then gulped the Medoc. Clearly, they drank a great deal before dinner because they were all quite drunk. They took handfuls of mashed potatoes and threw it at each other. One woman slipped off her chair and howled from the floor. Egon stepped to assist her, but Madam Vernay held him back.

"No," she said and slid open the dining room doors. "Your feast has ended, please return to the drawing room for coffee," she announced.

Egon helped the drunk woman off the floor while the rest of them stood unsteadily, uncertain.

"Well that was quick," one said, his voice muffled under the ridiculous long nose of his half mask.

"When the food begins to fly, dinner is finished," Madam Vernay said curtly, "but, please, enjoy your party back in the drawing room."

As the unrestrained frivolity drained from the guests, Kitty felt her anxiety rise. She glanced at Nancy, wondering how to convince her to give up the key without telling Madam Vernay. *Stop!* she told herself, it was useless. Nancy *was* an idiot, and Kitty could not afford to put her life in her hands. She tried to think of another way out of Ravenglass.

Morris entered, wearing a dinner jacket and a white silk scarf draped around his neck.

"Ahh, am I too late? My apologies." He reached for a glass of wine left standing on the table and gave a half bow.

"Your final dinner at Ravenglass, provided by none other than you all. Congratulations on your success, and yes, please step into the drawing room and continue the celebration!"

The guests revived slightly, as they wove back to the drawing room. The music started up again, and before Morris closed the drawing room doors, Kitty saw Egon pouring large drinks. Madam Vernay remained in the dining room. "Nancy will clean up tonight. You may go to bed," she told Kitty.

"What? That's not fair!" Nancy was outraged, "Why does she get off so easy!"

"It has been a long day for all of us, Nancy. Please remember that this is her first day at Ravenglass. Go! Do as I say. And you," Madam Vernay turned to Kitty. "Upstairs," she ordered. She went out with Kitty to the back stairway.

"Am I in trouble?"

"Upstairs," Madam Vernay said again, and followed her closely all the way up to the top floor. She said goodnight, turned and quickly went down and shut the door at the bottom of the stairway. When Kitty heard it lock, she ran down to try to open it. All the fear and dread she held at bay flooded through her. She sank down on the steps, trapped. And she did nothing when she had the chance! Kitty berated herself as she pounded on the door, knowing it was useless. She felt weak and faint and hopeless. She dropped her head onto her knees and sobbed. After several minutes she went up the narrow stairs and into the bathroom. She could faintly hear the music, and looked out the bathroom window. It was larger than her bedroom window. She pushed it up, and to her surprise, it slid open easily. She looked out. There was the same steep pitched slate roof, but instead of a three-story drop to the ground, the bathroom window was directly above the flat wing which was the servants' quarters.

Kitty ran into her room and pulled her duffle out from under her bed. She ripped off her dress and apron, and quickly dressed in her own clothes. She pulled on her boots, and got into her leather jacket, making sure the back hood and leather gloves were still tucked in her pockets. She felt stronger, and more determined, wearing her own clothes. She unzipped her backpack, hoping to find something sharp, but all she had was her wallet, mobile phone, lipstick, sunglasses, and hand lotion. Not even a pen to stab with! She dug to the bottom and found an energy bar. She ripped into it, wondering how long it had been there, grateful it had been forgotten. She pulled on her hood, gloves, and backpack, and returned to the open bathroom window.

The drop to the flat roof was nearly fifteen feet, but looked higher when she considered jumping it. She had no other choice, and waiting was wasting her time. Kitty climbed out, hung from the sill for a moment to stop herself from swinging, then dropped. She landed hard, sending a jolt up her spine, but felt no pain. She rolled onto her back to take stock of herself, and listened for any noise from inside the house. The only people who might have heard her hard landing were Berthe and Eunice. Kitty doubted they would do anything about it. She doubted they would bother to pour water over their own heads if their hair was on fire.

The night was bitter cold, and the wind gusted off the moors. Kitty sat up and looked around. She stood and carefully walked to the back edge of the wing to a shorter sloped roof. She crawled on her belly to that edge and saw that she was on top of the second-floor screened porch. Kitty hung her legs down and kicked at the screen, which easily gave way. She eased herself off the edge and made the short drop onto the wooden planks. She tried the door. It was locked, so she decided to keep climbing down. The drop to the ground level was over twenty feet, but instead of jumping, she wrapped her arms and legs around a pillar and slid to the frozen grass.

Kitty felt a sense of power when she landed, but stopped herself. She was outside, it was freezing cold, and she was miles from anywhere. Her next challenge was to steal a car. She ran down to the parking area, hoping they might have left keys in the jeeps, but found nothing. She thought of testing the doors to the other cars but didn't want to give herself away by setting off an alarm. She was growing cold. She looked around, trying to think, and saw the barn.

Kitty ran back up the drive to the barn door. It was closed, but she saw light through the cracks. She had no idea if anyone was inside and tried to peer through. She saw nothing, so she leaned on the edge of the door and pushed. It rolled a few inches and Kitty peeked in.

At first, she thought she was looking at a large shawarma from her favorite Halal grill, but it was too dark and bloody. It took Kitty a moment to realize she was looking at a headless butchered corpse hanging by its feet over a large metal bucket. She stepped back, stumbled, and fell, then screamed in terror. She clapped her hands over her mouth, trying to stop herself from screaming again.

"Don't think about it, don't think about anything except getting away," she said out loud to keep her control. She was alive, she reminded herself, she could run all night if she had to, run to a village or until someone picked her up along the road…and then she remembered Denny and Bilto were out there, driving around with guns. Kitty rolled over, buried her head in her arms, and screamed into the ground until she could not breathe.

When she looked up, there was Ravenglass. It seemed to mock her in its malevolence. It filled her with such fear, such dread, because she knew she had to go back inside. Her escape plan circled back to the key. Nancy and her damn key! She was going to take it, she had to, and she would tie Nancy up, gag her with her apron if she had to.

Kitty got up, crept to the kitchen door and looked inside. The kitchen was empty but she could see through to the scullery where Nancy was alone, still washing dishes. Kitty pushed back her hood and gently tapped on the door until Nancy looked up. She tapped some more until Nancy came over. Nancy's mouth dropped open when she saw it was Kitty.

"What are you doing out there?" she said as she opened the door, "And why are you all dressed like that?"

Kitty quickly stepped inside and grabbed Nancy by the mouth.

"Shut up and give me the key," she hissed at her.

Nancy shook her head, so Kitty grabbed the loose collar of her dress feeling for the chain.

"Where is it?" she demanded. "And don't you dare shout when I take my hand off your mouth or it'll be the last thing you do."

"Madam has it," Nancy whispered and started crying.

"Shit!" Kitty shoved Nancy against the wall and covered her mouth again.

"Do you know where it is?" Nancy shook her head. Kitty swore under her breath again, furious. She listened to the noises coming from the parlor. The party sounded like it was still going strong.

"Are Egon, Madam Vernay, and Morris still with the guests?" Nancy nodded. Kitty thought for a moment, and then she shoved Nancy down the basement stairs.

"Get me some rope and tape," Kitty ordered, looking over the chisels. She grabbed two, tucking one into each boot. Nancy stood dumbly before her holding out a roll of duct tape in one hand, and rope in the other. Kitty took the rope and slung it onto her shoulder. She grabbed the tape, ripped off a long piece, and slapped it over Nancy's mouth. She shoved her onto the floor, pulled her hands behind her back and taped them tightly, then taped her ankles together.

"You knew all along they weren't hunting pigs, and you knew it was wrong. Should have decided to be my friend Nancy, I might've taken you with me," Kitty said, and then ran up the back stairs to the second floor.

The wide hallway ended in large French doors that opened to a balcony over the front entrance of Ravenglass. Kitty tried one of the guest room doors knowing it would be locked. She pulled out a chisel from one of her boots and wedged the blade into the doorknob as quietly as she could. She did not hear Madam Vernay come down the hall.

"Aren't you clever?" said Madam Vernay, standing directly behind Kitty, towering over her.

Kitty startled and dropped the chisel. Madam Vernay kicked it away, then grabbed Kitty's wrist with an iron-tight grip.

"You are nothing but trouble, I *knew* it the moment I saw you."

"Let me go, please," Kitty begged, trying to back away.

"Oh, of course, let you go! And what, you run your mouth about what you've seen? Not on your life. You, my dear, are not going anywhere."

Kitty yanked herself free and ran to the end of the hall. She squatted to reach into her boot, but Madam Vernay was quick. She shoved Kitty hard against the glass doors, which swung open instead of breaking. Kitty fell onto the balcony, rolling away as Madam Vernay came out.

"Get inside," Madam Vernay ordered. Kitty backed away until she was crouched against the railing. She pressed down against it. The height of the balcony was too much to risk the jump.

"You sniveling twit, you are not going anywhere," Madam Vernay said as she approached. Kitty cowered until Madam Vernay was very close, then she jumped up and grabbed her arm. Kitty planted both feet and swung her around, slamming her against the railing.

"You bitch!" Madam Vernay gasped. Kitty kicked her squarely in her chest. Madam Vernay flipped back over the railing and fell head first onto the drive with a dull thud.

Kitty looked over the balcony at Madam Vernay's lifeless form. A large dark spatter surrounded her head on the light gray flagstone. She went back to the guest room door, pulled out her chisel and gouged around the latch until she was able to open the door.

Before going into the room, Kitty tucked the chisel back in her boot and listened. Music was still blaring from downstairs, although she could not hear any howls or yells. She shut the door behind her and turned on the light. It was a mess, clothes strewn about, rumpled bed sheets, and it smelled like someone had defecated on the floor. She scanned until she spotted a leather bag hanging off a straight back chair. As she dumped it out at her feet, she felt light-headed and nearly fainted when a set of keys with a car key fob fell on the floor. Kitty grabbed it, ready to bolt, but stopped. She forced herself back out to the balcony and looked over where the cars were parked, held up the keys with a shaking hand and pressed the unlock button. She gasped with relief when she saw a small yellow light blink twice in the dark.

Kitty went back into the hall, paused to listen, then went to the top of the stairs and looked down. It was dark, the doors to the drawing room were still closed, and she found herself grateful for the lengths the guests went to in celebrating their depravity. She pulled on her hood and crept down the stairs, pausing to look and listen on each step. When she reached the foyer, she looked down the back hall and saw nothing. She tiptoed to the drawing room doors and slid the rope off her shoulder, took up one end and wound it around the doorknobs in a figure eight pattern several times, then knotted it tightly. Even if they were able to escape, she hoped to cause them to panic. She wished she had a match; she would have set the rope on fire.

Not wanting to see Madam Vernay lying in the courtyard, Kitty hurried down the back hall to go out the kitchen door.

"Clever," came Morris's smooth, ingratiating voice.

Kitty froze.

"I think we could use some light," Morris said as he flipped the switch. "You really are dangerous in the dark." He was blocking the kitchen door, smiling. He pointed a long silver dagger at her chest as he approached her. Kitty backed into the scullery.

"Oh, Kitty. Kitty, Kitty, Kitty. What am I going to do with you? Don't bother to answer, it's a waste of my time."

"Shut your mouth, Morris." Kitty was furious to have come so far only to be caught by *him*.

"You're a waste of time, a waste of money, a waste of space," he went on. "If you were anything like your mother, you would have been on board. Fiona would have *loved* Ravenglass."

"Shut it, Morris. Don't you dare talk about my mother!"

"Sadly, you're just like weak little Henry. Helpless, spineless, I should have seen it." Morris looked up at the stained ceiling and laughed, "You are *pathetic*," and he lunged.

Kitty jumped up on the counter next to the sink, knocking a pile of dinner plates onto the floor.

"You little bitch," Morris clutched the dagger in his fist and came at her fast and hard. She reached into the sink full of cold, gray dishwater, scooped up a wine glass and threw it in his face. Shocked, Morris dropped the knife. He coughed and spluttered, frantically wiping his eyes. Kitty jumped down, snatched his knife, and stood ready, waiting. When Morris was finally able to focus, he spread his arms out to his sides as if in surrender.

"Now Kitty, let's not be foolish..."

"Oh my, no, Morris. Let's not be foolish," she answered.

"You wouldn't want to do anything you might regret."

"Good heavens, wouldn't want to do that, would I?"

"Don't toy with me, Kitty."

"Don't toy with me Kitty," she mimicked, then snarled, "Or what? You'll take me away from my home? Murder me? Butcher me in the barn? Eat me?" Morris looked frightened.

"What's wrong Morris? Run out of good lies to tell?" In a flash, she slashed him across the throat. Blood instantly poured from his neck. Morris's eyes bugged, and he opened his mouth to scream, but no sound came out. He grabbed his neck and sank to his knees as blood poured through his fingers. He tipped over, still holding his throat with both hands. Kitty came up with her plan as she watched him bleed. She reached into his left coat pocket and jangled his keys over his head.

"You know what? Let's take your car, more room in the back. And I'll be sure you can't get away from me," she said as she watched him gasp. She guessed over two minutes had passed since she cut him, and he was still alive, which meant she missed his major arteries, but slashed his vocal cords. Kitty grabbed him by his collar.

"Get up!"

He lay on his side making a rasping sound. She jabbed the back of his arm with his dagger and he jolted.

"Get up now!" she ordered. He stood shakily, before sinking back down to the floor.

"Stand up, coward," she said, and jabbed him in the shoulder. He gasped.

"The fact that you're not dead means you're coming with me. Now up!" She poked him in his side, and then showed him his knife.

"I can do this much longer than you can," she said, and jabbed him in his chest. His eyes widened in terror and he stood.

"What's the matter, can't talk?" Kitty yanked off his bloodied scarf and pulled his hands away from his throat. He tried to push her away but stopped when she held up the knife. She wound his scarf around his neck tight, but not quite enough to choke him.

"There now, wouldn't want you to die on me before I get you to the police." Kitty kept a tight grip on the back of his neck as she marched him to the front hall. The party continued inside the drawing room, and no one seemed to know or care they were trapped in the room. She shoved him out the front door.

Morris let out a gasp when he saw Madam Vernay's body and tried to run. Kitty hooked his foot, and he tripped onto his hands and knees beside her broken head.

"Take a good look, Morris. I hope it haunts you for the rest of your life."

She grabbed his scarf and yanked, making him jump to his feet. Kitty hoped he was in agony. She pushed him to his Land Rover, poking him in the back every few steps to keep him moving quickly. At his car, she opened the back door, shoved him in, and slammed hard.

"Hope you went to the loo," she said in the same sing-song tone he used on her when they had left London. Kitty started the engine, put the knife and the chisel on the passenger seat, and drove out the gates without a glance in the rearview mirror at Ravenglass. She turned onto the road hoping she was following the same route as they came until she saw a sign for A66 to Penrith.

"Good thing I didn't sleep the whole way, right Morris? Otherwise, I'd have missed the one police sign in this godforsaken place."

Twenty minutes later Kitty pulled into the Cumbria Constabulary Headquarters, a brick and concrete building off the main road, and parked as close to the front door as she could. It was locked, so Kitty banged until a wary, young police officer opened the door.

"Yes? Can I help you miss?"

"I...I need..." Kitty could not go on. She began to shake.

"Do you need help, miss?" the officer asked, coming out to her.

"Yes, I do. Please...I need to report something terrible happening at Ravenglass."

SANCTUS
Joey Phoenix

A figure crouches atop a marble base at the end of Faun Road. Faun Road leads to nowhere but the House. The House is a mile high. The House is boundless.

The figure is made of stone, tinged green by the weather that the house seems to generate on its own, a pea soup density to which the rest of the neighborhood appears to be immune.

The figure is barefoot, its hands splayed as if gripping unseen carpet, its eyes cast downward as if searching. The hollow at the base of the figure's throat is tensed as if to cry out, but the cry is caught in time, unable to escape into the open air.

When anyone passes by the figure, there is an impression that the visitor isn't alone on the front lawn of the House. There is a feeling of being inhabited, as if the figure is trying to possess the visitor but cannot make a foothold. This sensation is followed by a distinct sadness, a feeling of loss, of longing.

Of waiting.

A single word is engraved into the base of the statue. It may have been the name of angel, or maybe that of a demon, but it is a name, nonetheless.

***

She leaned over my shoulder and sneered. "Why don't you ever fucking draw anything other than guns and whores?" She smelled like booze and body odor.

"Sex and violence run the world," I said, not looking up. I was sketching a siren, half submerged.

She stood up sharply, her wrist banging against the edge of my chair in the rush, causing her to yelp and curse on her way out the door. Soon afterward I heard the shower running in the hallway. Relief drew spirals up my spine. This was my chance to get out.

Once I grabbed my bag and notebook, put on my hat and coat, leaving was the work of a moment. I didn't realize that I was running until I was three blocks away and at the bus station. I also didn't realize I had been holding my breath until my chest caved in and I nearly fell over, gasping for air. The chill in the night felt like the fulfillment of a promise. I decided not to take the bus and kept walking on toward the train station.

It had taken me three years to build up to that moment. Three years of wishing I had the strength to get out. Three years of listening to her degrade me and tell me how lost I was without her. Three years of wondering when the next time she would get drunk and threaten me with leaving. Three years of avoiding stairwells.

So I ran.

When I finally felt far enough away to be sure of myself and my feet, I pulled out a cigarette, there were only two left, and in one familiar motion brought it to my lips and lit it. The small blaze illuminated my ink-stained fingers and the warmth of it danced through me.

It felt like hope.

When I made it to the T stop, the tip of my nose had gone cold and my eyes were watering from the chill. It was unusually warm for January, but warm in January was still below freezing, barely tolerable.

The problem I now faced was that I hadn't really thought this part through. I had only decided on the leaving part, not the leaving to where part. I had spent months saving up, quit my job at the bakery two weeks before, and had picked the time to do it. To finally do it.

I decided that I would go to the airport and think about it there. That way if it took me all night to figure it out, at least they wouldn't kick me out. At least it would be warm.

I could go anywhere. The only thing I couldn't do was stay here.

***

I made it to Logan airport at just past 11:30 PM. The place was abandoned except for a few people working the counters, a French couple yelling at each other by the escalators, and a handful of solo travelers checking their phones.

My phone buzzed in my pocket. I took it out and looked at the message displayed on the lock screen. It was from her. "Where the fuck did you go? It doesn't take two hours to smoke a cigarette." I put it back in my pocket.

I walked up to the first counter I saw.

"Hello." I ventured, cautiously. "What's the first departing flight tonight?"

"No planes until tomorrow afternoon." The man said curtly, hardly looking up from the screen in front of him.

"What? Why?" I tried to keep the annoyance out of my question. I failed.

"Last one just left and there's a storm." He said and finally looked up. His eyes moved over my face as if he disapproved of my existence.

"What storm?"

He looked at me blankly. "The hurricane," he said.

This was the first I'd heard of it.

He continued. "Where do you want to go? I can get you a flight tomorrow afternoon maybe, but there's a bit of a waiting list. You should probably just go home for the night."

Home.

The word landed like a fist.

"Thanks, I'll figure it out." I walked unsteadily away from the counter, down the escalator, and found a seat in baggage claim to think. Maybe I could take a train. Did people still take trains? I brought my phone out of my pocket, ignoring the barrage of incoming messages on the screen. I quickly typed "Amtrak" into the browser and waited for the site to load. It took a moment, and when it finally did, an announcement was in red at the top of the screen. It read: "Due to extreme weather patterns, all trains from Boston are canceled until further notice."

"What the actual fuck?" I breathed, then looked out the airport window at the night, uncertain of myself. It was clear and empty. I checked the weather on my phone, and the forecast for the next few days said cold and cloudy with highs ranging from 25-45 degrees. Not yet ready to believe my bad luck, I ventured outside to look at the sky, and patches of black appeared in between the cracks of the concrete overhang. I couldn't see any stars. I couldn't see any clouds either.

"Oof," I said unwillingly as someone suddenly walked into me.

"Sorry," a voice said, walking past me and sitting down on one of the benches nearby.

I checked my phone again. Was there a glitch? I checked another weather service's website. I couldn't find any relevant information.

A noise snapped me out of my puzzlement; the person who had just bumped into me was hissing angrily into their phone.

"Goddammit, Mike, I told you I won't be there until tomorrow...The fucking planes aren't going anywhere." They checked their watch and sighed gruffly, apparently listening to "Mike's" response. They continued, "No, I'll be there tomorrow I swear...Or you know what, maybe I won't...Maybe I'll just stay here...Oh my God, don't fucking talk to me like that."

I tried not to laugh, but I couldn't help myself. This all felt surreal.

The person overheard my chuckle and looked up sharply. "Alright genius, bye," they said into the phone. Then they ended the call and stared at me poignantly.

"Something funny?" they asked. Then, softening, "I'm sorry. I don't blame you. I guess I was being kind of loud here. This whole thing is a fucking nightmare." They put their head in their hands. Dark brown hair spilled over their fingers in waves.

I smiled awkwardly and said nothing, looking away. I needed a drink. I needed to get out. I thought about pretending to take a phone call and walking back inside. I didn't think fast enough.

"Stuck here too?" they asked. I nodded and debated taking out another cigarette. "Where were you trying to get to?"

"Anywhere," I heard myself answer.

Go back inside, I told myself. My feet were frozen to the pavement.

I looked over at them again and watched as they were punching in something on their phone. They were wearing a brown floppy hat over their long, winding hair, which covered them like a cloak. Their chin was small but pointed, their lips were dried and blistered and hiding a smile behind them that was for a flash, dangerous. Then it was gone. A large green coat hugged their shoulders, hanging over a shin-length dress covered in something that looked like lizards. A pair of Dr. Martens finished the outfit. As they sat they were up on their tippy toes, back arched over, arms hugging their knees. They looked at me and caught me staring, their gaze direct. I looked away.

A taxi sped past us, the driver not even slowing down. I thought about calling a cab, but had no idea where to go.

"I'm Rhys," they said.

"What?" I answered. My head felt strange. Maybe I was more tired than I thought.

"My name," they explained, "Rhys."

"Oh," I said, dumbly. "I'm Sanctus."

"What are your pronouns?" they asked, politely.

"It's just Sanctus," I responded. Then, remembering myself, "What are yours?"

"She/hers," she said quickly, "but I might change my mind at some point." She glanced off to her right as if she heard something, then looked back to me. "So Sanctus?" She turned my name into a question.

"So Rhys?"

"My parents wanted me to be a boy. It's like some big joke or something that all the women in my family..." She trailed off. "I don't know. I don't feel cursed."

A tense silence filled the space upon this admission, and I watched as a question sprouted in the middle of her forehead, one that went unasked. I then noticed that her eyes were different colors, one hazel and one aquamarine. For a moment I didn't breathe. Her lips parted slightly, partially revealing an uneven row of white teeth.

"Have you heard anything about a hurricane?" I finally managed, compulsively looking down at my phone.

"Yeah. I was supposed to be going to see my friend in Detroit but there are no planes until tomorrow. I've been staying at my sister's house in Danvers, and I was so ready to get out and now I just have to go back. Where are you headed now?"

"I don't know," I said. "I hadn't gotten that far yet. But thanks to this hurricane I'm stuck here at least for the night."

A pause, and then I saw something shift in her face.

"I normally don't do this," she said, "but my sister's house has about 20 bedrooms, so if you want to come back with me that would be cool. I mean, you don't look like a serial killer, but if you are, just tell me now so we can get it out of the way." Her eyes were gleaming.

My laugh came out like a cough. I took a deep breath. "Thanks, but I'll probably just sleep here and catch whatever flight I can tomorrow."

She narrowed her eyes. "Ok, fine. It was nice meeting you, Sanctus." Then she stood up to leave and walked briskly away, her dress swishing against her ankles. I suddenly felt my insides lurch with the jolt of missed opportunities, of constantly choosing the known over the unknown, of being stuck.

Besides, it would only be for a night.

"Wait!" I yelled, running over to her. She stopped and turned around, eyes dancing and a twisted smile forming at the corner of her mouth. "But at least let me help with cab fare."

"No need," she said. "I have a driver."

"You have a what?"

"His name is Dick," she explained. "He's just around the corner."

***

After nearly an hour in the limousine, we pulled up the long drive to the largest house I had ever laid eyes on. "Thank you, Dick," she said lightly and jumped out of the car door he held open for her. I sat for a moment, feeling the warmth of the heated seats in this expensive vehicle. It was the first time that I had been driven by anyone other than my adopted parents or a cabbie. It was incredible. I couldn't process any of it.

"Are you coming?" Rhys said, popping her head back into the car. I nodded and started to move.

"I'll bring your bags inside," Dick said to her. He was a stout man with a broad smile and dimples. He wore black gloves, a waistcoat, and a flat cap. He didn't acknowledge my presence, except as I walked away, back facing him, I felt him watching me warily. Instinctively I turned to look at him and he was already moving her bags out of the trunk of the car, as if he had never glanced my direction at all.

Unnerved, I pulled the last cigarette out of my pack and lit it, cursing myself for not stopping earlier to get more. The familiar smoke warmed my lungs and diluted the oddness of the situation. I gaped up at the house, trying to see where it ended. I couldn't.

The driveway was lined with unusually shaped topiary: images of bears with wings, creatures with the body of a lion and the head of an eagle, a three-headed dog. Rhys caught me looking at them. They were extraordinary in their details.

"My family has this thing for mythology..." she apologized.

"They're beautiful," I said, entranced. I made a mental note to draw them later. "I didn't know you could do that with plants."

Why don't you ever fucking draw anything other than guns and whores? I shivered and pulled my coat closer around me.

"Well, if you like this shit wait until we get inside." She smiled and walked onwards.

I pulled myself away from the figures in the driveway, and stubbed out my cigarette. She was already at the front doors turning a key in the lock. These doors, stretching twenty feet high, unlocked with a thunk, as if they were being awakened from a deep sleep. She lowered her shoulder and drove it into the door, pushing it inward. It gave a hollow creak in protest that echoed through the first floor of the house.

"The door handle keeps falling off, so this is easier," she said by way of explanation and, stepped aside to let me in.

The doors opened to a foyer with a ceiling three stories high. The floor was black and white tiled marble, broken up by massive marble pillars holding up the mezzanine overlooking the space. Dark corridors stretched in several directions, leading to the various wings of the house. Some of the upper floors were visible from the entryway, many of them adorned with small gargoyles and beastly figures along the central columns and the inner balustrade.

While I was taking all of this in, I thought I saw a person move in the shadows on one of the upper balconies, but it was gone so quickly that I assumed it was just a trick of the light.

While my eyes adjusted to the dim, lit by ornate wall sconces, I took in a dozen or so white stone statues lining the atrium. Each of the statues depicted human figures in unusual positions. The one closest to the front doors was of a man in a top hat and Victorian finery. His hand was lifted over his face as if blocking a sudden stream of daylight on a cloudy day. The next was of a woman in a winding sheet, kneeling on the ground, her face lifted up toward the high ceiling. Another was of a woman lounging on her side, completely naked except for a cuff at her wrist. The cuff had a bird in flight on it, but I couldn't make out what kind of bird it was.

"Do you mind shutting the door? It's fucking freezing," I heard Rhys say and hastily did as I was told, pushing on it with all my strength, and stepped further into the room. She took off her coat and casually flung it over the base of one of the statues. She then stepped out of her boots and left them untidily by the front doors. I took off my boots too, but left my coat on. It was shockingly cold inside.

"Come upstairs, I'll show you to your room." She motioned toward the large stairwell to the side of the space that I hadn't noticed before. I froze. I forgot how to breathe.

Stairs.

"Well, come on," she said, and headed up the stairs two at a time until she was just out of my sight. Swallowing my fear like a shot of whiskey, I quickly crossed the space to the stairs and started to climb, holding onto the banister with a white-knuckled grip and keeping several paces behind her ascending form. As much as I wanted to look down on the odd statues in the room below, I kept my eyes up. As I stepped upward, I began to feel several tingling sensations on my neck, the backs of my shoulders, legs, and spine, as if many pairs of eyes were taking me in, and tugging at me gently. The sensation was accompanied by a sudden sense of loss. It caught me around the waist and I had to stop for a moment to clutch at my chest. I felt hollowed out, empty. I fought the urge to glance behind me, afraid of losing my balance, afraid of—I tried not to think about it.

I failed.

Rhys apparently noticed my pause and took a couple of steps back down to face me. "Are you alright?" she said, looking me in the eyes. I swallowed hard. My palms were slick with sweat.

"I'm just tired," I said. She nodded as if this made sense, then turned to go back up. I held my breath the rest of the way, relieved when we finally made it to the second-floor mezzanine.

"You have your choice," she said, waving her arms in the general direction of some open doors. "There are like nine unused rooms on this floor, so you can pick whichever one you like."

I poked my nose in the first one. It was filled with a large canopy bed and antique furniture that must've cost more than I'd ever made in my lifetime. It would've been fine, except that the curtains and the bedding were all a shade of jaundice yellow. I quickly backed out and looked at her, unsure of what to do.

"This one's my second favorite. Naturally, I'm staying in my favorite one." She motioned toward the third door on the right.

I shuffled to it and peered inside. The room was lit by an odd lamp on the bedside table. It was shaped like an angel. It was hairless, eyes lifted upward, and wearing a golden cape that fell in waves down its tiny form. In each palm it held a glowing orb, and the light cast a warm and welcoming glow on the walls. The wallpaper was a rich hunter green and gold brocade, which caught the light and shimmered subtly. A print of Edvard Munch's "The Scream" was opposite the bed, the only decoration on the wall, and the figure looked down on everything in the room with horror. In the center of a room, pressed up against the wall, was a large double bed with a forest green duvet, topped with several impractical throw pillows.

"This is great," I said, ready to pass out where I stood.

She nodded. "The bathroom is over there and if you need anything, I'm on the floor directly above you, the first door on the left. If you want water there are some glasses and a pitcher in the hallway. The maids fill those." She turned to leave.

Struggling to keep my eyes open, I said a quick "thank you and good night" to her disappearing back before going inside the room, closing the door behind me, and falling instantly asleep.

***

I woke up at dawn to the sound of thunder ripping through the skies overhead. Lightning struck the house and the power flickered for a moment before sputtering out completely. The accompanying thunder shook the house on its foundation, seeming to last a full ten seconds.

I rolled over toward the sound, and a weak light was creeping in through the window, rain was pattering the frames in a consistent pattern. Curious, I stepped out of bed and drew back the curtain, but through the rain and a haze that was tinted green, I couldn't see much of anything.

Unconcerned, I crawled back into bed and slept for a couple of more hours.

I woke up a second time to a light rapping on my door. I opened one eye slowly to see the door creeping away from its frame, and a shadowy form appeared and then spoke. "Are you awake?" the disembodied voice said. I opened my other eye and realized where I was and recognized my host. It had all been real then.

I had left.

"Nope," I said.

"Well, we just lost power but fortunately the cook made us breakfast before it happened and there's coffee, so if you want anything while it's warm, now is the time."

"Do you have any cigarettes?" I asked, slowly sitting up.

"Um, no. But my sister might. I'll go check."

"Your sister is here?" But no one answered, she had already gone.

I pulled on my pants which were in a heap at the side of the bed. Then I buckled my belt, threw on my hoodie, and put on a fresh pair of socks before going in search of food. The smell of warmth and coffee was rising up from the lower floors. The skylight in the ceiling reached all the way down to the marbled entryway, letting in a hazy glow. As I approached the stairs, the lights flickered on momentarily before going off again. I gripped the banister and began my descent one step at a time. I wished I had a candle.

"Here you go." She appeared at my side so suddenly that I lost my balance, my foot slipping off the step and my shin banging into something hard. I gripped the marbled edges like a screaming child holding its mother and fought back the feelings of vertigo and unease. A slight pain in my arm rose to the surface, and I realized she was gripping my shoulder, keeping me from falling. All I could do was stare up at her while the blood in my face drained into my knees. I tried to remember how to operate my feet.

"I can't navigate stairs when I'm pre-coffee either," she said, helping me get upright before passing me the brand new box of cigarettes. "Next time we can take the elevator." She flashed me a twisted smile before hopping down the rest of the way, throwing a half-concerned glance over her shoulder at me as I descended the final steps at a painfully slow rate.

She disappeared around a bend in the serpentine corridor, and rather than hurry up to follow, I kept my pace the same, finding my way to the kitchen by the smell of coffee alone. When I eventually got there, I found her at a small table with four chairs, busily eating the contents on the plate in front of her. It was eggs and hash and bacon, and the entire thing was covered in ketchup.

I gawked at her while she shoveled a fork full into her mouth.

"What?" she said. I pointed at her plate.

"Oh yeah," she responded, knowing what I meant. She covered her mouth so as not to show me what was in it. "Ketchup is one of the best creations of the modern world." I rolled my eyes and the cook, who I hadn't seen beforehand, came out of nowhere and handed me a steaming cup of coffee. "Thanks," I said, a touch disconcerted. The cook didn't reply.

I took a furtive sip before turning my gaze toward the kitchen door leading to the back of the house. The small window in the frame offered me a view of massive gardens with a central row leading down to a small labyrinth cut from hedges. The fog was growing thicker, and the rain was coming down in sheets. I strained my eyes to take in the sight. More of the odd stone statues lined either side of the central row; each figure seemed strangely alive in the rain and the flashes of lightning.

I suddenly felt Rhys appear at my elbow. "Do you want to go out and look?" she said. I nodded, setting my coffee down and pulling a cigarette out of the pack she had given me. I patted the pockets of my pants looking for my lighter. She disappeared for a moment and then came back carrying our boots. While I put mine on, she grabbed us each an umbrella from the stand by the door and then opened it and stepped outside. The shock of the wind was a slap as I followed.

The raindrops were like tiny shards of ice, against which the umbrella did little. I angled it into the force of the wind and tried to light my cigarette. Noticing me struggling, she came to my side and cupped her hands around the flame until the end caught fire, and together we ventured off down the central row, the stone figures looming over us.

We walked in silence for some time, past the creeping white figures and nearly to the beginning of the labyrinth before I found the energy to speak.

"So you live here with your sister?"

"I used to," she said quickly, her eyes darting to the right suddenly. "Now I live in Detroit with my stepdad and stepbrother Mike."

"The person you were talking to at the airport."

She nodded. "He's an idiot."

I shrugged, not knowing what to say to that. "Um," I faltered. Our steps were making odd noises on the stones beneath our feet, crunching and squishing at intervals. "What does your sister do?" I took a long drag of my cigarette, blowing out the smoke slowly. I watched it curve upwards, intermingling with the rain, becoming part of the fog.

"She doesn't do anything. She's not well. When my Mom died she left her the house and enough money to take care of me and for her to never have to work again."

At first, I wasn't sure how to respond. "I'm sorry about your Mom," I finally said, feeling awkward.

"Thank you, but it's been years. I was young when she died."

"How old were you?" I managed.

"About six. But she was gone a lot, so I didn't know her that well."

"Oh," I said.

We reached the end of the central row and entered the labyrinth, the hedges seeming much higher now that we were inside of them then they did from the house. The bust of a minotaur stood on a pillar at the entryway, the word "Beware" engraved at the base in elegant script. I paused for a moment, taking it all in.

"What's all that about?" I asked, not certain whether to take it seriously or not.

"Oh right, that." She laughed nervously. "Apparently this labyrinth is particularly difficult or something, and some kids from a local school snuck in here one time and weren't seen for three days. The gardener found them when he was trimming the hedges, and they were soaked and terrified and starving. It was really awful. Fortunately, no one has tried to do something like that since then, the place has developed a bit of a reputation I guess, but my sister put up the sign just in case.

"Don't worry, if you follow me we won't get too lost," she continued, seeing my discomfort, and picked up her pace. Her moves were swift and experienced and I kept up as best I could through the maze of hedges.

There were no distinguishing features anywhere, except for the occasional rod sticking out of the green at odd points.

"I come in here to think sometimes," she continued. "I know it so well, but I probably should let you navigate for a while, as it'll be more fun for you that way. I can always get us out of a tricky situation if you choose wrongly." She winked and stepped aside to let me lead. We were getting soaked but this was such a new experience for me that I didn't care. It was actually the most fun I'd had in years.

Suddenly a gust of wind came and knocked the umbrella out of my hand. It was accompanied by the flapping of large wings and a screeching form progressing quickly toward my face. Terrified, I ducked as the being flew over my head. I stayed down, convinced that whatever it was would come back.

Rhys laughed and held out her arm. "Hector!" she scolded. When I caught my bearings and stood up, a screech owl was perched on her outstretched arm, its talons flexing and stretching in turn, as if searching for the best foothold. The owl was enormous, the largest bird I had ever seen. Although, most of the birds I had ever come across before now had been pigeons.

"Um," I managed, quite bewildered. She brought her arm closer to her face so that she and the owl could both fit comfortably beneath her umbrella. Mine had disappeared. She finally looked up into my perplexed face and saw that she ought to explain.

"This is Hector," she said. The bird lifted its right wing as if to say hello. "He belongs to my sister. He helps with the snakes."

"Snakes?" I said, still not following.

"My sister hates seeing snakes on the property, but there's not a whole lot that can be done, they just love the grounds here." Rhys offered as a final explanation before adding. "I see the wind has eaten your umbrella, we should probably go back inside. We can check your flights too, if the power is back."

I just nodded and followed dumbly as she set Hector upon his rod perch and headed back in the direction of the house, turning left and right, and going straight, and curving when necessary. I paid extra attention to where I stepped, wary of things slithering in the hedges.

When we reached the central row, I paused. The avenue was empty.

"Where are the statues?" I asked.

"What statues?" she asked.

I shook my head, bewildered. Maybe the experience with the owl had messed with my head. "Nevermind," I said, and proceeded up the row toward the house, walking more quickly than usual.

Before I stepped onto the porch, I saw a flicker in the window overhead, the brush of a curtain against a pane of glass. "Is that your sister's room?" I asked, pointing up. Rhys nodded but said nothing.

Once we got back inside, she told one of the maids to light the fire for us in the parlor, then she turned to me. "You're soaked through." She said it plainly. Her clothes were marvelously, miraculously dry. She was wearing a burgundy turtleneck and a black skirt which reached her ankles, and there was an unusual pendant hung at her collarbone, an icon of two amphibious shapes wrapped around each other.

"Can I get you some clothes?" she asked, unbothered by my gaze. "A lot of people have stayed here over the years and left things that may fit you."

"No skirts," I said. She smiled and bounded off to search. I wish I had thought to bring more than spare socks and underwear. I also realized I hadn't checked my phone since the night before. I pulled it out of my pocket. It was dead. I hadn't thought to charge it. Did I even bring a charger?

Weren't you supposed to be running away?

The thought continued to gnaw at me. I tried to think about something else.

She came back downstairs within minutes carrying a pair of pants, a wool sweater, and a blanket. "You can change in the bathroom down here if you'd like." She motioned toward a room near the back. "The parlor is just through there. I'm going to go look up flight information on my sister's laptop." I said thanks, took the clothes, and went to change in the bathroom.

It was completely dark except for a small white votive burning in a dish on the sink basin. I unzipped my hoodie and pulled the shirt I wore beneath it over my head. The semicircle scars on my chest were still a deep purple, but had faded considerably since the last time I had looked at them. I twisted my torso around to view the one on my back. The six-inch gash had closed neatly into a jagged smirk, hiding all evidence of where the metal had dug in. I took a deep breath to keep the tide of memories from rising up. There wasn't room enough for bittersweet, there definitely wasn't room for bad.

I hung my wet clothes on the towel rack and put on the ones Rhys had given me. The pants were on the larger side, so I slid my belt out of my wet pants and attached it to the borrowed ones. The sweater was also too big, but it was warm and the empty space felt right. I looked at myself in the mirror again, the candlelight causing my features to distort, and for a moment I didn't recognize myself. My chin length hair, matted from the rain, the bags under my eyes, the split open lip that I had forgotten about, the bruise at my neck that was turning yellow at the edges.

I splashed water on my face from the basin, dried off from a towel to the left of the sink, and left the room to find Rhys. It didn't take long.

"Fuck fuck fuck!" she cursed. A laptop was open on her knees as she sat in front of the fire. I noticed that all the lights were on in this room.

"What's wrong?" I asked, sitting down next to her in front of the blaze, wrapping myself in a large blanket that had been lying close by.

She turned the screen to show me. The screen read: "All flights into or out of Boston canceled until tomorrow at 8 AM. Please contact your airline for more information. We are sorry for the inconvenience."

"Fuck," I said, agreeing.

"Well, at least the electricity's back on for now," she said. "Dick turned on the backup generator so the first floor at least will have power."

We both stared into the fire for a few moments before she broke the silence.

"Do you want to stay another day?" She turned to me, waiting for my response, her eyes uncertain.

"I'm happy to sleep at the airport."

She looked at me like I was an idiot.

"You're staying here."

I nodded and that was the end of it. Her mouth sharpened into its knife smile. I felt myself smile too.

A draft blew through the open door to the atrium and a slight sensation of pressure landed on the back of my neck.

"Rhys," a voice called from behind us, and I felt Rhys stiffen slightly before she turned toward whoever had called. I looked too, but there was no one there.

"I'll be right back," she said, before standing up and disappearing through the open door.

I stayed there for a while until my joints softened and the warmth coursed through me. A large grandfather clock in the corner chimed 15 minutes on the hour, then 30 minutes, then 45. The silence of the room was so pleasant that I didn't mind being left alone, at first, but when the next hour chimed began to wonder where she had gone. I stood up, gingerly, my knees cracking with the strain of sitting so long in one position. I folded the blanket and left it over a nearby armchair upholstered in ghastly orange brocade, then went to go see where she had gone.

We nearly collided at the end of the corridor, leading toward a part of the house I hadn't seen yet. As I walked, I had been looking up at the row of shields lining the hallway. Each of them seemed to be from not only different places but drastically different points of time. One was Napoleonic, one was probably Viking, another one depicted a woman whose hair was made of snakes and her mouth full of rows of sharp teeth, bloodied by a recent conquest.

"They've been here for as long as I can remember," she said, answering my unspoken question. I pulled my glance downward and turned to look at her. "My sister says she would like to meet you."

"Oh," was all I could say.

"We can take the elevator. It's through here."

She turned down one hallway, this one covered in Renaissance period art, then down another, decorated with daggers and swords, where the elevator stood at the end. None of the corridors were straight, but each bowed and winded like a long piece of string. While I was taking it all in, she pressed the call button for the elevator, pulled the sliding door open, and when the elevator made its way down to our floor, going, "clunk clunk clunk," the whole way, she pulled open the gate and stepped inside.

"Because the power's out, we have to crank it ourselves," she said. "It's a bit of a junker so I usually prefer taking the stairs. But you're obviously bad at stairs."

"Is it safe?" I asked, stepping inside, uncertainly.

"Sure," she said, unconvincingly. Then she closed the gate and started cranking. With a jolt, the carriage started moving upward. "Clunk clunk clunk," it complained until we reached the fourth floor with a final, "kapclunk."

"Before you meet her there's a couple of things you should know," she said as she stepped off the elevator and into a different hallway. This one was empty except for a long jade table topped with candles, and wallpaper covered in peonies that were hideous shades of pink and green.

I nodded, waiting for her to continue.

"When you go into the room, don't go all the way in. She hates making eye contact and, oh yeah, try not to speak unless she asks you a direct question."

"Is she agoraphobic?" I asked.

"Sort of," she answered, eyes shifting to the right, uncomfortably.

I followed her down the hallway and through another small parlor. "She's here, in the library," she told me, knocking three times on a tall mahogany door. Three more knocks came from the other side of the door, which made me jump. Rhys laid a hand on my arm to steady me.

"Remember what I told you," she said, and opened the door.

We stepped inside and she closed the door behind me. Rhys motioned for me to stay where I was and she went to sit in a small chair next to a roaring fireplace, the only source of light in the room. The walls were lined with several bookcases, stuffed to the brim with hundreds of books of all shapes and sizes. The ones closest to me were all folklore and mythology. Bulfinch, Hamilton, and Homer were all visible, but many more were in languages and scripts I couldn't quite make out. The bookshelves themselves were also something remarkable, as each of them was ornately carved with angels and demons, their faces shining in the wood, alongside trees and fruit and more mythical beasts.

But the most extraordinary thing in the room wasn't the fireplace, the books, nor the shelves that contained them, but the ceiling overhead. The entirety of the space, from wall to wall, was covered in the most magnificent mural I had ever come across. It depicted many scenes from a story I only half recognized. At the very center was a man, his head large and distorted and wearing a silver crown, fighting a massive sea monster. The sea monster was wrapped around his middle but the man was stuffing a spear into the sea monster's mouth. It was difficult to depict who had the upper hand in this particular battle.

"Have you ever heard of Perseus?" said a voice from the shadows. It was thickly accented, each consonant rounding out with musical tones, the timbre rich and sweet. The same pressure I had felt in the downstairs parlor earlier tickled my jaw, my cheeks, my temples. I didn't know whether to be frightened or intrigued.

"I believe so, yes."

I was both.

"He was an awful man," she said. "He was a thief, a murderer, but he eventually was murdered himself by the hand of the son of Menelaus, so everything comes around in the end." A small sound followed this, like a gurgle. I realized she was laughing. It sounded like bats leaving a cave.

I said nothing. I still couldn't see where the voice was coming from. I looked to Rhys, who was staring into the fire, her mind somewhere else. For a moment I thought a saw something move along the skin at her jawline, like fish just beneath the surface of a river. It sent chills along my ribcage.

"Where are you from?" the voice asked. I didn't want to be in this room anymore.

"Boston," I forced myself to reply, and noticed a slight movement at a space between the bookshelves. I kept my eyes on Rhys. Her knife mouth twitching, scales just beneath the water.

"Ah, that's a fine city. They have an excellent library. Do you like to read?"

"Yes, some."

"Good. Reading is the only pastime that's worth anything. It keeps you from feeling the need to adventure out-of-doors, into danger. The people of the world are filled with murderous intent."

I pursed my lips, feeling like I should leave. The room was icy, despite the fire.

"Thank you for coming to see me," she said. "I hope you enjoy your stay. This house is full of the most wonderful mysteries. If you have time to explore it, I encourage you to do so."

"Thank you," I said. Then Rhys stood up from the fire quickly, crossed the room in three steps, grabbed my elbow, and escorted me through the door. Neither of us said anything until we were out of the elevator and back on the bottom floor sitting in front of the fire.

"Um," I said.

"You're lucky," she said. "Normally she asks my friends how they feel about snakes."

"Oh," I said. "She's...um."

"Do you mind if I share your blanket?" she asked, and without waiting for me to answer, lifted the edge cover and pressed the side of her body against mine. A sudden warmth passed through me, accompanied by discomfort. I stiffened, uncertain of myself, but then realized how foolish I was being and forced myself to relax.

It worked, a little.

"Can I ask you a question?" she said. I nodded.

"What were you running away from?"

I sighed. She waited for me to answer. I realized there was no reason not to.

"It's not a what, it's a who." Again, she waited for me to continue. A log cracked in the fire and sparks flew up into the chimney.

"I met someone who wasn't who I thought they were. And then once I found out what they were really like, I found I couldn't leave. Not until yesterday."

"What happened?" she said.

"It started off ok," I began, falteringly, "and then after a while things went south really quickly. She would make all these little remarks about my clothes or my artwork, things that were jarring and uncalled for, and left me feeling worthless." I paused, reconsidering my words. "Then, when I started transitioning, her reaction to that became outright violent. She would say that she was too good for me and that she should've left me years ago. And then one time..." I found myself unable to continue. Rhys took my hand in hers, encouraging me.

"One day, we were fighting. We were in the stairwell of our apartment building, on the top floor. I told her I was leaving. She didn't like that."

"So I started to walk away and she reached out to grab my shirt and pull me backwards. Except, in doing so, I missed the step I had aimed for and tumbled downwards. She screamed as I fell, but I couldn't stop myself. There's nothing that either of us could've done.

"It was a shitty old building in Dorchester, and the railings were made of metal. They had rusted and broken off over the years, and no one had thought to do anything about them. At one part, the banister was all but worn away, and the railings stood like spikes at the base of the stairs."

I took a deep breath.

"The metal went into my right side, just barely missing my kidney. She called the ambulance and they were there within minutes. She rode over there with me and kept saying, 'I'm so sorry. I'm so so sorry,' over and over again as if that would make everything ok."

"And for a while, when I got out of the hospital, everything was like it had been when we first got together. But it was so short lived."

"Because a few months later, I said something that, apparently, she didn't like, and she slapped me across the face. I was so stunned that I couldn't say anything, but I knew then that I needed to get out as soon as possible."

"What I'm the most ashamed of was that it took me nearly three years to do it."

I looked over at her, her eyes shining up at me, one green, one blue. The skin of her face was luminous, I couldn't make sense of it. It was like looking at an Impressionist painting close up. The tones were somehow wrong. They were too light, too full of complementary colors. I felt drawn in and uneasy all at once.

"Can I kiss you?" she asked me.

"I don't think I'm ready," I said quickly. She responded by putting her head on my shoulder, and we sat there, huddled closely together, as the clock chimed again and again and again and the sun disappeared from the windows.

***

Sometime in the mid-afternoon, all the lights in the house turned back on, accompanied by the sounds of banging and clunking in the walls. Each time it happened, I startled. "It's an old house," she explained.

The storm outside had picked up considerably, with thunder cracking with violent force every few minutes. We eventually moved from our space in front of the fire, and she had the chef make us cups of tea and sandwiches, and we sat down at the table in the kitchen.

"So this house?" I began. I didn't know where to begin.

"What about it?"

"Um," I said. "I've never seen anything like it. It's enormous, it's old. It's weird. Don't you think it's weird?"

She laughed. "I grew up here, so I guess I'm used to it." When I didn't say anything she filled the silence. "When I was little it was my mom and my dad and my two sisters. My oldest sister, Steya, the one you met, is actually my half-sister. My mom moved with her from Greece when she was young. My mom met my dad at a dinner party and they fell in love instantly. My mom got pregnant with my second oldest sister, Anka, and then my parents got married. Then they had me a bit later." Her eyes danced quickly to the left and paused there, as if she were recalling an especially painful memory.

"Anyways, so the house has been in my dad's family for generations. It used to be Domus Serpens, the House of Snakes, but no one really refers to it as that anymore. Anyone from around here just calls it 'The House.'"

"If your sister hates snakes so much, why does she still live here?"

"I think out of loyalty to family. And besides, it's a beautiful place, the snakes are just more of a quirk, I think..."

A groaning moved through the walls as a gust of wind came through the hallway into the kitchen. The temperature dropped several degrees. I heard the doors in the entryway slam closed as someone began to shuffle about. I assumed it was the maid.

"Where is your dad now?" I asked. She flinched.

"He left," was all she said, before changing the subject. "So where are you flying off to tomorrow, have you decided yet?" I just shook my head in reply. "You could always come to Detroit."

"Isn't Detroit a mess?" I asked.

"Everywhere's a mess," she said. I couldn't disagree.

"Why don't you want to stay here?"

"I'm just ready for a change. Besides! I'm studying to be a sculptor."

"Oh yeah? What's your medium?"

"All types, really. But I love working with stone."

***

We spent the remainder of the day wandering through the house, me asking questions about this painting or that choice of wallpaper or once, where a door led to. She opened it to reveal a hidden staircase.

"Cool," was all I could say.

"The maids sometimes take it if Steya needs something. She rarely ever comes downstairs." Noticing my discomfort, she closed the door and we moved on.

At around midnight she announced that we probably should go to bed. She had to catch a flight right at 8, and she suggested that I might as well go with her to the airport, so I should get some sleep too. I agreed. She gave me a hug goodnight and tiptoed off toward her own room. I watched her walk away thinking that for her soon I could be ready.

Soon.

But I had to get away, properly get away, before that could happen.

I also realized that maybe me being afraid of the stairs was something I should get over too. This was a fresh start, an opportunity for reinvention. And not every staircase was dangerous. It couldn't be.

When I was sure she was gone, I walked over to the top of the stairs and looked down the steps. I knew I could do this. I would take one step and then the next one and then the next one. And if I made it to the bottom and it became too much, I could always take the elevator back up. My palms began to sweat and I wiped them off on my pants.

Slowly I made my descent. With each step, I felt more confident, more sure-footed. *This isn't so bad,* I thought. I made it down four steps, five steps, six steps, and before I knew it, I was at the bottom on the tiled marble floor, so relieved that I had made it. Feeling accomplished, I looked back up the staircase and the height of it brought me down to earth a little bit. Maybe I would go to the kitchen and get a cup of water before I tried to climb them again.

I started to turn toward the kitchen when my phone jumped out of my pocket, landing with a clatter on the tile and sliding beneath the pillar of one of the stone statues.

"Fuck," I exclaimed, dropping on all fours and trying to find it in the near darkness.

As I reached out to grab it, the great doors of the entryway opened with a sudden thunk, and a small woman stepped into the corridor. She took off her glasses to wipe off the raindrops, and I gasped in surprise, startled by her sudden appearance. She heard me, and glanced up compulsively at the sound I had made, her glasses still in her hand. Her eyes were amber, flaming. The skin along her jawline was moving in slow undulations.

Moving like snakes.

The pain was immense and sudden. It began like a fire at my ankles and shot upwards into my torso, my upper body, my arms, my hands, my face. I tried to cry out, but before I could, my body froze, making it impossible for me to shift my weight in one direction or the other. The only thing I had any control over were my eyes, and even that was going. I could hear, I could see, I could smell.

I couldn't move.

"Oh, Christ," the woman exclaimed, coming over to me quickly. "Who are you?" she asked, her voice like a gun. "Why are you here? No one told me there would be anyone here." She put her glasses back on and started pacing the room, frantic. All I could do was stare at the place where she once was, feeling nothing.

Hearing the commotion, Rhys came bounding down the stairs. When she saw the woman kneeling over me, she started shouting.

"Anka, what did you do? What did you do?! WHAT DID YOU DO?!"

Anka was still pacing, frantic, "I came inside and I took off my glasses just for a moment to shake off the rain. I'm so sorry."

"I don't care if you're sorry, we have to fix this. Sanctus can't stay like this. Fuck fuck fuck fuck fuck." She came quickly down the stairs and over to my side, kneeling down beside me. Another figure appeared at the top of the stairs, I couldn't see who it was but I knew who it was.

Steya.

Steya started descending the stairs, and out of the corner of my frozen eyes, I saw her fully. Her gown was a deep crimson, reaching down to her ankles. Her white arms hung limply at her sides. Her hair...she didn't have hair. Where hair would be was...was...

Rhys was talking to me slowly, her voice was sharp at the edges, panicking. "I should've told you." She was saying, "Anka wasn't supposed to be home until next week and Steya always stays well away so I thought it would be fine. I thought it would be ok." Her eyes had changed. They weren't in color anymore. They were gray. Everything was going gray. She started to lift her hand to my face, but stopped halfway, dropping it back to her side.

"Will anyone come looking for this person?" Steya said from the base of the stairs.

I felt panic rising. "No. Sanctus was running away," I heard Rhys say. All hope died in me.

"Then we have time to fix it," Anka said, coming back to kneel beside Rhys, looking at her intently. "You know where you have to go. You know who you have to see."

Rhys's voice was barely more than a whisper. "I don't even know where to look to find him now."

"We will help you," Steya said. Anka nodded in agreement. "But for now, it's best if Sanctus goes to sleep. It may be a long time before you can return."

Unable to do or say anything, I watched as Rhys moved her hand up my face to my temple, pausing only for a moment before she spoke two words, "Sleep now."

Then everything went dark.

***

A figure crouches atop a marble base at the end of Faun Road. Faun Road leads to nowhere but the House. The House is a mile high. The House is boundless.

A single word is engraved into the base of the statue. It may have been the name of angel, or maybe that of a demon, but it is a name, nonetheless.

Sanctus.

MATRIARCHY
Monique Bos

Miranda Reade flew into Denver on an August afternoon of stark brightness. She rented a car at DIA and drove west on I-70 into the mountains, past the palatial residences of football players and tech industry executives. When she had last been on this road twenty-five years earlier, the mining towns squeezed into narrow valleys had been decrepit, forgotten reminders of the tarnished side of the Gold Rush. Now casinos flashed neon signs high above the interstate, and row after row of windshields glittered in the parking lots.

Crystal Falls hadn't legalized gambling yet, but the attorney told her that marijuana legalization had brought an infusion of cash to the town. She thought of her high school classmates: Kirk Sullivan, with whom she had traded virginities during a game of kick-the-can; Jessica Cross, who had frozen Miranda's bra during a slumber party and then mocked her to the rest of the class; overweight Jerry Wilder with his perpetually runny nose. Were any of them still around? What kinds of lives could they have there?

The sun had set by the time she rounded the final curve into town. In the darkness of a night with no moon, the house on the hill faded into shadows, into the deeper darkness of the slopes that rose behind it, and she was glad not to see it yet.

The hotel where she had made reservations occupied the upper storeys of a block-long building that ran along Main Street. When Miranda was a teenager the street-level shops had been old and rundown. She remembered a soda fountain, a five-and-dime, a bank on the corner. Now the rutted sidewalk had been replaced by a boardwalk, and the hotel lobby occupied the corner position, across the intersection from the bandstand in the park.

Miranda found a parking spot and wheeled her suitcase past a trendy boutique and an art gallery. When she stepped into the hotel she caught her breath. The old bank had been floored with imported marble, but she remembered it as scuffed and dingy. Now it had been polished to a brilliant sheen, and artful lighting brought out hidden sparkles and veins of color. Where the tellers' cages had been, armchairs in Western kitsch sat in casual arrangements. Framed photos on the walls featured bald eagles, a cougar, a black bear.

At the far side of the lobby, a young woman stood behind a desk that looked like it was made of reclaimed railroad ties. "You must be Ms. Reade," she said.

Miranda didn't bother to correct her. She had worked hard for her doctorate but it didn't seem worth reminding people of the title. At least this girl didn't know who she was, or if she did know she didn't care.

"This is lovely," she said. "I remember when it was the Mountain and Miners Bank."

"That was before my time. They did a major renovation just before I moved up here."

Miranda raised her eyebrows. Throughout her childhood and adolescence, her family's money and the old sawmill were all that had kept the town going. No one back then could afford major renovations.

"I've put you in Room 25. It overlooks Main Street, but don't worry, traffic doesn't get too loud. You'll have a lovely view of Mount Zebulon in the morning."

Miranda murmured her thanks, accepted her key card, and took the elevator to the second floor. The room was comfortable without being ostentatious, but when she settled into the four-poster bed she couldn't sleep.

Sleep meant waking up, and waking up meant she would have to go to the house.

She texted her daughter. Then she lay on her back, staring at the canopy, feeling the moisture leach from her skin and eyes in the high desert air. Desiccating, turning brittle, like her grandmother before her.

***

As long as the old woman had lived, Miranda had avoided Colorado. She'd left the state as a sixteen-year-old runaway who'd attached herself to a punk band, and against all odds that story hadn't turned out a complete disaster: she and the charismatic, tortured vocalist fell in love, married, had a child. Then, of course, he'd cheated on her, and they had been in the process of divorcing when a rain-slick highway and a motorcycle had removed him permanently from her life. But with the contacts she'd made and the money he'd left—more of it after he died in such a headline-grabbing manner—she was able to start a career as a music journalist. In between raising her daughter and writing stories she managed to scrape her way through college, then graduate school, and now she was famous in her own right, arguably more famous than the late lamentable Jake Gallagher had been, certainly more famous than the flash-in-a-pan porn star he'd been going to see on that fatal night. But Miranda had never gone back to her hometown, had never even spoken to the old woman. She did not know whether her grandmother knew about Catriona's existence. For her daughter's sake, she had always hoped not.

Occasionally Miranda had experienced a flicker of curiosity about whether the old woman had written a will. To whom would she leave the house, that magnificently upright brick structure with its turrets and gables, superior on its overlook? Or would she die intestate, determined to create as many headaches as she could, even in death? That would have been perfectly in character.

What Miranda never expected was that her grandmother would leave the house to her, but after she got the call, she realized it was the only choice. It was the best and cruelest way the old woman could exact revenge: forcing her to return to that house, to deal with the fact of it.

***

In the morning she had an appointment with the attorney, James Wheldon, Esquire, of Wheldon and Wheldon. He greeted Miranda warmly. In his seventies now, he had always been known around town for his kindness as much as for being her grandmother's factotum. All the kids knew that if you ran into him in the five-and-dime, he'd buy you an ice cream cone when he paid for his newspaper. If he saw a group of them at the soda fountain, he'd pick up their tab. His daughter Suzanne was in Miranda's class, and one year when Suzanne didn't invite Miranda to her birthday sleepover, she had encountered Mr. Wheldon in the lobby of the movie theater on the night in question. He hadn't asked why she wasn't at his house; he'd simply paid for her ticket and popcorn and then said quietly, "Don't mind the other girls too much, Miranda. Things will be better for you when you leave Crystal Falls." She'd never forgotten his unobtrusive courtesy or that remark, which had proven prophetic.

As they drove up the mountain toward the house, they chatted about the estate. Evaline Brandon, Miranda's grandmother, had owned half of Crystal Falls and invested in nearly everything else. In every way that mattered, she controlled the town: kept the people she wanted, expelled those she didn't, chased away corporations and big-box stores who sent their scouts to investigate. She liked to be surrounded by people she knew, and by their children and grandchildren and great-grandchildren. She served as their benefactress and manipulated their gratitude. For seventy years Crystal Falls hadn't had a minister or a mayor or a city council member who wasn't hand-picked by Evaline.

During Miranda's youth, the children and grandchildren of Crystal Falls who knew and resented her grandmother's power took out their anger on her. After the town came to understand that Evaline did not care to protect Miranda, the bullying became almost unbearable. As an adult Miranda could understand that she had been the target of helpless rage and aggression that couldn't be directed at her grandmother. But understanding did not mean forgiveness.

They reached the end of the long driveway, and the house loomed ahead. Miranda shivered. It looked exactly as it had when she'd last seen it, twenty-five years ago. She even thought that the curtains hanging in the windows were the same.

When Miranda had fled the house, she took nothing except the clothes she wore. She left on foot, and she did not follow the road because she was afraid the old woman would come looking for her to finish what she'd started in the basement. Bloodied and bruised, she had slid down the side of the mountain, clinging to roots of scrub oak and twisted juniper. When she'd reached the Crystal River she'd crept along the bank, staying in shadows, feeling her way among the boulders until she was past the town. She did not knock on any doors because she could think of no one she might trust not to betray her. Later doctors would tell her that she should have died on that walk. It was five miles from her grandmother's house to the 7-11 on the highway, and she was badly injured.

She chose the 7-11 because it wasn't a local business, so the owners wouldn't owe the old woman loyalty. The clerk turned out to be the older brother of one of her classmates, but either he wanted to give her grandmother the colossal middle finger or he saw that something was deeply wrong, and so he did not call Evaline. Instead, he gave Miranda a packet of aspirin and a quarter for the pay phone. She told him she would pay him back when her great-uncle arrived, but he said not to worry about it.

She left a message for Ezra, her grandmother's brother, and huddled on the sidewalk next to the store, hoping desperately that he would return to his home before nightfall. Sometimes he stayed out for days, camping and hiking through the backcountry. She did not know what she would do if darkness came and he hadn't arrived. She had no friends, nowhere to go, no one to turn to. Certainly, she could not call Kirk Sullivan now.

For the rest of her life she would be grateful that Ezra was merely outside chopping wood that afternoon, and that when he came inside he noticed the blinking red light on his answering machine and listened to her message. He lived thirty minutes away and his old pickup reached the 7-11 well before night crept down from the mountains. When she stood, he saw the blood on the ground where she had squatted, and so he drove her not to his house but to the hospital in Golden.

They both feared what would happen if he walked into an emergency room with her, so he dropped her off at the hospital with a wad of cash. He told her to use a false name and call him from the nearby McDonald's after she was discharged. She said she would, although she knew staying with him would be complicated. Her grandmother would not give up control so easily, and even if Miranda told her story, Evaline would marshal a whole town of character witnesses to support her own version. Anyway, the courts would never award custody to Ezra, a grizzled old bachelor who spent weeks camping in the high country and could provide no structure or support for a teenager. So an hour after a social worker visited her hospital room, Miranda left what she thought was a reasonable amount of cash on the bed to pay for her care and walked out with the rest. She rented a cheap room on East Colfax, bought clothes at a thrift store, and went to work at a Goth shop. When she called Ezra, he drove back to Denver and rented an apartment for her in a better part of town. He paid the rent for three months, left money for groceries, and promised to come back and visit her the next weekend.

She knew she was breaking his heart and she knew there were no good options.

It was during those days that she began calling herself Miranda Reade, an homage to her favorite activity and to the character Miranda Reed in the horror film *Spellbinder*. It was pathetic, both as an attempt to hide from her grandmother and as a pseudonym, but the name stuck and twenty-five years later she still used it.

Four months after her arrival in Denver she saw an obscure punk band called Syphilitic Whore play, and she fell in love with the lead singer, a Mississippi boy named Jake Gallagher, who had a blue mohawk and deep dimples and brown eyes that softened when he looked at her. When Syphilitic Whore left Denver, Miranda went too.

***

Before they went into the house, Miranda asked James Wheldon to wait while she visited the family graveyard. The Brandons buried their own in a plot upslope from the house, surrounded by a stone wall and sheltered by aspen trees. She climbed the rocky path and went through the iron gate. A few green shoots already reached from the mounded earth that covered her grandmother's body. The marker, granite as humorless and rigid as the old woman it memorialized, read *Evaline Brandon: Beloved Matriarch. 1917-2015.* Miranda wondered who had chosen that inscription: probably Evaline herself.

Her mother's stone stood behind it and slightly to the side, like an afterthought: *Margaret Brandon, 1950-1974*, etched in letters so fragile they were already starting to wear away. Miranda had always felt that Evaline begrudged her daughter even the earth in the graveyard. The old woman never spoke of Margaret, and questions invariably were met with cross words. Miranda did not know how her mother had died or who her father was or, for that matter, who her grandfather had been. So far as she was aware, neither her mother nor her otherwise devoutly religious grandmother had ever married.

She walked past the rest of the graves. Sun flickered through the trembling aspen leaves and spangled the markers: *Coraline Brandon, 1892-1920. Hannah Baker Brandon, 1875-1894. Emily Moss Baker, 1854-1950.* Miranda noticed things that had not struck her as a child. That her great-grandmother too had, apparently, never married or identified her children's father. That most of the women did not live past their twenties. That for a century and a half, the family had produced one daughter in each generation, and she, herself, had unintentionally followed the pattern.

Except for Zebulon Baker, who had built the house, no men were buried in the graveyard, not even the first Mr. Brandon. Her great-uncle Ezra had been adamant in his refusal to be interred there, although she doubted Evaline would have allowed it anyway. When he felt his time had come, he'd called her to say goodbye, and then he went alone into the mountains. A hiker or rock climber might find his remains someday.

Miranda turned back toward the house and saw a flash of color on her grandmother's tombstone: a length of red velvet ribbon, tied into a bow. It had not been there when she entered the graveyard; she could not have missed it. But she had latched the gate behind her and it was still latched, and when she opened it, it let out a discordant creak, so no one could have entered without her notice either.

She shuddered and hurried back down the slope. Wheldon waited for her on the front porch. He unlocked the door and stood aside to let Miranda enter the house. She reached out to touch the door frame. Her right knee, which sometimes gave a little when she was tired, faltered, but she caught herself and hoped the attorney hadn't noticed.

The foyer looked like it had throughout all the years of her childhood: peeling crimson flecked wallpaper, a chandelier dangling with crystal teardrops, the curving staircase rising past a stained-glass window.

"I'd recommend having the furnishings appraised," said Wheldon. "My wife's got an eye for antiques and she says there's a small fortune in here."

Miranda nodded and traced a hand along the railing.

"I didn't ask what you're planning to do with the house," he added. "I don't suppose you want to relocate, but it might be a lovely vacation home."

Miranda shook her head. "I'll never sleep here." She studied him, trying to decide how much she could trust him. And then she decided it didn't really matter. "Do you believe in ghosts?"

A shaft of light from the stained glass window pierced him, rendering his pale suit crimson. He half turned away from her to look down the hallway toward the room Evaline had always called the parlor. "I don't disbelieve," he said softly. "Is there a reason you ask?"

Miranda shrugged and decided not to mention the velvet ribbon. "I always thought this house was haunted," she said. "My grandmother said it wasn't, of course. I'd hear footsteps, and she'd say it was just the floorboards settling. I'd feel things, and she told me I had a vivid imagination. Once I woke up and a woman was leaning over my bed. I saw her as clearly as I see you. But I screamed and just like that she was gone, and my grandmother told me it must have been a nightmare."

She could still picture the woman, limned in moonlight: long hair, white or pale blond; a white gown; a mouth opening, and the child hadn't known whether it was to speak or to consume her.

Wheldon gave her a considering look. "It doesn't seem far-fetched," he said. "I've heard my share of odd noises in this house. I wouldn't require much persuasion to believe in a ghost." And then, in a courtly and old-fashioned gesture, he offered his arm and tipped his chin toward the hallway. "Shall we?"

They walked through the ground floor: the front parlor, where Miranda had never been allowed except on special occasions; her grandmother's bedroom; the formal dining room. As they walked the weight of the house's past settled onto her shoulders. She thought she could not sell it any more than she could live in it. But it wasn't in good enough repair for either, really; the floor bowed under their feet, and stains carved out maps on the ceilings, and she caught a cockroach padding into a large crack in the wall.

"This place is in worse shape than I expected," she said as they stood in the kitchen. The refrigerator buzzed and the smell of rotting vegetables crept from the sink, as though her grandmother had forgotten to run the disposal for the last months of her life. "I almost think the best option would just be to tear it down."

She'd thought Wheldon would react with horror, but he actually looked relieved. "If you'd asked my advice, that's exactly what I was going to recommend," he said. "I had a general contractor in to look things over and give an appraisal of what it would take to get the place up to code. I thought that would be useful regardless of whether you want to live here or sell. I hope you don't mind."

"No, I appreciate it."

"Along with the issues you see," he continued, "there are significant structural problems and faulty wiring. It would take a small fortune to make the place habitable. Of course, tearing it down won't be cheap, either, but the best Realtor in town tells me that given the issues with the house, you could actually get more for the land without it."

Miranda walked to the windows. She could see daylight in the gap between the glass and the frame. On the hillside beyond, the hard sun beat against the graveyard's stone walls.

She'd tried over the years to write about her childhood. Since she'd met Jake little in her life had remained private, and she told him once that she had kept so many secrets as a child that she retained no taste for them. She'd published a memoir about her years with him, another about raising her daughter as a single parent, another about her struggles when she transitioned from freelance journalism to academia. When interviewers asked about her history before Jake, though, she always changed the subject. It wasn't that she was trying to cultivate a mystique, but in this age of social media and Wikipedia she preferred not to see the sordid details of her youth splashed across the internet. If those stories were told, she wanted to be the one to tell them, to fit words to the experiences, to frame them in the context of who she had become and what she had accomplished.

She had sat down to write about her early years more times than she could say. Every time she upgraded to a new computer or updated her files she left behind manuscripts in partial states of completion. The words simply did not coalesce in her brain. Her fingers on the keyboard felt like wooden blocks. The stories did not want to be told.

But now her grandmother was dead and Miranda's name was on the title deed of this house. She could walk again through the rooms of her childhood, see the way the light fell and how the mountains blotted out the stars at night, remember how simultaneously trapped and omnipotent she had felt within these walls.

And she thought she might try, one final time, to write it all down.

"I'll need someone to take charge of sorting and inventorying everything in the house," she said. "I can go through the books and papers myself, but I can't move heavy furniture down from the attic so an appraiser can see it. And the semester's about to start, so I don't know how long I'll be able to stay. Can you think of anyone local who would be good and who's available for at least a few months?"

"I know the perfect person," Wheldon said slowly. "Someone who can do the heavy lifting and coordinate with appraisers and manage an estate sale, if you choose to have one. He can see things through to the demolition and even after, and he's been out of work since the sawmill closed, so he's sure to be available. But you're not going to like it."

"Who?"

"Kirk Sullivan," he said, and the way he said it caused her to wonder just how much he knew about her life, about why she had run away.

***

She met Kirk that afternoon at the Columbine Coffee Shop. Since high school he had grown several inches and filled out, but he was muscular rather than overweight, and the dusting of silver in his hair distinguished rather than diminished him. She felt an unexpected burst of lust when he sat down across from her.

Kirk had been her first love, and they had coupled for the first and only time furtively in the shed behind Doug Palmer's house while everyone else played kick-the-can. At some point in their flailing amid unused clay pots and broken tools and old boards, Kirk must have pressed his knee into a black widow spider, which had responded by biting him. He didn't realize it at first; not until he was driving Miranda home, the Outfield's "Your Love" playing on the tape deck in his old Datsun, did he start to complain about pain cramping his leg.

The bite might have caused everything that happened afterward, or it might have given Kirk an excuse to do what he would have done anyway. She would never know, of course, but when he came home from the hospital he called her and told her the spider had meted out God's punishment for their sin, and they must no longer see each other.

Back in those days, almost everyone in Crystal Falls at least pretended to be Christian. Notwithstanding the fact that she, her mother, and her daughter had apparently all procreated without benefit of clergy, Evaline Brandon was a strict and censorious Calvinist. If you rented a house or a business from her, you damn well made sure you were sitting in church every Sunday morning, preferably close enough for her to pick out your unsteady voice warbling the notes of the hymns. And on the other side of the equation, the Satanic panic of the 1980s also reached tentacles into Crystal Falls: Miranda and her peers were raised on stories of intra-generational cults who bred babies for sacrifice in black masses. They listened to Judas Priest and Metallica, but always with a frisson of titillating terror, knowing they were risking their immortal souls to dabble in occult music.

So for Kirk to interpret a spider bite as divine retribution was not incomprehensible or even surprising. Nor was his inexorable stoicism in the face of Miranda's pleas and imprecations to reconsider.

Nor, perhaps, what he did later.

"It's good to see you," he said now, forthright in a way he had not been as a teenager. She saw the silver wedding ring on his tanned finger, but Wheldon had already filled her in. "I've always felt bad about...you know..."

"No need," she said. "It worked out for the best. Otherwise, I might have stayed in Crystal Falls forever." Then she realized that was exactly what he'd done.

But he laughed. "It's good you got away. You've led an interesting life. I've read all your books, you know. I've always loved your writing."

"Thanks," she said, touched despite herself.

"Do you give autographs? Maybe you could sign the books for me sometime."

"I'd be happy to."

He looked away for a moment and twisted his wedding ring. "I used to wonder..." he said softly. His eyes met Miranda's and she saw the question in them, but he didn't ask it and she didn't answer. He began talking, too quickly, too much. He told her the same story Wheldon already had: that during his senior year in high school, he'd married a junior, Eileen Gordon, and seven months later they'd welcomed a baby boy. Rather than going to college, Kirk took a job at the sawmill, and by the time their fourth son was born he was managing the whole operation. For a while he made a good living; Eileen could stay home with their kids, and they'd paid off the house. Then the mill closed. Kirk could not find other employment. Eileen started waiting tables at the diner, and during the summer she also worked as a cashier in one of the boutiques on Main Street. The oldest three sons had left Crystal Falls; one "drove truck," one played in a band, and they didn't know what the other was doing but Kirk suspected meth. Only the youngest still lived with them, and when he graduated from high school the next year, he'd be gone, too.

When he finally subsided, Miranda told him about the job she wanted to offer him. She asked his opinion of her plan to demolish the place. Did he think losing the house would diminish Crystal Falls in any way?

"Are you kidding?" he said. She hadn't noticed before how weary his eyes were, how faded their blue. "It crouches up there like a gargoyle, like a demon on this town's shoulder. Even the teenagers are too scared to go up there. I oughta know, I've raised four of 'em. Yeah, tear it down. Everyone here will thank you."

***

Kirk started work immediately, and he hired his son and a couple of other high school boys to help move furniture. He also found an antiques dealer in Denver who was willing to trek into the mountains for an appraisal after they'd sorted through the furniture, clothes, and books.

Miranda managed to wrangle a semester's leave from the college where she taught, even though she made the request at the last minute. She suspected the president had learned about the size of the Brandon estate and hoped the school would benefit from her largesse. Also, everyone knew how much interest there would be in a memoir about her childhood, and that would reflect well on the college, too.

Sooner or later she would have to look into her old bedroom on the second floor, but she hadn't yet found the courage. She didn't know what would be worse: to see that her grandmother had kept everything exactly as it had been, or to discover that the old woman had erased any trace of her. Nor had she convinced herself to descend the creaky wooden steps into the basement.

She set herself up at the kitchen table and began sorting through boxes of papers Kirk and the boys carried down from the attic: letters in one pile, diaries in another, newspaper clippings in a third. Her ancestors had, seemingly, kept every bulletin of every church service ever held in Crystal Falls, along with minutes from every city council and school board meeting, and the local historical society had expressed interest in those documents, so she set them aside in another box.

August melted into September as she worked. Outside the aspen began to turn gold, and the wildflowers faded away.

One afternoon, she found a diary buried amidst baptism announcements and wedding programs. It was tied with a red velvet ribbon, a threadbare and worn version of the one she'd seen on her grandmother's grave that first day. Or, thought she'd seen: when she had gone back to the graveyard the following afternoon, it was gone. She loosened the ribbon from the diary and saw on the inside flap her great-great-grandmother's name, Emily Moss Baker.

Before she could read more, she heard a creak above her head, and a moment later another came. She paused to listen, and more sounds followed: a distinct and unmistakable series of cautious footsteps moving across the second floor.

"Kirk!" she called.

He did not answer. Of course not. He and the boys were in the attic, and from the kitchen she could not hear their movements or voices. When they descended, they always clomped so noisily down the wooden steps that they sounded like a herd of elephants. It seemed unlikely that any of them could or would have sneaked down from the attic, past the third floor, just to tiptoe around on the second.

She heard another step, closer to the back staircase that emerged into the kitchen. This one was slower and softer, as though the person realized they'd been overheard and wanted to mask their movement.

She felt herself tense.

Then she thought, this is stupid. She refused to sit frozen like a spotlit deer. She texted Kirk and asked him to meet her on the second floor ASAP, and she picked up the knife she'd been using to slice open the boxes.

She crept up the back stairs. She'd never been in a knife fight herself, but in the old days Syphilitic Whore had drawn a rough crowd, and she'd seen a stabbing once after a gig. She held the knife ready, thinking about the shock on the attacker's face when he saw the blood he'd drawn, as though he hadn't understood until that moment what his weapon could do. The victim survived; when Miranda wrote her first book, a retrospective of her years with the band, she'd interviewed him. He hadn't done anything significant with his salvaged life: delivered pizzas and admitted to fathering three kids with different women, but still he was better off than his assailant, who'd been killed in a prison fight.

She pulled her mind back to the present as she reached the top of the stairs. No one was in sight. She called out again, but there was no response. Kirk hadn't left the attic yet; she would have heard him. She stepped into the hallway, and the floorboards groaned tellingly beneath her feet.

Her old bedroom stood to her right. It was characteristic of Evaline Brandon that although the second floor featured two spacious turret rooms, with windows that overlooked the river and the valley and the town, she had instead exiled her granddaughter to a cramped back bedroom with a view of the family graveyard. Miranda hesitated before the closed door. She thought she discerned breathing on the other side, but no, she told herself, that was just her overwrought imagination.

From the other side of the door, she heard what sounded like bedsprings squeaking.

Without giving herself time to think she flung open the door.

The room stood empty. Not just of people and ghosts, but of furniture, of any sign that Miranda or anyone else had ever slept there. The high, narrow four-poster bed with the white chenille spread was gone, and so was the ugly walnut dresser. The pictures, saccharine religious prints chosen by Evaline, had been removed from the walls. Miranda checked the back of the door, where she'd defiantly taped up Van Halen and Def Leppard posters a few months before she'd left. They were gone.

She crossed to the closet. It too was bare. She wondered what had become of all her clothes, her shoes, the fat Stephen King paperbacks she'd hidden behind the laundry hamper.

In a corner at the back of the closet, she had written "MB+KS 4Ever" in blue nail polish, tracing it repeatedly to make it thick and bubbly and permanent. She found the letters now, found them by touch because they'd been painted over in enough layers to obliterate even the suggestion of Sparkly Ocean polish. But the letters were still raised enough to feel. The legend endured.

"I got your text."

Miranda turned. Kirk stood in the bedroom doorway.

"I thought I heard steps up here," she said. "The boys have been with you, right?"

"All morning, except for the occasional bathroom break." He glanced at the box knife and raised an eyebrow.

"You were in the attic," she said a little defensively.

He nodded once. "How about we check the rooms on this floor together, and then I'll have the boys help me look through the rest of the house? It could be that you heard an animal, and I'd rather trap it and get it outside than deal with its dead body a week from now."

"Thanks." She realized her hands were shaking. "And thanks for not acting like I'm paranoid."

"It's a huge old house," he said. "People in town know it's been standing empty, and the boys and I haven't always been great about locking the doors during the day when we're all here. It's possible someone did sneak in. We'll do a thorough check, and then we'll all feel better."

"All?" she said.

He looked away from her. "Well...we didn't want to say anything to you, and I don't even know that there's anything real to report. Just that the boys have started joking about a ghost. It's small things. The other day Cody set a hammer down on top of a chest and ran down here to take a piss. I saw where he put it. Then I went into another part of the attic where the rest of the boys were working, and when Cody came back upstairs, he couldn't find the hammer. He looked all over for the damn thing. Joe finally found it on one of the windowsills. No one admitted to moving it, and I don't see how anyone could have without the rest of us noticing."

"That does sound creepy."

Kirk exhaled. "Yeah. Then yesterday I put what I could have sworn was a full bottle of Coke right next to the stairs. When I went back for a drink later, the bottle was standing on a box by the opposite wall and it was empty. I figured I just didn't remember drinking it, or maybe one of the boys did and wouldn't admit it. But things like that happen almost every day."

"Things like that have always happened in this house," Miranda said. Misplaced homework, a book left in one room that she'd find in a different room, sometimes in a spot where she'd already looked multiple times. Her grandmother blamed it on carelessness, even hinted that Miranda might be losing her mind, like her mother. And she'd more than half believed that, but after she got to Denver, and in all the years of her life since, her possessions had stayed where she put them, where she expected them to be.

Kirk cleared his throat. "This used to be your room, didn't it?"

"Yeah. How did you know?"

"Oh, Miranda," he said, and his eyes were both fond and sad. "I had a crush on you for years. I used to ride my bike up here at night, and I'd watch the windows to see what lights were on and when. It wasn't hard to figure out which room was yours. Besides, you didn't always close the drapes."

"Ohhh," she said. That had been a point of contention with her grandmother; Miranda liked to keep the drapes open at night, liked the sliver of sky she could see from her bed, the sense of openness and possibility and the mysteries of the mountain rising beyond the bedroom. Evaline stridently disapproved, insisting that "perverts" could see in, but Miranda countered that no one was going to camp out on the slope behind the house just for the possibility of glimpsing her through the window.

Evidently she had been wrong.

"It was a treat," Kirk said, and the slow smile that crossed his face was one she remembered well. The last time she'd seen it had been after everyone else dispersed for kick-the-can, and he took her hand and asked if she wanted to...you know...explore Doug's dad's shed.

She brushed past him. He smelled like Old Spice and sweat, and she felt unwelcome desire.

He's married, she told herself, but after that first day at the Columbine Coffee Shop, he'd never again mentioned Eileen. James Wheldon, who gossiped like he'd spent decades storing up tidbits in the hope that someday he'd find a confidant, claimed the marriage was not happy. "They stay together out of habit and for the kids," he'd said, "but I don't think they actually like each other very well. I wouldn't be surprised if they split after Cody's out of the house. They have the same problems as a lot of couples. He doesn't communicate. She nags. On top of that, they resent each other because they had to get married so young. They both wanted to go to college, but neither of them got to because they were too busy raising babies." He hesitated, and then, putting his hand over Miranda's, he added, "I think the real problem is that Kirk's never really gotten over you. He buys all your books the day they're released. Keeps them on a shelf in the living room, where Eileen sees them every time she walks into her house. Like a reminder that she was the consolation prize."

He was off limits, Miranda told herself. He had to be.

Together they went down the hallway, opening every door, checking closets, peeking under beds. They saw no sign of anyone, nor did they hear suspicious noises.

"I'm sorry," Miranda said finally, and she half laughed. "I guess I called you down here for nothing."

"It's not nothing," Kirk said. "We have to watch each other's backs."

"Thanks."

"Miranda..." They were standing close together. In the dimness of the hallway his eyes were in shadow. "I've always been sorry that I...I let you down. Over a stupid spider bite."

She stepped back too quickly. "Did it scar?"

"No," he said, looking surprised at the question. "Isn't that the devil of it? I don't even have a scar to brag about."

She turned away from him, but he said in a rush, "I never told you: that night when we were together, I...I felt your back. What your grandmother did to you. And I still did what I did. Because I was scared, because I was a stupid kid. I've regretted it ever since."

Miranda stopped but did not look back at him.

"You were the best thing that ever happened to me," he said helplessly.

Without turning she said, "You have no idea what my grandmother did," and then she forced herself to walk back down the stairs to the kitchen.

When she reached the table, the diary was gone and in its place was a skull. And that was when she screamed.

***

The police officer who arrived to take charge of the scene turned out to be Jessica Cross. Like Kirk, she had put on weight, and it lent her a solidity and heft she had lacked in high school. Miranda remembered her as a slight girl, flat-chested into the tenth grade; as an adult she understood that perhaps jealousy had been Jessica's motive for freezing her bra at the slumber party, and for subsequently sharing her cup size with everyone in school. She had walked up one day just as Jessica told a male classmate, "She totally stuffs her bra. There's no way you wear a C in the eighth grade," and when Jessica saw her she looked, not ashamed at being caught by the object of her gossip, but defiant. Miranda, who had prayed every night since she was nine that God would take away the unwelcome protrusions from her chest, ducked her head and scuttled away. The person she became later would have lifted her shirt to show Jessica and everyone else what actually filled her bra, but she didn't develop that level of reckless confidence until she'd left Crystal Falls.

While Miranda had called the non-emergency police number to report the skull, Kirk and the boys looked through all of the rooms on the first and third floors and found no trace of any intruder, human or animal. But, as they insisted to Jessica, there were so many nooks and crannies, corners and alcoves in the attic and the basement, they couldn't say with certainty that no one had been in the house earlier, or was hiding there now.

Jessica clearly thought Miranda and Kirk were playing an elaborate prank, and she threatened to charge them with filing a false report unless they told her the truth.

"We are," said Kirk. "Look, we're on a tight schedule. Miranda has to be back in Pennsylvania by the first of the year, and we've got more than a century's worth of stuff to sort through before that. We don't have time to mess around with a stupid prank. Anyway, we're not fifteen anymore."

"No," said Jessica, looking at him through slitted eyes, and Miranda remembered something else about her: she'd always mooned over Kirk. "We're not. But a mysterious skull could be great publicity for Miranda."

"Sure," Miranda said, losing patience, "if I wanted publicity for any reason. Look, you can either get our statements and figure out whose skull this is and where it came from, or I can call my attorney."

Jessica glowered at her. "You aren't your grandmother," she said. "You just remember that. You don't run things around here."

"I'm not trying to run things. I'm asking you to do your job so we can get back to ours."

"Yes, your jobs," Jessica said contemptuously. "Does Eileen know how much time you're spending with your ex-girlfriend, Kirk?" Her gaze flickered with malicious satisfaction toward Cody, but he didn't flinch. He either had heard already about Miranda's history with his father, or he didn't care.

"She knows who signs my paychecks," said Kirk.

Jessica stared at him for a moment with an expression Miranda couldn't read. Then she bagged the skull for transport to the station. She said it might need to be sent to a forensic archaeologist out of state, and she'd be in touch if the police had further questions.

After she left, Kirk and the boys returned to the attic, and Miranda went back to the stack of papers she'd been sorting. Not until that night, when she was back in her hotel room on Main Street and looking at the dark outline of Mount Zebulon, did she remember the missing diary.

***

"Do you know anything about my family history?" Miranda asked Wheldon the next day. At her request, they had met at the Columbine Coffee Shop. That morning, she had walked through the Brandon graveyard, thinking perhaps the skull had come from there, but the ground appeared undisturbed.

"Very little," he said, blowing on his latte. "Your grandmother was always extremely circumspect."

"Do you know who her father was?"

"She never mentioned him."

"What about my grandfather?"

"I was five or six when your mother was born," Wheldon said, "and for a time the identity of her father was a topic of such speculation that even the children wondered. There were no obvious candidates: when she needed repairs or painting, men always went up there in pairs. She was never seen talking to anyone in town, beyond what was required for business. Ezra had been gone for years by then. And she never left Crystal Falls, so although the idea of an illicit lover elsewhere was floated, it seemed unlikely. Of course, no one dared ask Evaline. Later I heard rumors that someone had broken in and assaulted her. That was the year her great-grandmother died, I remember, and everyone knew she was alone in the house afterward."

Miranda picked at the piece of lemon bread she'd ordered. She couldn't imagine anyone having the bald nerve to attack Evaline, but it seemed equally unlikely that she had ever been overcome by passion.

"I tend to think that whoever he was, whatever the circumstances, he wasn't from around here," Wheldon said. "I was the only attorney in town for a long time, and I've heard as many confessions as a priest, but never a whisper about your grandfather. It seems unlikely someone could keep that kind of secret in Crystal Falls for nearly seventy years."

She chewed her lip and then nodded. "What about my father?"

"Are you sure you want to hear this?"

"There are five generations of my family buried in that graveyard, and only one man. I'm curious about why."

He sighed. "You know your mother suffered from mental illness?"

"My grandmother always said she was crazy. But she would never tell me anything else. I don't even know how she died."

He shook his head and covered Miranda's hand with his. "It was suicide," he said. "And it wasn't her first try. She'd been in and out of institutions since she was twelve. The last time, she came home pregnant. If she told Evaline your father's identity or the circumstances surrounding your conception, your grandmother never shared that with anyone else."

Miranda tore the bread. "So he was probably some orderly who took advantage of her," she said bitterly.

"He could have been another patient," Wheldon said. "Someone as lost and desperate as she was."

Miranda looked out the window at Main Street, at the bandstand in the park. A group of teenagers were riding skateboards through the shell, practicing tricks on the steps. She wondered if the skull belonged to one of the missing men in the family tree. Perhaps her grandmother was a black widow, mating and then murdering. Or killing Miranda's own father: That certainly would be characteristic of the woman who had raised her.

***

Several weeks later the police called. The forensic scientist who examined the skull had drawn three significant conclusions: the skull was more than a century old, it belonged to a woman, and she had died of arsenic poisoning.

Miranda climbed the steps to the attic to tell Kirk and the boys.

"Someone was murdered?" Cody said. "Awesome!"

"Not awesome," Kirk said, with parental exasperation that Miranda still had trouble reconciling with the boy she remembered. "We're talking about a human life."

"Fine," Cody said. "Can I at least say it's awesome that we have an actual mystery?"

Kirk rolled his eyes. "If you must."

"It's not a mystery that's likely to be solved," Miranda said, "at least not officially. Given the age of the skull and the fact that the killer's long dead, the police aren't going to devote many resources to finding out what happened."

"Do they know who the skull belonged to?" Kirk asked.

"No." She shook her head. "I called James Wheldon right after I got off the phone with the cop, because it seems like he knows all the local history worth knowing. He said it was probably a prostitute, but the town's population was so transient that the disappearance of even a respectable woman might not have been noticed or reported. He did have a theory, though." She grinned at the boys, who were leaning forward, eager. "Allegedly, there was a well-known prostitute named Aurelie Laval who ran an upscale brothel called the Mother Lode in Elk Valley."

"Sure," Kirk said. "It's still there, and it's open for tours. They have docents dressed up like madams. We went a few summers ago, Cody, remember?"

"That place? It was so boring. Mom seemed to like it, though." There was something ugly and provocative in his tone. "Aurelie Laval vanished in 1894," Miranda said. "Went out for a drive alone one day and never came back, but her cabriolet and horse were found tied up at the local cemetery. Everyone suspected she'd been murdered, maybe by a jealous customer, but the body was never found."

Before she finished speaking, a clattering and a crash came from the opposite end of the attic. All of them jumped, and then they looked at each other uneasily. Kirk started toward the noise; he didn't ask them to follow, but Miranda didn't think anyone wanted to be left alone just then.

They found a box upturned on the floor. When Cody lifted it, fragments of china spilled out: remnants of an old tea set. A spout had broken off, and shattered remains of cups radiated across the floor. The pieces still in the box were wrapped in newspaper so ancient that it crumbled when Miranda touched it.

"The ghost!" Joe said, trying for spooky but sounding very young and frightened.

"Miranda," said Kirk. "Is there a date anywhere on that newspaper?"

She peeled a strip of it away from a saucer painted with elaborate flowers and scanned through the faded print. "1894." And then, meeting his eyes, understanding the significance, she said, "I'll see about having the whole set tested."

***

The ghost remained active over the next few weeks. They all were vigilant about locking the house doors, both when they were working inside and when they left the premises, but items continued to disappear, to reappear in other spots or not at all. Boxes opened themselves and fell over unaided; furniture was moved when the workers left for lunch or overnight.

One morning the boys went up to the attic while Kirk stayed in the kitchen with Miranda, discussing plans for the antique appraisal. Suddenly there was a stampede on the stairs, and all three boys appeared, breathless and tousled, in the doorway. Cody held up a faded red velvet dress, more gingerly than he'd probably handle a rattlesnake. "We found this," he said dramatically.

"We've found lots of old clothes," Kirk replied.

"Yeah, inside chests and wardrobes," said Luke. "Not laying on top of the exact stack of boxes we were planning to go through today!"

They managed to calm the boys, but the following week, Miranda came back from lunch to find a pair of women's boots setting neatly on the table where she'd been working. They were a dusty red, with velvet ribbons.

The diary did not reappear.

One October afternoon, when most of the aspen leaves had fallen to the ground and sunlight sifted through the stripped branches, Miranda stood to stretch and looked out the windows at the back of the kitchen and saw a figure in the family graveyard.

Recognition punched her. The tangled pale hair, the loose gown, the flowing movements: all of it brought to mind the vision of someone leaning over her childhood bed, someone her grandmother had insisted was not really there. Before she realized what she was doing, she opened the back door and flung herself down the porch steps. For a moment as she ran up the hill, she lost sight of the land beyond the stone graveyard walls, and by the time she reached the iron gate the plot beyond was empty.

***

The day Miranda received test results on the broken china set—traces of arsenic found not in the teapot but in one of the cups—she went back into her bedroom, as if she needed the comfort of those blank walls. The evidence seemed incontrovertible: one of her ancestresses had committed murder, and based on the dates she thought it had to be either Emily Moss Baker or her daughter, Hannah Baker Brandon. She wondered about the missing diary: who had taken it and why; whether it provided an explanation for the killing.

She hadn't revisited her former bedroom since the day the skull turned up. She pushed open the door and inhaled rotting wood. Yes, she thought, the house's days were numbered, and even the walls seemed to realize it.

She sat on the floor in a corner, cradling her head on her knees. She missed Catriona. She missed her life in Pennsylvania, her friends, her students. Normalcy.

She heard the attic door open and Kirk's voice say something. Cody answered from further away, and then the stairs registered Kirk's tread, heavier and less frivolous than the boys'. Miranda thought he was probably heading to the bathroom on the third floor, so she didn't move from her corner. Even when his steps continued down to the second floor she didn't stir. She traced his progress by the creaking floorboards, down to the first floor, through the hallway to the kitchen, but he didn't call out to her. Instead, he climbed the back stairs, the ones that ran from the kitchen to just outside her bedroom, and then he was standing in the doorway looking at her.

"Want to talk about it?" he asked.

She shook her head and held up the letter from the lab. He came forward and took it from her, scanned it.

"So one of your great-grandmothers was a killer?"

"It seems that way." She turned her head to look at the window. From where she sat she could see only a slice of blue sky. "I think she's our ghost."

"Aurelie Laval?"

"It would make sense, if she was poisoned here," she said. "The red dress Cody found? I think it was hers. The shoes, too. They don't match the measurements of the other clothes you've unpacked."

"They don't?" He obviously hadn't thought of making the comparison.

"I've tried some of the dresses on, just for fun, and everything else fits me pretty well," Miranda said. "Whether they're from the 1890s or the 1920s or the 1960s, the clothes are all tailored to my approximate size and height and body shape."

"Short, slender, with large breasts?" he asked with a kind of wistful lust.

"The shoes, too," she rushed on, ignoring the way his words pulsed all the way to her groin. "They're all designed for tiny feet. That's a characteristic of Brandon women, I guess; Cat and I both wear a 5."

Kirk looked blank. Miranda realized he was not the sort of man who knew anything about women's shoe sizes. He'd probably never bought Eileen a pair.

"The red dress is for someone taller but with a smaller chest," she said. "The shoes are for bigger feet, I'd guess at least an 8."

"So," Kirk said. He sat down beside her on the bare floor of the room that had once been hers. "If you're right and those are Aurelie Laval's clothes, then the next question is why your great-grandmother or great-great-grandmother was serving arsenic to a famous madam."

Miranda thought of all the missing spaces on her family tree: the fathers whose names didn't exist, who weren't buried in the graveyard. A prostitute somewhere up the line would explain one of those gaps. But the Brandons had always been eminently respectable, single motherhood notwithstanding.

"There was a diary," she said. "It belonged to Evaline's great-grandmother. The day I heard those footsteps on the second floor? They started right after I found the diary."

"And you texted me," Kirk said, "and we checked everywhere and didn't find anyone."

The urge to rest her head on his shoulder pulled at her with the physical force of gravity. "When I went back downstairs," she said, "the diary was gone, and the skull was there."

"And in all the excitement you forgot to mention it to anyone," he said, and he grinned at her, that lazy slow grin. "Look at us, finishing each other's sentences. It feels so natural, doesn't it?"

"Kirk..." she whispered.

His eyes locked onto hers, and the smile was gone, replaced by an intense hunger. No man had looked at her that way in years. "It should have been you," he whispered. "I threw my life away. I should have been with you."

"Cody," she murmured, glancing at the open bedroom door.

"Let him catch us," he said against her hair. "He'd be thrilled. Just the other day he asked when I was going to divorce his mom so I could be with you."

"This isn't right," she protested, but she didn't move away.

"This is the only thing that's right," he said, and then his mouth found hers. Since she'd last kissed him, she'd kissed plenty of other men and several women, too, and he was nowhere close to the most skilled among them. But after the initial awkwardness, technique stopped mattering because passion consumed everything else. He moaned and their bodies twisted against each other, and then his hands went around her waist and moved up her back.

And Miranda was on her feet and halfway to the door. Because his touch on the scars reminded her of everything: what he had done, what his actions had cost her and the greater sacrifices they had almost demanded.

"Miranda!" he said, sounding bereft, broken.

"Take the rest of the afternoon, Kirk," she said. "Go home to your wife."

***

After he left, taking his crew with him, she sat down at the kitchen table. It was the first time she had been alone in the house, but now that she understood the ghost's identity and purpose she didn't feel afraid. In fact, she thought the poisoning might make an interesting chapter in the book she still hoped to write, if she could find a plausible motive.

A floorboard creaked in the hallway.

Miranda ignored it. The ghost's behavior had been benign, perhaps a bit mischievous, but not threatening. She decided she had no reason for concern.

Another board creaked.

Miranda continued to sort through the latest stack of papers. She had found what appeared to be her mother's elementary school records: report cards, badly colored pictures of sunshine and trees and houses, a report on the history of the Colorado gold rush. Despite the overwhelming evidence she'd already found that the women who lived in this house had been pack rats, she was surprised that Evaline had kept these mementos. Holding onto clumsily scribbled Mother's Day cards from a daughter she refused to discuss seemed starkly out of character.

At some point, Miranda realized she was not alone.

She looked up. The figure from the graveyard, from her childhood, stood in front of her. She knew at once this was not Aurelie Laval. This woman was short and slender, with colorless hair and luminous blue eyes and a large bust. She held out a book tied with faded velvet ribbon. Miranda realized it was the diary that had disappeared.

She reached out to take it, and the woman turned and moved away, the ancient floorboards marking her steps. Not until she had faded into the shadows in the hallway did Miranda understand who she was, who she had to be.

"Mom?" she whispered.

But by then there was no answer.

***

In the late summer of 1891, Emily Moss Baker and her teenage daughter, Hannah, traveled to Colorado to live in the mansion Zebulon had built overlooking the town of Crystal Falls. Emily expressed trepidation at bringing their impressionable child to such a rough place, but Zebulon assured her that the raw frontier was rapidly settling into domesticity and that the location he had chosen was particularly amenable to family life. He described the churches in Crystal Falls, and he enlisted the Presbyterian minister and two of the town's most prominent matrons to write his wife and tell her how appealing, safe, and wholesome she would find her new home. He told her about the sawmill, about the hot springs bubbling out of the mountainside, about the sanitarium where tuberculosis patients rested in sunshine as the mountain air dried their lungs. And finally, Emily was persuaded to purchase train tickets to Denver for herself and her daughter.

It was their misfortune to arrive during the week that Aurelie Laval, the notorious madam of Elk Valley, descended from the mountains to order her winter wardrobe. It was their further misfortune to lodge at the same hotel. Perhaps what caught Aurelie's attention was Hannah's fresh-faced beauty; perhaps it was a sanctimonious, badly timed comment from Emily, who resented the innkeeper's willingness to accommodate a "scarlet woman" under the same roof as her respectable self and was further incensed to learn they'd also be sharing a stagecoach for the final leg of the journey.

Regardless, when outlaws on horseback overtook their coach and forced them from the road, Emily was convinced that Aurelie Laval gave a purposeful nod to the leader just before he and his men tore Hannah from her. Emily begged them to take her instead; she would have sacrificed her life, her honor, anything, but both the men and the madam mocked her. She was not the one they wanted.

They carried Hannah into the next valley, around an outcrop of rock. Emily could hear her daughter's screams and sobs, the raucous, brutal cries of the outlaws. Aurelie stood beside her, speculating about what the girl was enduring at each moment. "She's ruined now," she said, partway through the ordeal. "You'll never convince a respectable man to take her." And then she smirked, the expression of a predator who had done toying with its food and was ready to dine. "But I can always find a place for a girl like her."

At that moment, Emily felt a pure, piercing hatred such as she had never known before. Standing in the dust beside the road, hearing the sounds of her only child enduring an agony she couldn't begin to imagine, she resolved that Aurelie Laval would not prevail. She would not hand over her daughter to this evil wretch, would not force Hannah into the fate of a fallen woman.

She did not know how much time passed before she heard horses whinnying and galloping from the valley. She started toward the rock outcropping and then saw Hannah staggering alone from behind it. Emily rushed to her, stroked the tangled hair, put her own coat over the girl's torn dress. Her daughter did not speak, and although tears had run through the dirt and blood on her face, her eyes were dry now.

They boarded the stagecoach again in the madam's hateful company because they had no choice, but Emily guided her daughter off at the next stop. She paid a local man to take them back to Denver the following morning, and they caught a train to St. Louis. Before they left she bought a gold ring in a mercantile near the station, and when they checked into a boarding house at their destination, that ring circled Hannah's finger, the mark of respectable domesticity. "This is my daughter, Mrs. Brandon," she told the proprietress. "Her husband was just killed," she added in a low voice. "She's not been right since she heard, poor thing."

They knew no one in St. Louis, which was as Emily wanted it. She chose the name Thomas Brandon for her imaginary late son-in-law because a boy called Thomas Brandon had been a neighbor ten years earlier. She and his mother had fondly fantasized about a future match between their children, but Thomas had caught typhoid fever and died.

Emily withheld her daughter's sordid story from her husband. She spun a detailed fiction through a series of letters: Hannah had met a charming young man on the train, and they stopped in St. Louis to pursue an acquaintance with his family. In Zebulon's absence, Emily gave her consent to a wedding, and she agreed to spend the winter with the newlyweds, resolving to travel alone to Colorado in the spring. Then, tragically, Thomas was thrown from a horse. Although she had never seemed concerned that her husband would remember their old neighbors, she dared not further risk jogging his memory by giving the fictional man the same malady that had killed the boy. Instead, she wrote Zebulon several anguished and entirely invented accounts of days spent at a bedside, of delirium and fever, of a final succumbing and a solemn funeral. She ended, portentously, with the news that when she arrived in Crystal Falls she would, after all, be accompanied by Hannah, and by the "unfortunate issue of their too-brief union."

To her diary, she confided the hope that with time Hannah would heal enough to make an appropriate marriage and thus secure her future. Healing seemed increasingly unlikely, however. Hannah sat mutely in a rocking chair by the window day after day, week after week. She did not wash or dress herself. She did not speak. Emily feared very much that her mind had been broken. And as she watched the girl's belly growing, straining against her dresses, she thought that Aurelie Laval had succeeded in stealing her daughter from her in every way that mattered.

The baby was born in the spring. Emily named her Coraline, after her own mother, because Hannah still refused to speak. Coraline Brandon: a child whose father they could not name, claimed for a boy dead a decade.

When the baby was old enough they traveled west again. Hannah watched the golden prairie unfold outside the train windows and said nothing. She never cried except in her sleep.

Their lives in Crystal Falls were a pale realization of what they had anticipated once upon a time. Rather than presiding over local society, Emily found herself raising an infant and coping with an adult daughter who was little more than catatonic. Hannah sat in her turret bedroom and let herself be bathed, dressed, moved as if she were a doll. Emily engaged a woman, the wife of one of the Chinese coolies working on the railroad, to help. Mrs. Wu spoke little English and knew no one in their social circles, so her discretion was assured.

That fall Emily began to consider taking her daughter back east if her condition had not changed by spring. She thought they would go back to the town in upstate New York where they had spent most of their lives. She hoped that a different environment would help, that a return to the world Hannah had known might return the girl to herself.

Coraline was the sticking point: as she grew, as features emerged from the bland roundness of her baby's face, she came increasingly to resemble one of the outlaws. Emily would not have said she could recognize any of them; she had tried to remember their faces and could not, and she had been convinced that if she ran into them in the street she would not know them. But now she could see him in her granddaughter's face, his buck teeth, his weak chin, his beady pebble eyes. Not the leader, but an inconsequential leering man who had proven the most consequential of them all. Emily knew that if she saw him whenever she looked at Coraline, and if the resemblance bothered her so much that she could barely bring herself to be civil to the child, Hannah must be far more tormented.

Returning to New York would not help her daughter if this constant reminder accompanied them, but leaving the little girl alone with her grandfather was not an option, either. Emily regretted, over and over, not abandoning the child in St. Louis, where they might have brought her to an orphanage and, with time, forgotten her existence and what it meant. It was too late for that now. The pastor in Crystal Falls knew people in their hometown and had mentioned the situation to some of them. Emily's own sister had written to ask about the mysterious husband and baby.

So the family passed through tedious months, three adults who barely spoke to each other, locked into secrets and recriminations and wounds, and one child who seemed determined, so her grandmother claimed in the hidden pages of her diary, to be as difficult and disagreeable as any child could.

And then a letter arrived for Emily from Aurelie Laval. The madam said she had seen Coraline in Elk Valley with her grandfather and recognized who the father must be. *He would rejoice in knowing his child*, she wrote, *and I should hardly like to keep a parent from his offspring*. She then, in a roundabout way, asked for a substantial payment that might help her quiet her conscience regarding the matter. Otherwise, she said, the father would easily be moved to claim the little girl and disgrace the mother's family.

Emily might not have wanted Coraline, but she was damned if she was going to let the girl be taken away by a madam. She calmly went to the Crystal Falls general store and purchased arsenic, explaining to the manager that they were having problems with rats. And then she sent Aurelie a conciliatory note, inviting her to the red-brick mansion during a week when Zebulon had planned a trip to Denver.

It was perhaps a mark of Aurelie's confidence in her own triumph that she appeared not to suspect anything. She drove herself from Elk Valley and left her horse tied in front of the Baker house. She watched greedily as Emily placed a full purse on the table between them, and she inquired with facetious solicitousness after Hannah's health as she drank cup after cup of Ceylon tea. If she found the flavor strange, she did not remark on it. When Emily offered her a glass of cordial, she accepted eagerly, and she seemed to notice nothing amiss with it either.

Emily suspected her of using laudanum regularly and so she had put far more than necessary into the cordial in order to ensure that it would take effect. If it did not kill the madam, she at least needed it to leave her unconscious. She did not know how much time the arsenic would require and she dared not risk allowing Aurelie to return to Elk Valley, where an enterprising physician might diagnose and treat the poison. When Aurelie's head began to droop, Mrs. Wu slipped from the shadows and helped Emily maneuver the madam into her own bedroom, where they undressed her and tied her to the bedstead. If the Chinese woman had qualms about what they were doing, Emily did not allow her to express them. She had no concern that Mrs. Wu would reveal her secret; no one who mattered in Crystal Falls would believe a coolie's wife over the mistress of the mansion.

Emily asked her driver to return the brougham to Elk Valley. She gave him extra money to hire a horse for the return trip and for his silence.

Aurelie lingered for almost two days. Emily sat through the hours in a stiff chair by the bedside, watching her anguish, reveling in it. She knew that a part of her soul was dying along with the madam, but she told herself that she had no other choice. Not if she hoped to preserve any kind of future for Hannah or Coraline.

On the day Aurelie Laval finally died, Emily waited until nightfall, until Mrs. Wu had returned to the tent camp that housed the railroad workers, and only then did she roll the body from her bed onto a quilt. She dragged the quilt through the house, out the back door, down the steps. For most of that night she labored, digging a hole near the bank of the river that ran behind the house. Then she wrapped Aurelie tightly in the quilt and buried her there. She piled stones on the body to keep predators at bay before she replaced the earth. As the sun slid over the mountains to the east, she scattered leaves, twigs, and other debris over the bare ground until a casual passerby wouldn't have noticed it had been disturbed.

When she returned to the house, Emily stripped the sheets off her bed and shoved them into the woodstove. Mrs. Wu would dispose of them later. Too exhausted to make up her bed, she climbed onto the feather mattress and pulled another quilt around herself. She slept badly, tossing restlessly through the too-bright hours in the stuffy room. At last she rose, made her toilet, and dressed.

She found Mrs. Wu and Coraline in the kitchen. The little girl watched with her pebble eyes as the Chinese woman chopped vegetables at the counter. Emily wanted to hire a real housekeeper, an American woman who could oversee the cleaning and the cooking; a house like this demanded a full staff, not a lone immigrant, but she had always worried about what an American might notice, overhear, observe. Perhaps with Aurelie Laval out of the way...

She went up the back stairs, then down the hallway to her daughter's room. She thought of the ivory-handled hairbrush that she forced through Hannah's hair every day, pictured it waiting for her on the vanity table, imagined how she might speak, matching the cadence of her voice to the soothing strokes of the brush as she told her daughter that Aurelie Laval was dead. I killed her, she thought of saying, so you could have back the life she took from you.

Hannah was not in her room.

Emily stood in the doorway, blinking in confusion. Hannah never left her room.

But she undeniably was not here. Frantic, Emily checked everywhere a young woman might be able to hide herself. The bed was neatly made, the space beneath showing empty to the floorboards. The dresses hung tidy and undisturbed in the wardrobe, the linens folded in bland symmetry in the hope chest.

Calling her daughter's name, shrieking it, Emily burst back into the hallway. She checked the other turret room, then Coraline's nursery, and then she started down the main staircase.

When she had taken the red velvet dress off Aurelie Laval's body three days earlier, she had folded it and put it in a chest in the basement. She did not see how Hannah, in her self-imposed prison two storeys above, could have known that; but somehow she had found the dress. She wore it now, although her heavy breasts nearly split the seams of the bodice, and the skirt fell past her feet. It fell into the space around which the grand staircase coiled, the space in which Hannah swung, and the stained glass window washed her face and the rope with gentle color.

***

Miranda closed the diary. The night outside her hotel window was quiet; the fall-color tourists had faded away weeks ago, but the slopes didn't yet have enough snow to attract the ski and snowboard crowds. She could mark the shape of Mount Zebulon only by the absence of stars.

She didn't remember ever seeing a photo of her mother, but still she'd known the woman in her kitchen. It was like looking into a mirror and seeing her own face twenty-five years in the future. Clarity, sorrow, and determination had settled in the lines around the mouth as Margaret Brandon wordlessly handed her the diary. When Miranda came to herself she ran down the hallway, calling, but the woman had already disappeared.

On the way down the mountain she had called James Wheldon, feeling furious and betrayed. Surely he knew that her mother had not actually died during Miranda's infancy, but when she told the story he seemed as shocked as she was. He swore that he, like everyone else, had always believed Margaret rested in the graveyard behind the house. He talked about getting an exhumation order to see if her coffin was empty, but Miranda couldn't think that far ahead. Too much of what she had always believed she knew about her family was shifting, tilting.

She locked herself in her hotel room and read the diary from cover to cover, struggling only a little with the unfamiliar narrow cursive. At some point she called for room service, but the diary distracted her so much that her salmon and mashed potatoes were cold by the time she remembered to eat.

Those pages explained so much: her grandmother's resentment, the way she held herself apart from the town as if she had to prove she was better than everyone else, the stories she never told about her own childhood. For Coraline had been Evaline's mother, and Ezra's. Reading of Hannah's suicide and the revulsion Emily felt whenever she looked at the girl, Miranda imagined an ugly girlhood for Coraline, a warped and miserable upbringing at the hands of people who saw in her the embodiment of the villains who had robbed them of their beloved daughter. It was not difficult to conclude that she had, in turn, loathed her own children and twisted young Evaline into the bitter, self-righteous, furious harpy who had raised Miranda.

She went to bed early and did not sleep well. A weak-chinned, buck-toothed child walked through her dreams, staring at her with eyes smooth and expressionless as pebbles, and somewhere behind her horses whinnied and ran away.

***

She debated telling Kirk about her mother but decided not to. She wasn't sure what to say.

She remembered the face leaning over her bed, the long hair falling down on either side and almost brushing her cheeks. Remembered scattered snatches of song echoing through the old house, whispers, sometimes coming into a room and catching her grandmother in mid-sentence. The old woman would always look irate and say she was talking to herself. But was she? Had Margaret been there, leading a parallel and mostly invisible existence throughout Miranda's childhood? And if so, why had she remained hidden? And how? And how had she survived in the months since Evaline's death, months when surely she would have needed food, groceries, human contact?

At any rate, after she delivered the diary, she seemed content to stop playing ghost. The boys reported no further incidents of tools disappearing or boxes moving. None of them heard unexplained footsteps again or felt the chilling sense of a presence watching them.

Miranda bought a printer and began scanning copies of documents she wanted for her memoir. Kirk and his helpers moved the last of the furniture down from the attic, to the main floor where the appraiser could more easily see it, and started work in the basement.

And one day, as Miranda had known he would, he walked up the steps and down the hall and into the kitchen and stood uneasily before her.

"We found a big stain," he said. "In the first room at the bottom of the stairs on the left, in the center of the floor. I'm pretty sure it's blood."

Miranda's eyes went from the laptop screen to his face.

"It's obviously not fresh. But I think we should call the police to come up and take a look."

"That's not necessary," she said, and her voice sounded calmer than it should have.

"But it might be connected to...the skull. And maybe the ghost. Or to the missing men you keep talking about. Your grandfather, your great-grandfather..."

"It's not." The walls pressed in. Her breaths came like little explosions.

"How do you know?" He stared at her, and she wondered what he was seeing that he hadn't noticed before. What told in her eyes that she'd managed to keep concealed until now.

"It's my blood," she said.

"But there's an awful lot of it. I mean based on the size of the stain there must have been. It seems like more than someone could lose and still..." He subsided helplessly.

"I needed a transfusion."

"When was this?"

Her eyes remained locked on his. "The night I ran away. I called my great-uncle and he took me to a hospital in Golden where they gave me a transfusion."

He pulled out a chair and sat forward, intense, waiting.

"I was pregnant," she said.

He flinched. He knew. That night in the shed. After she took the pregnancy test she'd called him—so confused she would have accepted either a marriage proposal or money for an abortion, and she herself couldn't have said which she preferred. But he wanted nothing to do with her, he had made that clear already, God had sent the spider to bite him and God wasn't fooling around and it was probably someone else's kid anyway.

"What did you think happened?" she asked.

"I always assumed you had an abortion when you got to Denver."

"When I got to Denver," she said, "there was no need. My grandmother saw to that."

His mouth opened. He tried to speak, faltered.

"It's my blood on that floor, and our child's blood is mixed in, and she did her level best to make sure I'd never have anybody else's child either," Miranda said.

For years she hadn't been able to picture what had actually happened in the basement. She remembered her grandmother's terrible expression, she remembered the old woman's talons digging into her arm and the sensation of being dragged with a strength she wouldn't have believed a seventy-five-year-old could possess toward the stairs. But after that everything was a blank until she found herself scrabbling down the steep wash toward town. Later she knew what had happened, but it was as if she had read the words in a book, not lived them herself.

After Cat's birth, the memories had begun to return in fragments. What her grandmother had done, what she'd said as she did it: that Miranda should never have been born, that their family was an aberration, that their bloodline should have ended with Evaline herself and it was her duty now to make sure the curse didn't pass to another generation.

But even after she remembered, Miranda hadn't understood how to make meaning of those words; she had thought it must be madness. The history was there, after all, and insanity was a convenient explanation for so many of her grandmother's actions and behaviors. Insanity was preferable to the alternative: inexplicable malice, genuine evil.

Now that she had read the diary, she knew. The curse, the aberration. A bloodline borne from rape and sustained with murder. Little wonder that Evaline, whose own mother had played such a central if inadvertent role in that story, had sought solace in the rigid structure of her religion and had so loathed her own granddaughter.

"I don't think she would have cared if I'd died in that basement," Miranda said to Kirk now. "Probably would have just lugged me up the steps and out to the graveyard, hidden my body there, and told everyone I'd run away."

As she said the words she knew their truth. One way or another, she was always destined to have disappeared from Crystal Falls that night.

"My god, Miranda," he whispered. "I don't know what to say."

"You felt my back," she said dispassionately. "You knew she beat me and you knew how badly. Yet you called her after I told you I was pregnant. I'm not sure there's anything you *can* say."

He raised his hands as if to pray but clasped his head. His skin had gone gray and she almost felt sorry for him except she couldn't feel anything just then: no grief, no anger, nothing but a terrible quiet.

"Go back to the basement, Kirk," she said softly. "The boys need you."

She wouldn't have told him, hadn't planned to, but he had asked and she did not care to lie. Not anymore. He stood and shuffled away, face ravaged, shoulders hunched, made suddenly old by the realization of what his long-ago cowardice had cost.

***

"I didn't know," said a voice that sounded like a cross between Miranda's and a creaky gate. A voice that had sung to her in her dreams and crooned over her bed in memories she hadn't realized until this moment were more than fantasy.

Her mother stood in the shadows next to the door.

"I wasn't here then. I was...away," Margaret Brandon said. "If I'd known, I..." The voice quavered over the last few words.

"There was nothing you could have done," Miranda said. "She was in a rage. I've never seen anyone in a rage like that. She might have killed you."

"She had already killed me," Margaret whispered, glancing at the window, at the graveyard beyond it, where the sun warmed her tombstone, "in every way that mattered."

Miranda stood slowly and walked toward her, not wanting to frighten her, hoping she wouldn't vanish again. When she reached her mother she held out her arms and Margaret leaned passively into the embrace. She felt frail, not a ghost but barely clinging to humanity: bone and skin fragile as twigs bound together with twine, shoulder blades brittle as ancient clay. One paper-thin hand reached up and patted weakly at Miranda's back, a moth fluttering against a light.

Later there would be questions and answers, although the answers would be fewer and less satisfying than Miranda hoped. Margaret could shed little light on the generations of nameless men missing from the family tree; she'd read all of the diaries and letters in the attic, but some stories had never been committed to paper. She could talk, however, about the love story that had brought Miranda to life. She could describe her childhood in a house haunted by the women who had lived and died there—Hannah in the red velvet dress, hanging from the banister in the entrance hall; Aurelie Laval's clove and orange scent—and Miranda would not know whether these things were the result of a vivid imagination fed too young on grisly tales, or early manifestations of madness, or genuine ghosts. Margaret would describe stretches inside an institution and then, as anguishing, stints in a home where her daughter had been told she was dead and her own mother made dire threats about revealing the truth. She would talk about being restricted to the attic, emerging only when the old woman slept, and of the secret passageways between rooms and floors that even Evaline didn't know, of nights when she tiptoed into her daughter's room to watch by moonlight.

Later, too, there would be a Christmas celebration at Miranda's home in Pennsylvania, and Catriona would finally meet her maternal grandmother. Miranda would look at them and wonder whether the very act of bringing her mother and daughter together reignited a curse she found herself unable to fully disbelieve.

But in this moment they embraced in a kitchen that smelled of old wood and aged paper. Miranda's blood had soaked the basement floor through to the soil beneath the house, and that would always matter, there would always be a part of her lost to the violence inscribed on and by her family nearly a century before her birth. But as her hands stroked the frail contours of her mother's back and she felt the same tracery of scars she herself bore, she knew the part of her that had left this place was stronger than what remained. Her daughter had never known the touch of a whip, the absence of a mother, the daily presence of cruelty and malice. The old woman's bones lay in the ground upslope from the house, and Miranda was still alive to experience this moment, this reunion with her own mother.

She had triumphed.

They embraced, and the ghosts were silent, and hard sunlight beat against walls and windows that for more than a century had yielded to nothing.

D. R. Bartlette discovered horror at an inappropriately early age, and has been writing true crime and twisted fiction ever since. Follow her on Twitter @DRBartlette.

C. W. Blackwell was born and raised in Santa Cruz, California, where he still lives today with his wife and two children. His passion is to blend poetic narratives with pulp dialogue to create strange and rhythmic genre fiction. He writes mostly crime fiction, dark fiction, and weird westerns. You can follow him on Twitter and Facebook: twitter.com/CW_Blackwell, facebook.com/cwalkerblackwell.

Jaap Boekestein (1968) is an award-winning Dutch writer of science fiction, fantasy, horror, thrillers, and whatever takes his fancy. He usually writes his stories in trains, coffeehouses, and in the 16th century taverns of his native The Hague, the Netherlands. Over the years he has made his living as a bouncer, working for a detective agency, and as an editor. Amazon.com/author/jaapboekestein.com

Die Booth enjoys painting pictures and exploring dark places. When not writing unsettling lies, like his latest short story collection, *My Glass is Runn*, he chairs Chester Writers and DJs at Chester's best* goth night. He is currently working on a collection of short stories with transgender protagonists. You can visit him at diebooth.wordpress.com or follow him on Twitter @diebooth. (*and only)

Monique Bos grew up in Colorado, where her story for this anthology is set. She now lives in southeastern Georgia. Her short fiction has appeared in *Vestal Review*, *Muscadine Lines*, and several Blood Bound Books anthologies, including the invitation-only *Blood Rites*. Monique also reviews mysteries for *Publishers Weekly* magazine and belongs to the Lowcountry chapter of Sisters in Crime.

Nancy Brewka-Clark is a longtime published author of fiction, nonfiction, poetry, and drama who began her career as a feature writer for a chain of daily newspapers on Boston's North Shore. She's delighted that this is the fourth FunDead Publications anthology to include her work. For more information, please visit her website nancybrewkaclark.com.

Patricia Correll lives in Alabama with her family and two elderly cats. She likes mythology and folklore, being scared, and reading all the books. You can find her other work at amazon.com/author/patriciacorrell and herself on Facebook at facebook.com/authorpatriciacorrell.

Russell J. Dorn's work has appeared in numerous publications, including, most recently, *Asterisk Anthology: Volume 2*, *Horror Bites 4*, and *This Book is Cursed*. By day, he's a library assistant; by night, he's working on a collection of unnerving horror stories and content for his free, spooky website for kids (felipefemur.com). Visit his author website for more information: russelldorn.com. Or follow him on Twitter: @DornRussell.

Cody D. Grady is a pencil-pushing desk jockey who prefers imagination over real life in most instances. When not writing, he can be heard running and playing games on *The Rancor's Brothel* (rancorsbrothel.com), a tabletop gaming podcast. He would like to thank his wife and son for putting up with his shenanigans.

David Kotok was enthused to write whilst living in Jakarta, Indonesia. "The Nightmare of Nik the Necrophiliac," his eighth story selected for publication, was inspired by a figure dancing in a graveyard, although it may have been the sunset playing tricks in a mango tree. After many years of motivational travel, David lives with his beautiful wife in a converted Oast House in the English countryside, where hops were once gathered to turn into beer. Between writing he walks his dogs, feeds the birds, and throws pots. He wants to play the trumpet. Other short stories can be found at: cargocollective.com/davidkotok.

Dan Le Fever is just a guy from Lynn, Massachusetts who puts one word after another in the hopes that it makes sense in the end. His short story, "PANIC," can be found in *One Night In Salem* by Fundead Publications. He is currently working on his first novel, *The Ashen War*. When not writing, he focuses on his hobbies of video games, reading, and practicing martial arts. Follow him on Facebook: facebook.com/authordanlefever.

Joanna Logan-Costello is a horror writer who favors gothic literature and dark poetry. In addition to FunDead Publications, her work has been featured in *Hinnom Magazine's* H. P. Lovecraft Birthday Edition. She is originally from Pāhoa, Hawai'i. Follow her on Instagram @joeatscrow or visit her blog joeatscrow.wordpress.com.

Ellery D. Margay is a freelance food and fiction writer currently residing in New Orleans, Louisiana. His work has appeared in various online journals, the poetry collection *Untimely Frost*, and in previous FunDead anthologies. When not dreaming up tales and the occasional poem, he can be found sampling and reviewing the newest restaurants and wandering the world in search of weirdness, wonder, and misadventure.

Facebook.com/shadowscribbler

Callum McSorley is a writer based in Aberdeenshire. He graduated from the University of Strathclyde in 2013 with a degree in English, Journalism & Creative Writing, and in 2014 was selected for the Hermann Kesten Writing Scholarship in Nuremberg. His short stories have appeared in *Gutter* magazine, *Typehouse Literary Magazine*, *Shoreline of Infinity*, *Monstrous Regiment* and more. You can follow him on Twitter @CallumMcSorley.

Allister Nelson is a published poet, academic, and author whose work has appeared in everything from *Apex Magazine* to *Eternal Haunted Summer*. A communications professional by day and novelist student by night, she is passionate about science, mythology, nature, and world religions. Her work can be found at dancingwithtricksters.wordpress.com.

Joey Phoenix is a professional faerie with Moonrise Fae and the Managing Editor for Creative Collective, where they use their tendency towards manic scribbling to tell stories about exciting things happening in the creative community. They are working on a memoir in between dancing in clouds of glitter and conducting interviews with professional artists. You can follow them on Instagram at @faephoenix.

Christopher Stanley lives on a hill in England with three sons who share a birthday but aren't triplets. His novelette, *The Forest is Hungry*, was published by Demain Publishing in April 2019. His short stories have been published by Grinning Skull Press, The Infernal Clock, and *Unnerving Magazine*, and are forthcoming in SFFWorld.com's *Dying Earth* anthology and Dave Higgins' *Fears of a Clown* anthology. Find him at whenonlywordsareleft.wordpress.com or follow him on Twitter @allthosestrings.

E. F. Sweetman is a writer living in Beverly, Massachusetts. She is a thriller, crime, and noir reviewer for *SPINE*. Her stories have appeared in noir, crime, flash, horror, and gothic anthologies *Microchondria II*, *One Night in Salem*, *Switchblade V*, *Sixx*, *and Stiletto Heeled*, *EconoClash Review*, and *Broadswords and Blasters*. She lives with her husband, two sons, and three rescue dogs. When she is not working on her noir novel, which she hopes to finish before she turns 95, you can find her glaring out the window at her neighbors. For more fun, follow her on Twitter @EFSweetman.

Nicole Vasari writes from the US Northeast. She has been published in *The Audient Void* and *Vastarien*. Find her on Instragram at @hersphinxness.

ABOUT FUNDEAD PUBLICATIONS

FunDead Publications is located in Salem, Massachusetts, a city which has provided endless inspiration to writers of every genre for hundreds of years. Established by Amber Newberry in late 2015, FunDead released its first collection, *Shadows in Salem*, in October of 2016 with the help of co-editor Laurie Moran. Since then, FunDead has published four more books; *Night in New Orleans*, a Christmas anthology called *O Horrid Night*, a poetry collection, *Entombed in Verse*, and a Halloween anthology, *One Night in Salem*. Devoted to providing a space for scribblers new to publishing, as well as veterans of independent and traditional means, Newberry hopes to keep the age-old art of story-telling alive and well in The Witch City.

Since FunDead's first publication, the small press has become known for exceptional promotion of writers and for their unique events in uncommon locations. The woman-owned and led press also runs the now-annual Write Like a Girl live horror reading event each February, a celebration of female horror writers for Women in Horror Month. With upcoming anthologies, FunDead hopes to shine a light on diversity within the pages of their 2019 releases and by continuing to celebrate writers from every walk of life. With a love for horror, gothic fiction, and all things macabre, FunDead brings a little joy to those who prefer the dark side. *Sticks, Stones, and a Bag of Bones*, a collection of short horror for kids and nostalgic adults is in the illustration stage and is slated for Fall 2020. The editing team is also working on several special team-only projects for the 2020 docket!

Follow FunDead Publications on Instagram, Facebook, or Twitter for the quickest access to announcements!